Ellie Darkins spent her formative years devouring romance novels and, after completing her English degree, decided to make a living from her love of books. As a writer and editor, she finds her work now entails dreaming up romantic proposals, hot dates with alpha males and trips to the past with dashing heroes. When she's not working she can usually be found running around after her toddler, volunteering at her local library or escaping all of the above with a good book and a vanilla latte.

Melissa Senate has written many novels for Mills & Boon and other publishers, including her debut, See *Jane Date*, which was made into a TV movie. She also wrote seven books for Mills & Boon's Special Edition line under the pen name Meg Maxwell. Her novels have been published in over twenty-five countries. Melissa lives on the coast of Maine with her teenage son; their rescue shepherd mix, Flash; and a lap cat named Cleo. For more information, please visit her website, melissasenate.com

REUNITED BY THE TYCOON'S TWINS

ELLIE DARKINS

WYOMING SPECIAL DELIVERY

MELISSA SENATE

MILLS & BOON

First Published in Great Britain 2020
by Mills & Boon, an imprint of HarperCollinsPublishers,
1 London Bridge Street, London, SE1 9GF

Reunited By The Tycoon's Twins © 2020 Ellie Darkins
Wyoming Special Delivery © 2020 Melissa Senate

Special thanks and acknowledgement are given to Melissa Senate for her contribution to the *Dawson Family Ranch* series.

ISBN: 978-0-263-27876-7

0420

MIX
Paper from
responsible sources
FSC **FSC™ C007454**
www.fsc.org

This book is produced from independently certified FSC™ paper to ensure responsible forest management.

For more information visit: www.harpercollins.co.uk/green

Printed and bound in Spain
by CPI, Barcelona

REUNITED BY THE TYCOON'S TWINS

ELLIE DARKINS

For my girls

CHAPTER ONE

'MADELEINE, WHAT'S WRONG?'

Finn took in the scowling face of the woman on his doorstep and tried to reconcile it with the girl he had first met more than two decades ago and hadn't seen in more than two years. And then she let loose an impressive string of expletives and Finn's eyes widened.

This definitely wasn't the girl he remembered from his teenage years, loafing around her house with her brother.

He covered the ears of the baby he was snuggling on his shoulder, but the tirade came to an end and he breathed a sigh of relief, removed the emergency ear muffs and stepped aside so that Madeleine could follow him into the hallway of the townhouse, and then on into his apartment.

'Are you okay?' Finn asked, wondering why Madeleine Everleigh had turned up on his doorstep fuming mad.

When his best friend Jake had talked him into letting his sister stay and help with the babies for a few weeks, he had thought that he was doing her a favour.

'An idiot in a white van beeped at me,' Madeleine said, following him into the apartment. 'It's nothing.'

No doubt she had to put up with this crap all the time. He'd known Madeleine for ever, and it had not exactly been possible to ignore that she was a woman with lush curves and a beautiful face, however hard he tried.

'It's not nothing; you shouldn't have to put up with that. I'm sorry it happened,' Finn said, shaking his head and wishing he could take back the last few minutes. 'Come through. I'll put the kettle on.'

The baby on his shoulder gave out a little squeak and Finn shushed him and bounced on the spot, only slightly frantically, hoping for just five more minutes before his son woke. He'd only been asleep for half an hour—if his routine went out then his sister's routine went out and then the rest of the day and probably the night would be complete and utter chaos. They'd all spent the three months since his ex-wife had moved abroad trying to build a routine, but losing his nanny when they'd only just settled into one again had thrown a spanner in the works and, without help, everything was at risk of descending into madness.

'Look, I appreciate it and everything but...' She cast a look at Hart that reminded Finn of how he had looked at babies before he'd found himself the single parent of two of his own. She was not exactly ideal nanny material, but he had promised his best friend that he'd give his sister somewhere to stay and a regular wage while she was between jobs. Jake hardly ever asked for favours and after twenty years of friendship it was really the least that Finn could do.

'This is Hart, by the way,' he said, giving the baby a gentle pat on the bum. 'Bella's asleep too, but this one is allergic to his crib.'

He laughed at the horrified expression on her face.

'Only metaphorically,' he reassured her. 'I've tried everything but a lot of the time he'll only sleep on me. Which is why I need the help.'

'Yeah, I don't know if Jake mentioned but I really don't have any experience with babies. I mean, his were all older than this when he adopted them.'

Finn smiled, and hoped it didn't look too forced. 'Yeah, he did mention it and it's fine, honestly. I just need an extra pair of hands for a few weeks until I can find a permanent nanny—I don't want to rush into hiring someone so it's great that you could help out at such short notice.'

Her face tightened, and Finn could have kicked himself for causing that reaction.

'Well, one of the great things about being fired,' Madeleine said, 'is that you can be super flexible. Really, I can recommend it…'

He reached his free hand towards her, then let it fall, realising he didn't know what he had been planning on doing with it. There was something about being around Madeleine that was making him feel like a kid again, and he couldn't say that he liked it. Everything that he had said in the last five minutes had been utterly the wrong thing and he didn't seem to be able to get off the back foot. And he'd invited her to stay, in his home, for at least a few weeks. He must be completely mad. 'I'm sorry, Madeleine. Jake told me that they made cutbacks at the website...'

'Yep.' She folded her arms across her body, and her expression went from irritated to full on angry. 'I don't know why I'm surprised. I escaped the last round, but everyone knows that there's no such thing as job security in journalism any more. I knew it was coming but it was still a shock.'

'Of course it was. It's a lot to take in. But is it too much of a cliché if I say that their loss is my gain? You're doing me a massive favour,' Finn said, smiling, hoping to ease her bad mood, 'and I truly appreciate it.'

She did smile at that, and he saw her shoulders relax a fraction. That was good; he wanted her to be comfortable here. He was hardly doing Jake a favour if his sister was so on edge the whole time that she was here that she couldn't even get through the door without worrying about him ogling her.

'You're the one giving me a place to stay. I think you're the one doing the favour really.'

He didn't remember her being so prickly when they were kids. Of course she wasn't, back then. Nobody made it into adulthood without a major dose of reality to knock the idealism out of them. Or maybe that was just his divorce talking.

'Wait until the twins are both up at three in the morning. We'll talk then about who's helping out who,' he said with a wry smile. 'Anyway, can I take your bag? Let's go through to the kitchen—I'm desperate for caffeine—then I'll show you your room. Do you want tea or coffee?' he asked as he gestured for Madeleine to take a seat at the kitchen island, but she stayed standing.

'You sit,' she said. 'You've got the baby.'

He smiled. 'I've barely managed a sip of water all day so I'm not going to argue with you. See, this is working out perfectly already.' He watched as she grabbed cups from the top of the coffee machine, slotted in a pod and made a couple of espressos. He took one from her gratefully and she finally took a seat beside him.

'I'm sorry,' she said, as she drank half the coffee in one go, then let out a long sigh as she relaxed back on her stool. 'I turned up in a bad mood and I shouldn't have taken it out on you.'

Finn smiled, grateful for the change in atmosphere. 'You've been through a lot. It's understandable.'

Madeleine quirked her eyebrows in a gesture that spoke of untold cynicism. 'None of it's your fault, though,' she said. 'You've already been better too good to me.'

Finn frowned. 'Don't say things like that. You deserve good things happening to you, Madeleine. I don't like that someone's made you think otherwise.'

He held her gaze for a moment too long, feeling the atmosphere between them grow heavy, and then

Hart turned his head and nuzzled into Finn's shoulder, and he knew that they were on borrowed time.

'Could you take him while I make up a bottle?' he asked, and laughed at Madeleine's wide-eyed reaction. He chuckled softly as he transferred the baby into her arms. 'It's fine,' he said. 'Just bounce him a bit if he starts to cry. He's going to wake up hungry and that's not the best time to be showing you how to make up a bottle. We'll go through it all after.'

'Um, okay, I guess?' Madeleine said, bouncing the baby awkwardly in her arms. Finn laughed. 'Don't look so terrified, Madeleine. Jake said you didn't have much experience, but he didn't mention a mortal fear of children.'

'I'm not afraid!' Madeleine said with a flash of defiance that hit him straight in the gut. God, he liked that. But this was definitely not an appropriate thought to have about his best friend's sister. Or about his kids' babysitter for that matter. Temporary or not. He concentrated on the formula machine, pressing buttons and moving bottles on autopilot, until he had two bottles made up. If Hart was hungry, no doubt he would be hearing from Bella soon enough too.

With Madeleine taking care of Hart for a second, he allowed himself a moment to lean against the worktop and feel—really feel—how tired he was. If anything was going to distract him from his completely inappropriate thoughts about Madeleine, it would be that. Most of the time he managed to keep the fatigue at bay. But since his last nanny had left a week ago, he'd barely managed a minute's break.

His assistant was keeping the business ticking over, with him squeezing every minute of work into the day he possibly could, but there was only so long that that could carry on. He had built that business from the ground up and he wouldn't see it founder because he couldn't get proper childcare in place. With everything that the business had been through recently—their move to new premises, the enormous amount of money he had had to borrow to make that happen…

He had survived his divorce; he would survive this. But only if he stayed focused. Which was why he was so grateful that Madeleine had agreed to help him out. For the first time in weeks he could see himself actually getting back to the office some time this year, and without two babies strapped to him.

That was what he had to remember when he was tempted to sneak a look at her. When he was tempted to think of her as anything other than his best friend's sister or his temporary sitter. He and his business had survived the breakdown of his marriage by the skin of his teeth. They were still only surviving because he was generating enough income to service the debt that he had accrued in order to separate his and Caro's finances fairly and equitably. His company couldn't withstand any more disruption. His *life* couldn't stand any more disruption—he wasn't opening himself up to that again. Ever. So this sudden and inconvenient attraction to Madeleine didn't matter in the slightest.

He turned back to the kitchen island and smiled despite himself at the sight of Madeleine gazing thoughtfully at Hart. 'You two getting to know each other?' he asked, concentrating his gaze on the baby as the safest course of action.

'Babies are weird. He's a whole, real person,' Madeleine said, a little line creasing her brow. 'Only much, much smaller. And we don't know who he is yet. Don't you think that's a little strange?'

'A little,' Finn agreed. 'Don't worry. Spend enough time with them and you'll be too tired for philosophy.'

'You know you're really not selling this.'

'Too late,' he said with a laugh. 'You've already agreed.'

She rolled her eyes. 'I could change my mind.'

'And leave me in the lurch? You wouldn't. Jake would be mad.'

She huffed a little breath of a laugh. 'Aren't we a little old for threats like that?'

He smiled. 'Probably. Here, do you want to try him with this?'

She took the proffered bottle from him and stroked it over Hart's lips, then smiled down at him as he latched onto the teat, still only half awake. Madeleine beamed down at Hart, totally absorbed in watching him drink, and Finn forced down the warm feeling that was growing in his chest. It was just hormones, he told himself. It was natural to feel that when you were looking at a woman feed your baby. It was just nature. It didn't mean anything. It definitely didn't mean that he was interested in Madeleine because that would be more than inconvenient. It would be a complete disaster.

CHAPTER TWO

So...BABIES ARE OKAY, really, Madeleine thought, as she looked down at Hart drinking his milk, eyes rolling back in his head and cheeks wobbling. *Yeah, babies are fine.* It was the dads that were the problem. Well, one dad in particular. This one, whose eyes she could feel on her as she fed his son.

She was used to feeling men's eyes on her. They followed her down the road, fixed on her in lifts. Judged her from across a desk at work. They scraped on her skin from the minute she left the house until the minute she locked the door behind her at night, breathing out a huge sigh of relief as she did so.

She felt Finn's eyes on her occasionally since she'd arrived. Only, they didn't scrape. They...nudged. Suggestively, enquiringly, in a way that she was actually in danger of enjoying.

With some coffee inside her, and the baby on her knee, she could feel the tension leaching from her muscles and the rough start to her day starting to fall from her. There was something about the rhythmic sucking from the baby that held her attention absolutely. It wasn't until the bottle was empty and Hart was sucking on air that she looked up from him to find Finn watching her.

His eyes were fixed on her face, never wandering south, and she felt her cheeks warm.

'See, you're a natural,' he said, taking the bottle and the baby from her and laying Hart on his shoulder.

'I don't know about that,' Madeleine said with a shrug. 'But I'm glad I can help out. Did your last nanny leave in a hurry? Jake didn't tell me much...'

Like how you found yourself a single dad in the first place, she thought.

One minute Finn Holton had been the high-powered CEO of a company bringing ground-breaking technology to the world on a regular basis. The next he had been photographed with twin babies in a sling, and his wedding ring nowhere to be seen. The tabloids had gone understandably silly at this turn of events, but no one seemed to really know what had gone on. And she should know how hard they'd tried.

Not being a reality TV star or other such worthy, Finn's story hadn't made it to her desk at work. And thank God no one at the website had known about the childhood connection between her and Finn, otherwise they would have been harassing her for details that she didn't have.

It might have saved her job, she thought for a second, if she could have dished some dirt on her brother's friend. But she had none to dish. Jake had told her nothing, and Finn was hardly likely to tell her anything either. He knew that she was a journalist. To be honest, she was surprised that he had let her into his home at all. She couldn't imagine that he was going to start spilling his guts to her.

If only he knew that she didn't have the least interest in his personal life. She'd never wanted a career in celebrity gossip. But she'd left university without the double honours in politics and journalism she'd worked so hard for, and had found herself having to take any job she was offered. She'd thought the blog would be a stepping stone towards what she really wanted to be doing, serious political investigative journalism. But instead she'd found herself pigeon-holed. Doors slammed in her face and job applications unanswered. So she'd written clickbait, filed her copy and gone home at night with the sensation that somehow she'd found herself living someone else's life.

When the last round of redundancies had been announced, she'd been relieved as much as she had been concerned. A redundancy would give her a chance to make a change in her career. In her life. That was until her landlord had given her an eviction notice the following week, and she'd realised that she wasn't going to be able to get a new flat without a regular source of income. If she decided to go freelance—scrabbling around for the same work as all her colleagues who had also just been let go— it would be years before she had enough of an accounting history to pass a credit check. When she had called her brother and whined on the phone to

him, he'd told her he'd call her back with an idea—
and he had.

Which was how she had found herself in Finn
Holton's kitchen with a baby on her knee, wondering about the details of his personal life.

I mean, she shouldn't be curious. It was none of
her business how one of the country's leading technology moguls, and wealthiest men, had found himself a divorced single dad. If he had been a single
mum, no one would have given a second thought to
the fact that he was the one raising the babies. But
he wasn't a woman. And his situation *was* unusual.
Which made her wonder.

Her career might have focused more on celebs
falling out of nightclubs than on the business pages,
but that didn't mean she didn't have a journalist's
instincts at all.

'Jake was right, though. You're good at this,' Finn
said as he put the baby down in the Moses basket in
the corner. 'My children might be younger than his,
but you've got the knack.'

'Must be an auntie thing,' Madeleine said. 'I've
had enough practice with his brood. Who has four
kids, really?'

'They are great kids, though.'

She smiled but could feel her eyebrows pulling together even as she did so. Finn was not what she had
been expecting. At all. When she thought back to the
kid she had seen occasionally in her kitchen at home,
demolishing a loaf of bread's worth of toast with her
brother as they messed about on her family's com-

puter, there hadn't seemed much remarkable about him at all. She was pretty sure that she'd never paid him more than fleeting attention. I mean, who did, to their snotty little brother's mates?

If she'd known then the success that he was going to achieve, the enigmatic figure that he was going to become, would she have paid more attention?

Probably not, she admitted, letting her smile spread to her eyes. Teenage boys were unbearable. It didn't matter who they were going to grow up to be. She wondered if Finn remembered her as a teenager. Trying to swamp her emerging curves in giant T-shirts and baggy jeans. Whether he'd been one of the boys at school who had taken bets on whether they could sneak into the changing rooms while she was in PE and steal one of her bras.

No. Jake would have known. And he would never have allowed Finn in the house if that had been the case.

He looked nothing like the spotty, awkward-looking kid in worn-out trainers he had been then. She sneaked another glance at him while he was distracted by the baby, her journalist's eye taking a quick inventory, hitting the important points. Designer jeans, discreet but expensive watch, crisp white T-shirt, showing no sign of doing battle with two babies. Really, that wasn't fair. She was pretty sure her shirt had milk on it already and she'd only been here for an hour. But the clothes were all window-dressing, really.

It was the face that interested her. Because you

could change your clothes. You could drag yourself out of poverty and change your life and wear a new wardrobe. But you couldn't change your face. And when she looked at Finn, she could see him. The lost little boy who had spent more time in her family's kitchen than his own. Who had turned up starving, and had left stuffed to the gills with food by her mum, who'd known that he was probably going back to a cold house and an empty fridge. Who'd been packed off with clothes that Mum had just happened to find at the charity shop next door to her work, that wouldn't fit Jake and couldn't be returned.

He'd been a part of her family for years. But those years had happened to coincide with her later teenage ones, when she had spent as much time as humanly possible hidden in her room, avoiding her family. And anyone else for that matter.

Her teenage years hadn't exactly been a happy time, and being forced to revisit them, by virtue of the constant reminder that was Finn, hadn't been a part of her plan. But, as she had nowhere else to go, she was stuck with him, and the memories.

Finn was still making goofy faces at the baby, so she took another minute to look at him. To see the man, rather than the boy. There was no hiding from the fact that somewhere along the line he had become…beautiful. There was no other word for it. High cheekbones sloped down into a strong, stubble-covered jaw. Wide green eyes under dark brows, and a full mouth curved into a smile as he chatted gib-berish to his son. It was a pretty picture. If you liked that sort of thing. And the warmth low in her belly was all the proof—if proof were needed—that Madeleine absolutely did like that sort of thing.

She wondered if it had all changed him. The money. The success. The business. Of course it must have changed him. But *how* had it changed him? she wondered. Had it made him hard? Had he had to become tough, in order to break the cycle of poverty, finish his education, start his business? If it had, she couldn't see it now, with the sunshine streaming in through the windows and a baby chuckling goofily up at him. But that didn't mean that it wasn't lurking somewhere under the surface.

It didn't matter, she told herself sternly. Because she was staying in his home, she was looking after his children, and what she thought about him personally was completely out of bounds. It didn't matter if he was beautiful. It wouldn't matter if he was tough. Because any sort of a relationship—even the shortest of flirtations, the most casual of flings—was completely off the cards.

And flings were the only sort of relationship that Madeleine could tolerate. Get in, have fun, get out before they could disappoint you. That was what ten years of working and dating in London had taught her. So she swiped right and accepted blind dates and chatted to guys in bars, always safe in the knowledge that she was going to cut ties before they had a chance to disappoint her.

And there was no question that she would always be disappointed in the end. She'd learnt that early on in her love life, before she had even left school. When it didn't matter how sweet the boy was or how interested he pretended to be in her life; all he really wanted was to get a hand in her bra. And ever since she had worked that out, she had been happier. She accepted that no one saw past her body and her face, and all the assumptions that they would make about her. And as long as she didn't expect more, she could have fun with them for a few weeks. Relationships happened on her terms, met her needs and ended when she decided. It had kept her bed warm and her evenings full since she had been in London, and she was happy with that.

Except...that would never lead to this, she thought, watching Finn with Hart. It didn't lead to marriage and babies and a family of your own.

But she didn't care about that, Madeleine reminded herself. Single dad of twins wasn't exactly a nuclear family either. Nor were her brother and his husband and their adopted brood. She had other options if she decided that she wanted a family one day. Options that didn't include pretending that the guys she hung out with were able to take her seriously enough to be interested in anything more than her body.

And that was before she even got started on her disastrous professional life, which had never recovered from her decision to quit university in her final year. Which had led to her not being able to get the political reporting internships that she had wanted, which had led to her being on the entertainment desk of a second-rate gossip website, which apparently hadn't been generating enough income from its click-bait to actually continue paying its staff.

She shook herself, physically as well as metaphorically, causing Finn to look over at her.

'Sorry, we were ignoring you,' he said with a smile. 'I got distracted.'

She smiled at the pair, who were really too cute to be real. She'd had no idea what the sight of a beautiful man with his baby could do to a girl's ovaries, but she was pretty sure she'd just popped out an egg. And just as rapidly shut down those responses. This was just hormones. And stress. And…something of a dry spell. She wasn't sure what else she should be blaming it on. It didn't matter what the reasons were; the only thing that mattered now was that she shut it down.

'It's fine. I get it. I'm here to help, so just let me know what you want me to do.'

'Will you watch him again for a few minutes?' Finn asked, glancing at the clock on the wall. 'I should really wake Bella. If she goes too far off his schedule then the whole day falls apart. Pick him up if he starts to grizzle.' Which he started to do the minute that Finn moved away from him.

'Of course,' Madeleine said, taking Hart on her shoulder and rubbing his back out of instinct. Finn looked at her for a moment, and she felt herself starting to blush.

'Jake was right. You really are a natural at this,' he said, and Madeleine met his eyes, surprised.

'Yeah, well, I'm the fun auntie. I have the easy job.'

Finn nodded, and Madeleine turned away, uneasy under his gaze. And a little embarrassed. She had assumed that he had been looking at her because, really, it was what she was used to. But of course he had been looking at his son.

Maybe Finn wasn't attracted to her. That would certainly make life easier. Make the spark of attraction that she had felt for him a little less inconvenient too. Except…she had seen the way he had occasionally looked at her since she had arrived. It definitely wasn't as brotherly as would be convenient for her right now.

She tried to think back to the times that their paths had crossed in her childhood home, long since sold so that her parents could pursue their adventures abroad. Had Finn ever looked at her with adolescent heat in his eyes? Had she ever thought of him as something other than her pain-in-the-butt brother's pain-in-the-butt friend?

Of course not. Thinking back to her teenage years, it was unlikely that she'd peeled her eyes away from the floor for long enough to even get a proper look at him.

It had taken a long time for her to work out that the way to stop people looking at her was to stare them down rather than avoid their gaze. She had an expression that she knew could shame even the most hardened of voyeurs from fifty paces. It had taken time and practice to perfect, but she'd had no shortage of opportunities.

The pad of footsteps behind her made her spin on her stool, and Finn reappeared with another baby on his shoulder, the white of her Baby-gro as fresh and clean as the cotton of Finn's T-shirt.

'This sleepyhead here,' Finn said, half spinning on the spot so that Madeleine could see the baby's face, 'is Bella. Bella, say hi to Madeleine.'

Madeleine smiled at the baby, because who could resist a six-month-old, with their chubby cheeks and their chunky limbs, all energy stored up for crawling and walking and the chaos that was to come? But, for a little while longer, she would still be this gorgeous little chunk of babbling perfection, personality shining out of her, even when she was still half asleep.

'They're both so gorgeous. I don't know how you get anything done,' Madeleine said with a smile.

'I don't.' Finn laughed, though it sounded a little strained. 'That's why you're here. I think it would be a good idea if we all spent some time together over the weekend, get them settled in. Then next week I'll work from home but start building in a bit of time at the office. Get them used to it. Does that work for you?'

'*I* work for you,' Madeleine reminded him. 'It works how you want it to work.'

Finn narrowed his eyes at her. 'I'm not thinking of it that way. You're not an employee, Madeleine. I don't want this to be weird.'

'It's not weird.' She shook off the suggestion, tried to pretend that she was completely comfortable around Finn. Not unsettled at all by the attraction she was feeling for him.

'Good, because I thought we were just friends helping each other out. I'm really grateful for what you're doing.'

'And I'm grateful too, for the place to stay.'

'Good. You know that Jake is like family to me, right. Which means you're family too. Which means I want to help you out. Okay? The fact that you're able to take care of the kids for a few weeks, and I'm able to make sure that you are fairly compensated for that, that doesn't change how I see this, okay? If there's anything you're not happy with, if you change your mind or you find a new flat next week and you don't want to stay, you just tell me, right?'

She nodded, forced a smile, but it didn't matter what he said; this was already more complicated than he realised.

CHAPTER THREE

SHE LOOKED TRAPPED, and he hated that look on her face. Her expression when she said that she worked for him, he hated that too. He wasn't sure what it was, that haunted, distrustful look that told him that not everyone she had worked for had treated her fairly. It reminded him of how she had looked when he had opened the door to her earlier, when she had been harassed by the driver of a van.

'So…dinner tonight,' Finn said, changing the subject. 'My housekeeper, Trudy, has gone for the weekend, and I usually fend for myself.'

'My goodness, such a modern man,' Madeleine said with an eye roll. 'I'm sure I'm very impressed.'

'Save it for the stand-up routine,' Finn said, grinning. 'Fending for myself usually involves ordering pizza. If you're nice to me, I'll let you share.'

'Wow. Those millions sure have made you generous.' She smiled, but then felt awkward, seeing the look on his face when she mentioned money.

'I'm still just me,' he said, his voice low and serious.

'I know,' she said and smiled, reassuring him.

Even though, to be honest, she didn't really know him at all. But she knew entitled, privileged jerks when she saw them, and so far he didn't seem to be one. 'However fancy your kitchen gadgets. I like the apartment, by the way. How long have you been here?'

He produced a smile that didn't look quite natural. 'Since just before the babies were born. We sold the house when Caro and I...'

'Right, of course.' Madeleine tried to cover the awkward pause that inevitably followed accidentally bringing up someone's fairly recent divorce, not wanting to pry. But, at the same time, she was living with this man—albeit temporarily—and couldn't deny that she was curious about what had happened. I mean, she was only human.

'It was all very amicable,' he said, though a line had appeared between his eyebrows. 'We're still friends, of course. The twins, you know.'

Madeleine narrowed her eyes as she watched Finn. That all sounded too easy, and none of it explained the slightly pinched expression that he had assumed. The look of someone who had had too little sleep and too much worry in recent months, if she had to guess.

'It sounds like you were very grown-up about the split.'

Finn shrugged and gave a half-smile that came nowhere close to convincing her. 'We were, really. What choice did we have? She wanted to go; I couldn't make her stay. Squabbling over how we divided things up wasn't going to change that. I just needed it to be over. To concentrate on getting back on track.'

'And the babies?' Madeleine asked, surprised that Finn was opening up to her. And more than a little intrigued about what exactly it was that Caro had hated so much about her life with Finn. From where Madeleine was sitting, it had quite a lot going for it. And she wasn't thinking about the perfect espresso she'd just downed in two gulps.

'She didn't find out that she was pregnant until quite late on,' Finn said, and once again Madeleine was struck by his honesty. She couldn't believe that he was trusting her with the details of his marriage. Wasn't he worried that she was going to sell him out? 'By then our marriage was already over, and she had accepted a job doing emergency aid work abroad. She wanted the kids raised here, where it was safer. We both did. And she didn't want to turn down a job where she knew she could save thousands of lives.'

So their marriage was already over. That was interesting. She'd assumed that their breakup was a recent thing, with the babies and all, but it sounded as if it must have happened more than a year ago. And all of a sudden, sleeping in his home, with this spark of attraction she was finding hard to ignore, was seeming like a less and less good idea.

'And so now you're a full-time dad,' she stated.

'Well, I'm trying to work as much as I can,' he said with a shrug, that pinched look back around his eyes. 'But at the moment it's just not enough.

There's definitely more dadding going on, and I'm grateful for the extra time with them, but I can't let things slide any further with work. I'm hoping that's where you come in, while I find someone more permanent, that is.'

Madeleine nodded, thoughtful. 'I bet people were surprised.'

He frowned for a second before he guessed her meaning. 'That I want to parent my children?' he asked. She saw the hardness appear around his mouth and jaw and heard the sharpness in his tone, and realised that she had hit a nerve. But she hadn't been criticising—either him or Caro. She was just surprised. 'It's just unusual that you're doing it while Caro's abroad,' Madeleine said, pointing out the obvious. 'I didn't mean anything by it.'

'She's a good mum,' Finn said, his face still hard. 'She video calls every day. She comes home when she can. All that she wants is for them to be safe and happy. Thousands of men do the same thing every day and no one bats an eyelid.'

Madeleine sat up straighter, a little indignant that he thought she was judging. 'I wasn't batting! I never questioned that Caro is a good mum. But you can't deny that the situation is unusual, that's all.'

'Look at my life, Madeleine,' Finn said, the muscle in his jaw finally relaxing. 'Everything about it is unusual.'

She nodded. 'It's definitely different from when we were growing up,' she ventured, wondering how he would react to the reminder about his change in circumstances.

'God, I know. If you'd told me then…'

Madeleine smiled, sensing that this was as far as this conversation was going to go.

'So, this pizza, then,' she said, grasping for a change of topic. 'Are these kiddies going to co-operate and let us eat with two hands? Should we wear them out before bedtime?'

'That,' Finn said, standing suddenly, 'is an excellent idea. Let me give you the grand tour, and we can let them have a roll around on their play mat in the nursery while you get settled.'

Madeleine stood and parked Hart on her hip, where he gurgled and babbled as he reached out to Finn and his sister.

'I never knew they were so wriggly at this age,' Madeleine said, pulling Hart in closer so he didn't dive out of her arms.

'You should try it with two of them,' Finn said with a laugh as Bella decided it was her turn to try and escape.

'Just promise you're not going to leave me alone with them just yet,' Madeleine said, her smile fading when she realised that she was basically asking him to spend time with her. That verged dangerously close to needy—and she hated needy.

'I promise, not until you feel you're ready,' Finn said as he led them out of the kitchen and into the hallway, with its elegant sweeping staircase up to the first floor.

'I thought you'd be most comfortable in here,' Finn said, showing her into a guest room. The bed held an imposing number of soft furnishings, but it was the desk in front of the window that caught her eye. An elegant writing desk with a simple Scandinavian aesthetic sat in front of a Juliet balcony looking out on the garden.

Finn must have caught the direction of her interest because he said, 'I had Trudy bring that in here. I wasn't sure if you'd want to write, or if you were working.'

'That is so thoughtful. Thank you.'

'And if there's anything else that you need, just let me know, okay? I want you to feel at home here.'

And, surprisingly, she thought that she might, for the few weeks that she was planning on staying, at least. The luxuries made that easy enough: the sparkling decanter of water on her nightstand, the toiletries that she could glimpse through the open door to her en suite bathroom. It was a far cry from the mould-infested flat that she'd just been evicted from. But it wasn't just the luxury of the place. It just had…a vibe. She wasn't sure what it was. But she felt comfortable here. Maybe it was that she'd known Finn for ever, that he had been a part of her family for as long as she could remember.

But then she looked over at Finn and caught him looking at her. Not at her body—she could tell when men were doing that. But at her. And nothing felt comfortable any more. Because she wasn't sure that she'd ever seen anyone look at her like that. If she'd ever felt a man's eyes on her and not felt as if she was being flayed open and they were peering at her insides.

It was the same reason, she told herself. Finn didn't look at her like that because he'd known her before she had this body. When she'd been a child. Before everyone she met had started judging her on the curves of her breasts and her hips, as if they somehow broadcast something about her personality.

But he *noticed* her body. She'd seen and cringed at enough reactions to her over the years to be able to read a man's mind perfectly when he was looking at her. And Finn's was no different. He saw her curves. He liked them. But she was starting to have the suspicion that he saw beyond them too. That he would still look at her like that whatever shape her body took.

And that was deeply unsettling. Because if there was one thing that she had learnt over the years it was how reliably men reacted to her. What she should expect from them, and what she should ask of them in return. And if she was wrong about that, if Finn was going to tread outside of that familiar, safe territory that she had constructed for herself, then she wasn't sure what to make of it.

She met his eyes and he startled, and that gave her hope. Because, whatever this tension was between them, it seemed as if Finn was as wary of it as she was. And that was good. That meant that they were both going to be on their guard. That they were both going to be committed to keeping these feelings in their place.

She knew why she was so wary. But she wondered about Finn. She had strong suspicions that he was attracted to her. But it was equally clear that he had no intention of acting on that. Why? Was it the divorce? Was he still heartbroken over Caro? She didn't think so. He had sounded a little sad when they had talked about her earlier. But he wasn't yearning for her; she could read that much. But she still wondered what had happened—why they had broken up. They had been together for a couple of years before they had got married, so it wasn't a flash-in-the-pan relationship.

She could ask him, she supposed. But the way that he had shut down her questioning made clear that he didn't want to talk about it, and it wasn't her place to push him. She could ask her brother, but showing that level of interest would open her up to a whole lot of questions from Jake that she had no intention of answering.

Finn showed Madeleine around the apartment, wondering what on earth had made him think that it would be a good idea to spill the details of his marriage and divorce to a journalist. Because, despite their history and their shared childhood memories, Madeleine *was* a journalist. And, more than that, she was a journalist who had recently been made redundant and pitched into an enormously competitive job and freelance market. The woman had to eat, and if she chose to do that by selling the story that he had just willingly spilled to her then who could blame her? He certainly wouldn't.

Back in the day, there was very little that he wouldn't have done to put food in his belly and a roof over his head. And a decade of more money than he needed had done nothing to dull the memories of those decades of deprivation. And then recently, with his divorce and the developments at work, having to leave the home that he and Caroline had bought together, having to dismantle the life they had created together, he'd found himself staring at his spreadsheets and feeling that familiar nag of worry. An instinct that he'd thought he'd lost years ago.

And Madeleine hadn't forgotten his old life either. He used to turn up at her house with an empty belly, desperately ashamed of the fact that he would willingly raid their fridge for anything that he could get his hands on, and the fact that they all knew the score. They had always tried to cover it up. Looked the other way when their mum had given him the biggest portion at dinner. But they all knew, and he knew that they knew.

The alternative was going hungry, going home to a cold empty house while his mother worked her second job in a futile attempt to make ends meet. And hunger had won out over pride every time. He felt hot at the memories of how low he had had to stoop at that time in his life, and grateful that his children would never ever know that feeling. His mother had done everything that she could for him.

She had worked two jobs trying to provide for them, but it had never been enough. Without the Everleigh family, he would have been as lonely as he had been hungry. It was thanks to them that they had all made it through those years. Thanks to them that he had finished his homework and turned up at school.

Now that he was the one with the warm home and the food and the luxury lifestyle, he would never begrudge any of them a single penny. He could never repay what they had given him, no matter how hard he tried. Giving Madeleine his spare room for a few weeks was nothing. Not compared to what she had given him, what she'd shared with him, back when she'd barely acknowledged his existence. She could take it all, as far as he was concerned, for as long as she needed it, and he would still be in her debt.

Getting twin babies to sleep wasn't an easy task at the best of times. When they were overstimulated by a new face and a new playmate who was in no way as immune to their babyish charms as he had had to learn to be, it was damn near impossible. Despite Finn having managed to get two babies into the bathroom at six-thirty, right on schedule, it had been half an hour before they had escaped that steam-filled room with two overtired, giggling, wriggly bundles wrapped in towels. And that had only been the start of the fun and games. It had taken nearly an hour of rocking, bouncing and pacing the hallways to get them both asleep, and in that time he and Madeleine had barely exchanged more than an exasperated glance as they'd passed one another in the hallway.

He had seen the shock starting to fade and the reality of what she had let herself in for starting to sink in as the babies had fought sleep, or being put down in their cots, over and over. And over. By the time that they'd both slowly backed out of the nursery, breath held and the door gently closed, he was ready to sink into bed and call it a night. But Madeleine was his guest and he knew that Jake expected more of him than to leave her to fend for herself the first night she was here.

That was all it was, he told himself. He owed it to Jake to make sure that Madeleine was settled and happy and had everything she needed. There was no other reason that the idea of sharing a pizza with her had sustained him all evening. It would be absolutely inappropriate for him to think of her as anything other than Jake's sister and his temporary saviour. It absolutely was not—in any way—a date.

So why did he feel so nervous?

He didn't even get nervous before dates. At least he didn't think that he did. Since he and Caro had decided that their marriage was over, he hadn't been on one. Until the twins were a couple of months old he had seen Caro almost as much as when they were married—just because he was no longer her husband didn't mean that he wasn't going to support her through the pregnancy and take care of her afterwards, until she was ready to take up her new job. But, all that aside, what would be the point in dating when he knew that he would never have a serious relationship again? The last—as amicably as it had ended—had threatened everything that he had worked for over the last decade. Had seen him taking on financial uncertainty that he still wasn't sure that he was going to survive. He was never going through that again. He just couldn't take the risk.

Until he had opened the door to Madeleine Everleigh, and his decision to stay permanently single didn't seem quite so simple.

Which left his love life…where? In the realm of hook-ups and one-night stands and casual flings? And when it came to Madeleine…he couldn't think of a less appropriate relationship to have with his best friend's sister. Jake had been best man at his wedding. He couldn't even think about a casual hook-up with the man's sister. Except…he was thinking about it.

Oh, was he thinking about it.

And it wasn't even Madeleine's body he was thinking about. It was her eyes that he couldn't get out of his mind. The way that she looked at him and saw the smooth businessman and the frazzled dad and the scared kid all at once. They weren't separate people to her, the way that they were to everyone else in his life. The circles of his business life and his childhood friends and his social life never crossed. He squeezed himself into those different personas as he put on his suit for work or clipped himself into a baby carrier and headed to a playgroup. But not with Madeleine.

He'd never felt the strangeness of that with Jake. Maybe because he had never looked at Jake and had

the instant flash of desire he had with Madeleine.
With Madeleine? It was hard to think about anything
else. Especially now she was here in his home, settling in with her things, playing with his kids and
drinking his coffee. Merging their lives for the next
few weeks.

Even with Caro there had been barriers between
the different parts of his life. She had accompanied
him to work functions. Slipped smoothly through
the networking and the business dinners that were
expected of her. But she had never slipped so com-
fortably into his past, the parts of his life that were
harder to face. She'd never been comfortable with
his mother. He could never have taken her to see the
tiny flat where he had grown up.

Absurd, really, given that she was dedicating
her life to ending child poverty. She wouldn't have
judged him. But he didn't want to be a project to her.
He didn't want to be one of the kids she was rescuing.

With Madeleine, nothing had to be said. Or hidden. Or tiptoed around. She knew it all. She knew
how bad it had been, and how high he had risen, and
she saw that he was the same person wherever he
was living. And the thought of that, of the two parts
of his life being reconciled, was troubling. And in-
toxicating.

He showed Madeleine back down to the kitchen
and hunted out the pizza menus he kept in a drawer
for weekends when he couldn't be bothered to cook.
It wouldn't be long now before the babies were eating real food and he would actually have to produce

something that they could all eat together, rather than just steaming them some carrot sticks. But for a few more weeks, at least, his weekends could be eighty per cent pepperoni. He handed Madeleine a menu and headed to the fridge to find them both a beer.

'We can take the drinks out on the balcony if you like,' Finn suggested, glancing over at Madeleine. 'There's a nice view of the park.'

'Sure,' she replied with a shrug, eyes still on the menu. 'Sounds like a plan. I'll bring my phone and we can order from there.'

CHAPTER FOUR

MADELEINE FOLLOWED FINN up the stairs, still trying to keep her mind on the pizza menu in order to stop it wandering anywhere more dangerous than that. Like up a couple of steps to where Finn's behind was almost exactly at her eye line, and way, *way* too tempting to look at. He might have been a skinny kid when she'd first known him, but he wasn't any longer. He'd shown her the gym in the basement of the apartment building, and it seemed he made good use of it. She knew that if she let her gaze wander up over the edge of the menu she would see strong, thick thighs and a perfect firm backside.

All that from sneaking glances, then stopping herself as soon as she realised what she was doing. And it had been enough all day to keep her cheeks colouring, and illicit thoughts in her brain. She thought that she might combust if she actually allowed herself to get a proper eyeful.

Finn turned right at the top of the stairs, taking her down a corridor they hadn't covered in their tour earlier. And when he pushed open a door it took her a few moments to realise what she was looking at.

The duvet had been hastily pulled back on the bed, a phone was charging on the bedside table beside a creased paperback and half-empty glass of water. A pile of clothes had been discarded on the way to the bathroom, the door to which stood ajar on the far wall.

She took a step back, her heart caught in her throat as she tried to process this information. She'd thought they were going out onto the balcony for a drink. But instead he had brought her here, to what was unmistakably his bedroom. Was this a trick? She took another step back, her heart pounding in her chest as she tried to assess her options. She could just head for the front door. Run out and not look back. She could back away slowly, and hope that he didn't turn nasty when he didn't get what he wanted.

How many years had she been making these calculations—trying to find a way out of trouble when her body gave men ideas that she had no intention of going along with? Somehow, somewhere along the line, it had become her job to let them down gently. To avoid the nasty consequences she knew could follow if she didn't handle their fragile little egos carefully enough as she rejected their advances.

How had she really misread the situation here so badly? she asked herself. Sure, she had sensed that spark of interest from Finn. She guessed that he liked her body. But somehow she hadn't sensed danger here. Was that because she had been attracted to him too? Had that put her off her guard, led her into this dangerous situation? She tried to think again whether she had said something or done something to make him think that this was what she wanted.

Because this wasn't what she wanted. Just because she might have fantasised about more at some point, that didn't mean that that was where she was at right now. She wasn't so stupid to think that she could just have desires and act on them.

She heard a weird gargle form in her throat and had just about made up her mind to run when Finn turned and looked at her. She saw the expression in his eyes change from confusion to shock when he took in her expression. She gripped a little tighter to her phone, just in case she had to use it, and inched back when Finn squared up to her.

'Madeleine…' He spoke slowly, as if to a spooked animal, and she wondered what was showing on her face to make him think he needed to.

'This is your bedroom,' Madeleine spat out, taking control of the situation. 'You didn't say anything about your bedroom,' she went on, making sure he knew that she wasn't going to be swept along with something. That she knew what she wanted and didn't want right now and was going to stand up for herself.

'I'm so sorry,' Finn said, holding his hands up, still using that slow calm tone that made her think she had rabbit-in-the-headlights eyes. 'I should have explained we need to get to the balcony through my bedroom. Out there,' he said, gesturing towards the

French windows, covered with gauzy voile curtains. 'The lock is stuck on the other door out and at the moment this is the only way. I'm sorry I didn't explain that before we came up here.'

He looked at her for a moment longer, and she wondered what he was seeing. She was frozen in the doorway, her hand locked tight around her phone, her mind stuck in another moment of fight or flight. Another time where she had thought she was safe, only to be blindsided with a man's demands on her. She had run then, and it had destroyed her career before it had even begun. It had led her to the mouldy little bedsit she had been existing in until she had been evicted and found herself on Finn's doorstep.

So what should she do now? Fight? This was the only source of income, the only roof over her head, that she had for the foreseeable future, until she figured out what she was going to do with the rest of her life. Flight? She could run, to Jake's. He would make room for her, no matter how cramped it left his family. But she hadn't wanted to impose before and still didn't now. And he was Finn's best friend. What if he asked why she had left? *If?* Of course he would ask, and she didn't know what she would tell him.

Finn took a step towards her and she took another two back, glancing over her shoulder just for a fraction of a second to judge the distance to the stairs before looking back at Finn, making sure she had re-established the space between them. He shut the bedroom door firmly and leaned back against it, crossing his arms over his body, creating a barrier between them. His face was hard and tough, and she wasn't sure whether the suppressed anger she saw there was directed at her. There wasn't anyone else here.

'Madeleine, I'm so sorry that I scared you,' he said. 'That was thoughtless of me. I promise you have nothing to be afraid of. I didn't mean anything by bringing you to my bedroom, other than a way to get out onto the balcony.'

'I wasn't scared,' she bit out automatically. She could lie to him, but she couldn't lie to herself. Her mouth still carried the bitter tang of blood where she had bitten the inside of her cheek and she could still hear the pounding of her blood as it raced around her body, bringing oxygen to the big muscles of her limbs, readying her for battle.

She hesitated for a moment, let her blood pressure drop a fraction, and then a fraction more, Finn still standing dead still against the door to his bedroom. She looked behind her again, making sure she had space to run if she needed it.

'If you want to leave, I'll get you a car right away,' he said. 'It can take you to Jake's. Or a hotel. Wherever you would feel safe.'

'I can order my own ride,' she said on reflex, before she had really had a chance to process his words. He was offering her a way out. He was giving her sanctuary. Why would he do that if he was a threat to her? She looked up and met his eyes for the first time since they had left the kitchen, and the compassion she read there almost broke her. The adrenaline left her body in a rush, leaving her limp and soft, and she slumped back against the wall. Finn wasn't a threat. This apartment was safe. She was safe. He was the boy that she had known most of her life, and he wanted to protect her.

'I'm sorry,' she said, letting her head drop back against the wall and trying to slow her heart rate.

'Don't apologise,' he ordered, looking her hard in the eye. 'Are you okay?'

'Getting there,' Madeleine admitted, letting her eyes shut, blocking out the world for just a minute.

'Do you want to talk about it?' Finn asked, his voice as soft as she had ever heard it. She was tempted, for a moment. For no reason other than to explain what must have looked like truly bizarre behaviour. But she had carried this secret for more years than she cared to think about. And she had always believed that it was best that way. What was done was done, and talking about it wasn't going to change anything. More than that, talking about it was going to slice into a well-healed wound and make her bleed again, and she had absolutely no desire to give that a try.

Except…except how well healed could it be, really, when this was her reaction to something so minor? She had completely overreacted to an innocent move on Finn's part. Perhaps reopening that wound would be necessary, one of these days, and looking a little closer at what had got her blood pumping just then.

But she couldn't do it now. Not when her body was winding down from that burst of panic and her limbs felt like noodles. Not when Finn's eyes were on her, seeing more than she'd ever intended to show him.

'Pizza,' she said at last, loosening her grip on her phone and the sweaty flyer now scrunched in her palm.

Finn raised his eyes, assessing this change in the subject, whether he was going to push her more or let the matter drop. To her relief, he unfolded his arms and nodded.

'You order. I'm going to check on the kids and I'll meet you in the kitchen in a bit.'

Space. Silence. Thank God.

She walked down the stairs and perched on a stool in the kitchen, concentrating her whole mind on the simple task of ordering pizza. Because, if she let it wander, all she could see was Finn's face as she'd stood in front of him, looking at him as if he was a sexual predator, her body primed to fight him. She didn't want to think about what he was thinking right now. She couldn't afford to wonder what was going through his mind as he peeked in on the babies and made sure that they were sleeping soundly.

Maybe she should just go, be a burden on her brother for a few weeks. Sleep on her nephews' bedroom floor amidst the discarded Lego and Pokémon cards.

Or she could leave London. Go travelling. What, with all the money that she had stashed away for a rainy day from her subsistence-level wage from a second-rate gossip site? Maybe she could find a job at a local paper somewhere dull and anonymous and spend the rest of her life chasing stories about lost kittens and parish council in-fighting. Any of those options looked preferable to having to face Finn when he came back downstairs.

The buzz from the front door intercom interrupted her thoughts. Pizza. Whatever decisions she had to make, she would make them with a full stomach, even if that did mean facing Finn. She wasn't stupid enough to launch herself out into the night hungry.

As she brought the pizzas back through to the kitchen she heard Finn's footsteps behind her and felt the colour rising in her cheeks before she'd even turned around to look at him.

'Hey,' he said, his voice hesitant as she opened up the cardboard boxes and they were hit by the smell of melted cheese and crisp dough.

'Hey.' She forced a smile and hoped that it looked less creaky than it felt. She leaned back on the breakfast bar to eat. Last time they had tried to find an alternative venue it had gone so horribly wrong. And she felt secure with that huge chunk of granite between them. Not that she thought that she had anything to fear from Finn any more. It was just that she thought if he got any closer she might actually melt from shame, if the floor wasn't kind enough to simply swallow her whole before that could happen.

'Look, about what happened—' Finn started, but she jumped in before he could finish.

'Really, you don't have to… I'm sorry I overreacted. It's nothing.'

'It's not nothing, Madeleine. You're my guest and

I need to know that you feel safe here. I'm going to say this now so it's out there. I know that there's some sort of chemistry between us—I feel it, and I think you do too. But here's the thing—I'm not going to do anything about it. You have absolutely nothing to worry about on that front. I wasn't trying to get you into bed, and I'm not going to. You're Jake's sister, practically family, and I would never risk that over something… I just don't want you to think that that's what I had in mind when I invited you here,' he went on, 'I don't want you thinking you have to be on your guard around me. You're safe here.'

It was what she wanted to hear. She was safe. She was protected. She hadn't wanted him to be trying to engineer her into bed.

And yet…it still felt brutal, somehow. The way that he said it—he was never going to do anything about it. The absolute certainty in his voice when he told her that he wasn't interested in her.

Well, that was fine because she'd had every intention of shutting her own feelings down. This would only make that easier. She could carry on with her role as nanny, or babysitter, or best friend's sister, or whatever she was to him, without any added complications.

Fine.

She was absolutely fine with that.

CHAPTER FIVE

TORTURE. THAT WAS the only word that could adequately describe the past hour. First, that look in Madeleine's eyes when she'd thought that he was trying to trick her. Now this, having to tell her that he had absolutely no interest in following through on his feelings for her, because it was suddenly clear to him that this chemistry between them wasn't important. What was important was protecting Madeleine, and his place in her life—as part of her family. And that meant never following where that spark between them might lead.

There was no hiding the look in her eyes when they had been on the landing upstairs. She had been terrified. Looking for the exits, calculating risks. So sure that she was in danger. He couldn't believe that he had been so stupid. That it hadn't occurred to him to mention that the only way out onto the balcony was through his bedroom.

But there was more to the story too. He was sure of that. The look in her eyes and that reaction— they didn't come from nowhere. And that meant that someone in her past had hurt her. He had been surprised by the rage he had felt when he had realised that. The overwhelming desire to hunt down the person that had made Madeleine so afraid, and to make sure that he could never get to her again. But there was no way that he could say that to Madeleine. Because the minute that he had suggested that she might want to talk about it, her shutters had come down. She'd looked as terrified at the prospect of that as she had at the thought of him trying to trap her in his bedroom.

So he'd done the only thing he could think to do—he'd said what he had to, to make her feel safe. He'd decided that that was more important than any hopes he might have had that this chemistry might lead somewhere. Because of course he had been interested. In other circumstances. If things had been different. If his business had been more stable. If his divorce hadn't left him convinced that he needed to stay single to protect the life that he had built for himself, then he would *definitely* have been interested. But now that he had seen she was scared of him? None of that mattered anyway. He never wanted to see that look in her eyes again.

So now he wasn't interested, he told himself. It wasn't a lie. Because it didn't matter what chemical reaction his body threw up when he looked at her, he was more than just an animal reacting to his hormones or his basest desires. He was an adult with full control over himself. And he was using that control now to shut down any hint of attraction towards her. His only priority now was making sure that she felt safe. That nothing could hurt her while she was under his roof.

Thank God she had turned down his offer to get her a car. Because he had never felt such a strong urge to protect someone before. If he'd had to send her out into the night with no idea where she was going, he didn't think he could have borne it.

He hoped she felt safe now.

He risked a look at her over his pizza slice, and found her eyes on him. As their gazes met he hesitated, wanting again to ask her what had happened to provoke such a strong reaction. Wanting to ask how he could fix it. And then remembering that it wasn't his place to ask. She didn't want to share what had happened with him, and he had no right to push. He had no right to anything. She was Jake's sister, and that made her feel like family to him, but he had no expectation that she returned the feeling. To her he was probably just the annoying little kid at the end of her dining table, talking Lego and Nintendo with her brother. He was constantly surprised that she remembered him at all.

The fact that Jake thought of him like a brother didn't automatically extend that feeling to Madeleine. They had barely spoken when they were kids. The two-year difference in age had been a gulf that had stretched too far between them. Separating their lives into different worlds. She might as well have been an alien for all they had had in common when she was fourteen and he was twelve.

'Good pizza,' she said at last, when the silence had stretched out to unbearable. He looked away as she broke their gaze and started to lick the grease from her fingers. Principled he might be, but he wasn't a saint.

'Yeah, I'm a good customer,' he replied, trying to keep his mind on the food. He glanced up at the clock. It was still early, really early. But he had the perfect excuse to hide away from her tonight.

'Look, I'm sorry to leave you to your own devices your first night here, but would you mind if I turned in? The twins still have a midnight feed, and I could grab an hour or two of sleep before I have to do that.'

'Of course,' she said, looking relieved. 'Will you need my help—?'

'No,' he jumped in. The last thing that they both needed was an impromptu meeting in the middle of the night. 'It's fine. I can handle it. You need anything before I go up?'

She shook her head, and for a second he thought that she was going to say something more. But then she dropped her head and he knew the moment had passed.

'Goodnight,' he said, then turned for the door without waiting for a reply.

CHAPTER SIX

THE NEXT MORNING Madeleine fought the arrival
of the sunlight around the edges of the curtains in
her room and wished that she'd had the foresight to
close the shutters before she'd come to bed last night.
With how discombobulated she'd been feeling, it was
really a wonder that she'd managed to pull on some
pyjamas and wipe off her make-up, never mind fid-
dling with the pristinely restored period features of
the building.

How long could she get away with hiding up here?
she wondered. She was under no illusions that the
reason for Finn's ridiculously early night last night
was because the atmosphere had gone from awkward
to worse. All because of her stupid overreaction to
seeing the inside of Finn's bedroom.

A large part of her insides wanted to curl up and
die this morning, when she remembered how she had
reacted. The pumping blood. The wild eyes. The implicit accusation in her response.

Not implicit. Explicit. So explicit, in fact, that
Finn had felt it necessary to tell her in the baldest

possible way that he was not interested in having sex with her. She blushed again at the memory. She was meant to be his guest. But her hair-trigger reaction to the smallest of misunderstandings had meant she'd all but accused him of planning to try and molest her.

No wonder he had chosen to spend the rest of the evening away from her.

She wished that she could check out of her brain sometimes too. Leave the flashbacks and the panic aside, and just live like a normal person. React in a totally normal way to totally normal stimuli.

The sound of a baby crying reached up to her first-floor room and when the second baby joined in she knew that she had to move. She was meant to be helping out with the kids and hiding up here wasn't just childish, it was dereliction of duty. A duty that just happened to be keeping a roof over her head and her bank balance in the black.

She pulled a big soft wrap cardigan on over her jersey pants and sleep top, and pulled her hair back into a reasonably respectable ponytail. Drawing back the curtains, she realised she'd been missing out on a truly glorious day. The park in the middle of the square was bathed in golden sunshine and the sky was a deep clear blue. It was enough to blow the cobwebs off her bad mood and actually make her smile.

When she reached the kitchen, Finn was bouncing Bella on his shoulder while making up a bottle, and both babies seemed to be competing to see which could make the most ear-splitting noise. Hart, in a bouncy seat on the floor, looked—or sounded—to be winning, so she scooped him up, taking a moment to fuss over him before turning to Finn. She held her breath for a moment, not sure whether things would be weird this morning, and praying that he had scrubbed the previous evening from his memory.

'Oh, thank God you're here,' he said with a smile, hitching Bella higher on his shoulder as he scooped formula into little plastic pots. 'They don't usually gang up on me like this, but when they do—boy, do they go for it. Here, do you think you can manage Bella too?'

Before she had a chance to say no, she had a baby parked on each hip while Finn screwed lids onto bottles and wiped down countertops.

'I was thinking we should go out for the day,' Finn said. 'Enjoy the sunshine. There's only so much you can do to entertain these two indoors.'

'Sounds great. What did you have in mind?' she asked, grateful that they weren't going to spend the day inside. It didn't matter how luxurious the surroundings were. If the atmosphere was as tense as it had been the previous evening, then it would be completely unbearable.

'Well, I've never taken them to the beach,' Finn said, putting away the tin of formula. 'It's too nice a day to spend half of it in traffic getting to the coast, but there's a pop-up beach I read about that might be fun. It might also be a nightmare of sand-encrusted toddlers. But worth a try?'

'Definitely worth a try,' Madeleine said, marvelling that the twins were both quieting down as she bounced them gently. 'Do I even want to know what packing a bag for twins at the beach looks like?' she asked with a dubious look at the backpack slung over the back of one of the dining chairs.

'It's terrifying,' Finn confirmed with a laugh. 'But I'll talk you through it. And there should be enough stuff in the fridge to pack a decent picnic. Trudy has a habit of predicting my impulses on such a regular basis it makes me wonder how impulsive I really am.'

'Did you know that the best indicator of the number of barbecues on a Saturday is the temperature on the preceding Tuesday? Sounds like Trudy has a good grip on economics,' Madeleine said. 'Right, give me a list of what the kids need and I'll go find it in their room. Then we can raid the fridge together. Sound like a plan?'

'Great,' Finn said, before reeling off a list of clothing and supplies that Madeleine was sure could outfit a military unit for several weeks. But as she packed tiny clothes into an enormous bag she was glad of the practical challenges that a day out with the babies would pose. She wanted her time filled—every second of it, if possible—because the alternative was awkward silences or, worse, awkward conversation.

By the time that she got downstairs, Bella and Hart were in their car seats and Finn was looking at his phone. 'The car's outside whenever we're ready,' he said, looking up at her with a smile. 'Did you find everything?'

'I think so. I mean, how badly can it go?'

'Well, I've been out with them before and they've pooed through every item of clothing in the bag and I've run out of wipes halfway through the day. But sure, nothing worse than that.'

'We're going into central London. They have baby wipes there. We'll be fine,' she said with a confidence that she didn't feel.

'I'll hold you to that,' Finn said with a laugh, sliding his phone in his pocket and reaching for one of the car seats. 'Do you mind grabbing Hart? I cannot tell you what a luxury it is not to have to lug all this stuff on my own.'

'Sure. That's what I'm here for,' Madeleine said, and was grateful for the little reminder to herself. She was only here to look after the children. Last night had been awkward, but they just had to ignore it. It wasn't as if they even had a friendship that they had to rescue. Just because he was friends with Jake didn't mean he was her friend too. All they had to think about was the children—and she could do that.

Just from the half day she had spent with them already, she knew that they were more than capable of filling her time and her thoughts. But their dad did keep trying to muscle in there too. No, that wasn't fair. That made it sound like Finn's fault, and it wasn't. It was entirely her fault that she couldn't stop thinking about him. It had been bad enough, even before that incident on the landing last night. But this morning it was worse.

Because yesterday—it was a fun little fantasy. Something that she knew that she was never going to act on. Something that she knew couldn't hurt her. But today…today was different.

Because once Finn had mentioned his attraction— the chemistry between them—it had breached an unspoken rule where they were just refusing to acknowledge that it existed. And even though Finn had said that he wasn't interested in acting on their feelings, she wasn't sure that she believed him. It had felt brutal last night, when he had said the words.

But this morning she could see the bigger picture. She knew that there had been a spark there when she had arrived. And she knew what a fright she must have looked when she had freaked out about his bedroom. She didn't want him to be attracted to her. God knew she didn't want to be attracted to him. If they could go along with what he had said and just try and ignore these feelings, that would make life so much easier for the next few weeks.

As the car sat and idled in the London traffic she busied herself with fussing over the babies, glad that the four-by-four had enough space that she wasn't pressed against Finn's thigh. She wasn't sure how long she'd be able to kid herself that she had absolutely no feelings about him if she had the firm press of his muscle against her skin.

Up in her room, she had agonised over what to wear. A visit to the beach didn't usually see her at her most comfortable at the best of times, but she suspected that a visit to the beach with Finn by her side would make her more self-conscious still. The fact that the beach happened to be in the middle of London, the largest and most densely populated city in the country, was actually a godsend. There would be no room for relaxed, reclined sunbathing. She thought that they would be lucky to find somewhere to plonk the babies down on the sand, never mind find a space for them to sit.

And if there was no sunbathing there was absolutely no need for a swimsuit. She'd pulled on cropped culottes, a tank top and Wayfarer shades, sure that she would be grateful for the dark lenses to hide behind later in the day.

She couldn't shake those words from her head. He was attracted to her. Why did that bother her so much? No, that was the wrong question. She knew why she was so bothered by them. It was because she felt the same. Having that information out in the open was meant to defuse the situation, but it didn't feel like that right now. Once the shock of last night's encounter had worn off, the knowledge that their attraction was mutual had left an electric fizz in the air.

Not that it mattered any more, because after what had happened there was no way that he would be interested in her. Attraction—liking her body and her face—was one thing. Being willing to take on her trunkful of emotional baggage was quite another. And it was clear from the look on his face last night—even without him stating it as clearly as he had—that he absolutely wasn't interested.

And who could blame him?

Finally the car pulled up near to the pop-up beach, and she made herself busy fishing bags and sunshades and stray baby hats out of the boot of the car while Finn flipped out the pushchair with practised ease and started buckling Hart into one side. She fetched Bella from her car seat, stowed bags underneath and then took a step back to marvel at the sheer amount of stuff that they had brought with them.

'I am never ever doing this on my own,' she stated, only half joking. 'Can I be one of those completely useless nannies that you have to take time off work to supervise because you're worried they might leave the babies behind somewhere?'

Finn shrugged, all mock-casual in a way that had her softening towards him when she'd been so *so* sure that she could resist that charm of his. 'Only if you don't mind me telling Jake how useless you are.'

She laughed, her body instantly relaxing into it, despite her better judgement. 'You know it's really not fair to keep bringing him up like that,' she said, swatting at him good-humouredly as they clipped the babies into their pram seats. 'Pulling out sibling rivalry is below the belt. We left school behind more than a decade ago. We should really act like it.'

'I'm only joking with you because you know you will be completely fine. By the end of the weekend you're going to have the little ones wrapped around your little finger. You'll be making up a bottle with one hand and drinking a cup of tea with the other and rocking the crib with your foot.'

'Ha. I'm glad you have such faith in me.' She couldn't help but feel a little glow that his confidence in her was genuine. She knew that he wouldn't take risks with his kids and if he said that he trusted her she knew that he meant it.

They walked along the river, Madeleine enjoying the feel of the sun warming the top of her head. She could hear the beach before she could see it, the squeals of excited children building the closer they came.

'I'm starting to think this might not have been my best idea,' Finn said after a particularly piercing shriek.

'Ah, come on, it'll be fine,' Madeleine said, nudging him with her shoulder. 'And if it's not, there are plenty of places to escape to.' When they reached the beach—really just a huge sandpit—it wasn't as busy as Madeleine had feared. The summer holiday rush still hadn't hit, she figured, and there were just a few boisterous pre-schoolers making most of the noise.

She shook out the picnic blanket while Finn tackled the straps on the pushchair, and soon they had Bella and Hart rolling on the blanket between them, while Madeleine kicked off her sandals and leaned back on the changing bag as a makeshift beach pillow.

'This was most definitely an excellent idea,' she said, feeling herself sinking a little heavier into the sand, heat coming up through the blanket and the sunlight filtering down through the leaves of a nearby tree. The babies were contentedly gurgling as they lay on the blanket and the pre-schoolers had made a hasty exit when she had subtly mentioned that there were fountains to be run through nearby.

'I'm not going to argue with you. Good ideas are one of my many charms,' Finn said, his voice treacly and relaxed as hers. She didn't need to open her eyes and look over at him to know that he had adopted a similar position to her, stretched out on the sand.

Hart rolled over onto his tummy, nudging at her thigh with a fist, and she opened her eyes with a smile, her heart melting a fraction when she saw him grinning up at her with excitement in his eyes.

'Have they played in the sand before?' she asked Finn, rolling onto her side so that she could tickle Hart, and soaking in the sound of his gorgeous baby gurgle. Really, these kids were impossibly cute. No wonder Finn wanted to spend as much time with them as possible. If they were her kids, she wasn't sure that she would be able to tear herself away from them either.

'Nope. First time,' Finn said, cracking an eye open and smiling at the sight of Hart on his tummy.

'If only he would learn to roll back,' he said. 'In five minutes he'll be bored and annoyed that he's stuck like that.'

'Better give him something to do then,' Madeleine said, scooching him round so that he was at the edge of the blanket. Hart reached out into the warm sand, but then drew his hand back quickly in shock.

Finn laughed, and Madeleine couldn't help but join in. 'Maybe he needs backup,' Finn said, moving Bella so that she could touch the sand too. She reached out but, unlike her brother, buried her hand

and giggled as she found the cooler damp sand under the top layer.

'I guess we know who the thrill-seeker is,' Madeleine said. 'Are they always like that?'

'Hart's definitely more sensitive,' Finn said with a smile. 'He's braver when Bella's around. It's one of the more adorable things about them.'

'Are there less adorable things about them?'

'I'll let you ask me that at three tomorrow morning. Hey, kidding,' he added, and she wondered what had shown on her face. 'You don't have to get up in the night with them.'

'No, I'm here to help,' she said, drawing her eyebrows together and wondering why he was looking so warily at her. 'I'm happy to do it. That's the whole point of me coming to stay.'

'But…' He hesitated, and Madeleine knew from the look on his face that he was thinking about what had happened the night before. It wasn't going away, she realised. They had spent the last hour or two pretending that nothing out of the ordinary had happened, but it had been there the whole time, hovering over them, adding pressure to their day.

'Go on,' Madeleine said, aware that they were opening a can of worms. 'Say what you were going to say.'

'It's just… I wouldn't expect you to do the night shift on your own. And I'm worried that if we were to see each other like that—upstairs, in the middle of the night—that it would make you…uncomfortable. And that is the last thing I want.'

She sat up, drawing her knees up to her chest, and tried to fix him with a solid, stern look. 'You don't have to tiptoe around me, Finn. I'm not going to swoon or faint or have a panic attack if I see you after ten p.m. I'm really not the swooning type.'

'I never said you were,' Finn said, mirroring her body language and sitting upright beside her. 'But something happened last night, and I don't want to make you feel that way again.'

'You won't,' she promised, hoping that her voice sounded as sure as she felt. 'It wasn't you who made me feel like that anyway. It was me, being irrational.'

'I don't know about irrational.' Finn's face softened. 'Seemed like you were in a place where rational or irrational didn't mean much. You just looked frightened. And you don't have to tell me why, if you don't want. But you can't stop me wanting to do everything in my power to stop you ever feeling like that again.'

She shook her head. 'That's not your job.'

'I never said it was a job. But you're…we're… You're my friend, Madeleine, and I don't want to see my friend hurting like that.'

'We're not friends, Finn,' she said softly, meeting his gaze. 'We've never been friends.'

She didn't say it to hurt him, and she didn't expect the expression on his face—as if she'd struck him.

'I'm sorry,' she added quickly. 'I didn't mean it as a bad thing. It's just…true. We aren't, really. Are we? We've never hung out. You don't call or text for a chat. And that's fine. You're Jake's friend, and you're a part of the family. But I don't think we're friends.'

He stared at her for a long time, and she wished she could crack open that skull and see what he was thinking. What the narrowing of his eyes and the crease of his brow meant.

'I'd like to be,' he said at last. 'If we're living together, however temporarily, it would be nice if we were friends.'

She sighed. 'You're just saying this because I freaked out last night. You don't have to do this. I'm not some fragile little girl who needs looking after.'

He actually laughed at that. *'Fragile?* You think I think you're fragile? Last night I thought you might punch me. Or kick me in the balls… I never thought for a second you were fragile. Angry, yes. Frightened, yes. But never fragile.'

'Really? I looked like that to you?' She couldn't help smiling at the thought of that. Because she hadn't felt it. Hadn't felt strong. But it turned out she quite liked knowing how Finn saw her. She had felt cornered and vulnerable. But it turned out her reaction to those feelings had been very much in the fight camp, and she gave herself a little mental pat on the back for that. Once upon a time, she'd frozen. And then run. She wished that in the past she'd had that anger, that fire she had now. She could have directed it at the person who'd really deserved it rather than an innocent bystander.

'I… It wasn't you I was mad at.'

'I guessed as much,' Finn said, dipping his head

to meet her gaze when she tried to look away. She followed it back up, determined to be the fighter that he had said he'd seen in her, rather than meekly dropping her head as if she'd been the one in the wrong.

'Do you want to talk about it?' he asked. And she didn't. She never had. But…she couldn't bear the tiptoeing. Couldn't bear the fact that she'd come to stay to help him out with the kids and now he thought that she couldn't handle the night shift in case she bumped into him in the dark.

But talking about last night… That was complicated. Because it wasn't just how she had acted. It was what he had said. He had just come straight out with it. He was attracted to her. He acknowledged the spark and the chemistry between them as if it was the most normal thing in the world. But it didn't feel normal to her to be having that conversation. What was she meant to say—yes, you were right, I'm totally hot for you and desperately trying to ignore it because doing anything else would be a spectacularly bad idea? That didn't sound like a fun conversation. That sounded awkward and painful and suited to somewhere other than a kids' sandpit.

And if they acknowledged those feelings here in the daylight, out in the real world, then how were they meant to carry on as normal? Sure, he had mentioned it last night. But those were extenuating circumstances. He had said it because she was having a major freak-out and he needed to clear the air for her to feel safe. That didn't mean that he wanted to talk about it again, that he thought that those feelings meant anything—that they were important in any way.

They weren't important to her. How could they be? So, he was attracted to her. Big deal: a lot of guys were. Since she'd been a teenager, her life had been a string of guys making a big deal out of how attracted to her they were, whether she was interested in their attention or not. Usually not.

But not this time.

And when she thought back to what he had said, he hadn't actually said that he was attracted to her. Hadn't mentioned her boobs or her body, like half the guys who came onto her, thinking that that was what she would want to hear. No, he had talked about connection. About spark. About something mutual between them. And that was dangerous. She wasn't worried that he thought she was attractive. She was worried about the fact that he could see her attraction to him. That she wasn't imagining the spark of something between them.

How long had it been there? She couldn't be sure. It wasn't there the first time they'd met, when he was a skinny, scrawny eleven-year-old and she was a sullen thirteen. Had it been there at Jake's wedding five years ago? Thank goodness Jake and his husband had passed on the big traditional do and had listened to her insistence that she didn't need to be a bridesmaid. For a fleeting second she felt the horror of being matched with Finn as the best man. Except Caro had been there anyway, smiling at Finn's side for the best part of the day. Madeleine had given them a wide berth and had made polite conversation with Finn only when necessary.

No, she and Finn had never been friends, but now she found herself asking why that was. Why had there always been that distance between them, which had only seemed to get wider when he had married Caro?

Had she known on some level that these feelings had been growing under the surface all along? Had he? After all, he was the one who had called them out into the open now. Was it so difficult to imagine that he had been aware of them before this week?

Had she been aware of them? Never consciously. She was sure of that.

She had held Finn at arm's length for as long as she had known him, as she had every other man in her life. Even those who had made it into her bed were still considered with a healthy amount of suspicion—if all they were interested in was her body then what was the point of letting them closer? Had she done the same with Finn—what, out of habit? And missed the fact that he seemed to be an actual good guy?

'I don't want to go into details,' she said, shuddering at the thought, and wondering how to tell the story in as few words as possible. Writing tight copy was her speciality. This should be as easy as breathing for her. But when her life was the story it didn't seem so simple. 'I got stuck in a room where I didn't want to be. With someone I didn't want to be there with. I got out, but not entirely unscathed,

I think we can say after last night. I'm sorry that I tarred you with the same brush. I didn't mean to imply anything. It just triggered me, I guess, and I wasn't thinking rationally after that.'

She watched as his jaw tensed, then his eyes softened. 'I'm so sorry that that happened.' His voice was gruff, and she wished she knew him well enough to understand the emotion she heard in it. 'Is there anything else I can do to make you feel safe?' he asked.

Madeleine shook her head, wishing she could go back in time to a point where Finn didn't think that it was his responsibility to take care of her.

'I do feel safe,' she told him. 'I'm sorry that I made you think that I don't.'

'You have nothing to apologise for. I don't want you to ever feel like you have to say sorry for that.'

'I freaked out.' She sat up a little straighter, the memory of the previous evening making it impossible for her to relax. 'I basically accused you of…'

'You didn't.' He reached out a hand to cover hers and she started at the feel of his skin on hers. She had to force herself to remain still. Not to react how she wanted, to turn her palm over. To slide her fingers between his and hold on. 'You reacted to a situation instinctively to protect yourself.' He went on, 'Never apologise for that.'

'Well…thanks.' She pulled her hand away, breathing a sigh of relief at the clarity it brought. Trying not to think too hard about why such a simple touch made thinking so difficult. 'I feel like you're being much nicer about this than I deserve.'

'Why wouldn't you deserve me being nice to you, Madeleine?'

She stopped short at his words. No one had done this before. No one had made her stop and think about why she said certain things. Why she thought about her past in a certain way. But now Finn was holding up a mirror to how she had acted last night and, instead of looking away, she wanted to see more. Wanted to understand why she had made the decisions that she had. She'd been hiding from her past for more years than she cared to admit.

But it wasn't his job to tease that out with her. He had done enough by making her think of that time, that maybe it was time to reopen that wound and see if there was anything that could be done about making it heal a little smoother this time.

'I… I don't have an answer for that today,' she replied at last, realising that she had left him hanging. 'But I'm grateful to have you,' she added, meaning it. Whatever weird feelings she was having for him, she was thankful that she had freaked out on someone so obstinately determined to be supportive. 'Do we need to talk about what you said? About… chemistry? If you're going to find it awkward, me being here, maybe I should think about finding somewhere else to stay.'

'We can talk about it if you want. If you feel we need to. I'm sorry if saying it wasn't the right thing. But I was under the impression that we could both feel it, and it seemed safer to have it out in the open. I don't know. I feel like, if we ignored it, it could become this big…thing. And it doesn't have to be a thing. I thought it would be best to be honest, so you could make an informed decision about whether you want to stay. I didn't say it because I want you to go.'

'But isn't it complicated, me staying, now that we've said that?'

'It doesn't have to be. Because we're grown-ups here, Madeleine. Right? So there's a spark. You're Jake's sister. I'm hardly going to act on it.'

She wasn't sure how much of what she was feeling was showing on her face. But she was a little affronted, and she would be surprised if Finn wasn't perfectly aware of that fact right about now.

'Come on. I have six-month-olds. *Two* of them. I'm basically desperate for your help. I love Jake and I would never do anything that would risk my oldest and strongest friendship. You're like family to me, Madeleine. I love you and I want you to be safe. But I don't want more than that. I didn't think you did either.'

'I don't!' she said, her voice spiky with indignation. 'Why do you suddenly think that I do?'

'I don't. But everything is so awkward this morning and I just want everything to go back to normal. God, it's never this hard with Jake. Why can't it just be that simple with us?'

'Um, these?' she suggested, glancing down at her chest.

'No,' Finn said, meeting her eyes with a glare that caused a crease between his eyebrows. 'Don't accuse me of that. That's not fair.'

'Come on.' She forced a nonchalant shrug. 'It's just a body. You said yourself; it's just attraction.'

'Actually, I don't think I did say that.' That frown again.

'What then?'

'I'm pretty sure that I said we had *chemistry*. And your body…' he gestured towards her while his eyes remained fixed determinedly on hers '…lovely as I'm sure it is, is not chemistry.'

'Attraction. Chemistry. Whatever,' she said, trying to dismiss his words. But if what he felt for her wasn't based on how she looked, then she wasn't sure where that left them. He was easy to write off if he was only interested in how she looked. She had had plenty of practice dealing with that, after all. But chemistry was something else. Chemistry was something linking them. Something bringing them together. Something mutual. And it was definitely harder to ignore than attraction.

The worst thing was, he was right. There was something between them. She didn't want it to be there, and she didn't like it being there. But it was there, and she didn't know how to make it go away.

Pretty much her whole adult life, she'd only been interested in relationships where she knew the score because she was the one making up the rules. She'd dated guys who were pretty and shallow and uninteresting, because she knew that she could drop them without a second thought when they disappointed her. Which they invariably did. And now here was Finn. Totally honourable. Totally out of bounds. Totally confusing her.

Hart started to grizzle, growing bored of burying his hands in the sand, and Madeleine picked him up, standing and bouncing him gently on her hip, glad for the interruption to what had somehow become an uncomfortably personal conversation.

'Shall we walk for a bit?' she asked Finn, smiling at Hart as he quietened with her and made grabs at her hair and her earrings.

'So we're just calling it quits on that conversation?' Finn asked, looking at her sceptically.

'We are,' she confirmed. Though she had her suspicions that this chemistry wasn't going to fade helpfully into the background and allow her to concentrate on—say—her childcare responsibilities or job-hunting or finding somewhere to live.

'I'm feeling restless,' she announced, lifting Hart into the air and then planting a kiss on his forehead, pulling faces at him before parking him higher on her hip. 'Can we walk? Please?'

'We can go for a walk,' Finn confirmed, standing so that he could look her in the eye. 'But we started this conversation last night. And it feels like leaving it unfinished is adding to the tension here. If we keep walking away from it, it's going to become a thing.'

It was her turn to crease her brow, because he was making a lot of assumptions here. Ones that she didn't particularly care for. 'How do you know that talking about it is going to make it go away?'

'Because I'm sure that we've both got very good reasons why we want to make it go away.'

He thought it was just that easy? If it turned out to be, great. She would be delighted. But she couldn't help thinking he was being a little naïve here.

'So we just reason our way out of it?' she asked.

'Exactly.'

She envied his supreme confidence. But she didn't share an ounce of it. 'Not to play devil's advocate here—and I'm not talking about us specifically—but don't you think that if it were that easy to talk your way out of feelings like this, more people would do it? Like, there wouldn't be affairs, or star-crossed lovers. Or, I don't know, inappropriate workplace relationships.'

He rolled his eyes and she knew that he wasn't taking her seriously. 'I'm not talking about other people. I'm talking about us.'

'I noticed,' she said, voice dripping with sarcasm. 'Fine. Let's stop. You're right, it's not getting us anywhere anyway.'

'Good. We'll call a truce,' Finn said to her relief. 'We will ignore everything that we've been talking about this morning because we are grown-ups who know better. But I'm telling you, I can't live with an atmosphere. And if I feel like there is one, we're going to talk about this again.'

Madeleine nodded. 'Fine. But I don't think that's going to happen. We've acknowledged it. We've established that neither of us is interested in pursuing it. We're moving on. Now,' she said, strapping Hart into the pushchair and making moves to fold up the picnic blanket, 'let's go for a walk. I'm not used to lazing in the sunshine.'

He laughed at that. 'As if there's such a thing as lazing with these two around.'

They walked along the South Bank, past the squealing pre-schoolers who were running in and out of the fountains and past pained-looking tourists on the terraces of bars and restaurants, trying to look as if the incessant noise wasn't bothering them. At the foot of the London Eye she stopped and looked up at the pods, rotating so slowly around the centre that it hardly seemed as if they were moving. In her ten years in London, she'd never been up there. Never seen London from a different angle, a different perspective than being stuck right in the middle of it, just trying to get through the day.

'What is it?' Finn asked as she continued to stare up at the giant Ferris wheel.

'Do you think the babies would like it up there, or would they be scared?' she asked Finn, wondering whether she was really asking for the twins or for herself.

'You want to go up?'

She shrugged. 'I don't know. It's a beautiful day. I've been wanting perspective. But this seems a little literal, don't you think?'

He stuck his hands in his pockets and leaned back as he looked at her, his expression thoughtful. 'Perspective is a good thing, however you get it.'

'I'm not sure that going up there is going to find me a new job or a place to live.'

'No, maybe not,' he agreed, 'but I'm pretty sure it's not going to hurt either. So let's go,' he said, pushing the pram towards the Fast Track queue.

'You're just going to queue up?' she asked, laughing with surprise. 'Don't your sort arrange to hire the whole thing, or put on a special event or something?'

He stopped and looked at her, frowning. 'My sort? I practically grew up in your kitchen. How is my sort not your sort?'

She caught up with him, picking up the sunhat that Bella had thrown to the ground as a convenient distraction. 'Um, I don't know. Maybe because when we all left you went off and became a genius and a millionaire?'

'I was always a genius, you know.'

She met his eyes and laughed again at the smirk on his face.

She shoved him gently with her shoulder as she came back to stand beside him. 'You were always a pain, you mean. You were never a genius. You used to burn the toast.'

'And here was me thinking you never noticed me at all.' God, that grin of his really was too much. It spread automatically to her face without her even thinking about it. And it made her want to sway her body closer to his in a way that would be bad for both of their states of mind.

She reined in her libido and tried to keep her body on-message. 'I noticed the smoke alarm going off at regular intervals,' she said. 'It was kind of hard to ignore.'

'I had to get your attention somehow.'

She looked up and met his gaze, neither of them looking away long after the look had turned from friendly to intense to something much more concerning and she knew that, however hard they tried to talk about it or ignore it, this chemistry wasn't going anywhere. The thought sent a shiver through her, and she wasn't quite sure whether it was pleasure or fear.

'Don't tease me.' Her voice dropped to something more serious. Because they couldn't keep bantering like this. They were going to get themselves into trouble. They had to be more careful. 'You didn't think of me that way back then,' she told him with absolute certainty. 'You couldn't have cared less whether I noticed you or not.'

'God, you're so sure of yourself, aren't you? You can't bear to think that I might remember things differently.'

'Jake would have killed you. Or wanted to, at least.'

He nodded slowly, his eyes still never leaving hers. 'Then it's a good job that Jake could never read my mind.'

'You don't spill your guts to him like you do to me then?'

Finally, the grin was gone. She had got through to him. She saw the defences come back up. 'I don't spill my guts to you.'

'You've not been able to stop talking about this thing between us.'

'Because it's distracting,' Finn said, his voice shorter, spikier. 'It's taking up so much room in my head right now that I don't know how to talk about anything else.'

'Why not just forget it?' she asked.

He placed his hands on his hips, his body language matching the scowl on his face. 'Because it's important that I don't forget. I know I keep saying that there's this connection between us, Madeleine. And it's true. I feel it. The reason I want to talk about it is because I don't want to give that spark any power. I'm not interested in a relationship. I have the children to think about, I'm still processing a marriage that broke down and nearly took my business down with it, all because I... Look, my life isn't compatible with a relationship. With anyone else, I don't know...maybe I'd be up for something casual. I don't want casual with you. I don't want anything with you because Jake is practically my brother, which makes you family and I don't want to do anything to mess that up.'

God, she hadn't been expecting such a torrent of words. There was too much there to process, standing here amidst a chaotic queue of tourists in the middle of a London summer. She knew that she'd be killing herself trying to remember every word when she was finally alone tonight. But, for now, the gist of it was enough. He was as wary as she was, and he wanted whatever spark this was between them shut down fast. Good. She could get on board with that.

'Then I'm glad we're on the same page because I don't want anything either, casual or otherwise, Finn. It sounds like you're afraid I'm going to jump you. Or seduce you or something. For the record, I'm not interested in a relationship with you or anyone else. Now, can we please, *please* stop discussing this?'

He gave her the most intense look for a beat, and then another. And then, when she thought she couldn't bear it any more, he broke into an easy sunny smile and changed the subject. 'When you admit that you are desperate to play the tourist and go on the Eye.'

She was desperate to shut him up. She returned his smile, but couldn't quite convince it to reach her eyes. 'Fine, yes. Let's go.'

'So gracious,' Finn said, pushing the pram further up the ramp as the queue edged close to the embarkation platform.

The pod rose so slowly and smoothly that it was hard to even believe that they were moving unless she looked away from the skyline for a moment, then looked back again to find it that tiny bit further away. The crowded pod—twenty-five of them plus the double buggy—had them wedged into one spot, where for most of the ride up her view was mainly of the back of the six-foot bear of a tourist who had rudely pushed in front of her. She didn't want to look back at the hefty winding gear responsible for keeping nearly five hundred feet of Ferris wheel in the air.

And it didn't take long for her to realise that actually she had been pretty happy down on the ground, untroubled by thoughts of how sturdy that engineering really was.

But as the pod crested the top of the wheel and the bear of a man in front of her moved to another part of the pod, her cynicism fell away. The early summer sunshine flooded them with light and suddenly London was glorious beneath them, the river a living, moving ribbon through the landmarks of the city that had become so familiar that she'd stopped seeing it. From up here, she couldn't believe that she didn't spend her day looking around herself in wonder at the city where she got to live. And then, when she looked to her left, there were the Houses of Parliament.

She bit her lip, letting her hand rest on the glass as she took in the sight of the seat of British politics, the location of so many key moments in the history of the country. She'd dreamed of those Gothic buildings all through her degree course. She had been so sure that that was where she was headed. She'd be up close with the people making those decisions, holding them to account and providing the checks and balances that ensured a fair and accountable system of government.

But instead she was up here. Looking down on the Palace of Westminster like the tourist she would be if she turned up there now. From this height, it looked like a model. A toy. It might as well not be real for all the chance she had of working there now.

Finn's hand rested on her shoulder and she jumped, realising she'd forgotten that he was there. She had been so wrapped up in her dreams and her lost hopes that she'd forgotten she was meant to be helping him out. That was the whole point of her being here.

'Are the babies okay?' she asked, angling to try and see them in the pushchair.

'They're zonked. They must like the movement of the wheel. What's going on with you? You're miles away.'

She couldn't help a quick glance out of the pod towards Parliament before she answered. 'I'm fine. I'm great.'

Finn frowned. Really, this mind-reading ability was getting kind of annoying. 'You haven't taken your eyes off Big Ben for a full five minutes.'

God, why did he have to be so perceptive?

'You studied politics, right? I'm sure Jake told me that.'

Madeleine made a noise that she hoped sounded vague enough not to prompt any questions. But Finn was a talker. How had she not noticed that before? Because she'd never given herself a chance to. She'd dodged conversations with him for as long as she could remember.

'You know, the more you avoid my questions the more curious I'm going to get.'

She glanced up at him, finally taking her eyes off the view.

'I'm not going to push you. But if you want to talk, I'm right here.'

Right here.

He was. So close. The crush of people around them only served to push them closer to one another.

'I know.' But she couldn't talk about that. About university or her career—or lack of it. The spectre of what might have been. A weird sadness for how things might have turned out. It was too painful to touch. Especially with him; he had a way of looking at her that made her feel raw. Exposed. She wasn't going to volunteer to peel off another layer of skin for him.

She wrapped her arms around her body as she turned deliberately away from the river and pasted a sunny smile on her face. She waited for it to reflect on Finn's lips, but he just kept staring at her in that unnerving way. Well, he was either a sociopath or he could see straight through her fakery. At this point she couldn't be sure which of those two possibilities was the scarier.

'What do you want to do next?' Finn asked, and she breathed a sigh of relief at the change of subject. 'We could find somewhere for our picnic. Or choose one of the restaurants or cafés we walked past, if you've changed your mind.'

'No, a picnic sounds good. If these monsters wake up, I think I'll be glad of the lack of people staring.'

'Oh, people can still stare in the park,' he informed her with a laugh. 'Especially if they both get going.'

'Well, that's something to look forward to.'

She followed Finn as he pushed the pram out of the pod and down the ramp, and they weaved their way through the disorientated tourists standing around the exit gate. With barely a clipped ankle, he had them away from the crowds and exploring the streets winding away from the river.

'Where are we headed?' she asked as she lost track of where they were.

'I heard there's a little park down this way,' he said. 'I thought it might be quieter than staying by the river. You don't mind?'

A literal change of scenery was exactly what she needed after ruminating on the failure of her career. And her failure to come to terms with it in the decade that had passed since.

When they reached the gardens, she let out a long breath. Emerald grass was dappled with sunshine filtered through lush trees. Spring flowers lingered in the shady spots and the grass was yet to be scorched by a harsh city summer. But, most delicious of all, it was silent. Somehow, in the walk away from the riverside, the bustle and noise of the city had fallen away, leaving only a blissful quiet. She heard herself let out a long deep breath and for the first time since she had arrived on Finn's doorstep, tense and angry, she felt her shoulders relax.

'Oh, my God, this place is amazing,' Madeleine said, dropping to the grass and lying flat on her back before she could even be bothered to get the picnic blanket out. Finn laughed and dropped to sit beside her, his forearms resting casually on his knees.

'Starved of grass?' he asked with another laugh.

'God, I didn't even realise I was.' She feathered the blades between her fingers, letting them tickle against her palm and slip through her hands. 'And silence. I can't believe how quiet this place is. How did you find it? Tell me your secret.'

She kept her eyes closed as she realised how intimate that sounded. There was safety in closed eyes. But vulnerability too. If he was watching her, she didn't know it. She assessed her body, trying to sense whether his eyes were on her. But all she could feel was the sunshine, hot on her heavy limbs, and she decided she could live with that. She didn't need to know if he was looking at her. She was happy not knowing, just soaking up the heat and the light and feeling the ghosts of the past twenty-four hours melting away.

She heard Finn stand, then the flap and rustle of the picnic blanket. Then he was lying beside her again. And with the tension gone from her body, awareness crept in.

They had lain side by side in the sandpit before. But they had been protected by the noise of the crowds along the riverside cafés and the squeals of children playing in the fountains. In this private garden they had lost that safety net. They had left home that morning for the protection of being out in public, to escape the heightened tensions of their temporarily shared home. But now they were alone again.

She opened her eyes and glanced across at Finn, only to find him propped up on one elbow, watching her as if she were a puzzle he was trying to solve.

'What?' she asked, suddenly self-conscious, lifting herself onto her elbows. Too late, she realised what that did to her chest, but Finn's eyes never headed south of her nose.

'Nothing.'

'Then why are you staring?'

'I'm looking, not staring.'

'Said the serial killer.'

Finn laughed and rolled his eyes. 'You're not what I was expecting.'

'How can I surprise you? You've known me for ever.'

'You've known me for just as long. You think I couldn't surprise you?'

She thought back to last night. Not the mistaken assumption she had made, but the way that he had reacted to it. No judgement. No offence taken. Just concerned with making her feel safe. The whole focus of his quite brilliant brain directed at making her feel secure and unthreatened and safe. And it had taken some time to kick in but here, in the sunshine, she was happy. She knew her problems would be waiting for her when they walked out of this park, but in this quiet oasis she was calm and content.

Just as she thought she might actually drop off to sleep Finn's phone rang, surprising her out of her sleepiness. She watched as he dug in his pocket to retrieve it and guessed the identity of the caller from the slight crease on his brow.

'Caro, hey, how are you?' he said, and Madeleine turned away, knowing that it would be rude to eavesdrop, but not sure what else she could do when they were the only people here.

'No, they're asleep,' Finn said, and she knew that Caro must be asking about the babies. Finn angled the phone towards the pair of them sleeping in their pram, and Madeleine realised that they must be video calling. She wondered whether Caro could see her lying there on the grass. Whether Finn had told her that she was staying with them. It didn't matter, she reminded herself. She was just the help. Even if Caro did see her, it was up to Finn to let her know what was going on. Or not.

God, how had she even got herself down this train of thought? she asked herself. She sat up, trying to shake off the thoughts.

But, now that it had occurred to her, she couldn't help but see this situation as an outsider would—the two of them alone in a park, the kids asleep, lying on a picnic blanket. If that were her husband...

Ex-husband, she reminded herself. Finn was Caro's ex-husband, and had been for a year.

Why did that seem to matter to her all of a sudden? Both she and Finn couldn't have been clearer with one another that what they had was nothing more than a practical arrangement between friends. Not even friends. Between two people who cared for Jake and were happy to do him a favour.

So why did she feel so uncomfortable now? Why did she feel the need to explain herself? She heard Finn saying his goodbyes and stared at a flowerbed across the park, trying to look completely uninterested in Finn talking to his ex-wife.

'Sorry about that,' he said as he slid his phone back into his jeans pocket.

'No need to apologise,' Madeleine said, probably a little too quickly for someone who was not meant to be listening to his conversation.

'She hates it when they're asleep when she calls,' Finn said. 'She'll probably call back again in a bit if she can.'

'It must be hard for her. She must really miss them. Hard for you too.'

He sighed. The smile she was used to seeing on his face was missing.

'Her work is so important. But... I can't lie... This wasn't how I expected my marriage to turn out.'

'Were you sad when it ended?'

She wasn't sure what made her ask. Of course he had been sad. No one ended a marriage unscathed.

'Sad, but not surprised.'

Madeleine held her breath, with the distinct impression that Finn needed to talk about this. She stayed silent, curious about whether he was going to open up to her again. What would it mean if he did? They had only spent a day in one another's company, and already she had shared more about herself with Finn than she had with anyone else for years. If he was sharing too, then this wasn't an arrangement any more. They were…friends.

'I knew it was coming,' Finn said. 'The longer we were together, the more unhappy she became. I think when she decided to go, it was a relief for her. I… didn't find it easy,' Finn said, and Madeleine winced at what she guessed was a hell of an understatement.

'Did you try—' Madeleine started, then stopped herself. It was really none of her business. Even if they really were friends, it was surely an unwelcome degree of intrusion.

'By the time she told me she was going, she didn't want to try,' he said. 'Seems I used up all my chances without even realising it.' His voice was tinged with regret. 'It's not her fault,' he continued, and Madeleine could sense the false brightness in his voice. 'I wasn't a good husband. I worked too much. I never made time for her. I've spent my life building up the business, determined that…determined my life would be different now, and I didn't want to take the time out of the office to make sure that that was the most important thing to her too. I guess, in the end, I chose the business over her, and it nearly cost me everything.'

Madeleine looked at him for a moment and got the impression that he was expecting her censure. Well, he might be opening up about his guilty feelings, but he could keep on looking. She wasn't here to judge him.

'Marriage is complicated. I'm sure you tried your best.'

'That's the thing, though. I didn't. I knew I wasn't, and Caro knew it too. We were even able to cite it in the papers as unreasonable behaviour.'

She gave him a grim smile. 'You worked hard for that business. Your hard work changed your life. That's got to be a pretty difficult habit to break. But look at you now. Devoted dad. Here with me, not in the office, because you're determined to find the right person to take care of your kids. Looks like you've got your priorities right at the moment.'

'That's different,' he said, frowning, as if he was determined not to accept her assessment of the situation. 'They're my kids; it's not a choice, it's just what I have to do.'

'Plenty of people wouldn't do what you're doing. I'm not commenting on you and Caro. It's not my place, and no one can understand what a marriage is really like just from looking in from the outside. I'm not going to go along with your pity party. You're a good dad, a good person, Finn.'

He grimaced, but let the matter drop.

'Are we going to eat before these kids wake up?' he asked, breathing out a sigh of relief at the change of subject. He had never meant to get so heavy with Madeleine. And he *never* talked about what had happened with Caro. But after what had happened last night, after he had seen Madeleine so vulnerable, after she had shared a little of her past with him, it seemed wrong to hold out on her. Sharing a bit of his life made them equals again.

But it made them something more too—confidantes? Intimates? Whatever it was, she wasn't just his friend's sister any more. They were something to one another now, something that existed outside of their relationships with Jake.

He dug into the picnic bag and brought out cheeses and ham, salad and bread. There was a flask of coffee in there, and a bottle of Sicilian lemonade.

Madeleine swung her legs around, sitting cross-legged with the sun behind her, her hair highlighted by its rays and her skin glowing from the warmth of the day.

'So, how *is* the nanny hunt going?' she asked.

He narrowed his eyes, stopped short by her question. Was she trying to find a way out of their arrangement? Admittedly, it had already got more personal than he had planned, but she had only been there a day. And this mutual attraction that they had both acknowledged and then pledged to determinedly ignore had complicated matters beyond recognition. But that didn't mean that he wanted her to leave. She was staying with him because she had nowhere else to go. He had promised that he would look out for her, and he hated the thought that she might be making plans to leave because of everything that had happened over the past twenty-four hours.

'I've been speaking with the agency,' he said, wishing he could smooth the crease he could feel in his forehead, but not quite managing to get his muscles to co-operate. 'They're going to send some people over this week for interviews. It would be great if you could sit in, actually, if you don't mind?'

The crease in her brow at this request reflected his own, and he wished that he could see inside her head and work out what was going on in there. Last night had brought them closer, there was no denying that. But there was also absolutely no denying that she still had some very substantial protective barriers in place. She might have shown him more of herself than she had planned to last night, but she was making up for it now with reinforced defences.

'I… I don't know if that's a good idea. I don't know anything about being a nanny. I don't even know much about you or the kids.'

'I trust you. I trust your judgement. It would just be nice to have someone to talk it over with. If you don't mind.'

It was the sort of subject that he should talk over with his wife, except she had left him and the country as soon as she could be rid of him. Even the lure of their two children hadn't been enough to stop her wanting to get away from him. What he'd told Madeleine had been true. He hadn't tried hard enough to save his marriage. He had never put Caro first. He had been a spectacularly bad husband, and he couldn't blame Caro for wanting to put the whole catastrophe behind her.

But even he couldn't have imagined how devastating losing her would prove to be. For the first time ever he had thought that he had a stable home. For seven years they had lived in their beautiful house with their perfect life and full fridge and plans for the future. And then, all of a sudden, it was pulled from under him.

He'd lost it all: Caro, his home. Very nearly his business, if he'd not been able to secure the funding that they'd needed for the new premises in time.

Now he had the kids to focus on, he could tell himself that he didn't even miss her. And he didn't. Sure, sometimes he missed having another adult to speak to at the end of the day—he loved sharing the kids' firsts and milestones with her over video calls—but he didn't really miss her. And when their marriage was falling apart, all he could think about was how he was going to ensure that the financial consequences didn't reduce him to the poverty he had spent his life running from. What did that say about him—that he was more concerned about his bank balance than about trying to save his relationship?

It only went to show how much he'd let her down. It had been a long time since he'd been in love with Caro.

They'd married young, when his business had first started to boom and he'd realised he didn't have the skills or the experience or the connections to navigate the world he was suddenly living in. Caro had all that—had grown up in that world. She'd shared it with him, and he had honestly loved her, at the start. But as the years had gone on, and he had found himself further and further out of his depth, he had to work harder and harder. Spend more and more hours at the office. And what he'd had with Caro had...died. Because he had neglected it. And she had tired of the world of CEOs and easy money that she had grown up in and decided she wanted to do something more...worthy.

He looked over to where Madeleine was helping herself to the picnic and was hit with that stab of attraction that had been present since the moment that he had opened the door to her the day before.

If they hadn't had that misunderstanding yesterday evening, would he have acknowledged his attraction to her? Would he have ignored it—pretended it wasn't there? Or would he have flirted with her? Played with that chemistry, and seen where it might take them?

With Jake's sister? he reminded himself. No, he wouldn't. He couldn't. She was as off-limits today as she had been yesterday. He had to remember that. But her culottes had slid up her legs, showing smooth, toned calves, and he physically ached with the need to reach out a hand and feel the softness of her skin, the firmness of the muscle. He flexed his fingers and tried to concentrate on his food. But for once he could barely taste it. He was more interested in the curve of her lip and the close of her eyelids as she tasted an olive. The slide of her finger into her mouth as she sucked them clean.

He stifled a groan. That really wasn't helping matters.

'What?' Madeleine asked, opening her eyes and catching him watching her.

He opened his mouth to tell her *Nothing*, but no sound came out. Instead he held her gaze and watched as her expression shifted from quizzical to interested to knowing. He knew that what he was thinking must be written all over his face. But he had told her yesterday how he felt. It would be dishonest of him to try and hide it from her now. At least that was what he told himself so that he didn't feel he had to tear his eyes away. Not just yet. He just wanted another moment.

'Finn…?'

He waited in silence to see where that sentence was going. But it seemed either Madeleine didn't know or didn't want to share it with him, because her voice faded out. Her eyes dropped too. To his lips, and then back up again.

Her lower lip slipped between her teeth and she bit down, and he knew that they were thinking the exact same thing. How would it feel to press his mouth against her lips? To feel the slide and the power of them beneath his own? To taste and to test? To press against her until they were stretched out on the grass, the sun hot on their bodies as they explored beneath their clothes?

The cry of a baby behind him brought that stifled groan to life, and Madeleine took a breath as she glanced over at the pushchair.

Maybe it was for the best, he considered as he followed her gaze and saw Hart stirring.

And maybe he was going to spend the rest of the day wondering exactly where that look might have

taken them if they hadn't been interrupted. He had
a feeling he knew which way that was going to pan
out. And it didn't look good for his peace of mind.

CHAPTER SEVEN

OH. MY. HAD that been a moment? Had they just had a moment? One second she'd thought she was just picking at some antipasti, and the next Finn was looking at her like he wanted to eat her. In a really, *really* good way. He had watched her lips until her eyes had been drawn to his mouth too, and just as her body had begged her to find out what it would feel like—

Hart had woken up, and the moment was gone. Because she was not ready to deal with how much she'd wanted that kiss to happen.

Not like this. Not with Finn.

Because she knew what she wanted from her relationships. She wanted predictability, and the balance of power firmly on her side. She wanted to be able to walk away when she decided it was over because that was the only way that she knew how to handle this stuff. To be fair to herself, it was the only way that she had tried. Maybe, if she'd wanted to, she could have had a go at something different and made that work too. But she never had, because that meant opening herself up to getting hurt and she had precisely zero interest in doing that. Not with Finn, or with anyone else.

But when Finn looked at her like that—like he wanted to eat her, to consume her, to make her a part of him—she wanted to find out what that felt like. She wanted to give herself over to it and care precisely nothing about the consequences. Because she was pretty sure that the not knowing was going to kill her. The not knowing, and the being so damn close that she could practically taste him. Which was why she had to get up off this blanket and start walking and stop thinking before she did something she would regret later.

That night, Madeleine slipped between the cool cotton sheets and stretched out her feet, pointing her toes until she was sure that some part of her foot would just snap completely. After the babies had woken up they had played in the park with them for nearly an hour, pushing swings and taking gentle turns of the roundabout, rocking horses and adventures in diggers.

And then, with the picnic bag empty—and the coffee flask dangerously so—they had headed away from the green oasis in search of sugar and caffeine to keep them fuelled until the babies decided that they'd had enough of exploring and wanted to sleep in the pram. She wished she'd realised before she'd started how many miles you could cover with babies who would only sleep on the move. She couldn't have been more grateful when they'd woken and informed them—at some considerable volume, that it was time to go home now, please.

Once they were through the doors of the house, it had been a whirlwind of steamed veg and finger food and sterilising bottles. Bathing naked babies and wriggling them into Baby-gros and humming nursery rhymes.

By the time that she and Finn had collapsed in front of the TV she couldn't have cared less that they might have had a moment back there on the picnic blanket. All she wanted was spadefuls of the mac and cheese that Finn had found in the freezer, and the sweet, sweet oblivion of sleep. Neither of them had managed more than half an hour of the movie they'd stuck on before giving up any pretence that they would be awake later than nine o'clock.

It felt as if her head had barely hit the pillow before the crying began, but a glance at the time on the front of her phone told her that it had been a couple of hours. Turned out midnight really was the witching hour. She could leave Finn to it, she supposed—they were his kids currently screaming the house down. But she was here to help him out and what was even the point of these awkward living arrangements if she wasn't doing that?

She stumbled out of bed and threw on her cardigan, pulling on socks in anticipation of the tile floors downstairs. She pulled her hair into a ponytail high on her head, opened her door and nearly crashed into

Finn, who was holding a wailing Bella on his shoulder and a tear-stained Hart on his hip.

'Oh, thank God,' Finn said, shoving Hart in her direction. 'Would you take him? He's settled for now but I just can't get him down.'

'I don't—'

But her reply was cut short by the arrival of Hart on her hip and she didn't have any choice but to hold on. He gave her an uncertain look and his bottom lip wobbled, but no tears were forthcoming for now.

'Is there something wrong with Bella?' she asked as she followed him and Bella's cries down the hall.

'Teeth? Wind? Existential angst? Your guess is as good as mine at this point.'

'How long has she been crying?'

'An hour? Half an hour? A week…?'

'Do you want me to take her?'

Finn's face creased as he peered at Bella, and Madeleine could see the ruminations behind his eyes as he tried to work out what was wrong.

'Maybe she's sick of me,' he said with a shrug before completing some sort of superpower twin manoeuvre which resulted in her finding that she was now holding Bella and Finn was bouncing Hart.

'What do I do?' Madeleine asked, aware that her eyes were widening in alarm as Bella's volume picked up a notch and the bouncing and patting that had worked with Hart the night before only seemed to make things worse.

'This…this is the part where we pace,' Finn said, heading past her door to the end of the corridor, bouncing and patting as he went. And pace they did. Long past her feet hurting. Long after her back started to ache and her shoulders started to burn. She saw half an hour tick by on her phone. Then an hour. By the time that Bella stopped screaming, they had moved their pacing down to the kitchen so that the adults could at least dose with caffeine to get through what was feeling like an endless night and the babies could spit out the lovingly prepared formula that Finn had somehow managed to make one-handed.

When Bella finally exhausted herself in Finn's arms and Hart was asleep on her shoulder, Madeleine was left with a deliciously heavy bundle snuggled into her as she collapsed onto the sofa in the open-plan area. Finn leaned back against the kitchen island, pinching the bridge of his nose before rubbing a hand across his forehead.

'I can't believe you've been doing this on your own,' Madeleine said.

'It's not always like this,' Finn said with a wry smile. 'Wait here. I'll put Bella to bed and come back for Hart.'

Madeleine snuggled deeper into the corner of the sofa and her eyes were just starting to close when she heard Finn's bare feet padding across the tiles of the kitchen floor.

'I'm sleeping here,' she mumbled without opening her eyes. 'Possibly for a week.' She heard his smile in his little huff of breath. Didn't even need to crack open an eyelid to see the lines around his eyes that he always got when he grinned.

ELLIE DARKINS 103

'Let me take him,' Finn said, and her shoulder was suddenly cold where Hart had been snuggling and she heard the gentle swish-swish of his swinging chair.

'If you're sleeping, I'm sleeping,' Finn said at last, when they had both finally released their held breath. 'Budge up.'

She lifted her feet so that he could collapse at the other end of the sofa, and it was only when her thighs started to ache that she realised she really hadn't thought this through. She lowered them slowly and felt heat spark when Finn's hand cupped her ankle and guided her feet onto his thighs.

'God, you really need a nanny,' she said, trying to think of any topic of conversation that would distract her from the electric feel of his hands resting on her. Suddenly, her ankles were the most sensitive part of her body and she could feel the heat of each of his fingertips as they gently rested against her.

He's not even thinking about it, she told herself. *He's literally only touching you because you refused to give up the sofa.*

Except now one fingertip was tracing a feather-light circle around her ankle bone, so slowly, so gently that she suspected that Finn didn't even know that he was doing it. Had no idea that he was driving her so insane with the gentlest of touches.

'I've scared you off, haven't I?' he said. 'You're going to pack your bags first thing in the morning.'

'No, not that,' she said, trying to keep her mind on the subject of nannies and their arrangement, and definitely not on the sparks of heat that she could feel radiating out from his hands on her. From the feel of hard muscle beneath her feet. 'You must be desperate for someone who knows what they're doing, that's all. I don't feel like I was much help tonight.'

His grip on her ankle was suddenly firmer, the wandering fingertips that had been driving her so insane were still, and she could feel that the hardness in his body went beyond that. She had annoyed him. Perfect.

'Why do you do that, Maddie? You did great tonight. I hate that you won't acknowledge how capable you are.'

She cracked an eye open at last, trying to read the expression on his face from the half-light of the lamp in the corner of the room.

'Okay, I won't say it again. It's no big deal.' She shut her eyes, tried to get the swimmy, heavy feeling of nearing sleep back into her muscles but it was gone, and she was angry at Finn for that. It was bad enough that she was awake in the middle of the night. Worse that he was annoying her so much that she couldn't even get the sleep she so desperately wanted.

'Don't,' Finn said, holding onto her as she went to swing her ankles off the sofa and sit up. 'I'm sorry,' he carried on in hushed tones. 'I didn't mean to criticise.' The stroking fingertips were back, driving her insane, and really she knew that that was reason enough to take herself off to bed. But… But. But she was a complete idiot and clearly needed her head examined, and it felt so good to have his skin so near to hers that she felt herself relaxing back, her eyes drifting shut again.

She could feel the intimacy settle over them like a blanket, shutting out the real world. They were the only two people awake in London. She was sure of it. Never mind that she had been out in this city at every hour of the day and night and never found it sleeping. She was quite sure that she and Finn were the only people in the world right now. As if they had slipped through some sort of wormhole brought about by screaming and pacing and fallen into a universe where no one but the two of them existed.

'I didn't mean to snap.' She sighed. Finn's hands stilled and she let out an involuntary mew of displeasure and nudged him with her toes. Her feet ached. Her calves ached. Her toes ached. She'd had no idea that it was possible to walk so far without leaving the house. The circles around her ankle bone resumed, each one unwinding her a little looser, each one undoing her a little more, so when Finn asked, 'What happened?' she didn't have the energy to throw up her usual barriers. The words fell out of her.

'A professor, the last year of my university course. I thought he was taking an interest because I showed promise. I thought the grades I was getting were because I was working hard. But it was all a play. It was all to get me where he wanted me. To get what he wanted from me.'

The hand on her ankle stilled, and she nudged him again. If he stopped, if they returned to real life, there was no way that she could talk about this. The circles came back, and so did her words.

'When he made it clear what he really wanted… When he locked his door and stood in front of it so that I couldn't escape, I finally worked it out. God, what kind of journalist was I going to be if I couldn't even see that coming? I managed to get out of there, and that's when it all fell into place. It was never my work that he saw. It was my body. He thought that he could just take it. That I would hand it over. Well, I didn't. I wouldn't. I walked out of university and I never went back and I lost my career because of it. Well, the career that I wanted. That I might have had. Except I'll never know now, will I? I'll never know if I could have had that career, because everything I know about my ability has been cast into doubt. I never got a single grade that I don't ask myself whether it was for my insight and understanding and thorough research. Or whether it was just someone wanted to get a better look at my boobs.'

Finn was quiet, still for a long moment, and when he spoke his voice was ice. 'You should kill him.'

She gave a wry smile at his instinctive response to protect her. 'Too late. I thought about it, but a heart attack beat me to it. Two years ago. Glowing obits in all the broadsheets.'

'You could dig him up and kill him again.' The words were ground out, shocking her with their carefully harnessed rage. She opened her eyes and the expression on his face startled her. She had never seen his features contorted into such anger. Every line of his face was hard. His jaw was a slash of muscle beneath the hollows of his cheeks. The bones above were stark lines caught by the light from the lamp. The creases around his eyes owed nothing to laughter now. They were deep and harsh.

She sat up, her feet sliding under his leg now, her knees bent as she hugged herself smaller, brought herself closer to him.

He shook himself and she watched as he forced some of the tension from his face. When his eyes met hers she wanted to hide from the raw intensity there, but then her hand was on his face and she couldn't look away.

He gripped her other hand hard, and she could feel him shaking. 'I am so, so sorry that that happened to you,' he said. His other hand came to rest on top of hers, trapping it against his jaw. 'If you want to talk more about it, I'm here. I want to help—just tell me what I can do.'

She shrugged. 'There's not much more to tell. And there's nothing you can do.' His grip on her hand softened and she let her body follow, resting against the sofa cushions, still tucked into her little protective ball. But when she leaned against the sofa Finn's shoulder was right there and in a breath, no more than two, her cheek was resting against it, drawing the heat from it. When his arm circled around her back to tuck her more firmly into his side, she didn't fight it. With her toes tucked under his thigh and his arms a hard band of bone and muscle around her back and her waist, his shoulder the pillow under her cheek, she was surrounded by him.

If she dared open an eyelid, he would be her entire field of vision. He was the firm support under her head and the gentle strokes on her aching calves. He was the heavy weight on her feet and the rise and fall that was lulling her into sleep. He was the gentle huffs of breath, the slight movement as it nudged her hair.

The wormhole universe that they had created had shrunk around them until the only way that they could both exist inside it was by curling up tight. Tangling limbs around one another. Sharing a space that only seconds before had only been big enough for one. And for the first time in as long as she could remember she felt still. And quiet. And as sleep dragged her under she didn't care what she was going to think about all this in the morning. All she cared about was the aching perfection of their universes merging and colliding, and finding peace there.

CHAPTER EIGHT

MADELEINE WAS IN his arms.

She was practically in his lap. Her feet were still tucked under his leg, her cheek on his shoulder. One hand rested on his chest.

He had no idea how long they had been asleep, but the sky was lightening and Hart's swing had stopped moving. The dark circles had started to fade under Madeleine's eyes, and it took more self-control than he realised he had not to stroke the skin there, to try and soothe her tiredness.

He could kick himself. It was his fault that she was so exhausted. As if she didn't have enough going on in her life right now with losing her job and her flat, he had added sleep deprivation and crying babies onto her list of things to worry about. He should have just given her a place to stay, no questions asked, no strings attached. That was what she needed. That was what she deserved. Except he knew now that she wouldn't have taken it. Jake must have known too, and he silently thanked his friend for looking out for Madeleine in a way that he hadn't known how. From the moment that she had walked into his home she had thrown up walls between them so obvious that there hadn't been any point offering to do this another way.

But last night she hadn't shut him out. She had let him in and told him something that he had a sneaking suspicion she hadn't told anyone else about before. And then she had curled into him and slept and he had held onto her and sworn that he would keep her safe. It didn't matter that she was already gently snoring by then. It didn't even matter than she had been doing a pretty good job of keeping herself safe. He was there for her now. Whenever she needed him. Whatever she wanted from him. He would be there.

Except… Except how could he promise that?

With his failed marriage and the business that was desperate for him to return. With two babies who would always, absolutely and without exception, *always* come first. He had let Caro down, had been too distant, too absent, too distracted. What there was of him to share hadn't been enough for her, and that was even before the twins had come along. Now there was less of him than ever, and he wanted Madeleine to have more than that. She deserved someone who was devoted to her. Who she could rely on. Not someone who was already pulled in more directions than he knew how to handle.

But that was before he had woken up to her curled against his chest and tucked into his body. Now all his resolve was in very great danger of flying out of the window. What he wanted, more than anything, was to run his hands up the soft jersey covering her legs. To start at the delicate bone on her ankle that he hadn't been able to leave alone last night. To stroke up over those strong, toned calves that he knew must be aching from their afternoon walking along the South Bank, and then the hours that they had spent pacing last night. He wanted to sweep his hands up over her back. To stop at the nape of her neck and pull her closer, to tip her face up to his and...

'Finn? This is...'

Delicious? Incredible? Perfect?

'Awkward,' she finished, pulling herself away and tucking herself into a ball at the other end of the sofa. 'I'm sorry,' she carried on, wrapping her arms around her knees.

And he could see every single barrier that had dropped between them last night go flying back up. And he couldn't even resent it, because she needed those barriers. They both did, because his own were faltering badly and one of them needed to be doing the sensible thing here: nipping this chemistry in the bud before it could get out of control and hurt one or both of them.

Since she had first walked in here, they had both known that there was something between them. The way that they had avoided one another over the past few years, he wondered if they had known it longer even than that. But they also knew that it was completely out of bounds. It wasn't something that either of them was going to be permitted to explore. It was something to avoid. To push into a tiny, tiny space in his mind and ignore until he forgot about it. Simple as that.

'No, don't be sorry,' he said, standing and turning to the kettle. Anything for a distraction while he tried to compose himself and stuff his feelings into the tiny box where they belonged. Somehow both the babies were still sleeping. No wonder, he supposed, having been awake half the night. If they could keep it up long enough for him to have his first drink of the day then that would be just perfect.

When he turned back round with a cup of tea in each hand, Madeleine was perching on the edge of the sofa, cardigan wrapped tight around her. It didn't take a genius to work out that she was on the defensive. That cardigan, as deliciously soft as it had been against his skin when he had blinked awake a few minutes ago, was now being deployed as armour.

How could he blame her? If she was feeling anything like as conflicted as he was this morning then she would need it.

He glanced at his phone and flicked through his email, still not ready to look at Madeleine. Ah. The nanny agency. That was safe ground.

'They've sent me a shortlist,' he said casually, 'of nannies to interview. Are you still okay to help with that? They've said they can send them over tomorrow.'

'Sure. Do you need to go into the office today?'

'Not if I can help it. But I could do with getting a few hours of work in my home office if we can manage it?'

'Sure. Let me know what you need.'

If they could just stay out of one another's way today, maybe this awkwardness would wear off and they would find themselves back to normal tomorrow, he told himself. They'd go into his office and interview nannies and pretend that she hadn't spent the night in his arms, however unusual the circumstances.

Work was the distraction that he needed this morning. The reminder that his business still owed an unimaginably large amount of money for the new office building they had just taken possession of, and he couldn't afford another day away from his computer, Sunday or not.

By tomorrow, Madeleine and the twins would have had a couple of days to get used to one another and he could go into work with a clear conscience. But he couldn't leave Madeleine completely alone with them after the night that they'd had. Not just the lack of sleep, but Madeleine had opened up to him, made herself vulnerable, and it didn't feel right walking out and leaving her to deal with the fallout on her own. He had told her last night that he wanted to be here for her, and he'd meant it.

CHAPTER NINE

TWENTY-FOUR HOURS LATER, and he was pretty sure he had a handle on this Madeleine thing. They'd managed a whole day of being in the apartment together, caring for the babies, with him in and out of his home office, without a single personal conversation or ankle bone in sight. Even the babies had showed pity on them and had only woken for a quick feed in the night and gone straight back to sleep. Seemed everyone was as keen as he was to get them back on an impersonal footing. Well, good. They were both going to be grown-up about this and pretend that nothing had happened.

'How about this for a plan for today?' he suggested as they both sipped a coffee with their breakfast on Monday morning. 'We both take the babies into the office. They're treated like minor celebrities, so all you'll have to do is try and keep track of which one has been taken to which department to be passed around for cuddles. I'll make sure someone brings you a steady supply of coffee, and you can call me in for nappy emergencies. We'll do the interviews there after lunch. Does that sound manageable?'

'If that's what nannying for you is like then I want the job permanently,' she said with a slightly forced polite smile. 'Baby snuggles, no nappies, endless lattes. Sign me up.'

He reflected her creaky grin, wondering where the ease that he had felt before had gone. And then remembered where that ease had led them, and was grateful that they were both back to tiptoeing. 'That deal is just for you. If you tell our interviewees then the deal's off the table.'

'Fine, fine. What time do you need to go in?'

'Can you be ready by half seven?' he asked. 'It'd be good to be at my desk by eight.'

She glanced at the clock on the wall and nodded. 'How do you want to handle the babies? Take one each—divide and conquer? Or assembly line?'

'God, right now I just want to leave them to sleep. If you can give me a hand to get their bags packed we can stick a clean nappy on them the minute before we need to walk out the door. They can party in their pyjamas this morning.'

His kids could go out in their PJs. He could forgo breakfast. But the one thing that he absolutely, definitely could not skip this morning was the cold shower he seemed to be permanently in need of these days.

He watched Madeleine closely as they walked through the lobby of his office building and couldn't help the swell of pride that he felt when he saw the evidence of all he had achieved over the past few years. Seeing Madeleine had reminded him of where he had built all of this from in a way that never seemed to happen during his weekly drinks with Jake. His best friend had been there for him all along. He'd seen the first tiny office space that he had rented. And the larger building when the first investments started coming through. And then he had pored over the plans for this building when his company had outgrown its space again, and he had decided that he needed somewhere bespoke. Something that would help to create the vision he had of his company as somewhere creative and innovative and exciting.

Except that wasn't all he saw when he looked at his place. He also saw the scary number of zeros on his mortgage statement. The one that he wouldn't have needed if he'd managed to hold his marriage together. This was everything that he had worked for, and everything that he stood to lose if he lost control of his personal life a second time. Everything that he stood to lose if he forgot how vital it was to hold Madeleine at a distance and stop himself getting too close.

There were glass open-plan areas, private offices. Different spaces to suit different personalities and moods. A building full of employees relying on him to keep this company afloat, to keep their wages and their own homes safe and secure.

He chatted with the security guard as he got Madeleine signed in, and nearly lost a twin out of the pushchair before they had even left the lobby. This was always the problem when he brought the babies into work. They were whisked away to be showed off and he could hardly keep track of where they were. He had sold it to Madeleine as an easy morning out, but it was harder to keep track of the babies when they were here than it would be once they were toddling around a busy park by themselves.

'The babies stay in the pushchair until we are upstairs,' Finn said to the guy with a beard and a lumberjack shirt from the design floor who was swooping in to coo at them. 'I promised Madeleine coffee and a comfortable seat before she started having to shepherd them.'

He placed a hand on the small of her back as they crossed the lobby towards the lifts, but pulled it away when he felt her stiffen. So, normal service resumed, he confirmed with a small smile. Good. That was what they both needed. Something had happened between them that night on the sofa. Barriers had come down that he had feared would be impossible to rebuild. She had shared so much with him that he'd thought he had felt the substance of their friendship shift, but it seemed he had been wrong.

This wasn't beyond saving. They could get themselves back somewhere safe, where they could be friends who saw each other occasionally at Jake's family events. Finding the right nanny, and helping Madeleine decide what she wanted to do next, would make that happen even faster.

Madeleine's eyes widened further when he opened the door into his private office, and was it really so terrible to feel such a swell of pride at the expression on her face? It was only as he was hovering at the open glass door into his corner office that he realised how desperate he was for her approval. He stood back and waited while she took a step into the office and then abandoned the pushchair to cross over to the window and look out across the panorama of the London skyline.

'We didn't need to queue for the Eye at all,' she said as her eyes scanned first one way and then the other across the capital. 'We could have just come up here,' Madeleine said with a raised eyebrow and a wry smile.

He laughed and shrugged as he walked over to join her. 'Ah, but you were so keen to do the tourist thing.'

She bumped his shoulder in a friendly way that made him think that their intimacy maybe hadn't disappeared completely with the passage of a too-polite day.

'Seriously, Finn. This is amazing. I hope you're proud, because I am.' She glanced up at him. 'Does that sound really condescending? I'm not sure I care if it does because I mean it. I'm really proud of you. You built all this from scratch while I was writing terrible copy I don't even want to put my name to.'

She must have caught the look that he aimed in her direction at that self-deprecating remark and stopped herself short. Good. He hated that she talked herself down like that. After everything that she had told him over the past few days he wanted to destroy people and places and generally rage out on her behalf. But he couldn't. The only thing that he could do was support her and protect her, even from herself.

'Thank you,' he said, sincerity giving his voice a gravelly edge that surprised him. 'It means a lot that you think that.'

They stood in silence for a few moments more, transfixed by the sight of the city below.

'When we were up in the Eye,' he said, choosing his words carefully, 'you couldn't take your eyes off the Houses of Parliament. That's what you wanted when you were at university, right? Before you had to leave. You wanted to work there.'

He saw surprise on her face, indecision cross her features as she considered him and he prayed to whoever would listen that she would take the leap and trust him with the truth. If she could only be honest with him in the dimmed light of the early hours when they were half delirious with fatigue then this wasn't a friendship. It wasn't anything, really.

She looked him dead in the eye and he held his breath.

'Yes. I wanted to work there. Desperately. As far back as I can remember.'

'And after...'

'After I dropped out of uni I had to accept that it was never going to happen. I missed my chance.'

She took a few long breaths and Finn kept his eyes on the city, giving her the privacy he knew she needed to compose herself. He sensed her straighten her spine, push her shoulders back and he finally glanced over at her.

'It's not too late,' he told her. 'If you want to go back. You could finish your degree.'

She shook her head, her expression fixed and fierce. 'That ship has sailed. It's sunk. It was in flames as it went down. There's no way that I'm going back into that world. Not if it means explaining what happened.'

He laid a hand on her shoulder, wishing he could offer more comfort than that. That he could take her in his arms and protect her as every muscle in his body was urging him to do. But their lives were more complicated than following base urges. There was too much at stake to ignore all the reasons why she needed protecting from him as much as from anyone. What she needed was support, and the only way he could really give her that was by absolutely indisputably refusing to fall in love with her.

'But you still want it,' he said. 'You wouldn't have to tell anyone what happened if you don't want to. Lots of people go back to university.'

She whipped round to look at him. 'And how would I pay for it? It costs ten times what it did when I was there before. Even just repeating the final year is beyond what I can imagine being able to afford. I don't know if the credits from the earlier semesters are even valid any more so I might have to repeat those too. That's before I even get to the question of where I would live and what I would eat. It's impossible, Finn, so please just leave it.'

'Of course it's not impossible. I'll pay for it.'

The look of horror that she shot him hit him straight in the gut, and he recoiled at the anger on her face. He couldn't believe that he had just offered that. It wasn't that he couldn't afford it. His personal finances had been incredibly rocky around the time of his divorce, but some judicious investments had paid off, so that he could breathe easy again at night rather than lying awake, worried that he was bringing two babies into a world that was too precarious for him to be able to guarantee that they would always be well fed and warm.

'God. No, Finn. Absolutely not. That's never going to happen.'

'Why not?' He had helped hundreds, maybe thousands of people go to university by now with his scholarship funds and early intervention programmes he had started early in his career, wanting to see other kids like him follow him up that ladder. Of course he would pay her tuition. Her housing. Whatever she needed.

'Because it would be weird,' Madeleine said. 'And inappropriate. And uncomfortable.'

'Weirder or more uncomfortable than me eating breakfast at your house every day for seven years? Uncomfortable like me wearing Jake's hand-me-down school uniforms? Weird like that time I came on a family holiday with you?'

'That's different,' she said, though they both knew

it wasn't. He let it slide this time. 'Anyway, what would we tell Jake?'

'How about to mind his own business?' Finn offered. 'Or we don't tell him anything. Or, um, I don't know, something outrageous like I'm helping you out because you're family and because I want to and I'm in a position to.'

God, there were a lot of 'I's in that sentence, he realised as he stopped speaking. This wasn't about him. It was about her. If he didn't think that it was what she wanted, he wouldn't be pushing this. But there was something about the way that she had looked out the window that made him think that she hadn't given up on this dream just yet. That she still wanted it. That if he could help with the practicalities, clear obstacles from her way, she could go back to it.

'He'd ask awkward questions.'

'Like what? It's not like there's anything going on between us. We have nothing to hide from him. He can ask what he likes.'

His words seemed to freeze out the rest of the world, because he had never in his life heard something that was so completely true and such an enormous lie at the same time. They hadn't slept together, hadn't even kissed. They had both sworn that nothing like that was ever going to happen between them. And yet they were stupid if either of them truly believed that there was nothing going on. Because he was fighting the urge to kiss her every minute they were together. And the urge to fall in love with her every second.

Love? When had he started thinking like that? She had only been back in his life for a few days. For years of his life he had seen her every single day. Eaten meals with her. Gone on holiday with her. Why was this only happening now? Was it just because they were all grown up? Was it because she'd ditched the baggy clothes and raised her eyes from the floor? Was it because he was finally grown up enough to realise just how beautiful she was? Or because he was suddenly divorced and single again for the first time in years?

No, he knew that wasn't it because that was all superficial bull, and if there was one thing that he knew for certain about these feelings that had been growing for Madeleine these last few days it was that they were anything but superficial.

It was that for the first time in his life he was in a room with Madeleine and felt completely her equal. Something that he had never felt when they were growing up. But he had built this business from nothing and he was proud of it. Hadn't realised it was possible to feel prouder, actually, until she had said that she was proud too. And he had never felt so valued, so truly seen as he did standing here with her right now. She didn't see the kid he'd been, as he so often thought that Jake did. She didn't see the CEO he'd become, like everyone else in this building, the failed husband, the man who had lost his home and taken his business to the brink little more than a year ago. She saw the whole person. Everything he had been. Everything he had worked so hard to overcome and become. Everything he still wanted to achieve. No wonder things had been so intense between them. But that wasn't love, or attraction. It wasn't even friendship, he told himself. It was just knowing someone at two extreme moments in their life. He was almost sure that he could convince himself of that.

Hart burbled behind them and he crossed to the pushchair, his arm brushing against Madeleine's as she followed him and picked up Bella.

'Do you want me to take them somewhere so you can get some work done?' she asked, and he felt the *No* in his gut before it made it to his lips.

'Hang around for a bit,' he said, hoping his voice sounded more level than he felt. He crossed to the double doors of the supply cupboard at the far end of the office and opened them, flicking on the light with his elbow. It was only when he heard the warm chuckle from behind him that he realised how strange it must look.

CHAPTER TEN

'You keep the babies in a cupboard?'

Madeleine laughed and took a step closer to investigate. The floor was covered with soft play mats, layered two or three deep over foam tiles locked together on the carpet. Fairy lights and gauzy fabric criss-crossed the walls and draped from the ceiling, and when Finn hit another switch, swirling stars were projected over the whole space and the notes of a nursery rhyme tinkled from a hidden speaker.

'I know, I know,' Finn said. 'It's not ideal. This place was already finished before we found out Caro was pregnant. It was the best I could do in the circumstances. In my defence, at least it's a really big cupboard.'

But she was still smiling as she laid Bella onto one of the play mats—the baby reached straight for one of the squeaky toys and cooed as if she'd been reunited with a dear friend. Madeleine was willing to bet that the cupboard in Finn's office was one of the baby girl's favourite places—and really, who could blame her? Hart had started to reach out for his sister, so Finn put him down on the mat too. Madeleine took a step back to marvel at the cuteness of twin babies in a closet.

'It's a masterpiece,' she told Finn honestly.

'Baby sensory class in a cupboard. I should market it.'

'You'd make a fortune. Another fortune,' she corrected herself, glancing around his office and feeling again that strange mixture of pride and being utterly out of her depth that she'd felt when she'd first walked in here.

He had achieved so much. She'd bitten off her words earlier. Hadn't wanted to turn the conversation back to herself, but the contrast in the direction their lives had taken had never been starker. He had achieved so much. She was homeless and jobless. Had zero prospects for her future. Well, until Finn had proposed some. Paying for her to go back to uni. It was ludicrous. And offered as, what? Some sort of payback for the generosity of her parents? Well, she couldn't accept. Her parents' generosity had nothing to do with her. If he felt some misguided sense of duty, then he could take it up with them or with Jake. She'd never given it a minute's thought.

But she could take it. She let herself think about that for a second. She had no job. No ties. The offer of a generous benefactor. She could go back to university, finish her degree and stop wondering. Stop asking herself what might have been and actually go and *do* something about it.

If only it wasn't Finn making the offer. If only

it was some completely disinterested stranger offering her this money to go and follow her dream. Because… Finn. Her feelings for him were anything but disinterested. They were complicated, and growing more so by the day. If she were to take him up on his offer, what would that do to them? What would that do to these feelings that she didn't quite know how to name but was finding increasingly difficult to ignore?

What if there was another way?

When she'd been stuck on the treadmill of rent arrears and copy deadlines, she'd never had a chance to draw breath and work out if there was a way that she could go back to studying. For years she'd hated the thought of having to come into contact with the professor again. But that excuse had died two years ago. He was gone, and she was still here. What if her dreams weren't as dead as she'd thought they might be?

She brought her attention back to the babies on the play mat. This wasn't something that had to be decided now, right away—going back to university or getting a new job. Whatever it was she was going to do next deserved more thought than the reflexive denial she'd just given Finn. She'd had to abandon her dream once already. If she was being given a second chance, she had to at least think about it, however uncomfortable that might make her feel.

'I promise I'll think about your offer,' she said at last. 'It's incredibly generous. I'm sorry that I didn't start by saying that.'

Finn gave her a long intense look that had the colour rising in her cheeks.

'Take all the time you need.'

She blinked once, twice, then turned her attention back to the babies.

'Right,' she told Finn, her tone firm. 'You are meant to be at your desk. I'm going to play with the kids here, but if we're keeping you from working then I'm going to take them on a tour of the building. If we're making too much noise, let me know and I'll get out of your hair.'

The morning passed more quickly than Madeleine had known that time could. By the time that the babies had got bored of their play mat, Finn's assistant had arranged someone to give her a tour of the building, and she'd not needed to do much more than step back and watch as the twins were passed from department to department. A hot cup of coffee had been pressed into her hands whenever they had been empty, and as she passed through the art department the guy with the checked shirt had finally got his cuddle with the babies.

By the time that she had changed two lots of nappies and made up two bottles, fed both babies, burped them and got them back in their pushchair, she realised that she was starving, and had no idea where she could get herself some lunch. She was just looking around for someone to ask when Finn's assistant appeared behind her and let her know that lunch was ready in Finn's office. Cool, problem solved.

When she arrived back on his floor with—somehow, miraculously—two sleeping babies, she was ready to eat her own body weight in cheese. Or, well, whatever culinary delights got sent up to the CEO's office in a company like this.

It was a far cry from the grubby office that she had just been made redundant from. And it made her realise that all the years she had spent in that dingy office with those dingy people had skewed her perception until she had lost sight of what the alternatives were. There were people in this building who loved their job. Who were excited and motivated to get to their desk in the morning. Who believed in what they were doing—believed themselves to be important. She'd taken the first job she'd been offered, convinced that without graduating she wouldn't be able to get anything else. And then she had stayed for years as it had gradually eaten away her ambition and her passion. It was like a light being switched on, being here at Finn's company. And he had offered her the way out.

Not a job that she hadn't earned, but something more fundamental than that. He had given her the chance to go back and pick up where she had left off. To retrace her steps back to the moment that her life had taken a catastrophic swerve and try to correct its course.

She got to decide now, what she wanted from her life, how she was going to define herself, and it was Finn who was offering her that chance.

Why? Why did he care so much? Yes, there was that chemistry between them—so much more complicated and confusing than the desire that normally characterised her relationships. Men who wanted her for her body. Men she wanted for their shallowness, their inability to hurt her. What she had felt with Finn that night, when she had woken in the morning with her body wrapped around his, protected by his, that was a far cry from simple. It was anything but shallow.

She had been adamant that these feelings they were having were not welcome, and were certainly not going to be acted upon. But, even without that future, one that they both knew was impossible, she was in no doubt that Finn *saw* her. Not her body, but her. He'd recognised the passion, the yearning she felt for the career that she'd left behind. And more than just seeing, he'd talked to her about it. Given her chances and choices, if she wanted to take them.

She put her finger to her lips as she walked into the office, and Finn came to admire her top baby-sitting and the sleeping babies in the pushchair. Then he parked them just inside the door and gestured to the table where lunch had been laid out for them.

'Fancy,' she said with an impressed smile.

Finn shrugged. 'Perk of being the boss. No such thing as a free lunch, though. Do you mind if I pick your brains about CVs before the interviews?'

Madeleine grabbed a plate and a stack of resumes and started reading, raising an eyebrow from time to time.

'This is…impressive,' she said as she read about languages spoken and subjects tutored. Cookery skills and forest school trips and school entry exams. 'Though I think this is a little high-achieving for a couple of kids who aren't yet crawling,' she said with a shrug. 'I mean, it's great that she offers all this, but where's the care for the kids' emotional well-being? She hasn't mentioned that once.'

She grabbed another CV from the pile and started to read. Then laid it on top of the first. With the third, she broke into a smile. 'This one,' she said simply. 'Josie. The love she had for her last family totally shines through.'

Finn smiled. Josie had been top of his list too, and was lined up first for the interviews. Though why it should make him so happy that he and Madeleine agreed on this was anyone's guess. Oh, for God's sake, who was he trying to kid? He knew exactly why he was pleased that they saw eye to eye on this decision, and he knew exactly why he should be shutting down any thoughts that pointed in that dangerous direction.

'Well, I guess we could give them all a fair shot,' he said, glancing at the clock. 'I'll get this cleared away and have them send the first one through. Make sure you have coffee. These things can be gruelling.'

He was on his fourth cup of the day and it was doing nothing to keep his yawns at bay. The babies hadn't given him any trouble the night before, but he had lain awake regardless, desperately trying not to remember how it had felt to wake up Sunday morning with Madeleine practically in his lap. Saturday night had been long, and thankless. But then, right at the end, a kind of perfect.

He shook his head. Perfect. Except it never could be with her. He'd proved with Caro that he couldn't hold a marriage together. And failing again? Losing his home again? Compromising his business again? Never going to happen. He could feel the burn of bile in his throat at just the thought of it.

He couldn't afford to fail. Couldn't afford to lose any other part of the life that he'd built for himself. Everything up to this point had been about momentum. One success after another had changed his life beyond recognition. Losing Caro, his home—that had been his first failure and it had hit him hard. Hard enough to have learnt his lesson that he couldn't have both a relationship and his life. There was no way that he was starting something with Madeleine just to prove to himself that it really wasn't possible.

The stakes were too high to take that kind of risk. He had thought it bad enough when his marriage had broken down and he'd had to keep his life and his business on track. If he had let one more thing drop, he could have lost everything. If he had taken his eye off the ball once in the last year, when he was putting his life back together, it could all have been gone.

Now he had Bella and Hart to think about, the stakes were higher than they had ever been before. The dangers of failing were worse than ever. He wasn't going to ever let them be in the situation he had faced as a child. And that meant protecting what he had now. Much as he had strong feelings for Madeleine, he couldn't risk anything that would disrupt the careful equilibrium that he had managed to re-establish in the wake of his marriage failing. And if the only way to avoid that was to turn his back on this thing that was developing with Madeleine, then he'd do it, no matter how much it hurt, because the alternative was all too terrifying.

It would be easier, he supposed, if he could cut her out of his life completely. But he had promised Jake this favour. No. It wasn't about what he had promised Jake; it was about supporting Madeleine because it was the right thing to do and because he wanted to. He just had to draw that line between friendly support and falling asleep with her in his arms. How hard could that be?

Josie arrived—the nanny candidate who had topped both his and Madeleine's list—and he turned his attention to finding the best possible person to help care for his children. This was the way to keep his life on track—by concentrating on what his children needed, what would make their lives richer. If he could push his own desires into some tiny space in his mind and ignore them then he would be all the happier for it.

Madeleine kept one eye on Finn's expression as he conducted the first of the interviews, and couldn't put her finger on what was going on in that brain of his. She could sense him withdrawing from her, and if she hadn't been so relieved that he was fighting this as hard as she was then she would have been hurt.

Maybe it was just the business setting, but any closeness that had been there on Saturday night was well and truly gone by the time that the first interview was over. The twins woke up just in time to have a play with Josie, and as she and Finn took them over to their sensory cupboard Madeleine leaned back in her seat and watched them together. The nanny was perfect, and Madeleine felt a little sorry for the other candidates who were going to have to try and follow her this afternoon.

They're a perfect unit, Madeleine thought.

And this was what she would be leaving behind when she made a decision about what to do with her life. Finn was already making plans, and she needed to too. Tonight, she promised herself. Tonight she was going to sit down with her laptop and make a real plan.

'Would you walk down with me, Madeleine?' Josie asked, tucking her braids behind her ear, and Madeleine's eyes widened with surprise. She'd asked Josie a couple of questions in the interview, but she had wanted to give Josie and Finn and the kids some time to get to know each other without a practical stranger there making things awkward. She lifted an eyebrow in question at Finn, who just smiled and tickled Bella under the chin.

'Fine with me,' he said, smiling as Bella laughed.

Madeleine shrugged and Finn followed her and Josie to the door. 'Thanks so much for coming in,' he said with genuine warmth. 'I'll be in touch in a couple of days. If you have any questions in the meantime, just send them over.'

'Great,' Josie said with a final smile. 'I'll look forward to hearing from you then.'

'So,' Madeleine said as they crossed to the lift and waited, 'was there something you wanted to ask?'

Josie hesitated until the lift arrived and, once she was inside, said, 'I just wanted to ask how it is living with Finn? I've had some live-in jobs that were better than others, you know. Finn seems great and Hart and Bella are adorable. I just wanted to sound you out—woman to woman—if there's anything else I should know about living with them.'

Ah, the penny dropped. Madeleine didn't need to imagine the awkward situations a live-in nanny could face. Add a single dad into the situation and she should totally understand her asking the question.

She thought back to her first night at Finn's, when she'd misunderstood his intentions. When he'd done everything in his power to make sure she knew that she was safe.

'He's honestly a great guy,' she told Josie without a hint of hesitation. 'I wouldn't have any reservations telling you that you should totally take the job if he offers.'

Josie smiled and Madeleine saw her shoulders relax a fraction. 'That's such good news. I hope I'll see you again,' she said with a smile.

Madeleine waved her off and returned to the lifts feeling pensive. Well, looked like Josie had found her dream job. Finn had his domestic crisis sorted. She was the only one now who had to get her life in order.

She heard Finn speaking as she approached his office and hesitated in the doorway. He spotted her and gestured for her to wait—it was only then that she realised who he was speaking to. She recognised Caro from her voice, and from the way that Finn was angling the phone, showing the screen to two giggling babies; it was clear that they were video calling again.

'You'll Skype me into the second round interview?' she heard Caro say as Finn began to wrap up the call.

Madeleine concentrated on repacking the twins' changing bag, trying not to eavesdrop on Finn's conversation with his wife. Ex-wife.

From the way the interview had gone, and the tone of Caroline's voice, Josie was probably going to be receiving a job offer pretty soon, and that meant that she had to work out a plan for what she was going to do next. Once Finn had a nanny in place, he wasn't going to want her living in his spare room. She'd known ever since she'd been made redundant that she was going to have to make big decisions, and her thinking time was almost up. If she didn't act now, she was going to find herself running out of options.

Since she'd walked out on her university education, she'd gone from one precariously held flat to another. The only constant—the job that she despised—even that was gone now. She had nothing to show for her life, and nothing made that more clear than being in

Finn's office with his successful business and adorable children and his grown-up co-parenting.

So she had to think about Finn's offer. Had to think seriously about whether university was what she still wanted. Whether journalism and politics were what she still wanted. Because, for the first time in for ever, she could actually choose what she *wanted*. Not what options were left to her. Not what she could afford, or which seemed to throw the least hurdles in her way. She had been given permission by the universe to make a fresh start. To be whatever she chose.

Was Finn one of those options? They had both been upfront about the fact that they didn't want a relationship. God knew he had told her that enough times. Roughly the same number of times that she had said the same thing. But… But did she mean it? Definitely the first time she had said it, and the second. But she had been less and less convinced by her own internal monologue as the days had gone on.

More importantly, he'd made her see that no one was putting more restrictions on her life than herself. Now was the time in her life she could make a change.

Finn had told her that he would help her financially. If she was turning him down because of—what?—some need to do this without his help?—who was she hurting? Only herself. It didn't make any difference to Finn or to anyone else in the world if she didn't go back to university. The only person it affected was herself.

Didn't she owe herself another chance? What else had she worked so hard for all those years? It didn't matter how resolutely she'd tried to ignore her dreams, to pretend that they meant nothing to her, they weren't going anywhere. Finn had seen them. He'd made her see them again too. To look at them straight on in a way that she'd been afraid to do for years. He thought they were worth fighting for. What did it say that he had read them so plainly on her face?

It said something unsettling. Unnerving. That she was so easy to read. Or maybe that Finn could read her easily—that wasn't the same thing at all, and she knew which one was true. Finn understood her. He *saw* her. And she wasn't sure where that left any consideration on her part about accepting money from him.

He hung up the phone and she crossed to the stack of CVs that they had left on his desk to remind herself of the next candidate. But the words swam in front of her eyes as she considered her next move. If Finn was serious about funding her, she had so many options that it was dizzying. Once, years ago, she'd looked briefly at the costs of going back to her studies and it had been beyond anything that she could dream of. Even a distance learning course would have left her hopelessly broke. But if she got a loan from Finn to cover her living costs, a student loan would cover her fees. She needn't be entirely dependent on Finn. If she was going to take this seriously, she could apply for some of the grants and bursaries and scholarships that had been so overwhelming when she had looked before. If she really wanted to do this, she could start applying for them now, and do it all by herself.

When the knock on the door snapped her back into the room, Finn had a half-smile on his face that she didn't have to work hard to interpret. She knew that her excitement was showing on her face, knew that Finn knew her well enough to guess what was going through her mind. But she wasn't going to share. Not yet, when it was still so fresh and delicate and unformed in her mind. She'd share later, when she was ready, and she knew Finn wasn't going to rush her.

And at that thought she was hit by a wave of desire for him that stole her breath and made her look away for fear that he was going to see exactly what swerve her thoughts had just taken. Because these feelings that she was having for Finn weren't just a case of lusting after a pretty face. He'd had that face for years and she'd barely noticed it. It was about seeing the man he'd become—capable, successful, generous, kind—and desperately wanting to keep him in her life. And yes, the pretty face made these thoughts extra lusty, but the wanting wasn't about the face or the body. It was about nurturing this connection. This feeling of seeing and being seen. About taking care of someone she absolutely knew would take care of her.

And those feelings were huge and hot and terrifying—and absolutely undeniable. Now that she saw the truth of them, it was hard to believe that she'd ever been able to ignore them. They'd burst to life outside his bedroom door the first night that she'd spent in his home, when he'd seen her vulnerability and stood by her side as she'd found her strength, and she'd been kidding herself ever since that these feelings were something she could 'manage'.

These damn inconvenient feelings were about as far from manageable as she could imagine. But at least they were both agreed that they weren't happy about them. Right now, the fact that Finn was fighting them as hard as she was was just about the only thing stopping her doing something really stupid.

The knock on the door from Finn's assistant stopped that train of thought heading somewhere that would get them into trouble and she pasted on a professional smile as the next candidate was shown into the room.

CHAPTER ELEVEN

THANK GOODNESS THE babies have gone down with barely a peep, Madeleine thought as she sat at the writing desk in her room and opened her laptop.

It had taken all her considerable willpower to get through the afternoon without a cheeky search on her phone to look at what loans and scholarships and grants were available for mature students. Now, with the kids asleep, she had all evening to research and start to come up with a plan.

An hour later she had a list of politics and journalism courses in London, application details for her shortlist, and every scholarship, grant and bursary that she could hunt down.

The next job would be finding somewhere to live. She had no idea how she would pay for a place yet, not until she'd found some sort of work, but she had to start trying to find somewhere. If she got into university, she could maybe get a place in a hall of residence but that would be months away, if she even managed to make it happen at all. And she didn't have months. She needed somewhere soon. She pulled up a flatmates website to see what was available, and how much money she was going to have to come up with to survive the next few months. Maybe she would be able to find some freelance work just to keep her going until she had this university thing sorted. A house share might not need the same financial information and upfront deposits as renting a place on her own. It wasn't ideal, but she wasn't sure what else she could do right now.

She looked up at a knock on the doorframe to see Finn standing there watching her.

'Just wondered if you fancy dinner?' he asked, and she realised that she was starving. 'What are you working on?' he said and she turned the laptop to show him, then frowned at the expression on his face.

'What?' she asked.

'I didn't realise you were looking for somewhere else already.'

'Of course I'm looking. It's great of you to let me stay but it was always the plan to find somewhere as soon as I could. Josie is great, so it seemed like you wouldn't need my help much longer.'

'That doesn't mean you have to move out.'

'I'm staying here to help you with the babies, Finn. If you have a nanny, then what would I be doing? It would be…weird.'

'You could stay as Jake's sister. As a friend.'

'I think we both know that it wouldn't be a good idea, Finn.'

'Why not?'

Why not?

He knew exactly why not.

Which meant that he was asking the question because he wanted her to say the answer out loud. Well, fine, if he wanted to be reckless then so be it.

'Because you like me, Finn. We both know it. The same way we both know that I like you. And if we stay here together under this roof much longer then one of us is going to do something that we regret. Saturday night already went too far.'

'Saturday night was nothing,' he said, though the expression on his face proved that it was a lie.

'Well, it didn't feel like nothing at the time. It didn't for me and I don't think it did for you either, no matter what you're trying to tell yourself today. If it was nothing, then neither of us would be thinking about it, and I know I am.' In fact, she wished she'd had a minute today when she wasn't thinking about it. When her mind wasn't drifting back to the feel of him wrapped around her. It was way too distracting. 'I think the best thing for everyone is for me to find somewhere to stay and remove the temptation for both of us.'

'You've no money; how are you going to find somewhere to rent?'

'Wow.' She stood up, planting her hands on her hips. If he wanted a fight about this then she was game. 'Thanks for that reality check, Finn. It actually hadn't occurred to me that I'm broke and screwed. Thank heavens you're here to remind me. Nice swerve on the subject, by the way. Don't think I didn't notice.'

Finn walked over and leaned against her desk,

and she took a step away from him sharply; she was cross and the last thing she needed was him getting close and distracting her. Finn took a step back too, and she hated that he could read her so well.

'Sorry. I'm sorry. I didn't mean to be rude,' he said, looking genuinely conciliatory.

She rolled her eyes and didn't even care that it made her look like the stroppy teenager she was sure he must remember. 'I'm just excited,' she said. 'Getting ahead of myself, I guess, looking at courses and student loans and bursaries. I want it to happen now.'

'Don't apologise for being excited. I should be the one apologising. So you're thinking of going back to university?'

She smiled as she acknowledged to herself that she had already made the decision, and she wasn't going to change her mind.

'I'm going. I've been looking at courses, loans, scholarships. I'm sure I can do it. I just need to come up with a proper plan.'

'I've already said that I'll lend you the money,' he reminded her.

'And I've thanked you, and told you that I wouldn't feel comfortable taking it. I want to do this myself. I got myself here. I'm going to get myself out.'

Finn frowned, reached out to brush a hand against her arm. 'You *didn't* get yourself here, though, Madeleine. Someone did something terrible to you. That's why you're in this situation and I don't understand why you won't let me help you out of it.' He frowned at her, but she shook off his judgement. He didn't understand what it was like to be in her position.

'Because it's uncomfortable for me, Finn,' she told him. 'Because these feelings that I have for you are uncomfortable, and the thought of owing you thousands of pounds makes me feel sick.'

Finn shook his head. 'But you wouldn't owe it. I wouldn't expect you to pay me back.'

'Don't you see that makes it worse?' She sat heavily on the edge of the bed. 'Because then it would always be weird and I would never have the chance to make things equal between us.' She stood up again, needing to do something with her body to get rid of this fizz of anxious energy. Finn crossed his arms and held her gaze, not backing down for a second.

'You're making a big deal out of this when you really don't have to.' Finn perched on the edge of her desk, crossing his arms as he watched her pacing. 'It's just money. It doesn't make us unequal—you can take it without it meaning anything.'

'I just can't, Finn.' She shook her head. 'I need you to leave this now,' she said. She had made her decision, and nothing he could say would change her mind.

He rubbed a hand on his jaw and shook his head. 'Fine. I'll leave it. But I'm not going to pretend to be happy about it, Madeleine. It doesn't seem fair that I can owe you, but you can't owe me.'

She rolled her eyes. This again. 'I told you, you don't owe me anything, Finn. It was my parents, and Jake, who were generous. I didn't do anything.

Anyway. We've talked this subject to death. If you want to help me talk through my ideas and come up with a plan, that would be great. If you're going to bulldoze over my wishes and continue to insist on your own way then we're going to fall out. Now, let's change the subject.'

He looked as if he was going to go for one last argument, but then changed his mind. 'Fine. Dinner?' he asked.

'Yes. I'm starving. I can cook or…'

'Trudy left something for us in the fridge. We just need to heat it up. Do you want to eat together or—'

'Of course we can eat together, Finn. I'm not planning on hiding in here. All of this is meant to be keeping us friends. I don't want things to be awkward. I'm pretty sure we can still manage to eat a meal together without things imploding.'

'Good. Then I'll see you downstairs in ten?'

'I'll see you there.'

Finn checked the time on his phone again as he glanced towards the stairs. He was sure that once Madeleine was down here and they were talking again this anxious feeling would go. But right now, waiting for her to come down from her bedroom, he could feel his whole body on the verge of a twitch.

She was moving out. Of course she was. She had never really moved in because this was only ever a temporary arrangement. But seeing her browsing that site looking for flatmates—that had struck him in a surprisingly painful way. And he didn't want to have to think about why it hurt. He just wanted to convince Madeleine that she didn't have to rush into anything and leave in a hurry. He hadn't even definitely decided if he was offering Josie a job. He couldn't, not until Caro had spoken to her too. Madeleine was totally jumping the gun. She could stay as long as she needed.

Which meant this probably wasn't about him hiring Josie at all. This was about the other thing that she'd said. The words that had made his stomach twist in anticipation. *'We both know that I like you.'* He'd goaded her into saying it—he wasn't stupid, he could see that. But he'd expected her to bring up what they'd said before. About chemistry. He hadn't expected her to come right out and just tell him that she liked him. He hated that just hearing those words had fired his blood and it was now making it difficult to sit still. It was all so schoolboy.

But the words had hit him hard and he wanted to know more. He would die before asking if she *liked him* liked him. But he was desperate to know if she was thinking of him as often as he was thinking of her. If daydreams and fantasies made it as impossible for her to concentrate as it did for him.

He looked up at a sound in the doorway and was arrested by the sight of her in his home. How had this happened? How had he found himself so undone by someone he had known for twenty years? Someone who until a few days ago had been a distant presence in his life. Someone he might kiss on the cheek at family parties but who otherwise didn't have a place in his life at all. Until she'd moved into his apartment and his brain and hadn't allowed him a minute's respite ever since.

'You like me?' he said, and as the words left his mouth he knew how dangerous a move that was. He knew that one of them, or both of them, were going to end up getting hurt because he had no way of following this conversation through. Of taking this friendship to another level—taking it to where he really wanted it to go. He couldn't risk a relationship. Couldn't risk his life falling apart when he had so narrowly averted that disaster. He had lost his home once. He wasn't taking his chances by making the same mistakes all over again.

Why was he even thinking about his divorce? He pulled himself up. No one had mentioned marriage. A relationship even. All Madeleine had done was tell him that she liked him and he was the one who had jumped all the way to the altar. It didn't have to be that way. There was a middle ground between a kiss on the cheek and marriage—and it would never be enough for him, he realised. Watching her watching him, he was convinced that nothing would ever be enough where Madeleine was concerned.

He had never wanted like this. Even in those early days with Caro when he had been so sure that he was in love, what he had really felt was relief and gratitude and comfort, he realised now—that he had someone who had been born into the world of CEOs and OBEs that he had suddenly found himself trying to navigate. Someone who knew how to move in that world and stop him feeling like the poor kid eating at someone else's table.

He could never escape that kid when he was with Madeleine. She saw him every time that she looked at him. And he didn't mind, he realised with a jolt. That kid was a part of his story. He was a part of Madeleine's story too. They both accepted that he had a place at their table. No point in either of them pretending that he didn't exist.

Madeleine had held his gaze this whole time, watching him while he grappled with how big a mistake he had made when he'd asked her that question. He loved watching her think. Loved watching her grapple with herself, deciding exactly how much of herself she wanted to reveal, how brave she wanted to be. She always took the brave option. He knew that she would.

'I like you,' she said.

She shrugged, as if the words were nothing more than a bland observation. They both knew they were so much more than that.

'Don't move out.'

Her eyebrows pinched together at his impulsive words, and he couldn't blame her. Asking her to stay didn't make any sense. They both knew that the safest thing for them both to do right now was to keep their distance from one another. And yet here they both were. Alone in his house, eyes locked and guards tumbling.

'Why?'

She was calling his bluff, just as he'd called hers.

And she'd already set the bar with her bravery and her honesty. He wasn't going to let her down by doing anything less.

'Because I like having you here.'

'You don't have me.'

Again, that pinch in her brow. He half smiled at the innuendo, wondering which of them was going to rein this flirting in. Not him. Not this time. Not yet.

'Maybe I would, if you stayed.'

She crossed her arms and leaned against the doorframe, her eyes never leaving his.

'That would be a terrible idea,' she said. And the words would have felt like a shot of ice water if it hadn't been for the expression in her eyes. The one that told him she cared about it being a bad idea about as much as he did right now.

That was fire. Not ice. He didn't want to be smart. He wanted to be stupid, if stupid meant wrapping his arms around Madeleine or rubbing that crease from her forehead with his thumb and making her forget her demons for a while. If stupid meant that his hands got to circle that little bone on her ankle again but explore further this time. Up long calves and soft thighs. If his arms could circle her waist as he pulled her under him.

'I agree,' he said at last. 'It's a terrible idea. But I can't stop thinking that I want to do it anyway. And I think you feel the same way.'

'Just because we're both thinking the same stupid thing doesn't mean we should act on it,' Madeleine observed with a lift of her eyebrow.

He left his stool and walked over to stand in front of her, his hands in his pockets as she looked him up and down. God, he would die happy if she just looked at him like that one more time.

'Agreed,' he said with a half-smile. 'Want to do it anyway?'

The moan she let out hit him straight in the gut and he was hard even before she took that step towards him, wrapped her arms around his neck until she was all he could see and hear and smell.

'A really bad idea,' she said again, but the smile on her lips—God, her lips…so close…so full…so pink—told him she was past brave. She'd headed straight through courage to reckless and he was right there with her.

There was no hesitation when her mouth finally met his. She pressed firm against him, her lips tasting and exploring, while he was so overwhelmed that this was happening that he barely knew how to respond. It was only when she broke the kiss and looked up at him, that little crease back on her brow, that he snapped back into the present, stopped overthinking and realised that he had everything he had been dreaming about right in front of him. In his next heartbeat his arms were around her waist, he had pulled her into his body and crashed them both back against the doorframe, her body soft in his arms, her breath in his mouth.

CHAPTER TWELVE

FINN CREPT BACK into his bedroom after settling Bella back to sleep and paused to take in the sight of Madeleine Everleigh asleep in his bed. The sheets were tucked across her chest, her head turned to one side and her hair messy around her on the pillows. In the half-light, he still couldn't quite believe what they'd done. That she'd wanted him as much as he realised he'd been yearning for her these past days. But now the spell was broken and he was out of bed—where did they go from here?

Could he just slip back into bed, wrap his arms around her and pretend the spell had never been broken? Or did he accept that his alarm was going off in an hour anyway and he might as well be up for the day? That must be the sensible thing to do. Because when he was too close to her he lost his mind. That was the only explanation for what had happened last night, when they had both jumped headfirst into something that they'd both said—out loud and on numerous occasions—was a very bad idea. And now they both knew exactly what they would be missing out on, he wasn't sure how they were ever meant to make a sensible decision again.

Nothing had changed for them. The fundamentals of their lives remained the same. He couldn't start a relationship now, couldn't add that layer of complication to a life that he had kept on track by the skin of his teeth. But...but last night. He had never felt so connected to another person. Which was a bad thing, he reminded himself for the thousandth time. Because neither he nor Madeleine wanted this to happen. So when the sun came up they would go back to being so very sensible and not letting this happen again. Wouldn't they?

Suddenly he wasn't so sure that that was what he wanted—to give up on the idea of ever having a relationship. But there really couldn't be a worse time. He had dragged himself out of poverty. He had worked every hour for a decade to build this business up. He had made the sort of marriage he had thought that he needed to survive in that world. And he'd tried his hardest to love her.

And all of that had nearly been derailed when his best hadn't been good enough and he and Caro had had to find a way to unpick their lives and their finances. He had lost his home. He couldn't face that sort of instability again—not now he had the twins. If the idea of losing everything he had worked for had been frightening before he had become a father, it was unthinkable now.

And yet...it wasn't quite morning. The babies were asleep and there was still an hour before his alarm would go off. If last night was all they were going to have then he wasn't going to waste the final hour of it examining his conscience.

He slipped back beneath the cool sheets and reached for Madeleine, an arm sliding under her waist, pulling her back towards him until he could feel the heat of her skin from his chest to his toes. She let out a huff of breath and tangled her fingers in his, pulling his arm tighter around her waist.

'Mmm...' she said, barely more than a whisper. 'Don't tell me it's morning.' He pressed a kiss to the nape of her neck, sweeping her hair out of the way to follow that thought around to her ear, her jaw.

'We've an hour until the alarm,' he said, fingers now exploring the soft skin of her belly, the dip of her waist, the ample curve of her hip. 'Want to go back to sleep?' He could feel her smile, even with her back to him, as she pressed herself just a tiny bit closer.

'Not even for a second.'

By the time his alarm sounded he was boneless and heavy, his eyes sore from lack of sleep, his body deliciously fatigued. As he reached to silence his phone, Madeleine shifted from where her head had been resting on his chest to look up at him.

'What are the chances we can ignore that and go back to sleep?'

He smiled at her and kissed her softly on the lips.

'You know I wish I could, but I have to go into the office. Will you be okay with the twins here for a couple of hours, or we could all go in together?'

'No, it's fine, we'll hang out here. I'm sure you've

got lots to catch up on,' Madeleine said, pulling the sheet a little tighter around her. And like that it was over. Neither of them had even left the bed yet, but whatever it was that had allowed them to ignore their better judgement was gone, leaving awkwardness in its wake.

He caught her gaze and looked her in the eye, and was unreasonably pleased that she cracked him a half-smile. 'Are we okay?' he asked.

'Go to work,' she said. 'And stop worrying. We're fine, and if we need to talk we can do it later.'

If they needed to talk? On what planet did you sleep with your brother's best friend—the same person who also happened to be your temporary housemate and whose kids you were babysitting—and not need to talk about it? Maybe Finn would get home from work tonight and Trudy would have left dinner and they could just eat and put the babies to bed and not mention the fact that he'd made her see stars last night. Well, that was a perfectly reasonable plan, wasn't it?

She rolled her eyes at her own idiocy as she heard the shower in Finn's bathroom turn on and started to look around her and work out what had happened to her clothes. One minute they had been in the kitchen—all meaningful looks and barely concealed lust—and the next they were done with even barely concealing and they were crashing against doorframes and knocking into bannisters, shedding clothes as they went.

From here she could spot underwear, but she was going to have to grab Finn's shirt if she was going to make it out of here with any sort of dignity intact. Really, this whole morning-after thing would be so much easier if they had actually talked for even a second about how they were going to handle this today... They should just be going back to normal, right? Pretending that it had meant nothing and that they were little more than acquaintances to one another. Acquaintances who had seen one another naked and done any number of things that were making her blush now that she was thinking of them in the daylight.

But it wasn't going to go any further than that because...because what? Because this wasn't her style, getting involved with someone who she actually liked and respected. Because he was someone she could have a proper conversation with, someone she could rely on. Because he wasn't one of the shallow boys that she normally picked up and put down. Because she knew deep down that he saw her for who she really was. He was someone who supported and respected her.

Yeah, she told herself with a heavy touch of sarcasm. Why would she choose *that* for herself, when she had her life of meaningless, pointless dating to go back to? It wasn't as if the guy was a genius in bed or anything...

The shower stopped as she finished buttoning her shirt—his shirt—and for a moment she considered darting back into her own room. But that would be idiotic, she told herself. She'd got herself here—into this room, this situation—and she could get herself out of it with at least a little dignity intact.

'Hey, you didn't have to get up,' Finn said as he walked back into the room and clocked her standing beside the bed in his shirt. 'Looks good on you,' he said with a smirk that was one hundred per cent alpha male marking his territory. In a really good way.

On her way back to her own room she could hear Hart stirring in his cot and decided to go in before he could wake up his sister. Carrying him down towards the kitchen, she sniffed the top of his head and asked herself for the thousandth time what she was going to do next. Everything that had happened last night had stemmed from a conversation about making plans for her future—and instead of finding an answer to that conundrum, all she had done was make the status quo even more awkward—had possibly even tipped it over into untenable. As soon as she had had enough coffee—eight or so espressos should probably do the trick—she would fetch her laptop down from her room and resume her search for somewhere to live.

Her employers had promised her pay in lieu of the statutory notice period, as well as the redundancy pay she was legally entitled to, but so far her bank balance wasn't showing any sign of their making good on this. Great. She could get the money she was legally owed if she pursued it through the courts, of course, but that didn't help her a whole lot right this minute. And it would also suck up a lot of the time

she had earmarked for university research. She didn't
want to give that time to her crappy old company,
along with everything else they'd taken from her.

She picked up items of discarded clothing, glad
that Finn was still upstairs and therefore unable to
see the fierce pink staining her cheeks. It was only
when he appeared in the doorway, reversing their po-
sitions from the night before, that she remembered
that she was still wearing his shirt—and very little
else. Well, it was a bit late to be coy. There was no
part of her—literally, she thought, not a single part
of her—that he hadn't seen last night. Surely that
should make her less embarrassed rather than more.
But her cheeks were still glowing and there was no
point trying to pretend that Finn couldn't see it. She
handed him one of the coffees she'd made and started
prepping bottles for Bella and Hart, anything to avoid
eye contact or awkward conversation.

'That was great,' Finn said after hastily down-
ing his coffee. 'You have my mobile and my office
number, so if you're at all worried about the twins
then give me a call, yes? I'll jump straight in the car
if you need me back.'

She gave what she hoped was a neutral smile.
'We'll be absolutely fine. Now go to work.'

Finn paused before walking past her, and she
knew he was making the same calculation as she
was. Did they kiss on the cheek? On the lips? After
all the places he'd kissed her just hours ago it seemed
ridiculous that they could be paralysed by such a
question now. But here they both were, with their

rictus grins stretching wide, quite incapable of passing one another in the kitchen like normal adults.

Eventually Finn broke—he was the one who had to leave the house after all—and gave her a hasty peck on the cheek as he passed her on the way to the door. *Fine—no eye contact, don't turn back.* Determined not to lift her fingers to the spot where the impression of his lips was still burning her already pink cheeks.

It was only when she heard the front door close that she allowed herself to unstick her feet from the floor and resume normal movement, moving around the kitchen until she had a plate of toast in front of her and Hart was drinking enthusiastically from a bottle. And then somehow it was nearly lunchtime, and the morning had disappeared in another round of milk-feeding and nappy-changing and pram-rocking.

Finally, in an attempt to buy herself enough time to sit down with a hot drink, she loaded both babies—sleepy and well-fed and clean and dry—into the double pushchair and determined just to keep walking until they both gave in and had a nap.

The leafy streets and quiet gardens around Finn's townhouse were hardly a trial to kill an hour in, and she had an entertaining time trying to peer into expensively shuttered and curtained bay windows, spotting grand pianos and silk chaises longues, sleek kitchens and surprised-looking neighbours. By the time that she had done her third lap around the block with the delicious-looking patisserie on the corner, both Hart and Bella had succumbed to the motion of the pram and were peacefully asleep.

Sighing with relief at the sight of a free outdoor table, Madeleine parked the twins in the shade and pulled out her phone. She could have a coffee and get a spot of research done, and all before lunch. Really, she was better at this babysitting lark than she had thought. It was hard to consider this as anything other than gloriously successful.

She pulled up her online banking app and tapped in her passcode. She had been avoiding looking at it for the past few days, not keen on having a concrete reminder of exactly how dire things really were. But if she was going to find somewhere to stay, she couldn't hide from the ugly truth for ever.

She squinted as the balance loaded, trying to brace herself against the flash of panic that was her norm in this situation. But the number on the screen was so far from what she was expecting that her eyes widened involuntarily. Had her former employers actually come good on their promise of redundancy pay, and pay in lieu of notice and—what?—a year's back pay that she had somehow not realised she was owed?

She clicked through to her recent transactions, to find the unfeasibly large deposit in her current account. This just didn't make sense. How had they even found the cash to pay her this much? And then she saw the name associated with the deposit.

He hadn't...

Oh, my God.

If he had done this, she was never going to talk to him again. She was going to kill him. She was going to kill him and then never talk to him again, which would be considerably easier once he was six feet under.

And then through her anger came a crashing wave of shame. Heat that started in her cheeks before spreading to her chest, down her arms, until it felt as if her whole body was burning with it. Was that what he thought of her? That she would accept money from him after last night? Had he thought that she was expecting it? Had she done something to make him think that that was who she was—so mercenary? So grasping.

She picked up her phone to give him an earful but stopped herself before she dialled. She didn't want to do this in a rage, so emotional. She wanted him to see her ice cool and totally in control. By the time he got back that night she could be packed. Jake would put her up for a night or shout her a stay in a cheap hotel. She didn't have it all worked out yet, but she was absolutely certain that she wasn't spending another night under Finn's roof, and she wasn't touching a penny of that money. As the flush began to fade, her skin began to crawl as every moment from the night before was cast in a new light—one where Finn was planning on paying for the pleasure.

CHAPTER THIRTEEN

FINN HESITATED AT the door as he dug out his keys, wondering what he was going to find inside. His texts to Madeleine had garnered *We're all fine* as a response. Which was…fine. But at the same time the brusqueness of those three words made him nervous. If he had thought that finally sleeping with Madeleine would make it easier to concentrate on his work, then he couldn't have been more wrong. He'd thought about nothing but her all day. Through various meetings that really should have had his full attention. During the lunch that he'd grabbed at his desk. In the car on the way home.

All seemed quiet, he noted as he turned his key in the lock and opened the door. From the hallway he followed the sound of babies laughing right up the stairs until he found Bella, Hart and Madeleine all lying on the play mat in the nursery, staring up at the stars projected on the ceiling. The babies were in pyjamas, looking freshly bathed and content, and there were two empty bottles on the dresser beside the glider chair. He'd tried to get home for their bedtime, but had been waylaid on his way out and was back half an hour after they'd usually be asleep. But Madeleine had known, it seemed, that he'd want to say goodnight to them. His heart throbbed at her understanding that. And then he saw her spot him standing by the door.

She sat straight up and the playful look on her face was replaced immediately with pure fury. He took a reflexive step back as she walked towards him and scrambled to keep up with the abrupt change of atmosphere.

'They're ready to go to sleep,' she all but hissed at him as she approached the door. 'Hart will go sooner than Bella, I think. Trudy left dinner in the oven.'

He frowned as he watched her walk down the corridor, grab a bag from her room and head for the stairs. 'Wait!' he called, jogging after her. 'What's going on, Madeleine? I know things are a bit awkward after last night, but you don't have to—'

'A bit awkward? *A bit awkward?*' Madeleine whisper-shouted, anger radiating. 'This morning in the kitchen was *a bit awkward*, Finn. Now…now we are so far past awkward that I actually kind of miss it. We left it behind when you decided to pay me for my services.'

'Services? I don't know what—'

And then he did know. Saw how it must have looked to Madeleine and wanted to bang his head against the nearest wall to knock the stupidity out.

He'd deposited thousands of pounds into her bank account the morning after they had slept together.

Of course it didn't look great. But that wasn't what he had meant by it—not at all, but it didn't look as if Madeleine was planning on sticking round long enough to hear him out on it. And how could he blame her for that?

'Oh, no, Madeleine. I see how it looks and I promise it's not like that. Not at all. I just wanted to help and you were so excited about university and this way you could be sure you had the finances in place. *Please*, please will you stick around until I've got the kids to sleep and we can talk about it properly?'

He couldn't do this in a stage whisper, waiting for a cry from the twins. He just needed her to wait one hour and they could sort all this out.

She glanced at her watch and then at the front door, and for a second he thought that he'd lost her. But she dropped the bag and his heart started beating again, a tattoo of relief.

'I'll wait in the kitchen until seven-thirty,' she said, glancing at her watch. 'But after that I'm going and I'm not coming back, Finn.'

'I'll be down before then, I promise you, and we will sort this out.'

Madeleine sat in the kitchen nursing a cup of tea and texting Jake while she waited for Finn to get the babies to sleep. She'd dropped him a text asking if she could stay the night, and he'd texted straight back asking what had happened with Finn. And so it begins, she thought. Suddenly she could see endless questions about 'What happened with Finn?' in her future and had no idea how to answer them.

And if she didn't tell, then Jake was only going to ask Finn, and she didn't even want to think about what he would tell her brother. Surely he wouldn't be so base as to tell him what had happened. But then before today she hadn't thought that he would chuck a big lump of cash in her bank account after they had spent the night together either. Turned out she didn't know Finn as well as she'd thought that she did.

Which shouldn't have been a surprise, really, considering that they had only spent a handful of days together since she had left her childhood home for university. But in those few days he had really convinced her that he understood her. That he knew her. She had told him things that she had never told anyone else. And he hadn't listened at all. Not really listened, not if he thought that he could treat her the way that he had today and that she would be fine with that.

She thought about the explanations that he had given her: that he wanted her to have certainty about her university finances, as if she were some eighteen-year-old schoolgirl who needed someone to help her navigate the world of student loans, rather than a woman the other side of thirty who had been handling her overdraft for nearly half her life and was perfectly capable of finding a scholarship for herself.

He didn't think she could do it.

If the money wasn't payment for services rendered, then it was something else. It was a tacit acknowledgement that he didn't think that she would be able to do it by herself. He was rescuing her before she even needed it, so sure was he that she was going to fail. By the time that he walked into the room at seven twenty-five, she was halfway decided that she was just going to walk without hearing him out. What could he possibly say that would make up for his utter lack of faith in or respect for her?

'Madeleine, if you'll hear me out, I'd like to explain.'

'I don't think there's anything you can say, Finn,' she said, crossing her arms across her body and making it clear she was putting firm boundaries in place. As far as she was concerned, the intimacies of last night had never happened. 'I stayed because I didn't want to do this in front of the twins, and they needed to go to sleep. But you can't undo what you did, so I think it's best if I go. I'll return the money, of course. It's best if we keep out of each other's way for a while.'

He shook his head and came to lean on the kitchen island opposite her. She couldn't look him in the eyes, not if she wanted to remember that she was keeping her distance, emotionally as well as physically.

'You don't have to go,' he said. 'I realise now what it must look like, and I'm sorry. But I was always going to give you the money for university. It had nothing to do with last night.'

'It had nothing to do with what I actually wanted either,' Madeleine said, finding in her anger that she could look at him directly. 'I know you expect me to be grateful, but I didn't ask for your money. I didn't want it when you offered it to me. I can do this myself, and I have every intention of doing so.'

'But you don't need to,' he countered, looking genuinely confused that she might want to do this on her own. 'Why won't you accept a little help?'

'Why won't you accept that I don't need your help?' she said, sliding off her stool and standing opposite him. 'Yes, you did me a favour by letting me stay here, but I want to get back on my own feet. I've never wanted to be dependent on you. Not before last night, and definitely not after.'

He frowned at her, and she wondered if he was being dense on purpose. 'Would that be so awful, having to depend on another person?' Finn asked.

'Do you depend on anyone?' she asked. 'Do you look to someone else to pay your bills?' She planted her hands on her hips, trying to ground herself and stay rational. But he was so infuriating it was becoming an impossible task. 'No. You did it all yourself, but you don't believe that I can. If you believed in me, you wouldn't have to sneak money into my bank account like that.'

Finn threw his hands in the air, and she could tell he was as frustrated as she was. 'Of course I believe that you can do it yourself. I just don't think you should have to. This way you can be certain that you've got a place to stay. I don't see why that's a bad thing.'

'I was sure that I could find another way. You're the only one who wasn't.'

'But why risk the uncertainty?' he asked, and she could hear his frustration in the strain of his voice. 'Why risk finding yourself with nowhere to live? Again.'

She talked low and slow, so he couldn't be in any doubt about how angry she was with him. 'I can risk it because I believe in myself. It's called confidence, Finn. Faith. Something you seem to be lacking in me.'

His hands had dropped to the countertop now, and he was leaning heavily on it.

'I don't think you understand. If something went wrong…'

'You don't think I understand? I turned up on your doorstep with nowhere else to go, with no job and no idea of what I was going to do next. And you think I don't understand? If something went wrong, I would try again,' she said, still speaking slowly. 'And I would keep trying until I'd done it. Isn't that how you got to where you are?'

'Yes, but…'

She paused, looked at him, at the way the colour had drained from his face.

'You've never failed, have you?' she said, realisation crashing over her. 'You've gone from one piece of good luck to another and never had to live with the consequences when it's all gone wrong.'

'Ha!' Finn said with a laugh that didn't sound at

all genuine. 'You don't understand what you're talking about, Madeleine.'

'Sure I do. You're the head of a huge company, in beautiful new offices. You have two beautiful children and this gorgeous home. You've got everything that you ever wanted. You can't even imagine how I would survive if my plans didn't work out first time. I mean, look at everything you've achieved.' She watched him closely, trying to read his body language, his face. She had spilled more secrets to him than she'd ever thought she could, and now it was time to even the score.

'You don't know what you're talking about,' he said again, his voice lower, more dangerous. 'You look around and see an apartment. I see failure. I see the house I should have been bringing my children up in, sold in the divorce because I couldn't make my marriage work. It was gone. I didn't even know— still don't know—how my marriage disintegrated so fast. And my home was gone, and the business holding on by a thread. And I could so easily have lost everything. I still could.'

'You're terrified,' she realised, looking at him, really seeing his life for the first time. Suddenly it all made sense. The drive, the ambition. 'You're terrified that all this is going to fail and you'll lose everything.' And he had been projecting all his worst fears onto her rather than face up to them. 'You're so afraid of failure that you can't bear the thought that my plans might not work out, so you pumped my bank account full of money to make sure that won't happen.'

'That's not it,' Finn said. But she could read his face. His heart wasn't even in the denial. That was *exactly* it.

'Why are you so scared?' she asked. 'You have this apartment. You have your business. You could walk away now a rich man.'

'I could, and then there could be another financial crisis and I could lose everything and the apartment would be gone and the kids… What would we do? I thought I was set for life. I thought the business was good and my home life was good and I thought I could see how the future was going to unfold. And then Caro told me that she was unhappy, that she was leaving, and it all fell away. I thought it was all secure, and it wasn't. Not a single part of my life made it out of the divorce unscathed. And I can't risk that again. I won't.'

And there it was. This was what he was really afraid of—finding himself a hungry little boy again. Seeing his children live the same childhood that he had. She was hit by a wave of sympathy, taking the edge off her anger.

'Your mother coped with worse,' she reminded him, 'and you turned out okay.' Because, really, the huge chunk of money she hadn't asked for aside, Finn was a decent guy and she knew his mother was proud of him.

'She did. She coped. Every single day she worked two jobs, sometimes more, to keep barely enough food in the cupboard for me, and she coped. And that's all she did. So that by the time that I had enough money for her not to have to work any more she was too worn out and tired to enjoy the benefits.'

'And you're frightened of ending up like her. I understand that. But you did it, Finn. You worked hard for her, and yourself, and you're a million miles away from that life now. You're not going to wake up one day and find yourself back there.'

'But what's the difference, really?' he asked, looking haunted. 'It's the figures in my bank accounts. It's not real money; it's just numbers. It's intangible. When Caro and I got divorced, that number halved. The house went. I nearly lost the business too. Anything could happen. The business could still fail. One of the kids could get sick. There are a million things waiting around the corner that will mean that all that work wasn't enough and I'll find myself back where I started. Where my mum started.'

'Your marriage ended and that meant you'd failed. That's what you think, right? You failed, putting everything at risk.' She so had him sussed, and he was wrong, and she was going to make him see it. Not for herself, she told herself, but as a service to her friend. She had no interest in whether he was relationship material or not, because she absolutely didn't want one herself. But she couldn't let him go on with his life scared to start a relationship because he was convinced that he was going to lose everything. That he wouldn't be able to cope if that happened. He was a good guy, and he deserved better than that.

'Well, we're divorced,' Finn said eventually. 'I don't think we can call it a roaring success of a marriage.'

She rested her elbows on the countertop, leaning towards him in a challenge. 'You could call it two people growing apart and making a positive decision for their future happiness.'

'*You* could call it that, if you wanted to.' Finn took a step backwards and she knew that her words had hit home. 'I just see it for what it was. Something that should have been better. Something that would have been better, if I'd worked a little harder.'

She laughed, only stopping herself when she saw the hurt on his face. 'You think your marriage ended because you didn't work hard enough?'

'That was part of it.' He nodded.

'And the other parts?'

'What do the other parts matter?' She was pressed up against the counter now and he had retreated to the other side of the room. He was on the run, but she was going to make him face up to this. He had put her in this position by putting that money into her account when she had specifically told him not to. She wasn't going to hold off making him as uncomfortable as he had made her.

'I imagine they mattered to Caro.' He was the one with his arms crossed now. She saw the barriers he had thrown up and ignored them. This was too important. 'Did you talk about it, when things started to go wrong?' she asked.

'Yes, of course, but by then it was too late. We

wanted different things: I wanted to be settled here
and she wanted something...*more.*'

Madeleine shrugged. 'Doesn't sound like there's
a lot you could have done about that.'

'I could have tried to go with her.'

'Was that what you wanted?'

He hesitated, looked thoughtful. 'No.'

'Then I can't imagine it would have made for a
fulfilling arrangement for either of you. Sounds like
the decision to end the marriage was a pretty successful one for both of you. So why did it feel so
scary? Was it the money?'

He shook his head. 'We split things fifty-fifty.
It was fair.'

'I'm sure it was. What aren't you telling me, Finn?
I know there's more to this.'

His eyes snapped up to hers and she realised she'd
been thinking out loud. He dropped his head into his
hands before he answered, and pressed hard against
his eyes. 'I lost my home, Maddie,' he said when he
looked up. 'I waited so long to have my own home,
with food always in the fridge. With the heating always on. And I married Caro and we bought our
house, and I thought that that was it. That I never
had to worry again. And then—so quickly—it was
all gone. Just...gone. And at the same time we were
building the new business premises, and the numbers weren't adding up. And for the first time since
I was a kid I was *scared*, Madeleine. I was scared
that it wasn't all going to come good in the end.
That I was going to find myself hungry. And cold.

And back on Jake's doorstep, looking for someone to take me in. I couldn't bear that. I couldn't bear to lose everything that I had worked so hard for. For it all to come to nothing.'

She watched as he crossed to the fridge, grabbed a beer and slid a couple of slices of bread into the toaster, and wondered if it was conscious. That need to go and get the food that was always available now.

'No wonder you're not ready for this,' she said, and his eyes snapped to her. How could he be ready for a relationship when he was paralysed by his fear of what would happen if it all went wrong? Far safer to sabotage the whole thing before it even got off the ground. 'But, you know, just because things went wrong once before, that doesn't mean it would happen again. You lost an awful lot when Caro went, and I'm not talking about the money and the house. Or even your wife. I'm talking about feeling safe, and secure. And loved. But you survived it. And you have the twins and a lot to show for those years you were married. Would you rather you'd never met Caro? Never married her?'

She saw him think about it, and then the expression on his face softened. 'No. I wouldn't have the twins if I'd never met her. I wouldn't… Everything that has happened in my life has led me here. Tonight. And I'm not sure I can wish that away.'

When he shot her a particularly intense look she had to look away. It was *good* that he wasn't ready for this, she told herself. *She* wasn't ready for this. She didn't *want* this. Not with her new plans for her life buzzing and sparking in her brain. She didn't want to be distracted by a man. Least of all one who wouldn't give her the space or opportunity to make her own mistakes—forge her own path.

She wasn't ready for this. It wasn't that she didn't want him. It wasn't that she didn't want a relationship, she realised. It was that she wasn't ready.

But that realisation made her wonder—did she *want* to be ready? Did she want *him* to be ready? She'd spent the last hour trying to make Finn see that his reasons for not wanting to ever have a new relationship didn't hold up to scrutiny. They were based on fear, not a choice. Were her reasons the same? For years she'd kept her relationships exactly how she wanted them: non-committal. Non-threatening. And they'd left her kind of...empty. If she wanted more out of a relationship, she was going to have to give more. And that scared the hell out of her.

Maybe she shouldn't be trying to help Finn. Maybe she should be leaving him with his illusions because that would be safer for her. With both of them running scared from a relationship, she was doubly safe. If she made Finn face up to his issues and put aside his fears, there was one of her defences gone. If doing that made her see that her own approach to relationships was making her unhappy and needed to change, then there was the second front defeated as well.

But somehow that seemed less important this evening than making Finn feel that he was safe. That he would still be safe if he decided to take a chance on a new relationship. That marriages ended and houses got sold and the world didn't fall in. He would never be as vulnerable as he was as a cold, hungry child again. And not because he was rich, right this minute. But because he was tough and worldly and had—as he always did—people who loved him, who had his back. She wanted him to know that he could take a chance on falling in love without fearing that he was putting his children at risk. That the fears that he had been carrying around didn't need to control his decisions or define his future. She would put her own fears aside for now, if it meant helping him.

Which was pretty much a one-eighty from the shouting match that she'd thought she was preparing for when she had found that money in her account. But it was so clear to her that the money had nothing to do with his faith in her abilities. She believed that he believed in her. His doubts were all in himself. She knew that she couldn't change that by herself, but she hoped that by pointing out what was so obvious to her, he would start to believe her.

'Why are you so invested in this?' Finn asked her and she had to admire the way that he was turning the conversation away from himself. It was what she wanted to do now—to take a swerve rather than face up to her own feelings. But she wanted him to be brave, and that meant that she had to be brave too, no matter the consequences. Wasn't that what they'd been doing with one another since she'd arrived? Being brave.

'Why do you think?' she said. 'Because I care

about you. I think these fears are keeping you from being happy. I want you to be happy.'

'Because of what happened last night? Because you want more.'

She shook her head, smiling. 'You know that's not it, Finn. I said I didn't and I meant it.'

'I know that's what you said. Was it true? Is it still true now?'

She could turn this around on him again, if she wanted. She could be all *Do you want me to want you to want me?* and they could continue going round in circles all night. Or she could tell him what she was actually feeling and see if he was going to put himself out there with her.

'I don't know what I want. Before last night, if you'd asked me, I would have sworn that I want to keep things casual. That I don't want to get too involved. Not just with you. With anyone. Today… I'm not sure. I'm not sure that my reasons for keeping my distance in relationships are good ones. I need to think about that some more. Now, are you going to be honest and tell me what you're feeling too? Or am I out here on this ledge on my own?'

He came back across to the counter, leaned on it, their body language mirrored across this great hunk of granite.

Pretty pathetic that this is the closest I've been to someone for years, she thought to herself.

Yes, they had been physically closer last night— but this here was the real scary stuff.

'People fall off ledges all the time, you know,'

Finn said. 'Gravity is pretty unforgiving. They hurtle down and smash onto the ground below. Who walks into that situation willingly?'

She smiled at the metaphor because he was really throwing everything that he had at resisting what was starting to look pretty tempting to her.

'Everyone does, Finn. People do it every day. People pick themselves up after divorce, or harassment, or any number of other horrible situations, and they try again. Because what's the alternative?'

'Is that what you're doing?' he said, answering her question with a question. 'Trying again?'

She shrugged because at this point she honestly wasn't sure. 'I don't know. I'm thinking about it. But you're leaving me hanging here.'

'I care about you too.' Holy crap. He was tiptoeing out onto the ledge. 'You know that I care about you, Maddie. But I don't know how we decide to do this. That all the reasons—all the really good reasons—we have for not doing this don't matter any more.'

She thought about that for a second.

'Tell me what you think about my reasons then. Why do you think I've been fighting this?'

He smirked, and she knew how clearly he saw her. 'Because you like to be in control. Because someone took that from you once, and now you guard it with your life. Because you think that any man who shows you attention is only interested in one thing.'

She nodded, amazed that hearing those words coming from him could make her smile.

'Do you think I'm right?'

He stared at her longer than was comfortable. 'I think you have every reason to want to protect yourself.'

'But?' she prompted.

'But I think I've proven to you that not everyone who looks at you sees you that way. Some of us see *you*. And you deserve a chance. You deserve a chance to be happy.'

'So, to summarise, you think I should take a risk. But you're not prepared to take one with me?'

Oh, they were really doing this. Her heart started pounding and she could feel the heat in her cheeks as her face flushed. They were talking about their feelings and acknowledging that this was about to get complicated. And for all her pushing him to be brave, she was terrified. Of this. Of him. Of getting hurt if she decided she wanted to be brave again too.

But what was she afraid of, really? Now that she understood Finn, she trusted him. She had trusted him with her body last night, and today she knew she could trust him not to hurt her, because he wanted her. All of her. Everything that she brought to a relationship. He had seen the darkest, most fearful parts of her character and he hadn't flinched. The only thing that he had done that had made her mad was to give her the money to pursue her academic ambitions. It was hardly a capital crime. She calmed her breathing, felt her face gradually cool, and then threw down the gauntlet.

'So, what are we going to do about this?'

CHAPTER FOURTEEN

WHAT WERE THEY going to do about it? Right now, half his brain was voting enthusiastically for heading straight back upstairs, directly to his bedroom, saving the talking for later. They'd done pretty well communicating that way last night. But it had hardly made things less complicated.

What if Madeleine was right and he was holding back because he was scared? Was that who he wanted to be—someone who missed out on the thing that they desperately wanted because they weren't brave enough to take a risk?

And, God, did he want her. He had wondered yesterday if maybe this blinding lust was the result of a very long dry spell as much as it was about her—but he couldn't have been more wrong. He wanted her even more now than he had before and he couldn't imagine existing in a form that didn't want her. How had he thought that he could just walk away from feelings like that?

'You're right. I've been scared. I *am* scared. Divorcing Caro was the biggest knock to my upward trajectory since as far back as I remember. It floored me. And I was terrified that I was going to lose everything—that the business would fail and I would fail and it would be a slippery slope back into poverty.'

Madeleine watched him in silence, her expression serious as he looked for the words that would explain why he had taken so long to give in to the feelings that had been assaulting him since she had walked back into his life.

'And then you showed up and there was this connection between us and I knew it was something powerful. Something important. Something I knew I wouldn't want to stop, if it started.'

'Which is why you've been fighting it.'

'Yes. I mean, fighting it pretty ineffectually, but yes.'

'I think after last night we can agree neither of us did a great job at that.'

She smirked, and he felt it all the way in his gut. But he had been fighting it for a good reason. Because his life had fallen apart last year, and he had been scared in a way he hadn't felt since he was a kid. In a way he never wanted his own children to experience.

'I can't promise that if we try this it will work, Finn. There's no guarantee.'

'But you want to try?' he asked.

'Do you?'

God, why does this have to be so hard? Finn thought. *Why does it have to be so scary?*

He couldn't imagine contemplating this sort of risk for anyone but Madeleine. But, scary or not, he couldn't see how he could walk away now. He had fallen in too deep without even realising it. How could he walk away when he had had a taste of what it was to see someone and be seen? To have peeled away one another's fears and defences and looked one another in the eye, knowing that the only thing that would get in their way now was a lack of courage.

He knew that Madeleine had courage by the bucketful. She was the one that had brought them to this point. He didn't want to be another person who let her down.

'I don't need guarantees, Madeleine,' he said, examining his feelings, boiling it down to what really mattered. 'I just need you.'

She looked at him for a long moment. 'Why?'

He held her eye and knew exactly why she was asking. Knew how many times people had looked at Madeleine and assumed they could know everything about her by the way that she looked. He also guessed from the confidence in her posture right now and the hint of a smile at the corner of her mouth that she knew exactly how brilliant he thought she was. If she wanted to hear it out loud then he would tell her. He didn't want her to ever think that she had reason to doubt how he felt about her.

'Because you're brave. And determined. And fiercely independent. And you like my kids and we have the same taste in pizza. Because my home and my office and my life seem dull when you walk out of them. Because last night was incredible in a way that I've never felt before. And yes, you're beautiful. You know I think that, but I hope you know how unimportant that is to me.'

The smile spread across her lips, upwards, to crease faint lines around her eyes.

He laughed, walking around the kitchen island, suddenly desperate to have her close. She turned on the spot, following him with her eyes as he came closer, until she had her back to the counter, leaning back on her elbows as he stopped in front of her. He could lean in now, take her lips with his and, if the previous night was anything to go by, he wouldn't have another coherent thought until morning. But he wasn't ready to lose his mind just yet. Not when his senses were so damn delighted with what was right in front of him. Madeleine settled into her lean against the counter and quirked an eyebrow at him. She was going to wait for him to come to her. Good. He wanted to drink her in a little. Soak in the promise and potential of this moment before they jumped in.

He rested a hand either side of her waist, trapping her against the counter, but he still didn't lean in. Not yet. Instead he looked at her—looked inside himself at the riot of sensations that she provoked in him. But at the centre was a stillness, and he knew without having to think about it what that meant. He lifted a hand to her jaw, his thumb following the path of her cheekbone, his fingertips settling in a sensitive spot behind her ear.

'Nice speech,' she said, her arms lifting to rest gently on his shoulders, her gaze flicking between his eyes and his lips.

'I'm not done yet,' he said when his lips were just a breath away from hers. 'I love you. And I'm going to want you for ever. I hope that's okay with you.'

He felt rather than saw her smile.

'I think I like the sound of that. Because I love you too, and I wasn't planning on letting you go.'

EPILOGUE

'Bella! Hart! Get back here!'

Madeleine sat with Jake, watching Finn and Josie chase after the twins as they headed for the garden gate, running with their cousins.

'Still time to change your mind,' Jake said with a smile, and Madeleine rolled her eyes.

'Just because you want to keep him all to yourself.'

'Are you kidding? He'll be at mine all the time once you're married. Anything to get away from the ball and chain.'

She hit her brother on the arm and relaxed back in her chair as she watched Finn trying to wrangle the kids back into the garden.

'Honestly, though, sis, I've never seen him happier. You either. It's good to have you back.'

She felt her eyebrows pinch as she looked at her brother. She hadn't even realised Jake had seen how sad she'd been for so many years. And wondered, not for the first time, just what he'd been hoping for when he'd sent her to stay at Finn's place. Stupid interfering brothers with their insight and good instincts.

'Yeah, well, I guess he's all right really.'

'I should hope so,' Finn said behind her, making her jump. 'Otherwise I'd have to ask them to take that marquee down.'

'And tell the two hundred guests to stay home,' Jake added.

'And send back the cake.'

'Enough, you two,' Madeleine said. 'God, what have I done?' She shook her head, laughing. 'I'm not returning the cake. Fine, I'll marry you, even though you're really annoying. But I'm uninviting Jake.'

'Deal,' Finn said, leaning in for a kiss.

'Gross.'

But Madeleine grabbed Jake's hand before he could walk off.

'Seriously, though, little brother. He's a good one, and I'm not sure I would have seen it if you hadn't dangled him in front of my nose for, you know, the last couple of decades. I love you, and I owe you.'

Jake pulled her in for a hug before holding her out at arm's length and taking a long look at her. 'You're welcome. I'll redeem my Brownie points in baby-sitting time. I'm just glad to see you both happy.'

Finn pulled her into his lap as they watched Jake go over to battle with the kids, all six of them, and he wrapped his arms tight around her waist.

'Did I mention that I love you?' Madeleine asked, turning her head to look up at Finn.

'Once or twice,' he replied with a smile, dropping a kiss on her nose. 'But I can probably stand to hear it again.'

'I love you,' she said again, her voice turning serious. 'And I'm going to stand in front of all of those people tomorrow and tell them. But really, as long as you know, nothing else matters.'

'I know,' he said, bringing up a hand to cup her face, brushing a kiss high on her cheekbone. 'The same way that you know that I love you. More than I ever thought possible.'

She turned to watch Jake and the kids, the marquee for her wedding set up for the morning, her whole future playing out in the garden of their new home.

'I'm so glad you were brave,' she told Finn, and he pulled her in a little tighter. 'When I was out on that ledge, hoping that you were going to come for me.'

'How could I not be when you'd shown me how it was done?' he said softly into her ear.

* * * * *

WYOMING SPECIAL DELIVERY

MELISSA SENATE

For my mother.

Chapter One

Daisy Dawson's wedding ceremony was supposed to start any minute, and there was no sign of the groom. At nine months pregnant, in a pretty but scratchy white lace maternity dress and peau de soie heels that pinched, standing around wasn't exactly easy.

She poked her head out the door of the small room where she was getting ready. The special events hall of the Dawson Family Guest Ranch lodge had been beautifully decorated, thanks to her sister-in-law, Sara, who'd gone all out with pink and red roses, white tulle, and a red satin carpet runner to create an aisle. Thirty-six chairs were set up on both sides of the carpet. On the bride's side, she saw her five brothers in the first row, all decked out in suits and Stetsons and cowboy boots. She saw her colleagues from the ranch. She saw old friends and newer ones.

But the other side of the aisle was still conspicuously empty of guests. No relatives or friends of the groom had arrived. That was really weird. Jacob was late and so were all the people he'd invited to their wedding?

Sure, Daisy. Right.

She poked her head back in and looked in the mirror, reality hitting her right in the nose. Jacob wasn't coming to his own wedding. And since none of his guests had turned up, it was obvious that he'd let them know in advance that he was calling it off. How kind of him to tell everyone in his life but her.

Everyone who meant something special to her was waiting for her to walk down the aisle. And there wasn't going to be a wedding. She shook her head, calling herself all kinds of a fool for ever thinking this was going to happen.

Ping!

Daisy eyed her phone on the vanity table with all her cosmetics and the curling iron she'd painstakingly used to get beachy waves in her straight light brown hair. The text was either from one of her brothers asking if everything was okay—since the ceremony was supposed to start at 5:00 p.m.— or it was her fiancé, Jacob, the cowardly fink, not facing her in person.

She grabbed her phone. It was Jacob.

I'm really sorry. But it hit me hard this morning that we don't love each other and we've been forcing it. And I've been forcing that I can be a dad. I'm heading back to Cheyenne and might move east. Wish you and the baby all the best. J.

A burst of sadness got her in the heart at the same time that red-hot anger seized her. She stared at herself in the mirror, through her late mother's beautiful lace veil, which she should have known would be bad luck. She'd tried, at least. Tried, tried, tried all summer to make it work with Jacob— she'd thought they were going to build a future together. A family. But her baby wouldn't have a father.

She stuffed her phone in her little beaded cross-body purse and stalked out the back door and down the side steps, to where her Honda, with a Just Married sign with streamers on the back, waited to get her out of here.

She quickly got in the car and took a deep breath, flipped back the veil, then texted her brother Noah.

J called off the wedding. Need some time alone.

She reread Jacob's text. Wish you and the baby all the best. Like he was some distant uncle! How dare he? She banged the phone against the steering wheel and chucked it out the window, then pulled off her engagement ring and threw it out, too. She grabbed the headpiece and veil off her head and tossed them on the back seat.

Then she peeled out, seeing the ridiculous streamers floating behind the car in the rearview mirror as she took off down the drive toward the gates of the ranch.

Where exactly am I going? she wondered, trying not to cry so she wouldn't swerve into the wildflowers lining the road. She lived in the main house at the guest ranch, and no way could she deal with relative after relative, friend after friend coming to see her, feeling sorry for her. So forget about her sanctuary of her bedroom and pulling the quilt over her head for a few days.

Jacob had booked a weekend honeymoon for the two of them at the Starlight B&B in Prairie City, a half hour away. She supposed she could go there and lick her wounds and order their highly rated room service. Her cravings were insane these days. All she seemed to want was pasta in pink sauce with bacon and peas. And garlic bread. And chocolate cake. All B&Bs had chocolate cake, right?

Thinking of the food almost took her mind off being stood up at the altar and the sudden change to her future.

Not just hers. Her brothers' futures, too. Four of the five Dawson men had scattered across Wyoming, and she'd been hoping to steer them back home to stay. She'd had big plans for becoming a secret amateur matchmaker at the wedding reception tonight, putting individually irresistible women for the four remaining Dawson bachelors under their unsuspecting noses. But some case she could make to Ford, Axel, Zeke and Rex for sticking around Bear Ridge, finding true love and settling down in their hometown, if not on their home ranch, *now*.

One of her brothers—Noah—had already done exactly that, which had given Daisy hope for the others. One down, five to go, right? Her wedding had brought them all home when being at the ranch, being in Bear Ridge, made them all feel… unsettled. But they'd inherited the ranch last winter from their father, and only Noah had stayed to rebuild the long-closed, run-down family business.

Daisy, then five months pregnant and alone, had joined Noah in the mission, and no one had been more surprised than her when her baby's father had come after her, saying he was sorry, that he wanted a second chance, that they could do this, after all: be a family. He'd lasted four months.

She'd thought she was getting married today. She'd thought she could convince her brothers that true love really did exist, even if it hadn't for their father and various mothers—there were three moms among the Dawson siblings. She'd thought the Dawson clan could start fresh here together. She'd thought she could use the wedding festivities to show them they could be happy here. Among the guests she'd invited were at least eight women who would seriously appeal to each single brother for one reason or another. Falling in love would be just the ticket back. But after seeing their sister stood up at the altar—nine months pregnant with their little niece or nephew—the four remaining Dawson bachelors would hightail it out of Bear Ridge, which had always meant bad luck to all of them. Family was everything to Daisy. And not only had her dreams of building her own family with her baby's father gone *poof*, but Ford, Axel, Zeke and Rex would most likely leave tonight or tomorrow and come back for her baby's birth, then leave again after a day or two and return for Christmas. Maybe.

Family: the way it wasn't supposed to be.

Daisy let out a sigh and kept driving, teary acceptance and pissed-as-hell fighting for dominance. Fifteen minutes later, the two still going at it, she drove down the service road on the outskirts of Bear Ridge that would eventually lead her to the freeway. But then her car made a weird sputtering sound. *Crunch-creak.* Then another. *Crunch-creeeeeeeak.*

Oh no. She quickly pulled over, turned off the engine, then tried to restart. Nothing.

"Nooo!" she yelped, hitting the steering wheel. *Someone tell me this is all a bad dream.* She looked around, out the windshield and both passenger windows. She was on some rural stretch, hay bales for acres on either side of her. Not another car in sight. She tried the ignition again. Dead. One more time, because you never knew. Still dead.

She rested her head against the steering wheel for a moment, the stretch tearing the side of her wedding gown. Fine with her. The minute she got to the Starlight, she'd be rolling it up in a wad and setting it on fire in a garbage can out front like she was Angela Bassett in *Waiting to Exhale.*

This really wasn't her day after all.

Daisy grabbed her purse to get her phone to call for help, then grimaced. "Oh hell, that was stupid." Her phone was behind the rosebushes on the side of the lodge. With her engagement ring. Her mom had often said, *Daisy Rae Dawson, acting first and thinking later is gonna be your downfall, sweetcakes.* Her beloved mother was right about that. Especially now.

She sat there for a second, taking another breath when she was hit with a strange, pulling sensation low in her belly. That was weird. She grabbed her stomach and started breathing the way she'd learned in Lamaze class. A minute or so later, it hit her again. *Oh no. No, no, no.* Were these contractions? Maybe they were the false early ones the Lamaze teacher had mentioned yesterday, when Jacob was there breathing deeply beside her, making her believe he was really committed to her and their child. She wasn't due for another three weeks!

The pain got more intense. She stared at her silver watch with the mother-of-pearl face, a gift from her brothers for Christmas last year. The sweeping second hand told her the contractions were coming every minute and a half.

She was in labor. Left-at-the-altar, three-weeks-early labor.

Without a phone. On the side of the road. In rural Wyoming.

She got out of the car as another contraction sent her gripping the side of the door for support. She stared up and down the road, praying a vehicle would come by. Without an ax murderer in it.

She started pacing, keeping one hand on the car, but it was July and eighty-two degrees and the car was hot. Contraction! She bent over and let out the scream bursting from her. "Owww-weeee!"

Breathe, breathe, breathe, she reminded herself. She heard the sound of rushing wheels in the distance. A car! Yes! It was coming closer! She managed to pick up her head to look. Oh, thank God. Someone was coming and stopping behind her car.

A fancy silver SUV with Wyoming plates. Not one of her brothers' cars. Or anyone she knew. One of the guests at the ranch had a fancy silver SUV, now that she thought about it.

"Owww-weeee!" She yelped and doubled over as the contraction seized her.

She heard a car door open and close, footsteps rushing toward her.

"I'll help you get in my SUV," a male voice said, coming closer. "I'm not a stranger," he added quickly as he bent down where she stood to sort of make eye contact. "I'm a guest at Dawson's ranch."

She glanced up. It *was* him. He might not be a stranger or an ax murderer, but he *was* kind of mysterious. He'd been at the ranch for two days yet didn't seem remotely interested in the horses or activities. She'd even mentioned to Noah, the foreman, that something was up with the guest who'd booked Cabin No. 1, which slept four, all for himself, and then hadn't gotten on a horse the entire time he was here.

Maybe he *was* an ax murderer.

"No time," she managed to croak out as she dropped to her knees, then backward onto her butt. "The baby…is…*coming*! Owww-weeee!"

Over her earsplitting yelp, she still heard him gasp and saw him grab his phone, then listened to him frantically explain the situation to the 911 dispatcher.

"Okay," he was saying into the phone with accompanying nodding. "Okay. Okay. Okay, I think I can do that. Okay."

"Owww-weeee!" she screamed, eyes squeezed shut as she bore down.

"Oh God," he said, rushing to kneel in front of her.

He lifted up her wedding dress and cast it over her knees. She heard him run away and thought *noo, don't leave me*, but then he was back, and she realized he was cutting off her ridiculous lace maternity undies with a Swiss army knife.

She had the urge to bear down again. And grunted and did.

"The ambulance is coming," he assured her. "Just hang on, Daisy."

"I'll try," she said, squeezing her eyes shut. "But I can't!" she croaked out, opening her eyes. "You're…about…to…*owww-weeee*…deliver my… baby!" she yelped.

Harrison McCord's brain fought to catch up with what was happening. Not forty-five minutes ago, he'd seen Daisy, all decked out in bridal wear, walk into the ranch lodge with another woman who he recognized as her sister-in-law. Now, Daisy was still in the wedding dress, which was dirty in some spots along the bottom. But she was alone, no rings on her finger, he noticed, on the side of a road. And, if he wasn't mistaken, *in labor*. What the heck had happened between then and this minute?

"What can I do?" he asked, his voice frantic.

"Get…these pinching shoes…off me!" she barked out before leaning back and shouting, "Owww-weeee!" That was followed by four fast breaths. Then four more.

He took the white shoes off her feet, and her face relaxed for a second, then the panting, grunting and yelping, and breathing started again.

"The baby. Is. Coming!" she screamed. She scrunched up her face.

"Oh God," he said. Again he lifted the long lacy gown and flung the edge up over her knees. He could see the baby's head. Whoa.

He forgot everything the dispatcher had said. *What the hell do I do?* Instinct must have taken over, because he took off his dress shirt and held it carefully under the head as he guided the baby—a boy—out. He then gently wrapped the messy newborn in his shirt and handed him to Daisy.

"It's a boy!" he announced.

Her mouth opened in a kind of wonder as she took the newborn and held him against her, tears running down her cheeks.

He heard sirens in the distance, coming closer. "That's the ambulance," he said, relief flooding him. It pulled up in front of Daisy's car, and two guys and a woman jumped out, one wheeling a stretcher. An EMT took the baby while the other two helped Daisy onto the stretcher.

"Thank you so much," she said to Harrison, her blue eyes misty. "Thank you."

"Of course." His heart was beating a zillion

miles a minute. He had to sit down before he passed out.

"Call my brother Noah, the foreman at the ranch," she shouted out to him as the EMTs loaded her into the back of the ambulance.

"Will do!" he called back.

He'd just delivered a baby. On the side of the road. He was grateful he'd been wearing a T-shirt under his dress shirt or he'd have helped bring the newborn into the world half-naked.

The ambulance making a racket as it drove away, he was stirred to action. He pulled out his phone and called the guest ranch and asked for foreman Noah Dawson's cell phone number, adding that it was an emergency. He'd been watching Noah the past couple of days. Daisy, too. Watching everything. Unfortunately, the Dawsons seemed like good people. But as his dad used to say, that was neither here nor there.

He punched in Noah's number. He answered right away.

"Noah Dawson. What's the emergency?"

"This is Harrison McCord from Cabin No. 1," he said. "I just helped deliver your sister Daisy's baby on the side of the service road onto Route 26. She doesn't seem to have a phone with her. The ambulance took her to Prairie City General."

"What?" Noah bellowed. "Is the baby okay? Is Daisy okay?"

"They both seemed fine," he said. "It's a boy, by the way."

"We're on our way. Thanks for helping Daisy."

Harrison pocketed his phone and got back in his car, just sitting there behind the wheel for a moment, barely able to process what had just happened. A single workaholic businessman, he had no siblings to provide baby nieces and nephews, and he didn't think he'd ever held a baby in his life—until today.

He drove the fifteen minutes to Prairie City and pulled into a spot in the hospital parking lot, then stopped in the gift shop. There were congratulations balloons, get-well balloons and an entire section devoted to stuffed animals, big and small. He eyed a soft and squishy medium-sized light brown teddy bear with a plaid bow tie and bought it, then followed the signs to Maternity.

In the elevator he stared at the bear, unable to fully comprehend how he'd ended up here, holding this stuffed toy, about to visit a new mother he hadn't more than nodded at while seeing her at the ranch the past couple of days. A new mother who would hate his guts when she found out why he was really at the ranch.

Daisy was in room 508. He sucked in a breath and peered in the open door. Now in a hospital gown with a thin white blanket covering half of her, she was alone—well, except for the baby in her arms, her gaze so full of wonder as she stared at the infant that he felt he was intruding. He was about to turn around and flee when she said, "You! My hero!"

Harrison offered what had to be an awkward smile and walked fully into the room.

She smiled at him. "I'm sorry—as guest relations manager of the ranch, I'd normally know your name, where you're from, if you like decaf or regular for your cabin, but I took this past week off for the wedding. I wasn't even thinking I'd need to start my maternity leave so soon." She smiled a dazzling smile. Wow, she was pretty. All glowy and happy. "But I do recognize you as one of our guests. Guess you didn't expect your day to go quite like this."

He had to laugh. "Nope. Definitely not. But I'm glad I happened to be driving down that road. You didn't have a phone to call for help?"

She frowned and glanced down at the baby. "As you probably figured out from my outfit and the dumb sign on the back of my car, I was supposed to get married today. The groom, my newborn son's father, didn't show and sent me a Dear Jane text. I got pissed and chucked my phone out the window of my car. Dumb, I know."

The father of her baby had left her at the altar? When she was nine months pregnant?

"Sorry about the wedding," he said, unable to even imagine what that must have felt like. He'd never come close to marrying. Or proposing to anyone. But he'd been betrayed before and knew what *that* felt like.

"I'm sure I dodged a bullet. We weren't right for each other, and we both knew it."

So did he, despite not even having met her before today. Because he'd been keeping watch over the Dawson family and the only two of the six siblings who worked at the ranch, he'd made a point of taking a tailing walk whenever he noticed Daisy strolling a path with the fiancé, a surfer-cowboy type. Their body language was always so awkward. They never held hands or kissed, though they did take a lot of walks on the paths, which was how he managed to spy on them so often. He'd wondered about their relationship because they barely seemed like a couple, yet he'd overheard her tell the fiancé it was time to get to Lamaze yesterday, and off they'd gone.

She waved a hand in front of her. "Anyway.

That is old news. This," she said, smiling down at the baby, "is breaking news and all that matters."

The love and reverence and sincerity in her voice caught him by surprise, and for a moment, he just gazed at the baby with her. Finally, he cleared his throat. "My name is Harrison McCord," he said, stiffly sitting down in the chair by her bed. "I got you a little something. Well, I got him a little something," he added, gesturing at the tiny human lying alongside her arm. The newborn was skinny and cute with wispy brown curls. His eyes were closed at the moment. "I'm in Cabin No. 1 at the ranch. I booked it for the week."

"But it's just you?" she asked. "Cabin No. 1 sleeps four."

"Just me," he said.

She waited a beat, as if she expected him to elaborate, but now was certainly not the time or the place. He'd wait a couple days, give her a chance to settle back at the main house at the ranch with the baby, and then he'd ask for a meeting with her and her brother. And drop a bombshell. The timing wasn't good, but that couldn't he helped.

"So what's his name?" he asked.

"Tony. After my late grandpa, Anthony Dawson. I haven't decided on a middle name," she said.

"Given what you did for me—for *us*—I'd like to use your middle initial."

He gaped at her. *No, no, no, no, no. Noooo.* "That's very thoughtful, but there's no need for that."

"You came to our rescue, Harrison. You helped bring this little guy into the world. I'd like to honor that."

He swallowed, his T-shirt suddenly tight around his neck. "Um, I...don't have a middle name," he lied. He actually did—Leo. "I'd better get going," he added, bolting up. "I did call your brother. He's on the way." He put the teddy bear on the table beside her bed.

She tilted her head at him. "Oh. Okay. Well, thanks again. For everything."

As she turned her attention back to the baby, he took one last look at her, not wanting to leave—but how could he stay? Now that he'd met Daisy Dawson under these unusual circumstances—like delivering her baby and calling her brother and visiting her in the hospital and bringing baby Tony a teddy bear *and* hearing how she'd been left at the altar—he felt something of a connection to the new mother. The news he planned to deliver in a couple days wouldn't be as cut-and-dried as he'd expected.

It's just straight-up, on-paper business, he reminded himself. *Nothing personal.*

She wanted to give her baby his middle initial!

Things with Daisy Dawson had suddenly gotten *very* personal.

Chapter Two

Okay, Cabin No. 1 guest who very unexpectedly helped deliver her baby? Definitely mysterious. Her wanting to use his middle initial for Tony's middle name had him jumping up like an electrocuted porcupine. What was with the guy?

Then again, he'd had a pretty eventful last hour.

"Well, Tony," she said, looking at her baby son. "It's just me and you. And I think I'll use my mother's first initial for your middle name. Her name was Leah. Let's see... Liam. Lucas. Lawrence. Lee, Landon, Lincoln. Louis. Levi. Leonardo DiCaprio." She stared at Tony, thinking he didn't look anything like the actor. "How about

Lester, as in Lester Holt?" she suggested. "Tony Lester Dawson. Tony Lucas Dawson. Tony Lincoln Dawson. Hey," she whispered. "I think we have a winner. Very presidential, right? Anthony Lincoln Dawson, it is."

Luckily she'd gotten the name squared away, because the room suddenly filled with the five Dawson brothers and Sara, her sister-in-law and best friend. There were gasps and oohs and ahhs and so many flowers, balloons and stuffed animals, a few huge, that another person could not squeeze in.

"I present your nephew, Anthony 'Tony' Lincoln Dawson," she said. "Tony for his very special great-grandpa Anthony Dawson." Gramps had always been called Anth, interestingly enough, a nickname started by his mother when he was very young, but the moment Harrison McCord had helped place the newborn on her chest on the side of that road, she'd instantly thought: Tony.

"Gramps would like that," Axel said, and they all nodded reverently.

"The *L* in Lincoln for Mom?" Noah asked with a gentle smile.

Daisy gave a teary nod just thinking what a wonderful nana Leah Dawson would have been. The six Dawson siblings had three mothers among them. Ford from the first marriage, Rex, Zeke and Axel from the second, and Daisy and Noah from the third. The siblings had all gotten to know Daisy and Noah's mother pretty well since she'd been so kind and welcoming that their mothers had felt comfortable dropping them off for weekends and weeks in summer with their not-exactly-attentive father. That had stopped when Leah had died when Daisy was eleven, though. A few hours here and there were all the other two mothers had trusted Bo Dawson with their kids.

"That's really nice, Daisy," Noah said, and she could see how touched he was.

"So Tony for Gramps, Lincoln for my mom, and Dawson because Jacob called off the wedding *and* being a father." She explained about the text. Tossing her phone and engagement ring. And then about her car sputtering on the service road and Harrison McCord coming to her aid.

"We all owe him one," Noah said. "No phone, hot as hell out, rural stretch of road. Thank God he came along."

Daisy nodded. "I kind of wonder why he *did*, though. There's something up with the guy."

"What do you mean?" Ford asked in cop tone. A police officer in Casper, Ford didn't let anything escape his attention.

"Well, Noah can probably attest to how odd it is that a guest would book a cabin for four and then show up solo *and* not partake in a single activity at a dude ranch," Daisy explained. "I've only seen him walking the grounds. In fact, any time I've been out, I feel like he's been around. And then he's suddenly five minutes behind me on the service road to the freeway?"

Noah narrowed his eyes. "You know, now that you mention it, he does seem unusual. He wasn't interested in being matched with a horse. And twice I've looked up while in the barn or talking to the ranch hands, and there'd he'd be, suddenly pulling out his phone like he had to make a call that second."

"Sounds like he's watching you two," Axel said. A search-and-rescue expert, Axel wasn't one to believe in coincidence.

Daisy shrugged. "He did help me, though. And then came to visit me and Tony. He brought this," she added, pointing at the teddy bear. "I told him I wanted to give Tony his middle initial, and he turned white. Said he didn't have a middle name and made excuses to leave."

Rex, the businessman of the brothers, crossed his arms over his chest. "Hmm. Something is definitely up with him. But like you said, he did come to your rescue. You and Tony are safe and healthy."

Noah nodded. "That's all that matters right now."

"Couldn't hurt to check him out," Zeke said. This from the mysterious brother. Zeke had long refused to talk about his work and would only say it was highly classified, whatever that meant. Sometimes Daisy thought he was a spy.

"Couldn't agree more," Ford said, taking out his phone. "What's the guest's name? I'll start with a simple check on the guy. Just to be safe."

"Harrison McCord," Daisy told him. "Wyoming plates. Silver Lexus."

"Harrison McCord," Rex repeated, clearly thinking. "That name does sound familiar. I've heard it before. In business circles, I think." Rex lived out in Jackson, Wyoming, which was hours away from Bear Ridge.

Ford nodded and stepped out of the room, phone in hand. It was good having a cop in the family.

"I'll keep an eye on McCord," Axel said. "Turns out I'll be staying for a week or two. I'm on enforced R&R from my search-and-rescue team."

All eyes turned to Axel. He rarely said so much about his private life. She wondered what had happened to get him sent on "vacation."

"I'd like to stay at the main house with you, Daize," Axel added, "if you'd like the company."

She beamed. She'd be able to work on keeping Axel in town *forever*! She almost wanted to add a mock-evil *mwahaha*, she was so happy about the news. "I'd love it. But you'll be woken up all hours of the night by a shrieking newborn. Just pointing it out if it didn't occur to you."

Axel stared at the creature in her arms, his blue eyes widening slightly as he ran a hand through his thick dark brown hair. "Not like I'll be getting any sleep anyway, so bring it on, little nephew."

Daisy laughed, but as she glanced at Axel, she could see something was eating at him—something about the enforced vacation and whatever had gone down there. He could probably use a little distraction, right? She *would* put her matchmaking plan into action. Within two weeks, he'd never want to leave anyway, because he'd be too in love. With the woman she had in mind for him and with his darling baby nephew, who'd be the apple of his ole eye. He'd sign on with a new search-and-rescue team much closer to Bear Ridge and build a big, gorgeous modern log cabin on the edge of the ranch property. That was the dream—having all her brothers back home.

Yes, Daisy was feeling better about knowing

three of her brothers would be leaving later today or in the morning. Because Noah was here, of course. And now Axel would be, too.

"The baby looks just like you," her sister-in-law, Sara, said, her eyes misty. "I can't wait to introduce him to his little cousins. Cowboy Joe is watching them right now."

Daisy smiled. Cowboy Joe was the grizzled sixty-two-year-old cook at the guest ranch cafeteria. He adored babies.

Noah put his arm around his wife, and they gazed at the baby. "Welcome to the family, Tony Lincoln Dawson," he said to his nephew. "You're gonna be spoiled rotten."

Daisy grinned. She felt so lucky that her baby would have five incredible uncles, one amazing aunt and two instant baby cousins. Sara had five-month-old twins, Annabel and Chance. Sara's husband had died just a couple months after she'd given birth to twins, only one of whom had survived—supposedly. Within a half hour of the birth, Sara's twisted husband had actually left frail newborn Annabel on Noah Dawson's doorstep after telling Sara the girl twin had died. But the truth had come out seven weeks later, and Sara and her daughter had been reunited. Noah, who for all that time had taken care of Annabel on his own, thinking she was his baby—per the false, anonymous note left with her—had never looked so happy than on his wedding day, when he, Sara and the twins became a forever family.

Ford stepped back in the room, pocketing his phone. "Harrison McCord is a successful businessman—mergers and acquisitions—in Prairie City. Owns his own firm. Clean record. On local charitable boards. Highly regarded. From basic reports, a top-notch guy."

"Well, he did deliver Tony and ruin a really expensive-looking dress shirt," Daisy said with a grin. "So that's not a *total* surprise."

"He lied about not having a middle name, by the way," Ford added. "It's Leo."

"*L* for Leo!" Daisy said. "Turns out Harrison Leo McCord got a piece of the middle-name honoring whether he liked it or not."

"Probably just didn't want a fuss made over what he did," Rex said. "Likely he doesn't think he did anything anyone else wouldn't have done."

Except Harrison was the only person around. And he had come to her rescue. So that was all she knew.

"Still worth keeping an eye on," Axel put in, and Daisy caught Ford and Noah nodding.

She wondered what was behind Harrison's mysterious behavior. Still, when a nurse came in to check her vitals and bring Tony to the nursery, she forced herself to stop thinking about her impromptu birth partner so she could catch a much-needed nap. But between wishing she could have Tony back in her arms and wondering about Harrison McCord, she was wide-awake.

With visiting hours at the Gentle Winds hospice about to end, Harrison sat at the bedside of ninety-four-year-old Mo Burns, an over-bed table between them holding a deck of cards, Mo's favorite candy—sour jelly beans—and a full house. Mo had beaten Harrison at poker again.

"Gotcha, kid," Mo exclaimed in his whispery voice, his filmy blue eyes beaming with pride.

Harrison had been volunteering at Gentle Winds, where his aunt was a patient just down the hall, ever since Lolly McCord had moved in ten days ago. Lolly had stage-four cancer, caught too late to do anything, and she was often very tired. Harrison liked to be close by to his only relative, so he'd asked about volunteering, and every day, before or after he visited his aunt, he'd spend an hour or so with a few different patients, reading to them, talking sports, playing cards and often just listening to a lifetime of memories. Eighty-eight-year-old Clyde Monroe liked to talk politics, so Harrison read to him from the *Converse County Gazette* about national and local happenings. Danielle Panowsky loved reading true-crime books but couldn't see the tiny type anymore and couldn't stand e-readers or earphones, so Harrison found her a few great crime podcasts they could listen to together. And Mo liked poker and winning, so Harrison mostly let the sweet man win. But today, Harrison hadn't even had to ignore his good cards. His mind was not on the game.

"How's your aunt feeling today?" Mo asked, picking up his cards.

"Lolly was sleeping when I arrived. I'll check in on her in a little while."

Mo nodded. "You're a good nephew. I've got so many nieces and nephews and grands and great-grands I can't keep their names straight, but I love when they come see their old great-uncle Moey. They always bring me my favorite beef jerky. I can't chew it, but I love the smell of it."

Harrison laughed. He adored Mo. And he'd met quite a few of Mo's boisterous, large clan, a few always popping in every day. Harrison had figured he'd be paired with patients who didn't get many visitors, but he was assigned to anyone who'd filled out a form requesting volunteer visitors—or their families had. For Mo, the more the merrier.

Harrison's aunt Lolly wasn't the type to want someone sitting in the chair beside her and reading from *Anne of Green Gables*, her favorite novel. Lolly had always been private and a keep-to-herself kind of person. Harrison was a little too much like that, but he was working on it. He'd lost his father a couple weeks ago, and when the grief had grabbed him particularly hard one night and he'd gone for a drive and passed a health club, he'd gone in, signed up for membership, and taken out his frustrations on the treadmill and punching bag and weights, and he'd felt a lot better when he'd left. It was also good to be around people who didn't know him, unlike at work, where the looks of sympathy over his dad had gotten hard instead of comforting.

"You seem upset to me, buddy boy," Mo said. "Spill the beans. Back in the day, people told me all their troubles. I shoulda charged ten bucks a trouble."

Harrison smiled. "I'm all right." *Sort of. Except for losing my dad. And now having to say this hard goodbye to my aunt.* And then there was the matter of Daisy Dawson.

All the Dawsons, really. But particularly her now.

"Guess what?" Harrison said. "I helped deliver a baby on the side of the road earlier today." He felt himself smiling, the marvel coming into his face. "Isn't that something? A boy."

He thought of Daisy's big blue eyes. Little Tony wrapped in Harrison's shirt. Daisy wanting to give Tony his middle initial as a way to thank him.

He'd practically run out of her room after that. But he'd have to face her tomorrow. With some news she wasn't going to like.

"I did that once," Mo said, his eyes lighting up. "Hand to God. Lady went into labor right in front of me while I was showing a house. Did I tell you I used to be a real estate agent? It was just the two of us, and wham, the baby was coming. The ambulance got there a minute after I helped deliver the baby. I didn't know what the hell I was doing."

Harrison stared at him. "Are you serious? That *just* happened to me. How can it be this common?"

"Hey, we're a couple of uncommon dudes," Mo said. "Baby was a girl and squawking her head off."

Harrison laughed. "So what happened?"

"Well, a couple days later, the lady's husband came to see me and tried to give me a hundred bucks and a cigar. I took the cigar and told him it was something anyone would do. But I'll tell you,

I did feel like a hero. I told that story for months until my brother told me to shut up already."

Harrison smiled. "I felt like a hero, too." But then his smile faded as he realized he was the opposite of a hero. He'd helped bring little Tony Dawson into the world—but was about to take something away from Daisy.

Her family ranch.

Which was really *his* family's ranch.

How the hell was he going to tell her?

Every time he thought, *Why did I have to be at the right place at the right time*, he'd then realize—*thank God I was*. He couldn't imagine that beautiful woman, so full of life, literally, giving birth alone on a stretch of rural road. Yes, getting rather intimate with Daisy Dawson had thrown a monkey wrench into things, but he'd come to the Dawson Family Guest Ranch to right a wrong, and he would. Whether he'd delivered Daisy's baby or not. Whether he felt a connection to her—and that tiny baby—or not.

That's neither here nor there, he forced himself to think, recalling his father's favorite line when someone would try to inject emotion into business. Business was business. Signed documents mattered. The Dawson Family Guest Ranch was rightfully his father's property, and now his. And he'd get it back in the name of his father.

And for Lolly—there was a long story there that he didn't want to think about. Not with his aunt five doors down, barely able to consume even clear soups in the past couple of days. He had a lifetime of wonderful memories of family holidays and special celebrations with his dad and Lolly, and he'd hold on to those.

Mo's eyes started to flutter closed, so Harrison packed up the cards and moved the table and jelly beans. He patted sweet Mo's hand.

"I'll see you tomorrow, friend," he told Mo.

Daisy had mentioned she'd be getting discharged tomorrow afternoon. Harrison would stop by the main house at the ranch in the early evening and explain the situation. Who he really was. Why he was there. What the law said. He felt terrible about it, given the new circumstances, but he had to stop seeing Tony Dawson's little fingers and button nose and bow lips—and Daisy Dawson's big blue eyes, so full of *thank you* that he couldn't bear it.

You're righting a wrong, he reminded himself. *Just focus on that. Do what you have to do and leave and you'll never have to see those big blue eyes again.* He'd never stop thinking about them, though.

How in the world was he going to tell Daisy he was taking away her home and family business?

Tony's home and family business? A beautiful newborn he'd helped deliver.

Suddenly, *that's neither here nor there* wasn't working for him. Not one bit.

Chapter Three

"So I brought you some stuff you'll *really* need," Sara said with a smile, plopping into the chair beside Daisy's hospital bed. She had a big red tote bag on her lap.

Daisy grinned and sat up, baby Tony sleeping nestled against her chest. The Dawson crew had left a few hours ago, and since visiting hours were ending in about a half hour, Daisy hadn't expected to see any of them until tomorrow, when Noah and Sara would come pick up her and Tony to bring them home. She should have known her BFF would be back.

Sara pulled out three books. "Okay, you might

not exactly have time to read. But if you do, you'll want these. One," she said, holding up a hardcover with "*New York Times* bestseller" atop it. "*Motherhood for Total Beginners: Your Guide to Fusspots, Colicky Screamers, Nonnappers, Binky-Spitter-Outters, Diaper Rash and a Total Lack of Help.*"

Daisy laughed. "That last bit clinches it as definitely the read for me, since I'll be on my own." A second ago she'd been smiling, but the moment the words were out of her mouth, she frowned, that vague fear that sometimes gripped her now hanging on tight. She'd expected to be coparenting. With a husband, her baby's father. Instead, she'd be a single mother. Alone, alone, alone.

"Hey," Sara said, giving Daisy's hand a squeeze. "You've got me 24/7 a quarter mile away. Even if I'm in the middle of breaking up an argument between the goats or dealing with a guest issue, I'll come running. You know that, right? So will Noah."

She did know that. And she loved Sara and Noah for it. Having her family's support made everything about single motherhood a lot less scary. "I don't know what I'd do without you two."

Sara smiled and held up the next book. "*Your Baby's Development by Month*," she read. "This one is a little more boring but very informative. My own copy is already full of Post-its. Basically what to expect. Don't read ahead or you might get scared. Teething?" Sara mock shivered. "That's next for us." She held up the third book, a hardcover with pretty illustrations on the front. "This one is a baby book." She flipped a few pages. There were pages to write down baby's first word, laugh, step. "Every time Tony has a first, you can record it, and there are spaces for accompanying photos. Annabel's and Chance's baby books are full of blurry shots of them having their first spoonfuls of pureed peaches."

Daisy laughed. "I love these, Sara. And thank you."

Sara reached into the bag and pulled out a huge bag of lemon drops, which were Daisy's favorite candy, and waved it. "Also in here? Everything a new mother needs—from nipple cream to a sitz bath to Extra-Strength Tylenol to this coupon indicating that Noah and I hired a cleaning service to come every other week for a few months."

Daisy's eyes misted. "I could not love you more."

"Hey, that's what besties are for. Plus you're lucky that I'm also your sister-in-law, so you get the BFF love and the family treatment."

"Thank you, Sara. Seriously." She bit her lip and eyed the scary stuff in the tote bag. She'd read about those items but had forced them from her mind, so she hadn't bought them. She was grateful to know she'd have them stored in the bathroom when she'd need them. "I wonder what it'll be like, being home with him on my own. Doing this alone. I mean, I know I have you and Noah. But there's no dad, Sara. You went through that. I know you know it's scary."

"It is scary," Sara said. "But just like I knew I'd be all right, you know you'll be all right. You do what you gotta do. You accept support. You say yes to every offer of help. You ask for help when you need it. You learn on the job. And the job is everything, Daize—motherhood. And motherhood is truly instinctive. The incredible love you feel for Tony, that love you've never felt before in your entire life before you held him? That guides everything. Everything else you look up in these books or google it. Like sudden bumpy rashes on Tony's chest or a barking cough."

Daisy felt instantly better. Yeah—Sara was right. Daisy had felt an instinctive burst of love, protectiveness, commitment, everything the moment Harrison McCord had placed her newborn baby boy on her chest. She'd be a good mother—she knew she would be. And for all the scary stuff that would come up, she'd ask Sara, who had several months of experience on her, or she'd hit the laptop.

She breathed a sigh of relief. "Gimme a lemon drop."

Sara grinned and handed over the bag, two pounds' worth and tied with a red wire bow. A few minutes later, a nurse popped her head in and pointed at her watch. Visiting hours were over for the day. Sara gathered her stuff, assured Daisy she and Noah would be back tomorrow afternoon to bring her and Tony home to the ranch, and then it was just Daisy and her newborn.

Daisy was going to be just fine. She and baby Tony were a team, a family. And she had a big support system. Maybe even a new friend, the mystery man guest in Cabin No. 1 who'd helped bring Tony into the world. She wondered why he'd left so suddenly earlier. Maybe the idea of giving Tony his middle initial was overwhelming for him. After all, he was practically a stranger.

A stranger who'd shared the most intimate, most beautiful event of her life with her.

Hopefully he wasn't expecting his fancy blue dress shirt back. Daisy had a feeling he'd be happy never to see it again. But she would have it cleaned and save it for always. She'd never forget what Harrison McCord had done for her.

"I do wonder what our rescuer is up to," she said to a still-sleeping Tony. "Maybe he just likes coming to dude ranches, staying alone in a cabin meant for four and not partaking in a single activity." She smiled. "That's the thing, Tone. Could be any reason. A million reasons. Maybe he recently lost his parents and they took him to a guest ranch as a kid and he wanted to soak up the memories. Maybe they even took him to the Dawson ranch. You know, I'll bet it's something like that."

Tony's eyes fluttered open as if he agreed.

"I love you, Tony bear. I might be your only parent, but I promise you I'll do the best job I possibly can. We've got this."

Tony's eyes closed again as if he also agreed with that, as if he felt one hundred percent safe with his single mother. Daisy's heart almost burst with happiness and relief.

Late the next afternoon, Daisy stood in the farmhouse nursery with Noah and Sara and gasped as she looked around. She gently put down Tony's infant carrier and unbuckled him, carefully cradling him along her arm as she stepped around the room. The nursery sure looked different than it had a day and a half ago. She'd had the basics of the room set up for a couple months now—the crib, the dresser with its changing pad, the glider—all gifts from Noah a few days after she'd told him she was pregnant. But now there were surprises everywhere. In one corner was an adorable plush child's chair in the shape of a teddy bear for Tony to grow into. And someone had stenciled the wall facing the crib with the moon and stars. Tony's name was also stenciled on his crib, which was Sara's handiwork. And there were stacks of gifts in one corner that she knew were baby clothes and blankets and burp cloths. She wouldn't have to buy anything for Tony for a long time.

"Ford and Rex did the moon and stars," Noah said. "For novice stencilers who had to read the instructions twice *and* watch a tutorial, they did a great job."

"And Zeke and Axel hit up BabyLand and bought that adorable polka-dot rug and the yellow floor lamp," Sara added. "I didn't even go with them to make sure they didn't buy anything weird or clashing, and what they picked out is absolutely perfect."

The room was so cozy and sweet. "You guys are going to make me cry," Daisy managed to say around the lump in her throat as she surveyed the nursery. She used her free hand to swipe under her eyes.

She couldn't say she and her brothers were close—well, except for Noah these days—but they were always there for her. And they'd all been there to meet Tony the day he was born. That was the one lucky thing to come out of her nonwedding—her whole family had already been at the ranch.

This place had always held bad memories for all the siblings, but after inheriting the ranch from their father, they'd all invested in rebuilding and renovating and reopening the Dawson Family Guest Ranch. Noah had done the lion's share on his own; Daisy had been too pregnant to help much when she'd arrived a few months ago, and the four other Dawsons couldn't get away from the ranch fast enough.

Ford had once said hell would freeze over before he'd come back here, a sentiment shared by the other three brothers as well, but Ford, Rex, Axel and Zeke had surprised Noah and Daisy at the grand opening this past Memorial Day weekend. And now Axel was staying at the ranch for a bit. That meant three out of six Dawsons at the ranch at the same time. It was a start. And Daisy was going to run with it.

The Dawson Family Guest Ranch was a completely different place than it had been, beautifully renovated as a modern-rustic dude ranch in the Wyoming wilderness, and being here didn't whip up bad memories for the brothers as they'd expected because of the changes. They still didn't want to be here, though. But it was a good sign that they'd come visit, and Daisy could put her master plan into work on them: finding them love so they'd stay. The thought of having all Tony's uncles in his life on a regular basis, not just a visit at major holidays, made her so happy she could burst. She just had to change their minds about the place in general. Noah had done such a good job with the renovations that the ranch didn't remind them of home anymore at all. A good thing *and* a bad thing.

Noah grinned. "There's more in the living room. A baby swing that plays five different lullabies. A huge basket set up with everything you might need while you're downstairs, from diapers and wipes to pacifiers to burp cloths and a change of clothes. The six-foot-tall giraffe in the corner is from Rex—he had to head home on some emergency business at work."

She smiled at the giant giraffe. "He called me this morning to say goodbye. Ford and Zeke, too."

"Axel is doing my rounds for me," Noah added. "He called me while riding fence and said he took to the routine immediately, remembered everything he'd learned as a kid. It's good to have him back, even just temporarily."

Daisy nodded. It sure was. She did wonder what had gone down to cause Axel's enforced R&R from his search-and-rescue team. He worked primarily in Badger Mountain State Park, about a half hour away, where Daisy herself had once gotten lost on a typically disastrous family trip. He'd tell her and Noah when he was ready, if he ever was. Axel was pretty private. In the meantime, she would distract him with just the right possible romantic interest. She had someone in mind already—two someones, actually, both of whom had been guests at her nonwedding.

She looked around the nursery, her heart bursting. "I love you guys," she said, her eyes misting. She gazed down at Tony, napping away, his bow lips quirking. Her family hadn't let her feel like she'd lost anything with Jacob's abandonment. And last night, during the times she'd actually been alone in the hospital without a nurse in her room for this or that reason, she'd only had to look at Tony or think about him if he were in the nursery, and she felt so filled up it was insane.

"Hungry?" Sara asked. "I stocked your fridge and freezer with all your favorites. You won't need to go grocery shopping till Christmas."

She wrapped her sister-in-law in a one-arm hug. "You're the best." She turned to her siblings. "You're all the best. Thank you for everything. You've outdone yourself. Now go to work. I've got this. I'm just gonna revel in being home and not in the hospital. Since Tony's napping, I'll try to also."

There were hugs, and then Daisy was alone in the house. For months she'd decorated this nursery, bursting with excitement for the day she'd come home with her baby. And here that day was. Between that and the way her family had rallied around her, she really did feel filled up.

She certainly hadn't expected the house would still be so quiet, given the baby, who was now in the crib. He'd transferred without a peep. *May it always be so easy*, she thought with a grin, knowing that would never be the case. She stood looking at him, his chest rising and falling, one little arm up by his ear in a fist. *Welcome home, my sweet Tony bear*. She could barely drag herself away, but she was yawning herself and realized she'd better squeeze in that nap.

She had a monitor set up on her bedside table and cranked it up, then slid into bed with a satisfied *ahhh*. She did sleep for about twenty minutes and woke up kind of groggy and out of it. Tony was still magically sleeping, so she headed downstairs for a cup of coffee, and even though it was decaf, the brew faked her brain into waking up. She responded to texts from her family, who sent her the photos of Tony and her they'd taken that morning, and then the crying began.

Ridiculously thrilled, Daisy raced from the kitchen upstairs into the nursery and scooped up her son and brought him over to the glider to nurse him. When he was finished, she stood up and gave him gentle pats until he burped, and then she changed him, marveling at how beautiful he was. She was a bundle of nerves about whether she was doing everything the right way, but Tony seemed content, so that had to be the guidepost. "How about the grand tour?" she asked. "Did you know I grew up in this house?"

The doorbell rang. The grand tour would have to wait. She wondered who could be visiting, though. Her brothers or Sara would text her before just ringing the bell. And guests of the ranch were always informed upon arrival that the farmhouse on the hill was the family home. With Tony nestled securely in her arms, she walked very carefully downstairs and headed to the door.

She pulled back the filmy white curtain at the door. Harrison McCord.

What was he doing here?

Top-notch or not, and holding another gift for Tony or not—this time a long, floppy yellow bunny—and very attractive or not, with his tousle of dirty-blond hair and green eyes, he was hiding something. Daisy had no idea if it was something completely innocuous, but he was *definitely* hiding something. He seemed too…intense at the moment not to be.

"I'm sorry for just dropping by," Harrison said.

"But I do need to talk to you. And to your brother, the foreman, as well."

Okay, this was unexpected. What was going on?

She lifted her chin and narrowed her eyes at him and then at the manila envelope he held in his other hand. He wanted to talk to them both? "I was the guest relations manager until just last week, so I'm your guy—gal—" She grimaced. "I'm a good contact if you're having any issues with your stay, is what I mean."

"It's nothing like that," he said. "I'd really like to talk to you both—together."

Hmm. What was this about? "Well, Noah is pretty busy right at the moment. He was here a couple hours ago, but he just texted me he's dealing with our runaway goat, Hermione. Treated like gold but takes off every chance she gets."

He attempted a half smile, but it was so awkward that an alarm bell went off. Something was wrong here.

"Can I come in?" he asked, practically strangling the yellow bunny, whose head and long ears were sticking out of the small gift bag in his left hand.

Daisy reluctantly stepped aside, and he walked in. She closed the screen door behind her.

"Let's go sit in the living room. I have decaf coffee, lemonade, tomato juice, orange juice, cranberry juice. I like juice, obviously," she added, then rolled her eyes at herself for rambling out of sheer nerves.

"Cranberry juice sounds good," he said. "But let me get it. You've got Tony."

"I'll put him in the bassinet," she said, carefully lowering the baby down.

She noticed Harrison staring at Tony, his expression…what? Like a mix of apology and resolve. Just what did he have to talk to her about? Something that also concerned Noah.

She gestured at the gray sectional, and he sat down on one end, looking around the room. The stone fireplace with all the photos, particularly. He got up and walked over to them. He looked at one in particular, of her grandparents standing in front of the big banner on the gates of the Dawson Family Guest Ranch. "Opening day fifty-two years ago," he read from the banner. He then picked up the next photo. It was of the Dawson siblings in the same spot, Memorial Day weekend—similar banner, but this one said Grand *Re*opening. "Opening day two months ago," he added, putting the photo back.

"Noah really did wonders with the place," she said. "I came back only a couple months before we reopened. This was really his baby. But it became my refuge when I had nowhere else to go when

Jacob dumped me the first time around, back when I lived in Cheyenne." Oh cripes, she thought, embarrassed she'd said all that. "Hormones. Making me spill my guts like a crazy person."

He stared at her as if taking in everything she'd said. "I didn't realize Tony's father had a second chance. That makes it even worse."

Didn't she know it. "I usually abide by the 'once burned, twice shy' saying. But I wanted to try for the baby's sake." Why was she telling this man her personal life details? He was here to talk to her about something…serious, from the looks of him. *Get his cranberry juice and let him get on with it.*

"I'll be right back. You'll keep an eye on Tony?" she asked.

His eyes widened just enough for her to catch it. He was either surprised she'd ask him such a thing because he'd never been around babies much, or he was about to spring some bad news on her, like that he'd burned down his cabin or something. "Uh, okay," he said, shifting a bit closer to the edge of the sofa where Tony lay in his bassinet.

She came back with two glasses of cranberry juice and a plate of Cowboy Joe's coconut fudge cookies, which he'd sent to the main house this morning with Noah. Cowboy Joe had a big enough workload, but he'd kept her cravings satisfied with his delicious homemade fare and snacks. Sometimes treats she didn't even know she wanted until there they were, on a plate, beckoning her. She wasn't pregnant anymore, but she craved these cookies big-time.

She sat down across from the sofa on the love seat, where she could directly see Harrison and the baby. "So what's this about?" she asked. "Is something wrong? Are you leaving us a terrible review on TripAdvisor or something?"

He seemed so caught off guard that he smiled for a second, but then it faded. "I'm just going to come right out with this, Daisy. The Dawson Family Guest Ranch doesn't rightfully belong to your family. It belongs to mine."

She stared at him. "What on earth are you talking about? How could this place possibly belong to your family?"

"Your father, Bo Dawson, signed over ownership of the ranch to my father ten years ago." He reached for the manila envelope he'd settled on his lap, opened it and pulled out a folded, yellowing square napkin, the kind servers set down on your table before plunking your beer on top of it. "The proof," he said and reached over the coffee table to hand the napkin to her.

What the hell is this? she wondered, taking the napkin. Staring back at her was her father's unmistakable scrawl in black pen. It was dated

June 15 ten years ago. *I lost the bet and transfer ownership of the Dawson Family Guest Ranch to Eric McCord.*

Daisy gasped. Her father had bet the ranch?

"This is some drunken bar thing," she said. "It wouldn't hold up in a court of law." She eyed the napkin again, her stomach churning suddenly, and handed it back to him, wanting it away from her as quickly as possible. Her father had drunk way too much, particularly the last couple of years before his death. She had no doubt he was five sheets to the wind when he'd bet the ranch. And left signed proof.

"I've consulted two attorneys who assure me it will hold up," Harrison said, so seriously that she sat straight up.

Daisy lifted her chin. "I think I should get my brothers over here before we say more. They should be in this conversation. Only Noah and Axel are still here. Ford, Rex and Zeke left early this morning."

Harrison nodded.

She stared at him, half scared, half hating his guts, and then grabbed her phone off the coffee table. She texted Noah.

Emergency. Harrison McCord says the ranch is his family's, that Dad signed it over. Has napkin proof. He's in the farmhouse. Find Axel and hurry!

Be right there. Texting Axel, Noah responded.

Daisy sat still as a board, hands in her lap, clasping and unclasping. Harrison did the same. They looked everywhere but at each other.

A few minutes later, Noah stormed in, Axel right behind him. Harrison stood up, the envelope in his hand.

"What the hell is this?" Noah said. "Napkin proof? What?"

Harrison gave the envelope to Noah, who opened it and pulled out the napkin. Daisy waited for shock to register and his muscles to bunch, and that's exactly what happened.

"This won't hold up in court," Noah said, passing the napkin to Axel. "Clearly drunken nonsense."

Daisy shivered, despite the eighty-one-degree temperature. "I said the same thing. He said two attorneys assured him it *would*."

"What's the story behind this?" Axel asked Harrison after reading the napkin for himself and putting it back in the envelope.

Harrison practically snatched back the envelope and held on to it.

"Let's all sit," Daisy said.

They sat, not taking their eyes off Harrison McCord.

Harrison picked up his cranberry juice, which

Daisy now wanted to pour over his head. How dare he drink her juice after threatening to take away their family business? She watched him take a long sip.

"On his deathbed two weeks ago, my father told me that ten years ago, he got into a fight with a Bo Dawson to defend the honor of his sister, my aunt Lolly, who Bo was three-timing. Bo apparently said that his face was too good-looking to risk getting rearranged and he'd challenge my dad to a poker game. If my dad won, then he could beat Bo to pulp. But if Bo won, my dad would have to leave him be forever."

Oh Lord. That did sound like her father. "Where does the napkin come in?"

"At the bar where they were going to play in a back room, Bo started flirting like crazy with the waitress, who wore a wedding ring. My dad got even angrier at how Bo used and abused people that he demanded Bo up the stakes or he'd bash his face in right there. Because Bo had pissed off most guys around, no one was going to come to his rescue."

"So our dad bet his ranch?" Noah asked. "The family ranch his parents built from nothing? No way."

"Your father told my dad he owned his family's very popular dude ranch in Bear Ridge. My dad had heard of the place, so he said fine, put it in writing and we'll play for it. Your dad did." He held up the envelope."

"And our dad lost," Axel finished, shaking his head.

Harrison nodded. "The ranch, therefore, belongs to my family."

"Now, wait a minute," Daisy snapped, standing up and putting her hands on her hips. "It most certainly does not! A drunkenly scrawled napkin from ten years ago? Your own father could have written that. My dad never mentioned a lost bet and signing over the ranch. That napkin isn't proof of anything."

"Except it's your dad's handwriting," Harrison said. "I did some investigating."

Daisy gasped. "How dare you! Lurking around, spying on our history."

Noah and Axel both dropped down hard on chairs with pent-up breaths.

"It's not personal," Harrison said. "It's just business. And this is the business I'm in. Mergers and acquisitions. Your father signed over ownership, but when my dad discovered the place was a falling-down mess, he didn't collect. I'm here to do just that."

Steam was coming out of Daisy's ears. "Oh, right, suddenly after Noah rebuilds the place and it opens to rave reviews! If you think you're taking the Dawson Family Guest Ranch from us, you have another think coming, mister." She stuck her arm out, finger pointing at the front door. "Get out of my house!"

Harrison had the gall to look hurt. "I just found out about the bet and the napkin a couple weeks ago when my father died. My aunt Lolly rarely talks about her private life, but my father filled me in on how Bo destroyed her faith in men and love and romance. She never dated again after the way he treated her. She just gave up. Now she's dying in a hospice in Prairie City all alone."

For a moment, all Daisy heard was that his father had passed away two weeks ago and now his aunt was dying alone in Prairie City, which was the big town that bordered Bear Ridge. Daisy had lost her mom young and her dad last Christmas. Her heart went out to him. Until she remembered why he was here.

"I'm sorry about the loss of your dad," she said. "And about your aunt. But the Dawson Family Guest Ranch belongs to *us*." She crossed her arms over her chest.

"I'm sorry, too, but again, a deal is a deal," Harrison said. "The ranch belongs to the McCords in my father's and aunt's dual honor. So I will see you in court."

Daisy gasped. He was taking them to court? He couldn't be serious!

"I'd like you to leave," she shouted, causing Tony's eyes to slowly open. The baby scrunched up his face and let out a cry.

Harrison eyed Tony, then lit out of the house fast.

"And take your stupid bunny with you," Daisy yelped, throwing it after him.

It landed in front of the door that Harrison had just closed behind him.

"Tell me that idiotic napkin won't hold up in court," Daisy said, looking between Noah and Axel.

Her brothers looked at each other, then at her.

"It very well could," Noah said. "Social gambling is legal here—in private homes and bars. The napkin is dated, very clear in content and signed."

Axel sighed. "We'll get our own lawyer. We'll fight this with everything we've got."

Damn right, they would. This ranch was their legacy. Their children's future. No one was taking it away.

She looked at Tony. Tony Lincoln Dawson. Just yesterday she'd been tickled to discover that Harrison's middle name started with *L* and that she'd chosen a middle name with that initial. Well, from here on in, that *L only* stood for her mother's name, Leah. Harrison and his middle name could go jump in a lake.

Chapter Four

Harrison wished he had the magic words to make Aunt Lolly feel more at peace. She'd been at the Gentle Winds hospice for ten days, her condition worsening, he believed, by losing her beloved only sibling and attending the funeral, which had been hard on her. He knew his visits made her happy, and if she was asleep during his visit, he always left her a cheerful greeting card from the stack he'd bought in the gift shop.

Dear Aunt Lolly, I sat with you till they kicked me out when visiting hours ended. I love you. See you tomorrow. Your nephew, Harry.

He wasn't a Harry, had never been a Harry with anyone but Aunt Lolly. She always called him that when they were together. Now, as he sat at her bedside, a hard knot of grief formed in his chest all over again. Lolly was napping, as she often was these days. And as he was sitting there, staring up at the leaf-patterned ceiling tiles that his aunt had admired the day she'd arrived, Daisy Dawson's pretty, glowy face came to mind. And all that had gone down at her house an hour ago.

He'd left feeling like the biggest jerk in Wyoming. But as he looked over at his frail aunt, alone except for him, the tension in his shoulders started to loosen, his head cleared and his conscience wasn't poking at him. Being with Aunt Lolly reinforced what he was doing and why. The Dawson Family Guest Ranch belonged to his father. In honor of Lolly McCord.

Harrison visited his aunt every day before his daily volunteer shifts. In fact, he'd been headed to the hospice yesterday when he'd come across Daisy in labor. He'd stopped in to see Lolly after he'd visited Daisy and Tony in the hospital, grateful that Lolly had been asleep since he'd been so wound up. Daisy had wanted to give her son his middle initial. Because she'd had no clue about the bombshell he'd been about to drop.

And now had.

He leaned his head back. What a mess.

He was glad Lolly was sleeping right now, since he was so distracted he wouldn't be fully present. Then again, when Lolly wasn't sleeping, she said very little. She liked to keep the conversation light, about the weather and how nice her nurses were, particularly Patricia with the "lovely bright red hair" and how she just loved the butterscotch pudding and Patricia made sure she had that for dessert every night. And she loved talking about her younger brother, Eric—Harrison's dad—eight years her junior and her hero. Eric had always adored his big sister.

Now, Daisy Dawson's *Get out of my house* ringing in his head, he wished Lolly would wake up so he could focus on his aunt instead of the shock in Daisy's pretty blue eyes. She'd almost looked betrayed, he supposed, because of what they'd gone through together.

He shook his head. This wasn't about Daisy. Taking the ranch was about his father and Lolly. Period. Nothing against the Dawsons. Well, maybe against one Dawson—Daisy's father.

Lolly might not be one to talk about her personal life, but Harrison's dad had told him all about how that rat bastard Bo Dawson had destroyed Lolly's faith in men and love, and she'd just "given up" after discovering he was not only cheating on her with a good friend of hers, but with another woman, too. Apparently, Bo had told Lolly he was saving up for an engagement ring for her, two carats like she deserved, and at fifty-five and long divorced, with no children, Lolly had truly thought she'd finally met her second chance at love. But that had apparently been Bo Dawson's MO, charming his way into women's hearts, having them foot the bill for their romance until he either dumped them or they caught on.

Harrison had seen a photo of the guy—Lolly had a few of the two of them in the last album she'd made up. Bo Dawson had looked a lot like Pierce Brosnan, way back when. His aunt Lolly had been madly in love, then ended up losing her good friend, her faith in love and a solid chunk of her retirement fund to "spotting" Bo money for this or that she'd never seen again, and clearly the ranch hadn't, either. He'd obviously spent the money he manipulated out of her on other women, drinking and gambling.

And Lolly had never put herself out there again. Fifty-five had been way too young to give up on happiness, on a life partner with whom to grow old, and now Lolly was sixty-five and had been on her own ever since Bo had betrayed her.

Eric McCord had told him all this in the hospital bed Harrison had set up for his dad at home. Eric hadn't wanted to go to hospice, he'd wanted his son to take care of him in his final days, and Harrison had, delegating a good chunk of work at the firm he owned. His father had shown him the napkin and said that he'd heard the Dawsons reopened their guest ranch and that he wanted Harrison to get it back for Eric and Lolly's honor. Harrison assured him he would.

The few times Harrison had tried to bring up Bo with Lolly in her hospice room, she'd looked uncomfortable and had said she didn't want to talk about bad memories. Harrison's anger at Bo Dawson had ignited every time. That fink Bo had cheated Harrison's dad out of a punch in the face and the ranch he'd signed over to him, and he'd used Lolly and had broken her heart. Hell yeah, Harrison was going to right the wrongs of the past.

He opened up one of the photo albums that Lolly had stacked on the table beside her. Pictures of her childhood, with her brother and their parents, and their parents, and dog after dog over the years. Last night, since she'd been asleep, Harrison had looked through an album of when she and his father had been little kids. He couldn't believe the two of them had ever been that young. He couldn't believe *he'd* ever been that young. He felt like a hundred.

And he felt like hell. Telling the Dawsons that he was coming for their ranch was a lot harder when he'd shared one of the most special moments in Daisy Dawson's life with her. Maybe the most special.

And yes, that look on her face as she'd told him to leave. He'd never forget the worry, the sadness, the anger, the betrayal in those beautiful blue eyes. Making baby Tony cry.

He hung his head in his hands. He wished he could right that, too.

I'm doing what I'm supposed to be doing, Lolly, he silently told his aunt. *But doing the right thing rarely feels so wrong.*

It was wrong. And right.

Oh hell. He had to stop that, get out of that mind-set. Taking what rightfully belonged to his family wasn't wrong. His father had agreed to accept the ranch for the bet because he'd *believed* it was fully operational and profitable—not some dilapidated, run-down ghost ranch that hadn't had a guest in years. When Eric McCord had gone to see the property he'd won, the grass had grown wild and there wasn't an animal in sight, not even a stray cat. Bo Dawson was actually living there, in the falling-down foreman's cabin, since half the main house had been destroyed with what looked like a pickup truck running into it, his father had thought. Eric had thought about taking the ranch for the land, but he didn't need the money, and putting money into this wreck of a place? Forget it. So he'd walked away—but held on to the napkin.

Eric McCord had been a wonderful man, true blue, compassionate, kind. Harrison wasn't going to let him down. Or Aunt Lolly. The ranch was rightfully the McCords'.

I'm doing the right thing, he told himself, giving Lolly's hand a gentle squeeze.

And this time when Daisy Dawson's beautiful face and Tony's wispy curls and matching big blue eyes came into mind, he forced down a steel wall.

With her baby in a sling on her chest, Daisy stood with Sara behind the "Help Yourself" table at the back of the ranch's cafeteria. There, guests could always find muffins, cereal bars, fruit and beverages, especially coffee. Daisy and Sara were replenishing the trays and bowls and adding bottled water to the coolers that lined the rear of the table. Well, Sara was doing the replenishing, since Daisy was technically on her maternity leave and not officially on the job for the next six weeks. But she needed to talk to Sara, and she could certainly add more muffins to the case while she let off steam about the Harrison McCord mess.

"I can't believe he's really going to take us to court," Sara whispered, putting chocolate chunk, raspberry and oat bran bars in the big bowl from the cart she'd wheeled over from the kitchen. "How could he? On such flimsy evidence?"

Flimsy evidence was right. Humph. What was real evidence was straight ahead of them in the cafeteria. The happy guests, the hardworking staff, the smooth-running hum of the Dawson Family Guest Ranch. All the guests, except for you-know-who in Cabin No. 1, were here having breakfast.

The Monellos, young, usually lip-locked newlyweds on their honeymoon, had their arms entwined as they fed each other bites of the breakfast special, a western omelet. The Humphreys, who were a little argumentative with each other but seemed to dote on their teenaged son, had the round table with a view of the sheep pasture. Daisy could hear the parents arguing about salt consumption. They were trial lawyers, so perhaps this was just how they operated in daily life. Then there was the mother and daughter duo from Cabin No. 4, who snapped at each other constantly but at least were here together, having their breakfast and laughing over the antics of Hermione and Snape, the goats jumping onto big rocks in the pasture.

And the occupants of Cabin No. 5, a stylish couple from New York City who hadn't brought appropriate footwear for riding or hiking and actually had to go buy sneakers in Prairie City, were looking at the colorful blackboard of the day's activities

that hung on the left wall. Daisy heard them excit-
edly talking about their very first horseback-riding
lessons. The family in Cabin No. 6 had checked
out early this morning, and a new group was expected this afternoon. All the guests looked happy.

And the guy in Cabin No. 1? Hiding out? Planning a coup today? She wished he were here with
everyone else, watching how hard Cowboy Joe
and his staff worked on the meals, how much the
families—people of all ages—were enjoying the
breakfast, what it clearly meant to her and Sara to
see this room full again when for so many years
it was a run-down nothing overtaken by a family
of raccoons.

He couldn't take the ranch from them. Could
not.

Daisy liked the way Sara put it: flimsy evidence. "I know. A yellowed cocktail napkin from
ten years ago." She rolled her eyes, but then the
worry set right back. "Noah and Axel say it could
be binding because it's not only dated but signed
by my dad, and it's clearly his crazy handwriting
with the weird left-leaning all caps."

Sara shook her head, adding two bunches of
bananas to a cloth-lined basket. "I heard Noah on
FaceTime with Zeke, Rex and Ford last night. They
all sounded worried, too, and said if it came to it,
they'd hire the best lawyer in the state—a shark to

deal with a shark—and Harrison McCord would be sent packing."

Daisy plucked a purple grape off the bunch that Sara put in the big fruit bowl and popped it into her mouth, then another. "What I don't get is how he can even think of trying to take away our family business. That my grandparents started. That Noah rebuilt himself after ten years of ruin. Suddenly the Dawson Family Guest Ranch is open again and a big success, and he's laying claim. I don't think so, jerk face."

"Right?" Sara said. "It's hard to believe that a guy who'd help deliver your baby and visit you in the hospital with that cute teddy bear would be capable of such a thing."

Daisy nodded. "That's just it. It doesn't really make sense. I know he thinks he's doing it for his father's memory and his aunt's honor, and there's some real heavy stuff involved in all that. But the Harrison I got to know briefly seemed so kind and generous. He has such warm eyes. I had such a wonderful feeling about him. And then, wham, he shows up with that stupid napkin, making threats to see us in court."

"He didn't check out of the cabin, by the way," Sara said. "I thought he might hightail it off the ranch and deal with this from where he lives. But he's still here."

"Probably because he thinks the whole place is *his*." Daisy narrowed her eyes. "I'm going to tell him he can't try to take the ranch from us. He's gotten to know us a bit as people and not just as names on a piece of paper. That has to make a difference."

Sara gasped. "Daisy. That's it. That's it exactly!"

"What's it exactly…exactly?"

"Show that man who you are," Sara said. "Who the Dawsons are. What this place means to all of you. To this little dude," she said, leaning over to plunk a kiss on Tony's head, just visible in the sling. "If he has half the heart you think he has, there's no way he'd try to enforce a ridiculous drunken ten-year-old bet that takes away the legacy of the baby he delivered."

Daisy stared at Sara with growing wonder, the truth about what her sister-in-law was saying sinking in more and more. "You're right. Mr. McCord likes deals? Well, I'm about to go make him a deal."

Harrison had arrived at the ranch cafeteria at exactly seven o'clock when it opened for a hot breakfast. He'd had the entire place to himself. The special of the day was a western omelet, which he had along with Cowboy Joe's amazing home fries and three cups of coffee. The breakfast station also featured eggs, bacon, sausage, bagels, cold cereals, fruit and various juices. None of the cafeteria staff gave him the evil eye, which told him the Dawsons hadn't shared his real reason for being here with the employees.

He took a long walk after breakfast. At one point he saw Noah Dawson on a brown-and-white horse, doing what seemed to be a slow surveil of the property, and Harrison figured the guy was making sure everything was in pristine condition for when the guests got out and about, which didn't seem to be before seven thirty. The grounds were immaculate, somehow managing to be rustic and wild and manicured at the same time. If Noah noticed him walking along the creek, he didn't acknowledge him, which Harrison appreciated. An argument before 8:00 a.m., even after three cups of coffee, wasn't appealing.

Harrison had to admit he loved this place. The grounds, the horses and livestock, the beautiful red and yellow barns. The well-placed benches and signposts indicating how far they were from various spots, like the cafeteria or the lodge. Despite having a not-so-pleasant mission here, he was able to breathe, to relax—well, when not confronting any Dawsons. He didn't think about work while he was here. Or what happened with Bethany, the woman who'd blindsided him when he thought they were getting serious.

I know how you feel, Aunt Lolly, he thought, reminded of all his dad had revealed about her debacle of a romance with Bo Dawson. Ten years alone, though. And now dying. The idea of spending the rest of his life alone sounded pretty miserable. But so did even thinking about taking a chance on dating.

Daisy Dawson and her round blue eyes came to mind. Her long, wavy, wild honey-brown hair. Baby Tony, who looked just like her and his big chubby cheeks. He smiled, then felt it fade. *You just feel bad about what you had to do. First the woman is stood up at the altar. Then she goes into labor alone. Then she finds out some jerk is going to steal her family's ranch away. A single mother who just had a baby doesn't need that extra stress.*

He didn't pride himself on being "some jerk," but he did believe he was right to take back what should have belonged to his family for the past ten years. The Dawsons didn't seem to know anything about his father's bet or the transfer of ownership, but that was Bo Dawson's fault for not telling them what he'd done. The thing that kept tripping Harrison up was that this didn't feel like business. It was actually personal. All feelings, all emotions. Negative ones.

That, Harrison wasn't used to. He liked the black-and-white of documents with the deal laid out to be signed. That, he understood. He lived his life that way now, staying on point, staying all business. He'd tried letting his guard down with Bethany, a VP at a rival company, and found out she was using him to gain information about a corporation his company was interesting in acquiring.

Maybe Lolly's way was the way. She'd worked as a home-care nurse, had enjoyed her job, loved going to the movies and reading and taking Italian classes. She'd avoided friendships after finding out her own good friend was also dating Bo Dawson. Since she'd given up dating and the idea of marriage, she'd spent her time alone if her brother or nephew weren't around. No more broken hearts, no arguments, no dashed hopes or expectations. Just a simple, quiet life of her patients, family and hobbies.

Except now she was dying—all alone, except for Harrison. No life partner, no one at her bedside. He sighed, kicking at a rock and sending it skittering into a bush.

He'd never claimed to have all the answers.

He headed back to his cabin and was halfway there along the path when he saw Daisy Dawson, a blue sling around her torso, coming toward his cabin from the path leading to the cafeteria. Was she coming to see him? Or would this be a very awkward coincidental encounter?

They both stopped at the fork where the paths met. "Morning," he said. He peered a bit closer at the sling. He could see Tony's yellow-capped head.

"Mr. Businessman who likes deals," she said, her blue eyes flashing. "I have one for you."

"Oh?" he asked.

"Why don't we talk privately in your cabin?"

"Okay," he said and they resumed walking side by side.

"Didn't see you at breakfast," she said. "You missed a great omelet."

"I got there first thing, actually. By the time I left, none of the other guests had come yet. I had the excellent fresh-brewed coffee to myself. And one hell of an omelet and great home fries."

"Oh, well I'm glad you're not holing up in your cabin," she said, eyeing him. "Especially since you paid in advance for a week's stay."

"I don't feel entirely comfortable here now that you and your brothers know why I'm really here, but I was starving. I'll plan on checking out today."

She frowned, which confused him, since he thought she'd be thrilled that he was planning to leave. "Well, I'm glad you experienced Cowboy Joe's incredible home fries. I *craved* those home fries for the last few months of my pregnancy.

Cowboy Joe always put aside three servings for me. Those tiny peppers and onions and burned bits. Yum."

He stared at her. She sure was being…friendly. Chatty.

His cabin came into view, surrounded by trees and wildflowers, the pine hitching post, to the left of the small covered porch, that he'd never made use of. He walked up the three steps to the dark wood cabin with its hunter-green shutters. Two rocking chairs were on the far side of the porch, a small table between them. Flower baskets hung from the railing. Lolly would have loved the place.

He unlocked the door and walked in, the bright, airy open-concept layout welcoming. There was a small kitchenette to the left that opened into a living space. Upstairs were two small bedrooms, a king bed in the bigger room and two twins in the other, and a bathroom between them. The furnishings were comfortable and durable at the same time. A slipcovered sectional sofa, a braided oval rug.

"What can I get you to drink?" he asked.

"I'd love something cold and sweet."

"Ginger ale?"

"Perfect!" she said so amiably that he stared at her again, wondering why she was being so warm. She'd said she had a deal for him, and deals were usually not about warmth and friendliness. At least not in his world.

He headed to the half refrigerator, wondering what she had up her sleeve. Or lack thereof, since she wore a pale yellow sundress with white stitching. She had on a floppy sunhat and flip-flops with lobsters on them. He got two bottles of ginger ale and the muffins that Cowboy Joe had insisted he take back to his room this morning and set them on the wood coffee table.

She was sitting smack-dab in the middle of the sofa. He sat on the L of the sectional, a reasonable distance. "Tony's napping. He's turning out to be a champ at that. I had no idea I'd be so lucky. I even got a two-minute shower this morning. My brother Axel is staying with me, but I'd hate to ask him to babysit just yet. The poor guy is on some kind of enforced R&R from his search-and-rescue team. He works out of Badger Mountain State Park."

He handed her a ginger ale, completely perplexed as to why she was treating him like an old friend instead of the vicious interloper trying to destroy her family. "Enforced?" he repeated.

She shrugged. "He's not talking, not that I blame him. I have a feeling a mission got hairy, you know? All he said was that a toddler went missing for over two hours. He found the little guy. But somewhere in there is a story."

Harrison was riveted. "Does he work with a K-9 partner?"

"Yup. A gorgeous yellow Lab named Dude."

He laughed. "Is Dude a houseguest, too?"

She nodded. "Sure is. I love having a dog around. We never did as kids, since guests could be allergic or the liability of having him get loose. You know."

"I do know. A dog once bit me on the calf. One of those tiny ones, half a foot off the ground. Chomp. That bite hurt for a week."

She smiled. "Not that that's funny," she said on a chuckle. "Broke the skin?"

"Yeah. But the poor lady was so beside herself, sobbing and crying and telling Puddles he was a bad boy that I told her as long as I knew I didn't need rabies shots, we'd just call it a day. Luckily Puddles had on his rabies tag with the current year, so all was well."

She smiled that dazzling smile. "Puddles?" She chuckled, then eyed the plate of muffins. "Ooh, don't mind if do help myself to one of Cowboy Joe's chocolate-chunk masterpieces."

Now he smiled, enjoying watching her savor the bite she took, careful not to drop crumbs on her baby's head.

She sure was easy to talk to. They hadn't gotten to talk much while she was giving birth. Of course. Or in the hospital, since she'd shocked him into hightailing it out of there by wanting to honor his role in that birth and give Tony a middle name using his initial.

"Look, Daisy," he said. "For what it's worth, I am sorry about all this. I mean, the napkin and everything." He *was* sorry.

"Sorry enough to rip it up and forget it ever existed?" she asked, staring at him.

Awk-ward. "Well, no. And I'm sorry about that, too."

"You can stuff your sorries in a sack, mister!" she said with an exaggerated frown, then grinned. "Remember that episode from *Seinfeld*? George Costanza kept saying that when anyone apologized to him and no one knew what the hell it meant." She laughed and bit into the muffin again.

Okay, what was going on here? She should be furious and chucking throw pillows at him. Not talking old *Seinfeld* moments and grinning.

The sling around her torso moved, and a little cry burst out. Daisy adjusted the sling and stood, taking Tony out and holding him against her. "There, there," she said, moving back and forth along the side of the coffee table.

He stared at the baby against her chest. Tony was so little! Harrison had helped bring this tiny human into the world. He still couldn't quite believe it, that it had really happened. She glanced at her watch, and he noticed it had Mickey Mouse in the center. "Almost time for lunch, isn't it, my little darling," she cooed, her gaze warm on the baby. "Tell you what, let me just chat with Harrison for a minute and we'll be on our way. 'Kay, sweets?"

Tony did stop fussing, seemingly content to be in a different position. Daisy sat back down.

"You're so natural at motherhood," he said out of the clear blue sky. "I mean, two days ago, it was just you, and now you have a baby and it's like you've been a mother forever." He wondered if fatherhood would be that way. Not that he'd likely get to experience fatherhood himself considering he was heading for his aunt Lolly's route. No more romance, no more heartache.

"I take that as a very high compliment," she said. "Truth be told, I was scared to death that I'd do everything wrong. But three-quarters of this gig seems to be instinct. The other quarter is online."

He smiled. "Thank God for Google."

"Right?" She grinned and gave Tony a kiss on the head, then shifted her body a bit to face Harrison. She looked him square in the eye. "I mentioned a deal, Harrison. I'd like to make you one."

He was burning with curiosity. "I'm listening."

"Something you said earlier about being uncomfortable here now...that's a perfect segue. I mean, here you are, probably sure we're all making voodoo dolls with your face on them or something that you're planning on leaving three days into your week's stay."

He shivered at the thought of the six Dawsons each poking pins into a little cloth replica of him. "Well, not that exactly. But yes, I assume you all despise me, so I think leaving today is a good idea."

"Then I'm very glad I caught you before you did," she said. "Because my proposition is this. Stay for the days you booked. Five more days. In that time, get to know us. Me, Noah, Axel, Tony. Noah's wife, Sara, who's my best friend, and her baby twins, Annabel and Chance. Meet the horses and the petting zoo animals. Meet the staff. Walk the grounds. Ride the whole length of the creek. Hear our stories of growing up here and wanting to leave something special for the next generation. This little guy and his cousins and his cousins-to-be, if my other four brothers get their romantic lives in order."

He narrowed his eyes at her. "You're asking me to like you and your family so that I won't take away your ranch. That's pure manipulation."

"Yes," she said, gently rubbing Tony's back. "But according to you, this is business. A deal.

Transfer of ownership. A wrong righted. I'm here to tell you, Harrison McCord, that in five days, you will like us so much that you couldn't possibly take us to court."

He stared at her. She couldn't be serious. "Then why on earth would I agree to stay and like you?"

"Because you're a good person," she said. "A fair person. The man who stopped to help a woman in labor on the side of the road, who ruined a perfectly good dress shirt, who visited me in the hospital with that teddy bear, is a kind, generous person. I'm asking that guy to give us a chance to show you who we are so that, yes, you won't want to take our family business away from us."

Oh hell. He should get in his car and zoom out of here. He *already* liked her. And Tony. Five days? No. No way. He needed to leave and honor his father's request to right the wrongs of the past, to honor his father trying to avenge his sister's heart. Lolly was dying. His father was gone.

She stared at him, waiting. For an answer, he supposed. But what the hell was he supposed to say to this crazy plan?

"I wasn't going to resort to this, Harrison, but your hesitation leaves me no choice." She stood up right in front of him.

She was a little too close. Close enough that he could smell her shampoo or perfume. Or maybe it was Tony's baby magic. Either way, it was enveloping him. That and what she was saying.

He had to stay strong.

But suddenly he was sweating. "Resort to what?"

"Saying please. *Please* stay for the rest of the days you booked. Get to know me. Get to know my brothers and everything this ranch was and is now. Give us a chance to change your mind. That's what I'm asking. It's not manipulative if I'm saying it straight out."

He had to give her credit for that one. She was damned smart. And the sincerity on her beautiful face had him all twisted around like a hot pretzel.

Walk out now, he told himself. *Get in your SUV and go. Talk to your lawyer today, get this thing going and that will be that.*

"Please, Harrison," she said again, this time reaching out to touch his arm. "Just give me a chance. It's not manipulation—honestly. It's about changing your mind very openly."

Oh hell.

He glanced away from her hopeful, determined blue eyes and the baby in her arms. The one he'd helped bring into this world.

Blast it to bits. Of course he had to say yes. And anyway, every day when he visited Lolly, his resolve to take the ranch for his family would continue to be reinforced. He let that sink in, shore him up. Yes, so really, this plan of hers was all good. Daisy would feel she was doing what she could to stop him. He'd know he'd see them in court. Sort of win-win for both. Until the end, of course, when *he'd* take what he'd come for.

Tony began to fuss again. Harrison knew she had to get going so she could feed him and change him and all that stuff.

He stood up. "I'd shake your hand if both weren't occupied. You have a deal, Ms. Dawson."

Relief settled on her face. "Thank you. Neither of us will regret this."

"We'll see," he said. "I should warn you, Daisy. I *do* mean to take ownership of the ranch. Liking you people and this place or not. I want to be very clear on that."

She lifted her chin. "Five days," she said.

"Five days," he repeated.

She nodded, did some kind of wizardry with the sling and settled Tony back inside, then extended her hand.

He shook it, the feel of her soft, warm hand in his unexpectedly...charged.

"Let's begin with a tour of the ranch," she said. "You've barely seen the place."

"Okay," he agreed. "A tour of the ranch."

It's one little walk. She'll show you the lodge

and the cafeteria. She'll talk about her grandparents. You'll nod. You'll go your separate ways in a half hour.

Repeat for five days.

He could get through this. Intact. He was seventy-five percent sure.

Chapter Five

"I'd like to start the grand tour at the main house," Daisy said as they headed up the path. "There's something I want to show you." Yessiree, she was going for the kill. She knew *exactly* where to start.

"What is it?" he asked.

"You'll see." She smiled and patted Tony's back.

Harrison lifted his face up to the sky and closed his eyes for a second, the bright sunshine glinting in his thick blond hair, on his cheek, on his forearms. "Well, it's a nice day for a grand tour."

For a moment she let herself ogle how sexy he was. At just a few days postpartum, the fact that she kept noticing was something. She wondered what it meant. That he was so hot *of course* she would appreciate him on a purely physical level? That she was a bundle of hormones and who knew what craziness they were up to?

Or maybe she couldn't help being attracted on a personal level because he'd come to her rescue when she'd really needed help. She couldn't even imagine what she would have done if he and his fancy Lexus hadn't come driving down that road.

Just keep your head around this man, she ordered herself. She'd learned quite a lesson about her proclivity to act first, think second. Angrily chucking her cell phone out her car window into a bush had been plain stupid. Noah had thankfully found it—and her engagement ring, which she hadn't decided what to do with yet—but way after she'd sorely needed it. She would not be impulsive with the most important parts of her life again. And how she responded to Enemy Hot Stuff here was super important.

"No, *you're* the best, my little schmoopy-pie."

"No, *you* are, my turtle dove."

Giant eye roll. That could only be the Monellos. Daisy had been trying to avoid the twenty-something honeymooning newlyweds—walking, talking, constantly lovey-dovey reminders of her wedding that wasn't. But since Tessa and Thomas were headed right for her and Harrison, there was no escaping them.

Happy couples—fine. Newlywed couples who were so in love that Daisy's teeth ached and her heart clenched—not fine. *Take your unbearable joy elsewhere, people!*

Not that she begrudged them—or anyone— happiness. But the Monellos were now lip-locked and trying to walk at the same time. And managing half-okay. They stopped right in the middle of the path to make out, his hands in her hair, her hands crawling up the back of his T-shirt. They were both tall, slender, dark haired and attractive and wearing matching "safari" wear. The couple resumed walking, kissing every five seconds. They were so googly-eyed for each other that they didn't even notice Daisy and Harrison pass right by them.

Sigh. Daisy was just jealous as all get-out. She herself had felt that way a time or two about a guy. Okay, four times. High school boyfriend. College boyfriend who she thought was serious about her until she found him cheating on her. Two other relationships over the years in Cheyenne, where she'd lived before moving back home to help Noah. One of them had been Jacob, her ex-fiancé. Granted, her ardor had quieted down when she'd realized they weren't exactly right for each other. He was uptight about things she'd never be. She was dead set on things that didn't matter all that much to him. By the time they'd realized they were poorly matched despite their chemistry on other levels, she'd discovered she was pregnant. He'd run for the hills, then come back when she was five months along. Then he'd run again.

And just a few days before that second exodus from her life, Tessa and Thomas had gotten married in the events room of the lodge at the ranch. Right where Daisy's wedding was supposed to take place. The Monellos had hired a wedding planner with her own crew to set up the room, and of course Daisy had found reason to check it all out. She'd been surprised to discover the Monellos hadn't really dolled up the place. Wildflowers were in a rustic centerpiece on each table, and each tablecloth was imprinted with illustrations of horses. Turned out the Monellos were horse crazy, and according to their wedding planner, all they needed to make the wedding amazing was their undying love.

Daisy, nine months pregnant then, had almost tipped over at that one. That was how utterly envious she was. Of the *love* part. That was what Daisy truly wanted, but she'd been going for practical, for working with what *was*. Daisy had been so focused on wedding details the two or three days prior to the big day that she hadn't paid much attention to what Jacob was doing, which was slowly—or perhaps quickly—imploding. That had been how important it was for her to try, to give being a family a real shot, and she'd been willing to sacrifice a certain reality to make it happen. Maybe she should be grateful Jacob had blown that to bits.

Eh, why was she going down this lane? It was all in the past and would never be part of her future. A memory for the keepsake chest she wouldn't open, where all her less-than-happy experiences got filed.

She turned to find the Monellos had stopped again and now Thomas was dipping Tessa for a killer kiss.

"Ever been in love like that?" she asked Harrison, forcing her gaze off the lovebirds.

Harrison glanced over at the newlyweds. "I thought so. But now I'm not so sure."

She tilted her head, hoping he'd elaborate. "Why?"

"Time and space," he said. "Distance. I can see things more clearly now."

"Yeah, me, too." She eyed him as they kept walking. "Got your heart broken?"

He hesitated for a bit, seeming to chew that one

over—if he wanted to say so or not. "I did. Pretty bad, too. I found out I was more a stepping-stone for her than anything."

"Sorry," Daisy said, wondering what the woman who'd won his heart was like. What she looked like. An ambitious businesswoman type in an impressive pantsuit with a great little scarf and gorgeous heels, she figured. The opposite of Daisy Dawson, whose job, even with the semilofty title of guest relations manager, required a staff polo shirt, khakis and sneakers.

"Were you thinking marriage?" she asked. Nosily. She couldn't help it.

More hesitation. He glanced toward the Monellos, now distant figures holding hands. "I guess my feelings never got that far. I always knew something wasn't right between us. I think people know when there's a problem, even if they choose to overlook it or rationalize it. It kept me from going overboard."

And here I was willing to go whole hog. Marry. Take vows. "Do you think it's wrong to overlook your problems or issues for the sake of building a family together? I'm talking about me and Jacob, obviously."

He stopped and looked at her. "Of course I don't think that's wrong. That's different. That's about figuring out how to make something work for a greater good. The baby, a family. You tried, Daisy. Sounds like you were willing to put in the work so that Tony could have his mother and father under one roof, an intact family. You wanted that to happen, and you were willing to give up certain things for it."

She bit her lip, surprised that he understood. "My brother Noah told me a time or two that having sane parents who are happy separately instead of miserable together is just as noble when it came to a baby."

Harrison gave a gentle smile. "He's right, too. You're both right."

She kicked at a pebble. "Well, life happens when you're making plans and all that, or whatever the saying is."

"Nothing truer," he said.

They'd been yakking so much she hadn't even noticed they'd made it up to the farmhouse. It was situated on a rise, slightly out of sight of the rest of the ranch due to the cover of trees, but all guests were notified upon arrival that it was the family house and if the foreman wasn't available in his cabin or by cell phone, they could always come to the main house in an emergency. Her grandparents had always kept a room available to guests in the wake of any trouble—from family fights to plumbing problems. Daisy and Noah did that now, always making sure one room was available.

"Here we are, home sweet home." She stopped in front of the house, admiring it as she always did. Once a sagging, peeling, sad affair with a patchy roof, Noah had renovated it to its original grandeur, had it painted an antique white and the door an interesting shade of blue. The porch had an old-fashioned white wooden swing with a yellow cushion, and there were flowers everywhere. Daisy loved the house now. She loved the idea of raising Tony here. How great was it that Uncle Noah and Aunt Sara were just a quarter mile down the road with Tony's little cousins? And now Axel was right under her roof. Harrison's bombshell had blown every other thought out of her head, but once Daisy got her mind cleared and this craziness about the McCords owning the ranch taken care of, she'd focus on finding Axel true love and a new reason to stay in Bear Ridge. Then she'd work on her other brothers.

"So you and Noah share the house? And now Axel?" Harrison asked as they headed up the porch steps.

"It's just me. Noah lives in the foreman cabin with Sara and the twins—just a quarter mile down that path," she added, gesturing behind them. "Sara grew up there when her dad was foreman. Want to hear something nice about my dad? In his will, he left Sara the raised garden plot her late mother had started years ago. It's in the backyard of the cabin."

"That does sound nice. Sara must have been touched."

Daisy nodded. "She was. My dad didn't have two hundred bucks to his name at the end, but he managed to leave us all priceless stuff in letters."

He glanced at her, curiosity flashing in his green eyes. "Oh yeah? What did he leave you?"

She put her hand to her neck and reached for the necklace she wore under her shirt. She showed him the two rings hanging at the end of the eighteen-inch chain. Both were thin bands of gold, but one had a couple of diamond chips in the center. "My mother's wedding rings. My dad could have sold them so many times over the years but he saved them for me, knowing it would mean a lot to me to have them."

"And he left them to you in his will?" he asked as they walked up the porch steps.

With one hand on Tony's back in the sling, Daisy carefully sat down on the swing and Harrison sat beside her—moving as close to the end as he could, she noticed. "Yup. My mother died when I was eleven. I asked my dad for the rings then, but he put me off, saying I'd lose them, and he'd hang on to them for me. Noah told me not to get my hopes up, that our dad probably sold them already for his drinking and gambling habits. The night he told me that, I snooped in my dad's bedroom and found the rings under his socks. Every time I checked, every first of the month like clockwork, the rings were still there."

"That must have been a relief," Harrison said, his gaze warm on hers for a few seconds.

She nodded, the memories, all she'd felt every time the rings had been there, safe and sound, enveloping her. "More than a relief. My dad had always been a heavy drinker and couldn't seem to stay faithful to his wives. I knew, even at eleven, that he was cheating on my mom because I heard a couple of arguments. I knew the truth, but I still wanted to believe in my dad, you know, that he wasn't…a bad person."

"I can certainly understand that," he said—so gently that she almost burst into tears. Talking about her dad wasn't easy, even with Noah. That Harrison was listening so intently and being kind and empathetic had almost opened the floodgates.

"Finding the rings every time under his gnarly,

threadbare socks gave me back my dad in a way," she continued. "You know? No matter what he'd done, I knew he'd loved me, loved my mother. My mother had always believed he loved her despite being a cruddy husband and father, and I had, too. Finding those rings, month after month, kept me believing that love is real, that the word, the feeling can exist in someone even if their actions aren't exactly showing it. Do I sound nuts?"

He touched her hand for just a moment. "No. Not in the slightest."

She wasn't sure why that buoyed her so much, but it did. "About a year later, when I was twelve, I was arguing about this with Noah, who thought our dad was the worst of the worst, and he said Bo had probably drunkenly forgotten he even *had* the rings. So to prove him wrong, I took a risk."

"What did you do?"

"I decided to remind my dad he had the rings by asking him if I was old enough to be trusted with them now that I was starting middle school. My dad made excuses again, that I'd lose them, maybe when I was older, blah, blah, blah. The next day, the rings were gone from under the socks, and I must have cried for an hour straight."

"I can just imagine how painful that must have

been. Twelve-year-old you with so much faith in your dad."

She glanced at him, surprised again at how he seemed to get her. "I was crushed. Noah felt so bad he'd put it in my head to remind my dad about the rings in the first place that he helped me look again when my dad went out that night. The rings were back. Noah said our dad probably *had* forgotten for a while, then maybe put them in his pocket to sell, then realized he couldn't and put them back. I started checking every week, every Friday, and the rings would always be there."

"I'm glad, Daisy." Harrison looked so serious, so moved by the story that she wanted to scooch over a bit closer to him. She almost wished he'd just put an arm around her. She could use even a quarter of a hug right now. But come on—Harrison McCord was the last person on earth who could comfort her. He cleared his throat as if he'd realized the same, given his mission here, and said, "So you wanted to show me something?"

Why had she thought this was a good idea? Maybe she should forget this part of her brilliant plan, which suddenly seemed a little *too* personal. Just talking about her dad and the rings had her all verklempt. By bringing him inside her home and inviting him deeper into her past, into her family, she'd feel completely vulnerable. Exposed.

Personal is *the plan*, she reminded herself, standing up. *Buck up and get down to business. Personal business.*

"Right this way," she said, gesturing toward the front door.

Uh-oh, Harrison thought once he realized just what Daisy Dawson had planned for him. Two words: home movies. They were on the couch with iced tea and Cowboy Joe's three-berry scones on the coffee table. Tony was dozing in his bassinet beside them. The big-screen TV was straight ahead, now showing Anthony Dawson and his wife, Bess, beaming in front of the Grand Opening sign fifty years ago. The video wasn't preserved all that well, but that added to its charm. Harrison could see the family resemblance; Daisy looked a lot like her grandmother.

"Want to hear something wild? My grandparents, those beautiful, young, smiling people you see right there," she added, pointing at the screen, "they met at a dude ranch when they were teens. Gramps was sixteen and Gram was fifteen. They were both on family vacations. They lived over two hours apart but kept in touch writing letters, and the day Gram turned eighteen they got married. Their dream was to one day open their own guest ranch, and they made that dream come true."

He stared at the screen as Anthony Dawson gave Bess Dawson a kiss, both of them beaming with clear happiness and pride as they held oversize scissors and cut the red ribbon at the gates. He could just imagine them madly in love as teens, in their respective homes wishing they could be together, writing long love letters.

The video cut to the stables, where the Dawsons and two hands were helping a line of children get on ponies. Most of the kids were in cowboy outfits with straw hats like Daisy had.

"See the last kid, the one assuring that little girl that the pony is nice?" Daisy asked, reaching for a scone. "That's my dad. He was about ten then. My grandparents always used to talk about what a help he was as a kid. Showing other kids what to do, telling city slickers there was no reason to fear a horse or worry a sheep would eat them." She bit her lip, a wistful smile on her face. "Feels good to watch these old videos. My brothers and I watched hours of them when my dad died. That's what really spurred us all on to rebuilding the ranch."

Harrison watched the video for a moment. Bo Dawson at various ages, working on the ranch as a kid, a teenager. Bo had a big smile and cracked easy jokes that had kids laughing. At one point in the video, Bess Dawson said, "Now boys, less giggling, more listening to the instructions," and Bo gave the boy he'd been helping the side eye and a grin. The kids clearly adored Bo. He seemed good-natured and easygoing with a bit of troublemaker mixed in.

The video jumped ahead in years, the Dawsons getting on in age, Bo with his arm around three different women at various times—the mothers of his kids—the grandkids running around the ranch. There was Daisy as an adorable youngster sitting in a pen and reading a book to the goats. There weren't many clips of the six Dawson grandchildren together, but Harrison was struck by one— Anthony, Bess, Bo and the six kids sitting around a big table in the dining room of what seemed to be this very house, a cake with lit candles in front of one of the boys, Harrison wasn't sure which, but he seemed like one of the oldest. He figured Daisy and Noah's mom was shooting the video. Must have been nice to have such a big family, even if the kids didn't live together. As an only child without any cousins, Harrison had spent a lot of time alone as a kid.

He stared at the screen, watching the birthday

boy blow out the candles, the kids clapping. Bo
Dawson got up and cut the cake, giving the biggest
slice to the birthday boy, taking requests for frost-
ing edges or roses (that was Daisy). Bo didn't sit
back down until everyone had their slice and their
cups of milk refilled. After cake, Bo called out
that he had a special present for Ford. The troop
scrambled out of their seats, and the video cam-
era followed them outside to where a shiny silver-
and-orange mountain bike with twenty-one gears
was waiting with a big red bow on the handlebars.

Ford wrapped his arms around his father, and
for a second it looked like Bo Dawson might get
emotional and cry, but he hugged his son and they
watched Ford take off down the path, Gram calling after him to be careful.

A fussy shriek came from the bassinet beside
the coffee table, and Harrison had never been more
grateful for a crying infant. He stood up, his collar tight, his stomach churning.

"Uh, Daisy, I just realized I told my aunt Lolly
I'd visit earlier than usual, since I keep catching
her asleep. Maybe we can put off the tour of the
ranch until tonight or tomorrow." He needed some
air. Some space. Some head space away from the
Dawson clan. And their home movies.

She went over to the bassinet and lifted out

Tony, cradling him against her. "Of course. There's lots more video, but another time. The footage of what the ranch looked like before Noah started rebuilding to the day I helped put up the grand reopening banner—it's amazing."

He wasn't sure he wanted to see any of that. No, he knew he didn't. This was all too much. "Well, I'll be in touch about that tour."

That's it. Keep it nice and impersonal. *Be in touch* was a sure distance maker.

She eyed him and lifted her chin. "Oh—I almost forgot! I have a favor to ask, Harrison."

Gulp. How was he supposed to emotionally distance himself by doing her a favor?

She smiled that dazzling smile. The one that drew him like nothing else could. "If you're not busy around five o'clock or so, I'd love your help in putting together the rocking cradle my brother Rex ordered for Tony before he left town. It arrived yesterday, and I tried to put it together, but it has directions a mile long that I can't make heads or tails of. I can't ask Axel for help—don't tell him I said this—he's a wizard at GPS, maps and terrain, but give him instructions and he holds the paper upside down."

Ah. This was almost a relief. He'd put together the cradle *alone*. No chitchat. No old family movies. Just him, a set of instructions and five thousand various pieces of cradle. "I'm actually pretty handy. Sure, I can help you."

"Perfect," she said. "See you at fiveish."

A few minutes later, as he stood on the porch watching her walk back up the path, he had a feeling he was at a serious disadvantage in this deal.

Because the farther away she got, the more he wanted to chase after her and just keep talking. Which sent off serious warning bells. That Harrison might actually *more* than just like Daisy Dawson already—and it was just day one of the deal.

Chapter Six

Not only was Aunt Lolly awake when Harrison arrived at Gentle Winds, she was chatting with a woman around her age. Harrison had never met the visitor and didn't recognize her as one of the staff. She was petite and had short curly blond hair.

"Harry," Lolly said, sitting up a bit from her reclined position. He was glad to see her awake for once, but she looked sleepy and sounded kind of groggy. "Come meet my friend Eleanor. She has the cutest dog. I forget the breed. A cockasomething."

Lolly had a friend? As far as he knew, Lolly had kept to herself the last ten years. When he'd asked her if he could call anyone to let them know she was here, she'd said a firm no. That had been eleven days ago, and he'd asked a couple times since. The answer had never changed.

He extended his hand, and the woman shook it with a warm smile. "I'm Harrison McCord, Lolly's nephew. Very nice to meet you. Do you live in Prairie City, too?"

Eleanor nodded. "I live just two doors down from Lolly. We just knew each other in passing, but she always stopped to pet my dog and tell me how cute he is." She turned back to Lolly. "I had no idea you were even ill." She frowned, and Harrison knew she was thinking about how ill Lolly *was*. Terminally. She looked at Harrison. "As I was telling Lolly, I happened to ask our postal carrier if he knew if Lolly went away on a vacation or something, and he told me he'd heard she was in hospice. I was shocked."

As they both looked over at Lolly, it was clear she'd fallen asleep, as she often did, sometimes even midconversation.

"Lolly's pretty private," Harrison said. "But I'm so glad you asked after her and that you came. That's very thoughtful of you, and it clearly means a lot to Lolly."

"She's a lovely person. Do you know that she bought a box of dog treats just so she could carry some in her pocket and offer them to dogs she met on her walks?"

Harrison smiled. That definitely sounded like Lolly. "She always did love animals." He'd once offered to take her to the animal shelter to adopt a cat or dog, but she'd said she'd rather help by volunteering. He once asked if she was doing that, and she'd brushed him off. As he'd said: Lolly was private.

"The man she was dating must have been devastated," Eleanor said. "I saw them together a couple times, and they looked so happy, holding hands and swinging them."

Harrison gasped. "Wait. Lolly was dating someone?"

"Well, I only saw them twice, and that was right before I stopped seeing her around altogether. I once asked her about him, and she smiled and said she was testing the waters. She had the biggest grin on her face."

Huh. So what happened to the guy? No one had come to visit Lolly since she'd arrived at Gentle Winds eleven days ago. Except for him and now Eleanor. He'd double-check with the nurses.

"Do you happen to know his name?" he asked.

She shook her head. "I didn't recognize him from the neighborhood. He looked to be about her age, midsixties. More salt than pepper hair, thinning some. Tall. Wore silver-framed eyeglasses, I remember that."

He reached into his wallet and pulled out one of his business cards, then wrote down his cell phone on the back. "If you happen to see him again, will you tell him I'd like to talk to him about Lolly?"

"I will," she said, picking up her purse and standing. "I'll let her rest. It was nice to meet you, Harrison. I'm so sorry about Lolly's condition." She briefly put a hand on Harrison's arm.

"Before you go, Eleanor," he said, "do you know if the two of them were serious?"

"I really don't know anything. Just what Lolly said about 'testing the waters' and looking so happy."

So what happened? he wondered. Who was Lolly's mystery man, and why hadn't he been to see her?

He looked at his aunt, sleeping peacefully. He wanted to gently rouse her and ask about her new man. But Lolly hadn't mentioned him at all. Had they broken up? Had Lolly not told him how ill she was or that she was entering hospice? Lolly's cancer had been caught so late that she hadn't been treated; she looked frail, but she had her hair.

Maybe she hadn't told her new guy that she was sick at all?

His questions would have to wait until his next visit. It was nearing four o'clock, and he was due at Daisy's at five to put together the cradle.

Lolly "testing the waters" didn't change anything for him. Bo Dawson had bet the ranch and lost, and it belonged to the McCord family. End of story.

But he sure did hope that Lolly had let someone in her life. The thought of his aunt walking down the street, holding hands with someone who made her happy, lifted his spirits like nothing else.

The only thing that came close was the thought of seeing Daisy again, being close to her. He just had to avoid conversation and her television and he'd be fine.

"I don't know, Daize," Axel said as he poured himself a cup of coffee in the farmhouse kitchen. "Consorting with the enemy? What if you spend all this time with the rat bastard and he still takes us to court?"

Was the guy who'd listened so attentively, understood so much, and been so affected by the home movies and her stories that he'd run out of the house...a rat bastard? Daisy didn't think so.

She'd put her money on Harrison McCord having a bigger heart for the personal, for people, than the businessman let on. Or even realized himself.

Daisy sat down at the table with her iced tea. "I did consider that. I still think it'll be worth it. I'll know I tried. And I think my plan is having an effect already."

"I hope so," Axel said. "I saw McCord walking around this morning. I wanted to punch him right in the smug nose."

"I hear ya." She truly did. Though his face was so attractive, she would probably aim for the stomach or arm. Wham! Not that Daisy—or any of her brothers—were prone to hitting people. And besides, the whole subject reminded her of Harrison's father wanting to punch out their father, and Bo not wanting his handsome faced messed with. She rolled her eyes. Her father had been handsome, she'd give him that.

Axel looked so much like him. All the siblings did, but Axel was almost a carbon copy with his thick dark hair and the piercing blue eyes. Features that were somehow pretty and masculine at the same time.

"So how's it been being back here on the ranch?" she asked. Axel, like Zeke, Rex and Ford, had never wanted anything to do with the place.

He'd invested in the rebuilding like they all had, but he had memories of dealing with a drunk, negligent Bo, watching him quickly turn their grandparents' hard work and legacy into a dilapidated mess, and the cowboy had basically been knocked right out of him. She knew Axel loved his work as a search-and-rescue expert, Dude, his hardworking partner and buddy always by his side. That partner was curled up in the big dog bed Axel had brought with him, half a rawhide bone protectively under a front paw.

Axel took a sip of his coffee. "Like Ford said, the changes Noah made are so big that it doesn't remind me of the old place or what Dad did to it. It feels new. Dawson Family Guest Ranch 2.0 for real. It feels like true progress, you know?"

"I totally agree. I'm glad to hear it, too. It's nice having another brother here." *And you're going to stay forever!* she wanted to add. *We have this great big family and yet we're scattered, barely connected to one another's lives.* Daisy wanted to change that.

She bit her lip. If Harrison McCord did take the ranch away from them, her entire dream to have the six Dawsons settled here would go up in the ole smoke.

She'd just have to make sure Harrison didn't take the ranch.

Axel smiled and looked around at the country kitchen, with its antique charm despite the fact that everything in it was brand-new, from the cabinets to the tiny cabbage roses wallpaper to the tile floor. "I admit, I like the place. I know I spent a few years living in this house as a kid and teenager, but not much of it reminds me of that old dump. Oh, and by the way, Daisy—stop *not* asking me to babysit if you need some time to yourself or to do something."

"You noticed that?" she asked, sipping her iced tea.

"Yes. I want to spend time with my nephew. So ask, okay?"

"You'll regret that fast," she said with a grin. But wasn't this a great sign? Axel wanted to spend time with a baby! A newborn who cried and spit up and pooped. The man had it in him to settle down, start a family of his own. Of course, she had no idea if that was the case. But wanting to hang with little Tony meant something very good.

He laughed. "Maybe. But seriously. I'm fine. I'll stay for a couple of weeks and then go back to work." He turned away, picking up his coffee, his mind traveling, she could tell. He was thinking about what went wrong on the rescue mission. She was pretty sure, anyway.

She eyed him. "You gonna tell me what happened out there on the mountain? With the mother and little boy?"

He put down his mug. "Let's just say I got too personally invested in the mission, and I broke a couple rules involving my own safety to make sure that boy was reunited with his mother before the day was over."

"I get it," she said. That was Axel. He cared—hard. And he'd risk his job to save someone.

"Some people are sticklers for rules. Like my boss. Apparently there's a right time to bend a rule and a wrong time, and I went too far." He looked away, taking a long drink of his coffee. "Let's change the subject. How about I take my nephew for a walk around the ranch? He could use some Uncle Axel time, starting right now."

Daisy grinned. "He absolutely could. And perfect timing, because I asked the interloper over at five to put together the cradle that Rex sent. I showed him some old videos this morning of Gramps and Gram starting the ranch, and I'm going to share more of their amazing history."

"I doubt he'll care too much about old stories," Axel said, standing up. "The man wants to avenge his father getting swindled out of beating Dad to a pulp and winning a *working* guest ranch. Anyone would have felt that way after looking at the trash heap with storm-damaged buildings and overgrown fields and also noticing Dad had sold off all the animals and equipment to pay for his drinking and gambling habit."

Daisy bit her lip. She thought about how moved he'd seemed this morning by the videos and what she'd told him about her family. "I have a feeling about Harrison McCord. I might be wrong. But there's a good guy in that businessy exterior. And don't forget—he helped deliver that nephew you're taking out for a walk."

Axel sighed. "I suppose. I'll reserve a quarter of my judgment. How's that?"

Daisy laughed. "Sounds good."

In a few minutes, she had Tony's tote bag packed with the necessities, and she watched her brother wheel the stroller down the ramp and onto the path leading to the big barn. She'd assured him he could bring Tony right back if he needed to be changed, but Daisy figured Tony would be A-okay for a good hour.

She stood on the porch, breathing in the gorgeous summer air, so fresh and breezy today with temperatures hitting the high about now at eighty-four.

Maybe before it got dark she'd walk down to the creek and dip her feet in. She'd spent a lot of time at the creek as a kid, and now Tony would. The thought made her smile.

She felt so hopeful—about changing Harrison's mind, about Axel not wanting to leave the ranch or at least the town, that she realized she could hold another thought in her head other than the fear of losing the family business. She ran inside for a pad of paper and pen, then went back into the gorgeous afternoon breeze and sat on the porch swing.

At the top of the page she wrote, *Axel's Type.*

Axel was two years older, and she'd seen a bunch of his girlfriends during high school and the couple years after until he'd stopped coming around. So what was his type? What kind of woman did Axel go for?

Hmm. She tapped the pen against her chin. All Axel's dates and girlfriends had absolutely nothing in common as far as she could recall. There were blondes, redheads, brunettes. Short, tall, medium. Curvy, skinny. Super brainy and totally ditzy. Outdoorsy hiking enthusiasts and stiletto-wearing fashionistas. The woman she'd had in mind for him at the wedding was a pretty redhead who led wilderness excursion tours for the ranch. Daisy had figured on introducing them at the reception,

and their first date would be a midnight hike after-
ward and they'd fall madly in lust and that would
be that. But of course, there was no reception, and
the two had likely not met.

Now she just had to figure out the best way
to bring them together. Invite Hailey Appleton to
dinner? Arrange a blind date? Nah, since Axel
would likely say *no way*. Yup, she'd invite Hailey to dinner. In fact, she'd make it a little dinner
party. She'd invite Enemy Hot Stuff, too, so that
she could work on him. Two birds with one stone!
She also thought about inviting Noah and Sara, but
Noah would shoot daggers at Harrison all night,
and who needed that tension?

Dinner at the house. Something casual, like an
interesting pasta dish, or maybe she'd grill. And
then true love would take its course.

She froze for just a second. *Holy cannoli: this
means I actually still believe in that pie-in-the-sky
fairy-tale stuff.*

Good. She wanted to believe. She hadn't lost
that part of herself as a kid when her parents' marriage started going south. And she hadn't lost it
when Jacob had ducked out on their wedding. Love
was real, even if it had clunked her on the head
and in the heart in the past.

Axel, you'll never know what hit you. She

grinned and was about to go in to check the time when she saw Harrison coming up the path. He wore faded, low-slung jeans and a navy T-shirt and a straw cowboy hat to ward off the bright sunshine. His shoulders were so broad. He was just so... sexy. She was surprised she could find anything sexy at three days postpartum. But as he walked, she couldn't take her eyes off his long, lean form. Or his tousled blond hair and how green his eyes were against the blue shirt.

He waved, and she did, too. She glanced down at her white cotton maternity capris and stretchy pink tank top. She couldn't be *less* sexy. But hey, this was the interloper and stealer of family businesses and legacies, not a man she'd ever think of romantically. And she had just given birth three days ago, so she could give a fig about looking good, let alone remotely sexy.

"Ready to work," Harrison said as he came up the porch steps. "Let me at that cradle."

She was surprised his enthusiasm could make her smile, but it did. "I have it in the living room. I think I'll keep it down there as another sleeping spot for Tony."

He followed her in. It was crazy to think that just yesterday, she'd kicked him out of this very room. Then she'd shared her couch with him and showed him scenes from her life, her history. Now he was putting together her baby's cradle. As if he were a cherished family friend. Ha.

She was *that* sure her plan would work. It had to.

"How was your visit with your aunt?" she asked.

He paused as if he wanted to say something but thought better of it. "She was actually awake for a bit, which was nice. And a friend was there when I arrived, someone who hadn't known she was terminal or in hospice until the postal carrier mentioned it. Lolly's pretty private."

"I'm glad to know she has a friend who cares," Daisy said.

Again, hesitation. "Me, too," he finally said. "This would be a nice spot for a cradle," he said, glancing at the big window on the wall adjacent to the stone fireplace.

"I think so, too," she said. If there was something on his mind regarding his aunt, he'd tell her—or not—when he was ready.

He smiled, took off his hat and sat down in front of the big box, the five pages of instructions on top of it along with her grandfather's old tool kit. "Tony sleeping upstairs?"

"Actually, my brother Axel took him for a stroll. I love that Axel is here. For the past several months, it's just been me and Noah. But now another Dawson uncle will get to spend time with his little nephew."

Harrison set down the instruction booklet and reached into the tool kit, taking out a few items, then he slid out the contents of the box, placing the pieces of wood and dowels and nuts and bolts in their little baggies around him. "I'm surprised only you and Noah came back to get the ranch renovated. Were the others just too busy?"

"Well, busy, but more like bad memories kept them away. My father was really hard to be around even in the years before he inherited the ranch from his parents. When he did take over about fifteen or sixteen years ago, the foreman and staff did the heavy lifting for as long as they could, but they weren't the boss—and the boss was either out living it up or passed out in a field somewhere. Within a year, the place fell apart operationally. Within five, it looked like it did before Noah rebuilt."

Harrison raised an eyebrow. "Your dad couldn't have been *that* bad if my aunt fell so hard for him."

"Oh, that was the one part of his life that always went right. He attracted the loveliest women. Kind, softhearted women who truly loved him and thought they could tame him, get him to settle down and stop drinking."

He stared at her, then turned his attention to

the directions. "So he didn't stop drinking? Was he an alcoholic?"

"Yes to being an alcoholic. No to stopping drinking or even trying. It's why he let the place go the way he did. He lost his days to sleeping off his benders, and when our foreman, Sara's dad, finally had enough and quit, my father eventually had to sell the animals that required the most care. He actually loved them—the horses and goats and sheep—which was really sad."

Daisy's eyes almost welled as she remembered how he'd sold Champ, his favorite gelding, who was twenty-six years old. Their closest neighbor, ten miles away, had bought him for their farm and he'd lived out a good life, but Bo Dawson had been so ashamed of having to sell him—for money and because he couldn't care for him—that he'd vowed to clean up his act. But that had lasted all of two days.

Daisy shook her head, trying to replace the sad memory with one that would make her angry instead. "He must have crashed his truck into the barn by the foreman's cabin three times coming up the road drunk," she continued. "Noah would tell me he hid our dad's keys or clipped a wire so he couldn't drive, but Bo would just call a lady friend and find the keys, and once he even hit Noah to get him off his back."

"That sounds really rough," Harrison said. "Noah was just a teenager. And back then it was just him on the ranch with his dad and the staff?"

Daisy nodded, guilt socking her in the stomach. "I was an hour away at college, living in the dorms, and Noah had an open invitation to visit, which I'm glad he took me up on often. We had a lot of weekends together, just talking about everything. The day he turned eighteen, he left the ranch. Once Noah was gone, there was no pull home for any of us." Tears stung her eyes, and she blinked them back hard.

"I'm so sorry," Harrison said, his expression so stricken she knew he really meant it. All that had been hard for her to actually say, hard to remember. Hard to live. But it was in the past.

"I think his alcoholism is why he never mentioned the bet and the napkin," she added. "He was probably drunk as usual, and since your dad didn't want the ranch upon seeing its condition and demanded something else, they both gave up when there *was* nothing else."

Harrison put down the instructions. "So you think I should give up, too. Now that the ranch is what your father made it out to be when he bet it."

"Yes," Daisy said. "I do. This is ten-year-old stuff, Harrison. Both parties are gone."

"My aunt is still here," he said.

She winced. "I didn't mean—"

He shook his head, his tousled blond hair falling in his face. "I'm sorry. This isn't your fault, Daisy. Or your brothers'. I'm sorry I'm making it your problem."

"I have a solution for that," she said overly brightly. *Please say you'll back off from this unfair situation. Please.*

But he just looked at her for a moment, then back at the instructions and contents of the box spread before him. "I doubt I'll ever put this cradle together if we keep talking. Maybe I should just get it done, work alone."

This was exactly what her deal was supposed to do. Get them talking about things that made them both uncomfortable. Get them talking, period. But she was done with this conversation and so, apparently, was he.

"I think I'll go put away some of the gifts I received for Tony in the nursery," she said. "If you need anything, just let me know. And help yourself to a drink or snack in the kitchen." Not that the thought of him walking around her house, poking around her fridge and cabinets didn't make her spitting mad.

She got up and headed toward the stairs. She wanted to flee from him and stay and talk at the same time. She'd been so confident that her plan would work. But suddenly she wasn't so sure that Harrison McCord would budge one inch, liking her and her family and the ranch or not.

You're not going to be able to convince him in one single day, she reminded herself. *You've got five days total. Use them. Make him see. Make him understand.*

But right now, she needed a break from him and everything he represented.

"C'mon, Dude," she whispered to the sweet yellow Lab. "Come keep me company in the nursery and then I'll take you for a walk along the creek. Maybe we'll run into Axel and Tony."

The dog tilted his head and followed her up the stairs like the good boy he was. If only Harrison would be so agreeable.

Chapter Seven

Harrison had just finished the cradle—took a solid forty-five minutes—when he heard the front door open and saw Axel push the stroller inside the foyer.

"Daize?" Axel said as he closed the front door. "We're back."

Harrison was kneeling on the floor, gathering cardboard and baggies and wrappings. "I think she's in the yard with the dog," he called out.

Silence. And then Axel appeared in the doorway of the living room. "Oh, it's you."

Harrison almost smiled. He had to admit, he liked that Axel wasn't trying to be his friend. None of that would work, anyway. "I put this together for Daisy. It's all set for the little guy."

Axel eyed him, then stared at the cradle. He walked over and examined it closely, pressing down on it, giving it a rock, checking the screws. "Seems solid."

"It is," Harrison said. "I didn't help deliver Tony so that he'd fall *out* of the cradle."

Axel raised an eyebrow. "Touché. But you're the enemy *now*."

Harrison stood up, his hands full of discarded wrapping to throw away. "Understood."

The word stung. *Enemy.* Had Harrison ever been anyone's enemy? He didn't think so. He'd always tried to be fair in business. He treated everyone with respect. But to the Dawsons, of course he was the enemy. He didn't like it.

A door opened, and Harrison could hear the tapping of nails on the tile kitchen floor. Dude came padding into the living room and beelined right for his person. Axel bent down and gave the dog a hearty rub and even a kiss on the head.

Daisy stood in the doorway looking both beautiful and surprised that he was still here. He supposed he *had* finished a good ten minutes earlier and had spent a little too much time picking up random bits of plastic that the nuts and bolts had been wrapped in. He hadn't wanted to leave before Daisy returned. Because it would seem rude to just finish up and go? Because he wanted to see her, talk to her? To look busy, he kept picking up little tubes of cardboard and stray foam pieces and stuffing them all into the big box.

She glanced at Harrison and gave a slight nod, then turned her attention to her brother. "Little guy give you any trouble?" She went over to the stroller and peered in. "Ooh, fast asleep. Good job, Uncle Axel."

Axel smiled. "He's as easy as you said. And I think every guest on the property stopped me to look in the stroller and ooh and ahh at the baby. A few even asked how fatherhood was treating me. Lord."

Daisy grinned. "One of these days, it'll get you. You'll see."

"Yeah. No," Axel said. "Anyway, I'd better get going. I promised Noah I'd sit with Sparkles until her tummy troubles go away."

"Ooh," Daisy said. "Poor Sparkles. She's one of my favorite goats. But don't sit *too* close, if you know what I mean."

Axel grimaced. "Gotcha. Apparently, Noah caught one of the guest kids feeding Sparkles jelly beans from his pocket. There are four new signs up about not feeding the petting zoo animals anything but pellets from the treat dispensers."

"Give her a belly rub for me," Daisy said. "And no worries about Dude for a few hours—we went for a long walk along the creek."

Axel gave Dude a scratch on the head and behind his ears. "Thanks, Daize. See you later. Bye, Tony," he added, then headed toward the door, finally giving Harrison a politeish nod of acknowledgment before leaving. When the door shut behind him, Harrison picked up the last of the wrapping and stuffed it into the box.

"All done," Harrison told her, giving the cradle a little push to make it rock.

"Very nice!" she said, surveying it. She pulled out her phone and snapped a photo. "I'll send it to my brother Rex, who bought the cradle." She looked at the photo she took, then put her phone back in her pocket. "I was hoping that while I was gone, I'd come up with the magic words to make you stop all this craziness about the ranch and just let us be."

Why did she have to be so straightforward? And earnest? And so lovely?

She had him all tied in knots. He took in a quick breath, forcing himself to focus on facts. "You didn't come up with them because a deal is a deal,"

Harrison said. "If my father had taken possession of the ranch ten years ago, you and your brothers would have accepted that, right?"

"What? Of course not!" she said, hands on hips.

He crossed his arms over his chest. "I thought the issue for you was that the ranch had been rebuilt and had reopened to great success."

She glared at him. "Harrison McCord, my grandparents bought this land. Anthony and Bess, who you got to know from the videos. They built the ranch. They opened a business, hospitality at its core. They raised my dad here, and he raised us here—well, until my brothers' mothers left him and moved on. This ranch is our family history, our legacy, our future. It's *us*." Tony let out a fussy sound, and Daisy went over to the stroller and picked him up.

She held her son against her, gently patting his back, cooing softly at him. For a moment he couldn't take his eyes off her, off *them*.

"Harrison," she continued, "my problem with what you're trying to do isn't about timing. It's about the ranch itself. A falling-down mess or this," she added, waving her hand around. "Didn't your father leave you a piece of your family history when he died? No matter how big or how small?"

"Everything in his condo," Harrison said. "But

my father wasn't very nostalgic. He had some old photo albums, some mementos of his parents. But except for the black leather recliner he loved watching TV in, the old Timex watch he wore every day despite being able to afford an expensive one, nothing really jumped out at me that meant all that much to him."

"Oh," she said, looking a bit defeated. "From the way you were talking, I got the sense that family meant a lot to you."

"The people, yes. Not necessarily the *things*."

"This ranch isn't a thing, Harrison. It's our *family*."

"I don't think the law would see it that way. It's property."

"You're absolutely maddening," she said. "Do you know that?"

He stepped closer, but she stepped back. "It's not—"

"I know, personal. It's supposedly not personal. Well, guess what, Harrison? It is."

He was out of things to say here. Part of him wanted to forget all about the ranch issue—for the moment—and tell her what Lolly's friend had said, about the man she'd been dating. He wanted to ask her opinion if maybe he should try to find the guy. But suddenly he didn't want to talk about his aunt's private business with a *Dawson*. Daisy was out to protect her family—period. He should do the same.

"And in fact," she added, "I'd like you to really understand how personal it is. So please come to dinner tonight. I'll expect you at seven."

Dinner? Here? With all this tension—of various kinds?

"Look, Daisy, I don't think—"

"You made a deal," she reminded him. "So I'll see you at seven. It'll be just you and me. Axel is working the dinner shift with Cowboy Joe since one of his assistant cooks called in sick. I'll be making honey-garlic chicken stir-fry with my secret recipe rice."

Home movies. Putting together a baby cradle. Now dinner—and a really good-sounding home-cooked meal.

"Are you sure you really want to make a fancy dinner?" he asked. "You did just have a baby three days ago. You should be napping every chance you get. Or putting your feet up. Or just taking it easy."

"Who said anything about fancy?" She grinned, and he relaxed a bit. "I've got this. Tony's an easy baby, and I have so much help and support from my family. So no worries."

He smiled. "Okay, then. I didn't know rice had secret recipes."

"This one does. And you'll see why when you taste it."

"I guess I'll see you at seven, then," he said.

He took the box and started to lug it toward the door.

"Axel will drive that out to the recycling center for me later," she said. "You can just leave it."

Her family really *was* there for her. Every step of the way, it seemed, with everything, big and small. She made it very clear that she knew she was lucky in that regard. The whole family was lucky. Maybe not when it came to old bets that were signed and dated. But with relatives.

Harrison dragged the box back to the corner and out of the way, then headed toward the front door, pausing in front of her. "See you later, Tony," he said, reaching out to give his head a gentle touch. He was almost surprised she didn't jump back.

"Thanks again for putting the cradle together," she said. "Tony says thank you, too." She turned sideways so that he could see the baby's face.

He peered at Tony of the big slate-blue eyes and giant cheeks. The little guy was wide-awake and alert and staring at him. "Anytime. Really. It was my pleasure."

That was the problem, though.

It really was his pleasure to assist her. To spend time with her.

He had to put up some kind of magical barrier so that he'd stop liking her so much. And being so damned attracted to her.

He had about an hour to work his potion.

After Harrison left, Daisy made sure she had everything she needed for her honey-garlic stir-fry and secret recipe rice. Good thing she checked, because she was completely out of garlic and had to borrow two bulbs from Sara, who loved to cook. Daisy could make a couple of decent meals—her stir-fry and a couple of pasta dishes—but overall she was a breakfast-for-dinner, pizza, Chinese or Mexican takeout, and cookout type. Before she found out she was pregnant, she'd even be happy with a bowl of Cap'n Crunch for dinner, but she'd stepped up the healthy living for the baby's sake. Now that she'd be cooking for her little family of two—although she had a ways to go before Tony would even start solids—she'd have to up her game. Might as well start by practicing on Harrison.

Although it did feel wrong to *want* to make him dinner. Cooking for someone, sharing a meal with them, felt intimate. Still, she needed him to owe her, right?

Ugh. All this suddenly did seem as manipulative as Harrison had complained about. But the stakes were high, and she was playing to win here. And winning meant that her family kept the ranch. If her honey-garlic stir-fry had an effect on him, good.

But if she were really honest, she'd have to admit that she liked being with Harrison. For a man who was looking to take away her family's business, a business that *would* one day be left to Tony and his cousins and cousins-to-be, she found him almost soothing to be around. Something in the way he listened. Really listened. He looked at her when she spoke, his emotions plain as day on his handsome face, and his responses were always honest and thoughtful. How he made her feel so comfortable was beyond her. Then there was the matter of wanting to kiss him.

That was craziest of all. Hormones, had to be. But there was no denying the man drew her like no one had in a long, long time.

Maybe she'd invited him to dinner so she could figure him out. Figure out her feelings for him. Because her feelings made no sense.

Once she had dinner prepped, she put Tony

in the sling and set out to enjoy a fifteen-minute walk around the ranch—for reinforcement more than anything. When Harrison would arrive later, she'd need to be fortified with how much this place meant to her. Every time she noticed his chest or the way his jeans skimmed over his lean hips, she'd picture the ranch and get herself back on track.

Tony had fallen asleep on the way to the barn. She waved at the Humphrey family, who were on horseback in the far pasture, getting lessons from Dylan, one of the ranch hands. Daisy stopped to smile at Hermione and Juanita, busy-bee goats who were jumping onto logs in their pen. She breathed in the gorgeous late-afternoon air, warm and breezy, the Wyoming wilderness never failing to restore her.

But wait—was that crying she heard? She glanced down at Tony's tiny head. The sounds certainly weren't coming from the sling. It was a *woman* crying. She stood still and listened. Yup. That was definitely someone crying. And it was coming from around the side of the barn.

Daisy walked to the edge and peered around. Uh-oh. Tessa Monello, the newlywed, was sitting against the barn, her head on her arms on her knees. Crying and sniffling. "Tessa?" Daisy said softly. She pulled out the little packet of tissues she always carried in her back pocket and handed it to Tessa, who took it and used a tissue to dab at her eyes.

"Did you and Thomas have an argument?" she asked, having no doubt they did.

Tessa's face crumpled, then her hazel eyes flashed and she looked like she might explode. "Do you want to know what he had the nerve to say to me?"

Oh boy. Did she? Daisy wasn't sure she should be getting in the middle of this.

Tessa didn't wait for an answer. "He said I was being Team Tessa instead of Team Monello. First of all, I've been a Monello for barely a week!"

Daisy lowered herself to the ground, her feet straight out.

Tessa looked over inside the sling. "Aw. So sweet." Then her face crumpled. "Thomas wants to have a baby right away. Is he kidding? I'm twenty-two!"

"Did you guys talk about all this stuff before you got married?" Daisy asked.

"We were too busy having sex," Tessa said, rolling her eyes. "I'm such an idiot!"

"Uh, exactly how long were you a couple before you got married?"

"Exactly a month. But it felt so right. I truly believed he was it, the one, the only guy for me. Now he's turned into Mr. Traditional? *What?"*

A month. She hadn't known Jacob much longer before she'd conceived. *Hindsight is definitely twenty-twenty, but we all need to be much more careful with ourselves and our futures,* she thought. She was so happy to have Tony, but she certainly didn't have even the faux fairy tale she'd been hoping for. She sighed inwardly. Fairy tales were never going to be real life. Her family, her brothers' families, could speak to that. Noah and Sara seemed to have it all right now, but they'd had one rough start. They'd fought for what they had. If you recognized that what you did have was that special, then you had to make it work.

She believed in love, but she also knew it didn't always come easy.

She supposed that would be her advice for Tessa.

"So he wants to start a family right away? Did he say why?"

Tessa grimaced. "He wants five kids, and he 'read some link on Twitter that younger mothers have healthier babies.'"

"And what do you want?" Daisy asked.

"Last month I sold two photographs to the *Converse County Gazette*," she said. "I want to be a photojournalist. I want to travel all across the state, taking photos, documenting what stands out."

"Congrats!" Daisy said. "That sounds amazing. And your new husband is not on board with this?"

"He's supportive of my being a photographer—for weddings, family portraits, pets. That kind of thing. But I have this idea for an entire series on female ranchers in Wyoming. I actually got inspired by your sister-in-law. You should see the shots I've taken of Sara. She told me that she's now assistant forewoman but that she'll be promoted to forewoman in the next few months as her husband, the current foreman, takes on more of an administrative role."

Daisy was thrilled for Sara. She knew how much being forewoman of the ranch meant to her, how hard she'd worked for it—and had worked for it since she was a teenager on not only this ranch back in the day but other prosperous operations. She and Noah had made a plan for childcare, and since the ranch was "bring your baby to work"–friendly, they could both see the twins often throughout the day.

"Guess who thinks *forewoman* is a made-up word?" Tessa asked. "I had no idea I married a Neanderthal!"

"Here's what I think," Daisy said. "I think you

and your brand-new husband need to focus on getting to know each other. You've got the love, right? You've made a lifetime commitment. With those vows in mind, put in the time to really listen to each other. The two of you simply have to talk, really talk, about what matters to you. Yes, Thomas might have some old-school ideas that need to be knocked out of him. You'll do that. And you might have to think about how traveling the state might affect your marriage—same if he was the traveler."

"Huh. I guess. I just got so mad I stalked off."

"The both of you will probably be doing a lot of that," Daisy said. "But if the love is there, Tessa, that's your base. Come at Thomas from love— which means respecting that he may have a different point of view. What I'm trying to say is, try to put aside the indignation and anger and *talk*. If you can't agree on fundamentals after that, that's a different story. But don't give up on each other before then."

Tessa's face lit up, and she threw her arms around Daisy as best she could with a baby between them. "You're absolutely right. One hundred percent right."

Phew. Daisy didn't want all her jealousy and envy over the Monellos to have been in vain. "Talk to your husband. And listen. And make sure he does the same. You both need to listen as much as you talk."

"Got it!" Tessa said, leaping up and dashing off.

Daisy smiled and slowly stood up, dusting off her tush. "Well, guess my work here is done," she said to Tony, giving his head a gentle caress. She thought about inviting the Monellos to her dinner party to help facilitate the discussion a bit, but that was going *way* too far—if they started bickering about such fundamental stuff, she'd scare Axel right out of the idea of settling down. She'd heard what he'd said about fatherhood—pertaining to himself—earlier today loud and clear. Fatherhood might not be on his radar right now, but he hadn't said anything about marriage being off the table. Baby steps. From dinner party to dating to settling down in Bear Ridge for all eternity.

She shook her head at herself, but hey, she had to think big.

She'd done what she could for the Monellos at the moment.

Now to get through to one stubborn businessman.

Chapter Eight

*C*an. Not. Lose. My. Edge. Harrison repeated his new mantra before heading down to the creek. He had twenty minutes before he was expected at Daisy's, and being alone in his cabin and staring out the window at trees was making him think too much about her. He had to keep the focus on *his* family, not hers. And he had to keep his mind off her face and her blue eyes and how attracted to her he was.

As he walked under the canopy of trees, he lifted his face to the sunlight poking through and breathed in the fresh air. Ahh. He could spend weeks here just walking along the creek and skimming stones and never be bored. He supposed soon enough, that would be an option that wouldn't cost him a cent.

He turned right instead of left to avoid where many of the guests tended to walk or fish or dip their toes. He wasn't in the mood for chitchat. The direction he walked in would lead near the gates to the ranch and there was a lot of brush cover, so not many people came down this way.

He stood on the bank and skimmed a few rocks, the ripples mesmerizing. Just what he needed to get Daisy Dawson and Tony Lincoln Dawson off his mind. The creek truly did set his head straight, calm him, soothe him. The whooshing sound of the current, the birds, the critters that called the creek bank home. He hadn't spent much time around brooks or rivers growing up; his parents had always liked living in the center of Prairie City with its shops and restaurants and businesses, including his dad's accounting practice, where he'd been in high demand for area ranches. A month or so after Harrison's mother died when he was twenty and in college, his dad had sold the house, unable to bear living there without her. Eric McCord had bought a condo and after a few years sold that for a smaller one when it wasn't so necessary for him to have space for a six-foot-two college student. So there was no family home to leave to him. That was gone, another family living in it.

What Daisy had been talking about—nostalgia, sentimentality for the past—Harrison wished he did have more of that. There were old photo albums in his attic, some family videos, but instead of them filling him up, the memories made him feel kind of alone. Sometimes Harrison thought he was too much a lone wolf. What had his mother said a few times? *Wolves are pack animals.*

But six months ago, after catching his ex-girlfriend in her lies, he'd felt himself harden up, his trust in anyone and anything obliterated. His father's story about Bo Dawson and how he'd been cheated by that rat had only made Harrison turn away from people more. He started delegating less at the office. Doing the big deals himself. Working out harder and harder at the health club, the punching bag his last and most satisfying stop before heading home. Alone. He hadn't exactly been having a great time lately.

He thought about how Daisy had to live in a world of trust, starting with having to put herself— and her baby—in his hands when he showed up on the side of the road. A half hour prior, she'd been left at the altar in her maternity wedding gown, her trust blown to bits. Maybe that was how trust worked—taken away and restored. Repeat. Repeat. Repeat. Except when it came to Harrison. It was as if *ye of little faith* had been written about him.

He sat down on a big rock and watched the water flow down the creek, his attention on a beaver— or at least he thought it was a beaver—scurrying among the brush and twigs at the creek's edge. He really was losing his edge here. Here at the Dawson Family Guest Ranch. Here with Daisy. He had to stop thinking about her. Her and that little infant with the big slate-blue eyes. Tony had had Harrison at first cry. He was being pulled in right before his eyes, right under his watch. He cared too damned much about the two of them.

He wanted to do right by his family, but he wanted to do right by Daisy, too. He wasn't sure how that was possible and no answers were coming to him, so he got up and headed up the path to the main house.

As he took the steps, he could smell something amazing wafting from the screen door. His stomach rumbled. He tapped on the door, and in seconds there she was in a light blue sundress, her long honey-brown hair loose around her shoulders. Did she have to be so pretty? "Must be the secret rice recipe that smells so good," he said because he was flustered. He could barely drag his eyes off her face.

"Oh, it is." She grinned and opened the door.

He felt like he should have brought a bouquet of flowers for her. She'd invited him to dinner, for heaven's sake. And he'd shown up empty-handed. But this wasn't a date—far from it. It was an ambush, and he knew it. Still. "I should have gone into town to the bakery I pass every time I drive to and from Prairie City and picked up some of their amazing bread."

"Nope. You're my guest, so all I need is you." Her eyes widened, and two pink splotches appeared on her cheeks. "That came out weird."

He laughed. "I've always liked weird."

"Me, too, actually."

He held her gaze a beat too long, and she didn't look away. Trouble. "So can I help with anything?"

"Sara stopped by earlier and beat you to it. Everything's ready." She led the way into the dining room. The table was set, interesting big blue flowers in a vase in the center. Daisy sat on one side and Harrison on the other. She lifted up the lids of the platters. The stir-fry made his mouth water, and the secret recipe rice looked savory and delicious. She heaped both on his plate, then served herself.

"Bon appetit," he said, forking a big bite. He

smiled. "My mother always said that. Guess I picked up the habit."

"Was she a great cook?" Daisy asked.

"My dad was actually the cook in the family. My mom hated to cook."

"Like me!" Daisy said. "Well, I don't totally hate it, but I'm not great in the kitchen."

"Then why is this food so good?" he asked, taking another big bite of stir-fry. He already wanted seconds.

"It's my one thing," she said. "So I'm really glad you like it. In fact, I'm going to make it again for a little dinner party I'd like to host, and I could really use your help."

Oh no. What subterfuge was this? The crazy part was, she knew he knew what she was doing. Reeling him in. Making him care. Making him feel needed.

Oh God, it really was working.

"Need a waiter?" he asked.

She smiled. "No. I have this grand plan. Another grand plan," she added with a wry chuckle. "Wow, I really am a busybody. But this is important."

"What's this second grand plan? The one that thankfully doesn't involve me?"

She ate a bite of her stir-fry. He could barely

take his eyes off her again as she looked at him, her blue eyes full of determination and hope. He wanted to reach out and touch her face, her soft skin.

He was losing it.

"I told you how my brothers have bad memories of the ranch and Bear Ridge, despite how much renovations changed the place. Just being here reminds them of times they want to forget permanently."

He nodded. "I can understand that."

"But you can probably also understand how much it means to me to have my family back together on the ranch my grandparents started fifty years ago. Right now, it's just me and Noah. And I get it—even I ran far away and wasn't the slightest bit interested in coming home. Until I was pregnant and needed family, needed that history and connection to not only Noah on the ranch but to the ranch itself. I finally understood what that meant. And now being here, living here, working here, fills me up, Harrison."

This wasn't about manipulation or subterfuge or reeling him in. She was speaking from the heart, deep down, and he knew it. She'd meant every word of that.

And every hour they spent together, he saw

more and more of how the place made her happy, did fill her up, gave her peace and security.

He mentally shook his head. Still. The napkin wasn't about Daisy Dawson and what she needed. It was about his family and turning a wrong around. It was about what he'd promised his father.

Lolly has a boyfriend.

The thought slammed into his head. So what if she did? How did that change anything? Ten years of living like a recluse, then she knew she was dying and she'd let herself have a few weeks, a couple months, maybe, of romance with a man she felt attracted to. That had nothing to do with Bo Dawson being a rat bastard who'd cheated Harrison's father out of a bet in good faith.

He wanted to get up and leave. And not. He needed this conversation—and his thoughts—back on track. "The other grand plan, then?" he asked.

"Love," she said. "Specifically involving my brother Axel and a nice, outdoorsy redhead named Hailey. I was planning to introduce them at my wedding, but we all know that didn't happen."

"And where do I fit in?" he asked.

"Well, I'd like to do a little matchmaking between Axel and Hailey. I want Axel to have a reason to stay in Bear Ridge, to build the fancy log cabin he's always talked about right on the property, at the far end, where he'd be comfortable. My plan is to invite Axel and Hailey to dinner at the house, a casual dinner party kind of thing. Because I don't want it to feel like a setup, I'm inviting you, since we're barely even friends let alone anything resembling a couple." She let out a dry chuckle as if she was speaking and thinking at the same time and wanted to take back what she'd said. "It's just a few people over for dinner. No big whoop."

No big whoop. Except that Axel wasn't going to be able to build on the property. It would soon legally be McCord land and belong to Harrison.

But he couldn't say that. Wouldn't say that. She had to know it, though. Right?

"I think we're friends," he said without meaning to, his voice unsteady. Even he knew it was a dumb thing to say given where his thoughts had just gone.

Everything about his life was upside down. He'd lost his dad. He was going to lose his aunt. And Daisy, whom he now realized he wanted with every fiber of his being, could never be his, would never be his.

"Nope," she said, disappointment on her face. "Not friends. Friends don't do what you're trying to do, Harrison."

He felt that zap hard in his chest. She was right

about that. One of them had to remember it, and he was glad she did, because he was too far gone. He stared down at his plate for a moment, pushing his stir-fry around to give him a minute to come up with a response. He had nothing.

There had been no mistaking that zap. Daisy was *in*. Her plan had worked—to a degree.

You can have feelings for the woman, be attracted to the woman, care about the woman—and still insist on making things right for your family, he reminded himself.

He cleared his throat. He drank some iced tea. He ate more special-recipe rice. Anything to avoid talking, because who knew what would come out of his mouth? Daisy Dawson had him all crazy.

He had to back off. Among Eric McCord's last words had been "do what's right for me and Lolly, son." Yeah, it was a bum deal for the Dawsons, but it had been a bum deal for Eric McCord for *ten years*. Same for Lolly.

They turned their attention to their plates, eating in a kind of glum silence. He had so much to say and couldn't say any of it.

"Just let me know when to show up for that matchmaking dinner party, and I'll be there," he said, standing up. "Thank you for dinner, but I need to get going."

Daisy bolted up. "Wait. You don't have to go, Harrison. You shoveled my one great dish in your mouth in two seconds and now you're running away. Because I got to you. Admit it!"

He stared at her. She didn't pull any punches. Said it like it was. "You got to me because we *are* friends. If I never see you again after the five days are up, I'll always remember you, Daisy. But you're trying to manipulate an end, and it's not fair. My father has been owed this ranch for ten years now. His dying words asked me to get it for him. I'm going to do that. If my dad had taken over the property back when your dad made the bet, we wouldn't even be having this conversation. Or dinner. Or anything. This would be McCord land."

She shook her head, and he could see frustration and tears forming in her eyes. "This isn't right," she said, but her voice was shaky. But the way she was looking at him—not with anger, not with *You're the enemy*, but with *Help me out here, dammit, because there's something between us*, he knew he had *her*. The playing field was suddenly even.

And it sucked. This was what he wanted? To best Daisy Dawson, a brand-new mother who'd been stood up at the altar days ago? Who'd gone into labor alone on the side of a flipping rural service road?

There *was* something between them. He felt it to his toes. He felt it everywhere. And he knew she did, too.

He put his hands on her shoulders, and she stared up at him in such surprise that all thought went out of his head. He leaned his head forward. She leaned her head forward.

And when their lips met, it was as if they were both so damned happy to be there that they went for it, both clearly eschewing thought and rationale and deepening the kiss. His arms went around her back, one up into her silky hair, the other around her neck, her shoulders, drawing her closer. Her hands were on the side of his face, in his hair, her breathing fast and slightly moany.

He kissed her and kissed her and kissed her and could stay here all night, just standing here doing this. She started backing him into the living room, right onto the couch, and suddenly she was on his lap, her arms around him, her soft lips on his neck.

"Whoa, whoa, whoa," she said, pulling back a bit and staring at him, her eyes wide but full of delicious desire. "This is *not* part of my plan. *What* are we doing?"

He missed her lips immediately. "What felt right in the moment. Crazy, but there it is."

She sat back, taking a deep breath. "Well, I sure shouldn't be doing this! In fact," she added, turning to him, "we *can't* be doing this—for two very good reasons."

Took him a second, but he did know what she meant. One: they were supposedly enemies. Two: it would be a good six weeks before she could even consider sex. Standard doctor's orders.

"I could kiss you all day," he said—because that was exactly what he was thinking, what was echoing in his head.

"I *really* don't want to say 'same here,' but same here. Ugh! How can that be? You *are* the enemy, Harrison. Now I'm making out with you?" She sighed and turned away.

"My aunt had a boyfriend," he blurted.

Daisy turned toward him again, curiosity lighting her beautiful blue eyes. "She did? I thought she was all alone the last ten years, that my father broke her heart to the point that she never dated again and was miserable."

"That's what my dad said. And they were very close, so I thought he'd know. But Lolly doesn't talk about her personal life with me. She's never mentioned a man in her life—or not. And no one has been to visit her until today—a neighbor who said Lolly was sweet to her and her dog when she passed them on dog walks. Apparently, this neighbor saw Lolly holding hands with a man around her age—twice. And looking happy."

Daisy smiled. "Really! That's wonderful. It's a huge relief to know she did find some happiness in the romance department. I felt so terrible about my dad taking that from her."

"I was relieved, too. But if Lolly was truly involved with this man to the point that they were holding hands, why hasn't he come to see her?"

"You said she's private. Maybe she didn't tell him she was sick? Or *how* sick?"

That sounded like Lolly. "I can't stop picturing her walking down the street with her new guy, holding hands, happy. Coming back from dinner or headed to the movies. I thought she was all alone. But turns out she wasn't."

"We have to find him, Harrison!" Daisy said.

He was so grateful that the despair was out of her eyes, but he didn't know about trying to track down the mystery man.

"But if she didn't tell him she was going into hospice, she clearly didn't want him to know," he pointed out. "Maybe she said her goodbyes in her own way, you know?"

Daisy bit her lip, her expression turning wistful. "Sometimes people think they're saving someone from a heap of trouble and so they don't share their biggest problem or darkest hour. Maybe your aunt didn't want her terminal illness to enter into their happiness. Or maybe she felt they hadn't known each other long enough."

He'd thought about all that at the riverbank earlier. He should have asked the neighbor how long ago she'd seen Lolly with the man. It had to have been before his dad died, since Lolly had taken such a turn for the worse after the funeral and had moved in to Gentle Winds four days later. Harrison had been the only person by Lolly's side at the funeral and later at his dad's house, where they'd welcomed mourners.

When Eric McCord died suddenly from heart trouble, Lolly had been dealing with stage-four cancer for only a few weeks at that point and was not seeking treatment. Perhaps between losing her brother and being so ill herself, she'd turned away from the new love in her life. Harrison had a feeling that was exactly what had happened. But this was all just speculation. Harrison had no idea what had gone on.

He shook his head. "You know what I can't stop thinking about? This new man, being there for her, if only she'd let him. I could just picture him sitting at her bedside, reading from her favorite books or just holding her hand. Bringing her those fuzzy socks she likes. What if he'd want to be there for her? And what if that would actually make her happy?"

"I guess it depends on how she felt about him. But from what you described, it sure sounds like she was in love."

"I can't imagine Lolly holding hands otherwise," he said.

"You'll have to ask her. Go see her now. Maybe she'll be awake."

He glanced down at the floor, then back up at Daisy. It felt strange, poking into his aunt's private life this way. "Or…maybe I should leave it alone. Let her have the happy memories without her illness a part of it. I'll ask her about it, of course. But she's sedated for her comfort and not fully herself." He shook his head. "I don't know. I don't know what's right here."

Daisy put her soft hand on his arm, and he wanted to hold her against him so badly that he had to close his eyes for a moment to squelch the urge. "Maybe you can mention him, that you'd heard she'd been seeing someone, and watch how she reacts. Then go from there. You'll know whether to leave it alone or try to find him."

He nodded, feeling better about the whole thing. "That's exactly what I'll do. I'll go see her tomorrow morning." He stood up again. He wanted to stay. He wanted to go. He mostly wanted to just wrap Daisy in his arms and stay that way all night. But this was getting all out of hand. "But she's often napping. I might just investigate who the guy is on my own and get a sense of whether I should try to find him or not." He headed over to the door, hating to leave her presence.

She followed him to the door. "That's a good idea if you can't ask her about him directly." She tilted her head. "Did you really have enough to eat? You barely had one serving."

I only want you, Daisy, he thought out of nowhere. Which meant he really *should* go.

"Yes," he said, and it was true. "You're a much better cook than you think you are. The stir-fry and rice were delicious."

She smiled and took both his hands. "Thank you." She let go and stepped back, and he supposed that was her version of a hug. There would be no more kissing.

She put her hand on the doorknob, then hesitated. "Let me ask you something, Harrison. Let's say that stupid napkin does hold up in court and you *are* entitled to the ranch. What would you do with it?"

He hadn't even thought about that. "I suppose I'd change the name to the McCord Family Guest Ranch and keep on all the employees. Nothing would change except ownership. Management wouldn't even have to change. I'd be happy to keep Noah on to run the place and Sara as assistant forewoman."

He was getting to know her so well that there was no mistaking the sparks flashing out of her eyes. Barely contained anger.

"Turns out Noah promoted her to foreman— fore*woman*," Daisy said through gritted teeth. "He's going to be more administrative and focus on growth and new programs and initiatives."

"Perfect," he said.

She glared at him. "So that's just hunky-dory to you. All their hard work, all their plans, all their dreams. And you'll just take it away but let them keep their jobs. Aren't you a saint! Give me a flipping break."

Dammit. "I've been honest with you from the start. I intend to take the ranch, as it belongs to my family. No one loses their job, at least."

"Oh, how big of you!" She narrowed her eyes

at him, but now the anger was mixed with frustration and worry.

He hated this. Hated making her feel so awful. This was definitely not what he wanted. "We can't separate like this," he said. "With you angry and upset. Take me on the tour of the ranch. We can talk more."

"About what, exactly? How you'll order a big wrought iron *M* for the gates to replace the *D*? What is there to say, Harrison *McCord*?"

A lot. But what? Right now he didn't know how to smooth things over. They were at an impasse. They always had been.

"My plan is supposed to work!" she yelped.

He smiled. "It is, Daisy. Trust me."

She shoved her long hair behind her shoulders. "No, because if it were working, you wouldn't have just said you still intended to take over the ranch."

"I kissed you. I held you in my arms. Your plan is working."

"That's just straight-up lust," she said with an eye roll. "Please."

He looked directly at her. "No, Daisy. It isn't. I mean, yes, I want you. Clearly. But it's not just about lust."

He could see her trying to surreptitiously study him, read him, tell if he was being honest.

"Fine. Then the plan continues," she said, lifting her chin, her voice a bit uncertain, if he wasn't mistaken.

"Ah, yes," he said, grateful she wasn't kicking him out of her life. "The tour you promised me of the ranch. Tomorrow morning?"

"Tomorrow afternoon. Tomorrow morning I'd like to help you track down Lolly's mystery beau. Sara has the day off and can watch Tony for a few hours. We'll go to Gentle Winds in the morning—with me waiting in the waiting room, of course. If your aunt isn't able to talk, I think we should investigate the guy on our own—ask around Lolly's neighborhood. Maybe we'll run into the neighbor."

He didn't realize how much he wanted her—needed her—by his side for this unexpected detour until she'd proposed the idea of joining him. This was all uncharted territory for him, and he really didn't want to face it alone. "I'd appreciate your help in tracking him down. Lolly might not be able to give us answers."

She gave him a warm smile and squeezed his hand.

She likely thought that finding the boyfriend and hearing how in love his aunt was or had been would mitigate the past and her father's role. But it wasn't just about Lolly and how Bo Dawson had treated her. Bo had cheated Harrison's father. Lied, swindled and made a phony bet when the ranch was a hunk of junk. Besides, Harrison wouldn't ignore his father's wishes. Eric McCord had wanted unfinished business taken care of. Harrison's dad had made that clear.

When did you get this hardened? he wondered. *Bethany's betrayal? Bo Dawson's con job on two of your relatives? Your last two relatives on earth?*

Now there was only one. And soon he'd be the last McCord.

He needed to keep that steel surrounding him, but walking out the door of Daisy's home was among the harder things he'd done lately.

Chapter Nine

"Maybe I should tell Harrison to leave," Daisy said to Sara the next morning.

They were sitting in Daisy's kitchen, having coffee, and it was just past seven thirty. Harrison was picking up Daisy at eight for the trip to Prairie City. Axel had already had his coffee and was helping Noah reconfigure the petting zoo stalls now that they had two llamas and two alpacas. Good thing he wasn't around to listen to her and Sara's conversation, because he'd be really worried about how close Daisy was letting herself get to Harrison.

"To pack his stuff and go home and we'll see

him in court," Daisy added. She wrapped her hands around her mug. Most of her wanted to go with Harrison today. But a piece of her knew she was asking for trouble. What if she let herself really acknowledge how she felt about Harrison? What if she started seeing his point of view about the ranch ownership? What if she found herself trying to talk her brothers into accepting that Dawson Family Guest Ranch truly belonged to the McCords?

She'd tossed and turned last night, grateful to get up with a hungry Tony at 2:30 a.m. She'd sat with him in the glider for a long time after he'd fallen back asleep, wondering how today would go. Wondering what was going to happen in the end. She and her brothers would never, ever give up the ranch—not without one hell of a fight. No matter how Daisy felt about Harrison, the ranch was the Dawsons' property. It *was* the Dawsons. She'd felt better after that, more secure about not warming to Harrison's way of seeing things.

Sara sipped her coffee, the same chocolate-pecan decaf brew Daisy was having. "Yeah, this plan of yours seems to have backfired." Sara shot Daisy a smile. "But at least you're in love."

Daisy's mouth dropped open. She wouldn't go *that* far. Right? "I am not! I just kind of can't stop thinking about him. And his face. Every time I want to hate him, I keep seeing him handing Tony to me, bundled in his blue dress shirt, on the service road. I see the glistening in his eyes, the wonder of what he'd just helped do. I keep seeing *that* Harrison. Why does he have to be so easy to talk to? Everything I say, he *gets*. And every time he gets me, I think about Jacob, who I almost actually married. He never understood anything I said. He'd look at me funny, and I just knew he couldn't make heads or tails out of what I meant about so many things."

Oh God. She really was in love. And she'd just detailed why.

"Uh-oh," Sara said, nodding. "This is dangerous territory."

"I know. Here I was, trying to hit Harrison with the warm fuzzies about me and the family and the ranch. Who got smothered by the warm fuzzies instead? Me. Did I not just get dumped on my wedding day? Is the man who wants to take away our family business the very man I'm head over heels for? What. Is. Wrong. With. Meeeeee?" She dropped her head gently on the table with a little thud and then straightened with a sigh.

"If you're in love, Daisy, Harrison must be wonderful. I know you. I've known you almost all your life. He has to be something special if he's won your heart."

"Aw," Daisy said, squeezing Sara's hand. "What would I do without you to make me feel better about the crazy things I get myself into?"

Sara took a sip of her coffee and smiled. "Hey, I know the feeling. When Noah and I reunited, I should have been super wary of him based on our past. But the minute I was with him on this ranch, it was like I was home. *He* was home."

But Harrison was trying to take *home* away. Daisy didn't know what to do with that truth, that undeniable fact—one Harrison himself kept pointing out at every opportunity. He wasn't hiding it at all. *I will take the ranch. I will see you in court.*

"And thank heavens," Daisy said, shaking off her thoughts about Harrison. "Because I got my BFF back and now you're my sister-in-law."

Sara smiled, and they both looked over at the three bassinets when a fussy cry came from one of the little ones by the window. Annabel and Chance, Sara's twins, were happily gazing straight ahead and Tony was the fusspot, his little face getting red in the cheeks.

Daisy stood and picked up Tony, holding him vertically against her and giving his back little pats. She'd learned his gas face, and yup, a satisfying burp came out. She sat down, loving the soft weight of him in her arms.

"I'm glad to watch my adorable nephew this morning," Sara said.

"I appreciate it. That way I can really focus my attention on Harrison and helping to track down this mystery boyfriend."

Sara finished her coffee and glanced at the clock. It was almost eight. "I hope you find him. I'll be rooting for you two. In both regards. You're both knee-deep in each other's family affairs now."

His family affairs. She'd really have to watch herself. She'd been trying to pull him into her family's history and who they all were so that he'd care about them. Now she would be pulled right into his—and she already cared about Harrison McCord. She just had to remember what was at stake here—her family's livelihood and future.

She looked down at Tony. The ranch was his future. "Maybe I shouldn't go on the search. I'm already too involved, Sara. Now I'll be even more involved." Had it just been days ago that she'd thought being left at the altar and figuring out single motherhood was her biggest problem?

"Look, from what you've said, Harrison is the good guy with a heart and a soul. Your big plan was always a good one, and now you've kind of gotten entwined in his version of the plan—not that I think he has one. I kind of feel like everything that's happening between you two is supposed to be happening, like you're meant to figure this out together. Not as adversaries."

"We can't be friends, though."

Sara gave a wicked smile. "All that hot kissing you told me about means something, Daisy. You're *beyond* friends."

This was insanely confusing. "So I should go with him to Prairie City. And be sucked into his life." She let out a breath. "I do want to help him find his aunt's boyfriend. And not because I want the news of this beau to feel more real for Harrison to make him stop being so angry at my dad. I just want Harrison to have that peace. To know that his aunt's final weeks were filled with love and romance and swinging hands and dates."

"You know why?" Sara asked. "Because you *really* are in love."

Oh Lordy, she already knew that. But now she *really* knew that.

Harrison liked Prairie City, which was still a small town but a bigger small town than most in the area with a bustling two-mile downtown. But the minute he turned onto Main Street, both sides lined with shops and restaurants and businesses, he missed the open wilderness of Bear Ridge and the Dawson ranch.

"Ooh, I love the burritos at that place," Daisy

said, pointing at Burrito Mama. "And not because of the mama solidarity." He glanced at her when she got quiet. "Now I miss Tony."

He smiled. "We'll just take a couple hours tops. Then I'll bring you back home to your little guy."

"Feels weird not to be with him," she said. "Like something is missing."

He stopped for a woman in the crosswalk, a black pug on a bright yellow leash on either side of her. "Like having your heart walk around outside your body. I've heard people say that about parenthood."

She gasped. "That's exactly what it feels like!"

He had no idea, but he could certainly imagine it. She was a devoted mother, and he admired her for it. He admired a lot about her. "Is motherhood like you expected?" he found himself asking. The question hadn't even been in his mind thirty seconds ago, but he wanted to know everything about Daisy. How she felt and what she liked and didn't. What she thought about this and that.

"It's so much more," she said, joy radiating on her beautiful face. "Instant love and so powerful it blows me away a hundred times a day."

"I'll bet," he said. "For a tiny human, Tony sure is something."

Her smile lit up her face. "Right?" She laughed,

and he wanted to kiss her so badly that he had to look away.

"Planning to become a dad one day?" she asked.

He coughed—so unexpected was that question. "Not sure. Sometimes I wonder if I'll ever settle down at all."

"I see it," she said.

"Do you?" He glanced at her before turning his attention back to the road.

"Yup. I believe in you, Harrison McCord."

She did. He felt it in his bones, in his cells.

But if she believed in him, then she also believed he wouldn't take possession of Dawson Family Guest Ranch. So he didn't know what more to say about that. He'd gotten to know Daisy well enough to know she wasn't playing him or saying what she thought he wanted to hear or trying to butter him up with compliments. She was a straight shooter. Earnest.

She believed in him. Why did that mean so damned much to him?

"You were a natural out there on Route 26 when a certain pregnant woman in labor needed help," she said. "So I think you'll make a great dad one day."

He laughed. "A natural? If the 911 operator hadn't told me what to do, I'd have been in a blind panic. I forgot half of what she said, too."

"Well, you did everything right. Doc said so."

"So how's it been?" he found himself asking. "Being a single mother?"

"Honestly? It's hard. Emotionally. Financially. There's no dad to help with anything—but the hardest part of that? No dad to care with me, worry with me, marvel with me. I think I wanted that most of all. Someone who'd feel about Tony the way I feel about him because that person is also his parent."

He hated to think of her struggling in any way. "Well, you're a great mother, Daisy." And that seemed to be very true. Devoted, loving, committed. Tony Dawson had the best of the best.

"Thanks for saying that. I do have great support. I know I'm lucky in that regard."

He smiled. "I was just thinking how lucky Tony is to have you for a mom."

A smile lit up her face again, and he could tell by her expression and body language that she was truly touched by the compliment.

"Your family really seems to stand by each other," he said quickly to douse the intimacy of the moment. "The way your brothers and Sara decked out the nursery. The way Axel helps out Noah on the ranch—at the crack of dawn, too. The way Sara has taken over your duties as guest relations manager in addition to her own work."

"That's family. Always there. And the ones who are not—physically, I mean? I've got plans for them, too." She grinned and rubbed her hands together.

"Ah yes, the matchmaking. When are you having the dinner party for Axel and the woman you think may lure him into staying in Bear Ridge forever?"

Her eyes lit up. "I'm thinking in a few days. I'll ask them both when we get back."

"Well, I'll be there."

"Thanks," she said. "You've certainly been there for me lately, too. Starting with the side of the road."

"You can always count on me, Daisy."

"Don't say something like that when it's not true. You're going to try to take the ranch away from me and my family. I can't count on you."

He frowned and turned his attention back to the road, pulling into a parking space in front of the yoga studio next to his favorite coffee shop. He'd planned to head straight for Gentle Winds, but the coffee in their cafeteria was seriously weak, and he needed the goods right now. "Coffee?" he asked. "I could use an Americano."

She glanced at the logo for Java Jamboree. He could see the wheels turning in her mind, fighting with herself not to tell him off, that they were on a special mission here and to let it go for now. She wanted to scream bloody murder at him, though; he could tell. "Definitely," she said, the subject changed for now. "Decaf iced latte with a mocha swirl for me. Oh, and whipped cream."

Relief hit him that he hadn't started a miniwar after all. "Let's get fortified, then we'll go to Gentle Winds. It's just about a mile from here."

They were in and out of Java Jamboree with their coffees, Daisy sipping her iced latte and lifting her face toward the sun. It was another gorgeous summer morning. Low seventies and bright sunshine.

"I love that fish and chips shop," she said, upping her chin across the street. "Ever been there? They serve everything in a little cardboard boat with newspaper lining. Amazing tartar sauce, too. I used to dream of the tartar sauce when I started my final trimester, and I'd wake up planning to be here the moment the place opened."

"It was my dad's favorite place to go for lunch," he said, staring at the few tables just outside the small restaurant. "It was one of the last places we—" He felt himself getting choked up and couldn't continue speaking. He looked away, his heart throbbing. He missed his father so much.

"I'm so sorry, Harrison," Daisy said, reaching up a hand to his cheek. "I know how badly it hurts."

He squeezed the hand that had been on his face, never wanting to let it go. "I know you do. Times two just like me."

She nodded. "Worst club to be in."

That got a small smile out of him, and he felt the knot of grief loosening a bit. "That's for damned sure."

"Well, should we get going to Gentle Winds?"

He nodded, and they got back in his SUV, driving the mile to the hospice, which was down a side street. The building was warm and welcoming, painted a dusty salmon, and the brick path to the front door was lined with rows of flowers. Lolly's room was on the second floor. They took the elevator, staff and fellow volunteers greeting him as he and Daisy headed down the hall. One nurse stopped him to ask if he was switching up his volunteer shift, noting that he usually came later in the day, and he explained he was just trying to catch his aunt awake. The woman wasn't on Lolly's care team, so she wouldn't know if his aunt was napping or not.

"I didn't know you volunteered here," Daisy said as they continued down the hall.

"Yup. I come every day. Before or after I see my

aunt, I sit with a few patients, read to them, play poker, listen to them share life stories."

"That's really lovely, Harrison."

He stopped in front of room 216. "This is Lolly's room."

"I see the sign for the waiting area up ahead. I'll go there and finish my latte. Take your time if she's awake."

He thought about just having her come in and meeting his aunt, but the last name would throw Lolly off and could upset her; he certainly wouldn't risk that. He'd talk to her about the boyfriend, and then maybe she'd open up some about her past and the situation with Bo Dawson.

"Thanks, Daisy. I'm glad you're here."

She smiled and walked down the hall, disappearing to the right where the waiting room was.

He knocked on the door. No answer. He gently opened it and found Lolly asleep. Her ash-blond hair was in a little ponytail, and her nails were red. Lolly liked her manicures, and the staff often came around for spa treatments. He'd come back this afternoon. There was no real routine to when Lolly was awake. The first two days, she'd been awake and alert in the late afternoons, so he'd continued coming at that time, but then she'd been asleep the next two times. He started coming in the morning before work and found her awake but not consistently. So he tended to just come in at random times and hope for the best.

He stepped back out of the room and gently closed the door behind him, then walked down to the waiting area. "Asleep."

"Let's take a walk in her neighborhood, then," Daisy said, standing up and putting her almost empty cup in the trash can in the corner. "We can knock on the neighbor's door—the one with the dog. And maybe we'll run into the postal worker. We can even go to the post office to talk to him if he's not out delivering."

"I think we should start in her condo," he said. "She's always been a bit old-school and wrote appointments on a magnetic wall calendar on her fridge. Maybe she jotted down the guy's name and the time they were meeting for dates. Or maybe we'll find something with his name and address or phone number on it."

"Does she have a cell phone?" Daisy asked. "You could go through the contacts and see who sounds likely as a friend versus a plumber kind of thing."

"Good idea. She did have one but didn't want to take it to Gentle Winds. It's in her condo."

"Let's go," she said, excitement on her face. "We're so close to finding the mystery beau!"

He wanted to take her hand. That was how

close, how connected to her he felt at the moment. But she started heading to the elevator, and he kept his hands to himself.

Lolly's condo was on the ground floor of a garden apartment–style complex with lush lawns and beautiful garden beds. There were two red doors side by side—identical one-bedroom apartments—Lolly's was on the right. He used his key that his aunt had given him when she'd moved into Gentle Winds. She'd given him permission to go in whenever he might need for whatever reason. He hoped she'd be okay with *this* reason. Was he invading her privacy or about to bring a smile to her face in the last remaining days she had? He'd bet everything he had it was the latter. Yes, Lolly was private and didn't talk much about herself, but Harrison knew his aunt, and he believed she'd be happy to see the gentleman, even if she hadn't set it up so that he could visit her. He had to trust his gut on this.

"Wow, so tidy," Daisy said as they entered a sunlit foyer.

That was Lolly. Spick-and-span. The living room had the usual furnishings and some interesting abstract paintings he'd always liked. He took Daisy on a brief tour of the small place—spotless kitchen, spotless bathroom, spotless bedroom with its blue-and-white quilt and seashells decorating the bureau.

Back in the kitchen, they stood in front of the refrigerator, studying Lolly's magnetic calendar featuring photos of dogs. It was mid-July, and Lolly had been at Gentle Winds for most of the month. Except for a note on July 2 to buy brie and apples, there was nothing else jotted down. He flipped up the page prior, for June, and that was much busier, though he knew Lolly had slowed down a lot last month. His name was all over the calendar, as he'd come over for dinner three times a week. He'd hired a housekeeper to prepare meals and keep the place to Lolly's standards, and a private nurse, who Lolly had adored, had come every day. There were notations about checkups and diagnostic tests, which he'd taken her to. But no male name was anywhere on the calendar at all.

"Maybe she has a planner," Daisy said. "The old-school kind you keep in a purse." She glanced around the kitchen. "There!"

Harrison looked at where she was pointing. A small red leather case sat on a stack of opened mail. He picked it up and unsnapped it. "Bingo." Daisy came over and stood tantalizingly close to peer at the pages. He could smell her shampoo.

He flipped back to June.

Robert, coffee at Java Jamboree. Robert, din-

ner. Robert, gallery hopping. Robert, movies—
talk him into the rom-com and not the thriller.
Robert, dinner and theater. Robert, dinner. Robert, walking tour.

The entrance of Robert into her life seemed
to start in early June. The first entry was coffee.

"We found our mystery man!" Daisy said, her
blue eyes shining.

"Robert." Harrison flipped to the start of the
planner, which had an address/phone section. He
went through page by page until he found Robert
Chang—with not only home and cell numbers but
an address. Yes! He was the only Robert there, so
it had to be him.

He added the contact info into his phone. "Now
what, though? Do I really call him without talking to Lolly first?"

Daisy bit her lip. "Harrison, I lost both my parents. Both to car accidents, almost twenty years
apart. With my mom, there was no time for goodbyes. With my dad, the six of us just made it to the
hospital from where we were scattered across the
state. Axel had been up a mountain, and a chopper
flew him over and he got there five minutes before
our dad passed away. One of the last things my father said was, *You're all here.* And he said it while
sobbing with such surprise on his face. He left this

world knowing that no matter what, we cared, we were there for him. That means so much to me."

He was already so close to her that he put his arms around her before he could tell himself not to. She relaxed against him for just a moment.

"I'm okay," she said, but he could see she was feeling emotional. "I'm really going to need those fish and chips after this."

He smiled. "We'll definitely go before we leave Prairie City." The fish and chips shop would remind him of his dad, of his whole reason for going to Bear Ridge and booking Cabin No. 1, and suddenly that was both good and bad. He liked the good memories called up by being in places he and his dad had frequented. But now the reinforcement of his dad's final words, to get back what was rightfully his, was beginning to feel like a fifty-brick load on his chest.

She stepped back, and he missed having her in his arms immediately. "Well, here's what I think. We don't know why Lolly didn't tell Robert Chang she was sick or let him know she was at the hospice. Hey, for all we know, she *did* tell him, and he dumped her. Maybe he's a total jerk. We don't know anything. So let's find out. Lolly often isn't able to talk, so let's just ask him."

"I'll call and explain who I am and ask if we

could meet to talk about Lolly. I'll see how it goes from there."

"Perfect," she said.

As they left Lolly's condo, the woman who must live in the apartment right next door was on her knees in front of a patch of soil, pretty yellow flowers in little green containers at her side. Lolly had mentioned she had new neighbors a couple months ago, but Harrison hadn't met the middle-aged couple or their teenage twins.

"That's not the neighbor who visited Lolly," he whispered.

The woman turned at the noise and stood up, dusting off her hands. "Are you Lolly's family?"

"I'm her nephew, Harrison, and this is my friend Daisy." He knew Daisy didn't consider them friends, but they *were* whether she liked it or not.

"After a week of not seeing Lolly, I figured she was on vacation, and then when I saw our mail-woman, I asked her if Lolly was away, and she told me the bad news. I'm so sorry."

"Thank you," Harrison said. "Sounds like she barely told anyone she was sick, let alone that she was going into hospice."

"My own aunt was like that. Didn't want a soul to know or worry."

Harrison glanced at Daisy, then back at the

neighbor. "Did you happen to see her with a man in June? She was dating someone."

"Oh yes, I saw them a few times holding hands—the last time about two weeks ago. A couple times when we ran into each other here, she'd mention she was just getting home from gallery hopping or dinner or the movies with her significant other. She always had such a gleam in her eye when she said that." The woman smiled.

Huh. Lolly and Robert had been holding hands as late as two weeks ago, Lolly referring to him as her significant other. Something told him she'd broken up with him when they'd gotten the news Eric had died, followed quickly by Lolly taking a turn for the worse and knowing she'd have to go into hospice. Why she'd denied herself the comfort of having him at her bedside was for Lolly to say. But Harrison definitely wanted to talk to Robert.

"It was nice to meet you," Harrison said. "Thank you for the information."

The woman smiled and resumed her gardening. Harrison and Daisy got back into the SUV, and he told her his theory—that Lolly had turned away from everyone, perhaps not to worry them or to need anyone. The doctors and nurses hadn't been able to explain why she slept quite so much, and now Harrison knew why. Because she was sad.

Plain and simple. She'd closed herself off to avoid causing others heartache.

Oh, Lolly.

Daisy had tears in her eyes. "I think you're right about that. It's almost as if she broke her own heart to save his."

"I'm going to call him right now." He pulled out his phone, hoping he was doing the right thing by Lolly *and* this total stranger. He truly believed he was.

Harrison tapped in the numbers and waited. But the phone rang and rang, and voice mail picked up. "Hello, you've reached Robert Chang. I'm away for the next ten days, back on the twenty-second, and will return your call then."

The twenty-second was the day after tomorrow. *Please let us have that long*, he sent heavenward, then left a detailed voice mail for Robert.

He put his phone away and explained to Daisy about the voice mail messages. And the necessary wait.

"At least he didn't just leave today. We just have to wait two days. Let's go get fish and chips. You can help me plan the dinner party to find true love for Axel. I've never felt more like matchmaking than right now."

He knew what she meant. The story of Lolly

and Robert seemed a really beautiful thing. Love was in the very air.

Even he felt it. He stared at Daisy for a moment, taking in her long, honey-blond hair and blue eyes, the beauty mark on the side of her left eye. He had to fall out of love with her immediately.

Then he remembered they were going to Franny's Fish and Chips, his dad's favorite restaurant in Prairie City. Everything about Franny's reminded him of his father. And when he thought about his father, he thought about his final wishes. The bet. Taking the Dawson ranch. Bo Dawson's crappy treatment of Lolly.

Spending thirty minutes in that small restaurant would do a lot toward reminding him what his real purpose was. And it wasn't to fall in love with Bo Dawson's daughter.

Chapter Ten

As Daisy looked over the menu in Franny's Fish and Chips, she thought she should probably be past intense pregnancy cravings, but she wasn't. Ever since she'd spotted the restaurant earlier, she'd been imagining the fried catfish sandwich and Franny's amazing, creamy coleslaw she'd soon be enjoying. She ordered exactly that. Harrison went for the fried haddock and french fries, and hopefully he wouldn't mind when she swiped a few.

"What's Lolly like?" she asked when the waiter took their menus and left. "I know you said she was private, but what else? I'm trying to figure out what Robert Chang might be like."

"She always surprised me," Harrison said. "Overall she tended to be on the reserved side, didn't like to stand out, but then she'd come out with a hilarious joke or show up for lunch wearing a bright pink jacket or huge dangling earrings. So she can definitely be a little unpredictable. She's smart, kind, crazy about animals and loves old movies, particularly anything starring Bette Davis. I always had a great time whenever we got together."

She could easily see the sadness that passed over his expression. His aunt Lolly was the only family he had left. "Well, I can see why Robert Chang fell for her. She sounds wonderful. Eclectic."

"I'd like you to meet her," he said, then quickly took a long drink of his iced tea as if he hadn't meant to say that. "I don't know if you should—I mean, based on what you said before about your last name and the connection to Bo and if the memories will upset her."

Daisy gave something of a nod. Harrison was important to her—of course she wanted to meet his dear aunt. But because of this cold-case situation between their fathers, everything was a mess. And up in the air. Daisy hated *up in the air*. "I wish I could meet her. But I don't want to stir up any heartache. Especially not when she'll be reunited with Robert."

"I have a good feeling about inviting Robert to

visit her," he said. "On one hand setting this all up feels weird, but on the other hand, it feels right. It feels *necessary*."

Like you, she thought unbidden, wondering where the hell that had come from. But it was true. He had become necessary. She was in love with the man, trouble or not. Future heartbreak or not, and she had no doubt this was going to get messy. At some point, he'd demand they turn over the ranch. And they weren't about to. Not without a court order.

How could this possibly end well?

Ugh. Now her appetite was disappearing. Luckily, the moment the waiter set down the plates, which smelled so good, her cravings came roaring back and she could hardly wait to take a bite of her sandwich.

"What was your dad's favorite thing to order here?" she asked. Gulp. Maybe that was a mistake. Should she bring up his dad, who'd hated her dad? Whose final wishes were to right the wrong done to him? And to Lolly?

"Every time we came here, he ordered something different. He always got a basket of fries for the table—the fries here are too irresistible not to—but he always ordered a different entrée and a different side."

Daisy smiled. "I love that. Adventurous. My

dad was a creature of habit. Same beer. Same burger joint. He had a favorite Mexican restaurant, too, and went there a few times a week."

Harrison smiled and swiped a fry in ketchup. "I can be like that, too. Tried and true."

"Some people just know what they like," she said.

He held her gaze for a few seconds.

"Can I have a fry?" she asked. "And by a fry, I mean a few."

He laughed. "Help yourself. They definitely give you a ton here."

She heaped a small pile on her plate and dipped a fry into the spicy mayo that came on the side of every plate. "Heavenly," she said.

He glanced up at her. "My dad used to say that while dragging his fries through that very mayo. He loved that mayonnaise and tried to make it at home but never got the proportions right. He'd learned to ask for a few little containers of it to go, and they always obliged. When he was in the hospital right before…" He trailed off and looked down at his plate.

"I'm so sorry, Harrison. I know how much it hurts." She reached across the table and took his hand.

He cleared his throat and pulled his hand away, ostensibly to take a drink of his iced tea, but she could tell he needed some distance. "I went to his condo to pack a bag for him, and there were three containers of the mayo in the fridge. I admit, I broke down. We'd just been here the day before."

"What happened?"

"We were on our way to a cardiologist, actually—just a few blocks from here. My dad had been complaining of chest pain the past few days, and I insisted he ask for an emergency appointment. He grabbed his chest right in the middle of the sidewalk just a block from the medical office. An ambulance came and took him to the ER instead, his doctor hurrying over. He was admitted and monitored, in dire condition."

Her eyes were glistening. "You didn't leave his bedside."

Harrison shook his head. "No, and my aunt was there often, in tears. The final morning, very early, around three or four, Lolly went to get the two of us coffee. We'd been up all night keeping vigil, and that's when my dad told me the story of the bet and Bo Dawson and Lolly."

Daisy glanced down at her plate, willing herself not to burst into tears.

He clearly realized that. "I'm sorry, Daisy," he said, his voice soft. "You're just very easy to talk to, you know?"

She gave a little smile. "I could say the same

about you. Makes me tell you too much." She took a breath and looked at him. "Did you lose your dad right after that?"

"Couple hours. I was seeing red over the bet and the ranch. I kept hearing him say, 'That ranch belongs to us. Get it back.' And that's been burning in my gut ever since."

She suddenly understood how he must feel right now. Sitting in the restaurant that represented his father to him. With Bo Dawson's daughter. Pulled into her grand plan to stop him from fulfilling his dad's dying request.

Daisy could not feel more like dog doo.

But this was not her fault. It wasn't her brothers' fault. The ranch did not belong to the McCords because of a drunken bet. There was supposed to have been a punch in the face—a stupid punch, and it would have ended right there. But it had escalated—Eric McCord insisting on upping the stakes. And so Bo had bet the fallen-down ranch.

There was no way she could say that. Certainly not right now when Harrison's grief was palpable. Bo hadn't been the best dad in the world, and they certainly hadn't been close. His death had still knocked her upside the head, the sorrowful pain of it still catching her to this day, several months later. But from everything Harrison had told her about Eric McCord, he had been dad of the year, they'd been very close and Harrison had just lost him a little over two weeks ago.

She knew his grief was at work in his determination to take ownership of the ranch. Maybe she should just back off from even talking about it? Harrison would need time—deserved time. She of all people knew that.

She stared at her fries for a moment. She wanted Harrison to have what he needed, but what he needed was to make everything okay for his family, to avenge the swindle, and that was something she'd fight him on with every ounce of strength she had.

"You okay?" he asked.

The voice and looking up at his face changed everything. What she and Harrison had, if they had anything, was between them and had nothing to do with the past or her father or his. Something truly special had come out of something hard. It had started on that roadside, and it had blossomed from there without either of them able to stop it. Because it was that strong.

Given how they'd kissed yesterday, that she was sitting right here with him, on this quest to find his aunt's boyfriend, listening to him talk about his father and losing him, Daisy knew she wasn't alone in what she felt.

But what were they going to do about it? He

couldn't walk away from the ranch. How could he? Let his father's last request go unfulfilled? The way he saw it, the ranch really did belong to his father. And despite how he might feel about her and how unfair it was from the Dawson point of view...

She shivered in her seat, the air-conditioning suddenly giving her goose bumps. What was she going to do?

"I'm okay," she lied, picking up a fry she had no appetite to eat.

"No, you're not, and neither am I."

She smiled, and he reached his hand across the table.

"Whaddaya say we get home to Tony," he said, and she watched him stiffen.

Daisy herself was frozen in place for a second.

"I mean get you home and me to my cabin," he rushed to add. "Home being the ranch for the next few days for me."

She held on to his hand. "We really are in trouble, Harrison. Let's just call it out. We've got a problem." They knew what it was, and there was no need to talk about it.

"Yeah, we do."

"You like me and I like you," she said.

He nodded. "Yup."

Except for her it went much further than *like*.

* * *

Neither said much on the drive back to Bear Ridge. Daisy called Sara to let her know they'd be back in about twenty minutes, and Sara reported that Tony had been a perfect gentleman the whole time and had spent a lot of his waking hours staring at his comical cousins having their tummy time or in their baby swings. Daisy couldn't wait to get home to see him and hold him and take care of him. She'd missed him so much these past five hours.

When they drove through the gates of the ranch, she waved at Carly, the greeter in the welcome station, which was a hunter-green shed full of creature comforts so Carly wouldn't get bored. Noah liked having a receptionist of sorts at the gate, and so did guests, who always mentioned in their comments online about the ranch that they always felt safe and comfortable coming and going, because someone was always there during business hours (which in ranch terms were seven to seven).

Finally, they'd arrived at the farmhouse. Daisy was glad Harrison didn't turn off the engine and make any moves to come in; they clearly both needed a breather from that whopper of a lunch, some time to think. "How's around six o'clock for the tour of the ranch?" he asked.

Did she even have a tour in her? She wasn't

sure. But she did like the idea of having plans with him. "See you then."

He looked relieved. They were two peas, that was for sure.

She dashed up the porch steps and turned to watch him drive down the road toward the guest cabins. She closed her eyes for a second and sucked in some air, then ran inside.

"Where's my precious boy?" she called out. One was outside driving away—another was in this house.

Sara came into the foyer with a big smile, Tony in her arms. Her sister-in-law carefully transferred him to Daisy.

She could see Annabel and Chance having more tummy time on play mats, each gurgling and happy. "How do you make taking care of three babies look this easy?"

Sara grinned. "Oh, trust me, I had help all morning. Axel was here for a good hour and a half, then Noah came over and we took all three tots for a walk." Her phone pinged, and she pulled it from her back pocket. "Noah. He's waiting for me at our cabin. He's going to be on twin duty while I get back to work."

Just as Sara and the twins were leaving, Axel came in. Which reminded Daisy of the dinner party—that whole thing had gone right out of her head today. And she wanted to keep this plan of hers at the forefront. If she was trying to keep Axel in town, it meant she wasn't putting much stock in the ranch getting swiped out from under them.

Was she delusional? Ignoring reality? Being a total fool? Maybe.

But when Harrison was talking about his dad today, it reinforced how important, how special, family was. Two Dawsons had unexpectedly come home to the ranch to stay. There was a chance for a third right now. How could she not take it and run with it?

With three here, maybe the three scattered across the state would look at the idea differently.

As Axel came over making peekaboo faces at Tony, whom she was holding, she realized a last-minute, very casual invitation to a dinner party would work more in her favor to get a yes out of Axel than some long-planned event. Then she'd just have to pray that Hailey was mysteriously free tomorrow. She knew Hailey was a bit of a home-body when she wasn't working, so there was a good chance.

"Axel, I thought I'd have a few people over to-morrow night," she said. "I'm making my spe-cialty—honey-garlic stir-fry and that delicious rice you love. You'll be there, right?"

"I do love that stir-fry. Count me in." *She* loved

that he didn't ask who else was coming. That was Axel. He wouldn't much care who'd be there. Her brother wasn't exactly a people person. He was a wilderness person. *Like Hailey*, she thought with a happy, inward smile.

Axel made funny faces at Tony, played another few rounds of peekaboo and then told Daisy he was heading upstairs for a shower before helping out with the horseback riding lessons in the main pasture by the big barn. He sure did seem to like working on the ranch, even if he viewed it as temporary.

Maybe *because* he viewed it as temporary.

All she knew was that she had a yes out of him for dinner tomorrow. Now she just needed Hailey to say the same.

She put Tony in his bassinet and grabbed her phone. *Please don't have plans*, she prayed as she dialed. Hailey worked part-time at the ranch but wasn't scheduled to work today.

"Hi, Hailey, it's Daisy Dawson. I'm having a few people over for dinner tomorrow night, and I'd love if you could come."

"Is this a fix up?" Hailey asked on a laugh.

"Is it okay if it is?" *Please say yes. Please say yes.*

"Does it involve your gorgeous brother Axel?" Hailey asked.

"He'll be there. You two sure have a lot in common. He's a search-and-rescue specialist. You lead wilderness tours. You could talk about trails and mountain cliffs for hours, I'll bet."

She was reminded of something Noah once told her when she tried to fix him up with someone years ago, a woman who was a cowgirl through and through like Noah was a cowboy. *Just because you have everything in common doesn't mean you'll have a lick of chemistry. And it's the chemistry that counts.*

He'd turned out to be right about the cowgirl, but Daisy later figured out the real problem with Noah and all the women he'd dated back when was that none of them was Sara, who'd always been the love of his life, even though they'd been apart for years before finally reuniting this past May.

Still, having something big in common had to help with conversation. So she was keeping a very positive view of her matchmaking notions.

Hailey laughed. "I hate fix ups, but I have to say, I have noticed Axel. He's hard to miss."

Axel was a good-looking guy, that was for sure. "I'll see you tomorrow at seven," Daisy said and pocketed her phone. She picked up Tony from his bassinet and gave a triumphant spin. Not only was Hailey free, but she was totally into the setup! Yee-haw!

Axel, you'll soon be madly in love and building that fancy log cabin.

Of course, there might be technical difficulties with that last bit, but right now, that was the fairy tale she had in her head, so she was going with it and forgetting all about where Enemy Hot Stuff fit in.

She had a real chance here for Axel to see that the ranch was part of him, that Bear Ridge didn't have to be about the past, but about the future.

If only she could get that through to the guy she was crazy about in Cabin No. 1.

There was a knock on the door, and Daisy went to see who it was.

"Tessa, hi," Daisy said, noting that the pretty newlywed looked much happier than the last time they'd spoken. Her red cat's-eye sunglasses were atop her head, holding her dark hair off her face. "I was hoping to run into you to ask how things were going."

"Thanks to your advice—a lot better. Tom and I really needed to sit down and talk, put everything out on the table. He doesn't like some of what I had to say. And I didn't like some of what he had to say. But we're working through it. So thanks."

"I'm really happy to hear that, Tessa." Hmm, maybe she should invite Tessa and Tom to the dinner party. An extra couple would make it seem truly more like a dinner party and less like a double date, she just realized. And the Monellos were in a good place. "I'm having a small dinner party here tomorrow night at seven. I'd love to have you and Tom join us."

Tessa beamed. "That would be great! Tom could really use some exposure to older people with life experience."

Hey! Daisy was thirty, not a hundred!

"Great," Daisy said. "See you here at seven. I'm making a stir-fry. Come hungry!"

Tessa smiled and practically skipped away, and Daisy felt good about the invitation. She'd helped a young couple with their love. She'd help her brother *find* love. And as far as she and Harrison were concerned, she wasn't going to think about it.

"I don't know what's going to happen with us or that dumb napkin," she said to Tony, giving him a gentle rock as she moved over to the windows and looked out down the hill toward the cabins. She couldn't see them through the thick cover of trees, but she liked knowing Harrison was down there, probably sitting on the love seat in his cabin and thinking the same thoughts she was.

Namely what they were going to do about their crazy feelings for each other.

Chapter Eleven

"So you've seen the main house," Daisy said as she and Harrison stood in front of it later that night. Harrison was here for his tour, and he was jumping out of his skin. There was so much to say—again—about so much, but neither of them was saying it or wanted to. He had this need, this almost aching desire to be near her, so he'd just focus on that. Actually, scratch that. He shouldn't focus on that.

A mess. This was one hell of a mess.

"Ooh, there's that twinge again," Daisy said, rubbing at her lower back. "I don't know what the heck happened. I bent down to pet Dude earlier and got this little wrenching feeling."

"Uh-oh," Harrison said. "When that happens to me, it can mean a few days of soreness. But you did just have a baby, Daisy. I can drive you to the doc—"

"Eh, I'll hold off for a bit and see how I feel. But talk about great timing. I've got a baby in a carrier strapped to my torso and a dinner party tomorrow night. I'll be bending and twisting every which way getting pots and pans and stuff from the fridge and cabinets tomorrow."

"Tell you what," he said. "Let's start by you putting that contraption on me." He pointed at Tony. "I know he doesn't weigh much, but still."

"Really, you wouldn't mind? Tony loves the carrier, being all snuggly next to a warm, beating heart."

"I don't mind at all." Actually, he wasn't sure about this idea of his, but he'd offered, and now he'd have a baby—Daisy's baby—*this close* to his chest. His beating heart. Which was already too affected by both of them.

She plucked Tony out of the carrier and carefully gave him to Harrison, wincing a bit from the movements. Then while Harrison held Tony awkwardly along one arm, Daisy managed to get the carrier strapped to him, giving it a good yank to make sure it was all latched in place. Then she slid Tony back inside. He glanced down at the little

profile. Tony seemed quite content, the little bow
lips quirking, his eyes closing.

"Next step," he said, "run inside and take two
pain relievers. Maybe we should cancel the tour
and you should just rest up."

"Nah. A sore back isn't gonna keep me down. I
got through three months of awful morning sickness. I can take a little twingey pain here and there.
But I will go take some ibuprofen."

She gingerly walked up the porch steps, one
hand rubbing at her lower back. It didn't escape
him that he wished he could take her aches and
pains away.

He looked down at the baby, putting one hand
against the back of the carrier. "This is a first,"
he whispered to Tony. "And I can't say I ever expected to be wearing an infant on my chest, but
here you are."

A surge of…something gripped him in the re-
gion of his heart. Protectiveness? He cared about
Tony Dawson. Of course he did. He'd helped at his
birth. This baby would always be special to him.
But the feeling, the sensation was more than just
protectiveness.

"Everything I figured would happen once I met
your mother has gone topsy-turvy," he added to
the baby. "Days before I ever met you on the side
of that road, I thought I'd sit your mom and uncle

down, tell them what's what, show them the proof and then be on my way—temporarily. I figured I'd be in for a fight. There'd be court involved. And then I'd win and that would be that. Well, a few steps before 'that would be that' haven't exactly worked out like I thought. For instance, I never did get on my way, did I? I'm still here."

Holding you.

Crazy about your mother.

Crazy about this ranch. Simply because it's truly special.

His big mouth had Tony's eyes fluttering open, so Harrison swayed a bit to the left and right to rock the baby back to his nap.

"Your mommy has a backache," he whispered even though he was supposed to let the tot fall back asleep and stop yammering to him. "Do you know who gives great massages? Me. Should I tell her that? I don't know. That probably isn't the best idea." Touching Daisy, intensely kneading her lower back, might drive him off the edge. "We'll see how things go, right, Tony? That's often the answer to everything."

Daisy came down the porch steps. "The meds should kick in soon. Follow me, sir," she said, sweeping her arm out toward the big barn about a quarter mile down the path. "Your tour begins."

They nodded hello and waved to various guests,

some on horseback, some at the petting zoo, the mother and daughter, whose names he forgot, headed toward the creek with fishing gear.

"My dad used to take me and Noah fishing a lot," Daisy said, "and whichever older brother might be around, usually Zeke, who was the last to stop wanting to come at all for weekend visits."

There were so many Dawsons, he forgot who was who. "Zeke—is he the business guy or the one who won't say exactly what he does for a living?"

Daisy smiled. "We truly have zero clue what Zeke's job is. He'll only say it's 'sort of classified,' whatever that means. Government spy?"

"Maybe so. You never know."

"*That* is the truth. You never do." She glanced in the direction of the mother and daughter carrying their gear—poles and tackle boxes. "Our dad would bring us to the creek with our fishing poles—homemade ones. We had real fishing poles once, but one day they all disappeared, and Noah was pretty sure Bo sold them, but he never fessed up to that. So we used whatever cast-off odds and ends we found on the ranch that would make a good substitute, added the bait, and one of us would always get a bite. Sometimes it took a couple hours."

"That's a lot of waiting around for one person to get one fish," he said.

Daisy nodded. "That was back before my dad turned a corner—the wrong way, I mean. He was still halfway attentive and we just wanted his time, you know?"

Harrison knew. His father had been almost too attentive, always wanting to go to the mini golf course or go fishing or take in a game at the local university. Eric McCord liked listening to Harrison talk about what was going on in his life—school, college, work, women. And despite all that attention, Harrison couldn't get enough time with his dad. Eric McCord had been Harrison's favorite person on earth.

"It's amazing how forgiving you are," Harrison said. "You didn't forget, but you did forgive."

"Well, you have to, really, for your own peace of mind," she said. "My dad had some good qualities, and in the end, the very end, he made sure we knew he loved us and cared about us, even if he hadn't always shown it."

"With the letters he left you all," Harrison said. He remembered Daisy talking about them. "He left you your mother's rings."

She nodded. "And he left Sara, his foreman's daughter, her mother's garden plot behind the foreman's cabin. Sara and Noah weren't even speaking at that point, not that my dad would have known that. But Bo Dawson thought of his old foreman's daughter who'd lost her mother at a young age, and he bequeathed her that garden bed."

"Did he keep up the garden?"

Daisy laughed. "You can't be serious."

"Well, it sounded possible based on what you were saying. But yeah, given the condition of the ranch ten years ago, according to my father, your dad didn't keep up anything on this place."

"More like he was a one-man wrecking crew." She shook her head. "I really just want to remember the good stuff at this point. He was kind in the end. That's what I want to focus on."

"He made amends for you," Harrison realized aloud. "Same for your brothers?"

"For Noah, definitely. My dad turned Noah's entire life around without even realizing it. Noah had been following in Bo's footsteps until we inherited this place and my dad's letter to Noah asked him to rebuild the ranch."

He glanced at Daisy. She'd told him this before, but now he had a lot more context for the information, and he understood what a big deal it must have been on many levels. "Sort of like your father's trust and faith in him gave him purpose?"

"And helped him forgive," Daisy said. "Noah let go of a lot. And my other brothers and I wanted to help Noah, so we all rallied around the idea of rebuilding the ranch. Having a reopening. Giving my grandparents back their hard work and us the legacy they'd meant to leave us with."

And now she was working on bringing all her brothers home. Part of him—a huge part—wanted her to succeed. Part of him—the part still very focused on his father's last request of Harrison— knew she wasn't going to.

Something in his chest twisted, and now it was him wincing. How could he do that to Daisy?

But how could he avoid it?

Move along, he told himself. *Change the subject in your head.* He looked at the big red barn, the wrought iron weather vane with its rooster on top. There were sheep in one pasture and goats in another. Farther down, at the stables, he could see a ranch hand going down the line of half-open stalls, giving each horse an apple slice.

"Ranch tradition?" Harrison asked, nodding up ahead.

Daisy smiled. "Yup. They get their apples two times a week and carrots two times a week. For dealing with city slickers and people who'd never been on a horse."

"The stories the horses could tell," he said. He could just imagine.

"Yup. So I'm glad they can't talk. But we keep a very careful eye. Even when our guests are out riding, a couple of us are always patrolling for their safety, and the horses', too."

Tony let out a little whine, and they stopped walking to see what was up with the little guy.

"Maybe someone needs a back rub," he said, giving the baby pats through the material of the carrier.

"Yeah, me," she said, giving her own back a rub. "It's a little better, but I can still feel a knot."

Let me at it, he thought. Maybe when they got back to her house, he'd suggest it.

Tony let out a burp, and they both laughed.

"You're pretty good at this," she said, stepping closer to peer at Tony.

"No one is more surprised than me. But Tony and I have a bond, right, buddy?" he said to the baby.

He felt her looking at him, and he kept his gaze straight ahead, once again worried he'd said the wrong thing. Or the right thing. Because if they had a bond, he couldn't possibly take away Tony's future, Tony's legacy, Tony's family history.

"I had my first kiss right behind that little barn," she said, pointing up ahead at the lemon-yellow structure that housed the petting zoo animals. He'd never been so grateful for a change of subject. Out front, in a large pen, a bunch of little goats were grazing, and some were standing on stumps, the youngest guests staring in awe and giggling. "We were both thirteen and so awkward. His name was Charlie, and I was nuts about him. We were a couple for a whole two and a half weeks in eighth grade. He became a fancy state legislator and didn't even acknowledge me when I passed him in town a few months ago. Snob."

"Considering your kisses are unforgettable, he clearly is a snob. Hopefully he'll be voted out next term."

Daisy laughed, then bit her lip and turned to look directly at him. "I haven't been able to forget kissing you, either. I've tried, too. Hard."

"Yeah, same here."

"That's probably why we're getting so close," she said. "We're going through the same thing. Badum-ch!" she added, slapping her thigh. "Not that it's a joke," she added quite seriously. "It's true."

"I know," he said, wanting to take her in his arms more than anything. Luckily, he had a baby against his chest who'd get squished, so he'd keep his hands to himself.

She took a breath and glanced around, then pointed at the gate to the small barn. "Oh—and right here, Skippy Peterman asked me to the junior prom. I was also nuts about him."

"What did Skippy Peterman end up being?" he asked.

"A big-animal veterinarian. That's all he ever wanted to be from the time he could talk."

"And what did young Daisy Dawson want to be?"

She shrugged. "I was always so envious when friends would talk about their dreams and plans. I had no idea what I wanted to do with my life. I guess I just fell into jobs, and none of them really interested me. Once I even worked as a research assistant for a private investigator in Prairie City. You wouldn't believe half of what his clients hired him to do. One guy in the middle of an awful divorce wanted to find his old girlfriend from middle school, and we thought, *this is not going to end well.* We found the woman, and she couldn't even remember the client. She was happily married with four kids."

"What was your favorite job?" he asked as they continued walking past the petting zoo.

"You might not believe this, but it was being a ranch hand here. My grandparents hired me at one dollar an hour when I was seven—their rate for grandchildren depended on age. Every year I got a dollar raise. My first job was mucking out the sheep pen, and I adored those furry bleating creatures so much that I was happy to care for them."

"So you didn't keep on being a hand?"

She shook her head. "When I turned eighteen,

it was just me, Noah, who was sixteen, and my dad left on the ranch. I wanted to escape, get away from my father. I felt so terrible leaving Noah here, but he was so rough around the edges back then I guess I wanted to get away from him, too." She frowned, and her eyes got misty. "I thought college would give me options, but I just floundered. Want to know a secret? I didn't even graduate."

He stopped walking, and so did she. He reached up a hand to her face. "Jobs don't make you who you are, Daisy. Neither does a degree. You're one of the finest people I've ever met."

"Why do you have to be damned nice and always say the right thing?" she asked, a small smile finally appearing on her beautiful face.

"Just comes easy with you. And I mean everything I say."

The smile faded some. He knew she was thinking about how he'd said, multiple times, that he intended to fight for the ranch.

"Well, you've gotten half the grand tour of the ranch, Harrison. I should go lie down, rest my weary back."

"And you want some space," he said.

She nodded.

"I'll walk you home and put Tony in his bassinet for you so you don't have to bend."

"I appreciate that."

They turned around and started heading back toward the main house. Both were quiet, Daisy lifting up her face to the sun, Harrison's mind churning in many directions. He was so aware of the baby against his chest, of the woman beside him.

"Oh no, there goes Hermione again," Daisy said, pointing up toward where the land sloped to a hill. A brown-and-white goat was practically galloping from the pasture. "She keeps getting away, despite how strong Noah makes the enclosure."

"She sure is fast." He glanced down at Tony's sleeping face. "Hey, Tony, you're missing the runaway goat. It's like a cartoon in front of your eyes."

Daisy laughed. "Did I ever tell you that a runaway goat is why Axel became a search-and-rescue specialist?"

"Nope," he said. "I would have remembered that." Harrison pictured tall, muscular Axel Dawson and his brooding stare while giving Harrison the evil eye. Only one Dawson didn't want to chase *him* off the ranch. Make that two. Tony liked having Harrison around.

"When Axel was around eight years old, maybe nine," Daisy said as they continued to walk, "his favorite goat ran off, just like Hermione. Back then, my grandparents would let us name the baby goats, and part of our jobs was to care for the goat we named. So Axel named Flash, and that reddish-gold goat was as good as his name and took off so fast one night when a kid guest left the pen open that no one could catch him. Axel saw it happen and ran after him, but Flash was gone up in the hills toward Clover Mountain."

"Please tell me this ends well," Harrison said. "I need one happy ending."

Daisy smiled. "No spoilers. Well, my grandparents were older then and couldn't go traipsing after Flash. And my dad was the cowboy on duty that night, so he wasn't supposed to leave, but he called in one of the ranch employees and paid him a small fortune to cover for him. My dad took Axel up into the hills and into Clover Mountain, and after two hours of looking, there was no sign of Flash."

Uh-oh, Harrison thought. "So it doesn't end well?"

"Hey, I said no spoilers! Well, there are lots of foxes and coyotes on the mountain, and my dad was sure Flash was gone for good. But they'd dressed right for the trip, both had their fleece hoodies and hats with the headlamps, and Flash's favorite treats, peaches and sunflower seeds to lure him, so they weren't leaving the mountain without the goat—no matter what. Now this was about twenty-three, twenty-four years ago, and we didn't have cell phones. So there was no way to get in touch with my dad. When they weren't back by midnight, my grandfather called the sheriff for help, and the sheriff called his brother, who was a search-and-rescue specialist."

"For that mountain specifically?" Harrison asked.

"Nah, Clover Mountain's summit isn't very far to hike, but there are a lot of twisty trails. Gramps was afraid my dad might have been drinking, despite saying he hadn't, and gotten hurt, leaving little Axel to fend for himself. But the sheriff's brother got a team and went up into the mountain, and guess what they found?"

He grimaced. "Please tell me they found your father, your brother and Flash all sitting around a campfire, roasting marshmallows and telling ghost stories."

Daisy grinned. "Not quite. But—turns out that about halfway up the mountain, Flash had gotten himself trapped on a ledge that they couldn't get to. Axel, only eight, was a wreck. Axel refused to leave the goat, so my dad said they'd wait it out, that help would eventually come, since that was the Dawson way. And finally, at one thirty in the morning, the cavalry arrived. The sheriff's brother used a special pulley thing to get Flash onto the trail. Axel gave Flash a piece of peach and threw his arms around him, then hugged my dad, then the search-and-rescue guy, then the sheriff, who wasn't too happy about having to climb even an easy mountain at that hour."

Harrison threw his hands up. "Thank you, Universe, for the happy ending."

Daisy laughed. "Well, when they got to their vehicles, the sheriff radioed in and had someone call my grandmother, who was beside herself. And we were all awake and waiting when the trucks came in, Flash leaping out on his lead. My gramps strengthened that pen, and Flash never did get away again. And that's why Axel became a search-and-rescue guy. Because he never forgot how he felt when Flash was lost. Or when people cared that he was. And when people rescued him."

He stopped by the porch steps. "I'm glad for Flash and for Axel and for all of you." He thought of the photo he'd seen of Bo Dawson, a tall and rangy cowboy in a Stetson, with a way-too-easy smile and flashing blue eyes, and imagined him parking himself on the mountain at midnight after hours of searching for the goat because his eight-year-old son was sobbing over the idea of leaving Flash there to get eaten by a coyote while they went for help. The more Harrison heard about Bo Dawson, the more he realized he truly did have a good side. Maybe even equal to the bad side. Which was saying something.

"Well," Daisy said, "now we know how long it

is from the petting zoo to the main house—one very long story."

Harrison smiled. "It was a good story." He followed her up the porch steps. "I'll just put Tony in his bassinet and let you rest."

Please say, "Or you can come in and give me a back massage, sailor."

She didn't say that. And he didn't suggest it.

They went inside, and Harrison found himself very reluctantly taking Tony from the carrier and setting him in the bassinet. He missed that soft weight against him, the subtle scent of baby shampoo. He could not for the life of him figure out how to undo all the latches on the baby carrier, so Daisy did that, standing so close to him he could move half an inch and be kissing her.

But then the carrier was off and she was putting it in a basket by the door, and he had no reason not to trail her there on his way out.

And then a really bad-for-his-head-and-heart idea occurred to him, and he blurted it out before he could stop himself. "So how about if I help you out with the dinner party prep tomorrow?" he asked. "You can sit and direct me, and I'll do all the heavy lifting and twisting and bending."

She tilted her head and stared at him, and he could see she was touched. And thinking. Deciding. She gave her lower back a rub, which must have made the decision for her, because she said, "That's really thoughtful of you, Harrison. Everyone's coming at seven, and I'll need a solid forty-five minutes to prep and cook—for *you* to prep and cook—so how about you arrive at five forty-five and we'll get right to it?"

"Do you need anything from the grocery store? I don't mind driving over and picking up anything."

"Could you stop being so thoughtful? And no, I've got everything. But thank you. You're a peach—like the one Axel gave Flash when he was rescued."

His aunt Lolly always used to call him a peach every time he did something nice for her. For once, though, the thought of Lolly was just a sweet one instead of making him all knotted up. "See you tomorrow at five forty-five, then," he said and dragged himself out the door.

As he headed back down to his cabin, he thought about sitting across from her in Franny's Fish and Chips, telling her all about the day he'd lost his dad. How his father told him about Bo and the bet and Lolly. Harrison hadn't understood why he'd told Daisy all that. Not to hurt her, certainly. Or even to make her understand.

But he got it now. He'd told her because he was in love with her. Crazy in love. There was no denying it or trying to ignore it. He'd wanted to share with her—and he'd gone *way* overboard.

Now, *she* was sharing—much more than when they'd first made their deal. Her willingness to be so vulnerable shook him at times—quite a few times the past hour alone. He wasn't sure if she was being so open because she felt the same way he did and wanted to bring him inside her world. *Or* if she really was still working on her grand plan to sway him against taking the ranch. They'd both come clean that they had feelings for each other. So maybe the plan had gone out the window.

He had a feeling they were way past that.

Chapter Twelve

Since Daisy's sister-in-law was working tonight while her husband would be home with their twins, Sara had kindly asked Noah to babysit Tony since he was in baby mode anyway. Sara wholeheartedly approved of the plan to entice Axel into sticking around Bear Ridge and hopefully on the ranch, so she'd casually mentioned to her husband that Daisy "might be fixing up Axel" at a small dinner party. Knowing Noah would not want to know a detail more and that he'd agree just to not get involved, Sara had gotten Daisy a top-notch sitter for Tony, as Noah had taken care of a newborn on his own for seven weeks before

Sara had arrived at the ranch and changed his entire world.

The doorbell rang, and when Daisy opened it, she almost swooned. Standing there was gorgeous, sexy Harrison in black chinos and a black polo shirt, looking as mysterious as he'd seemed the day she'd met him. In one hand he had a huge bouquet of pink flowers, and in the other a little shopping bag from Heavenly Bake, which he held out to her. She peeked in to find a delicious-looking round loaf of crusty bread from the excellent small bakery right in town.

Daisy felt so underdressed in her yoga shorts and a flowy tank top. She planned to change for dinner once everything was all set. She could hardly take her eyes off Harrison. Even speaking was beyond her for the moment, but she managed to thank him for the flowers and bread.

"You sit," he said, pointing at the upholstered red velvet armchair in the corner by the window. "I'm at your service." He took one of the three stained glass vases on the counter and filled it with water, then put in the flowers, even giving them a little arranging before setting the vase on the kitchen table. "I'll bring these into the dining room later."

She smiled and sat, the twinge in her back still nipping, but it was better than earlier. "The flowers are gorgeous," she said, admiring them. "And this was Gram's chair, if you were wondering why a living room chair is in the kitchen. She would plonk down in it while something cooked or baked so she could keep watch." She rubbed her hands over the arms. "It reminds me of her, so I kept it here. I think it brings me luck."

"Well, if I don't burn dinner," he said, "we'll know it really does."

He seriously had to stop making her adore him. She eyed his clothes and realized he'd better wear an apron. "You look way too nice to risk getting splattered with chicken- and garlic-scented sesame oil. You can wear my apron—hanging on that peg." She pointed at the wall.

He put it on, tying it around his waist. He glanced down at himself. "'Baby on Board,'" he read aloud. "I guess this apron is only true for nine months at most."

"Yup. It was a gift from Noah when I first came back to the ranch. Hey, it was true for you during the tour earlier. You had a baby on board." She smiled, despite being aware that the memory of him walking around with Tony strapped to his chest would haunt her every night forever.

"Hey, where is the little guy? Upstairs sleeping?"

She shook her head. "Noah's on baby duty tonight while Sara works, so he's watching Tony, too. He's great with babies."

"Does he know I'm here?"

She gave a half shrug. "I told Sara, so I'm sure he knows."

"And what does the foreman of the Dawson Family Guest Ranch, the man who rebuilt this place, think of you cavorting with the enemy? He and Axel must not think it's too wise."

"They don't," she said. "But they know it's all part of my plan to change your mind by making you crazy about us, so they're grudgingly accepting it."

He let out a breath. He sure was crazy about Daisy. And everything he knew about her brothers had him respecting them immensely. But his mind was far from changed. It was more temporarily stalled—as in he wasn't going to focus on it until he had to. The five days weren't up. A deal was a deal.

"Okay, less chitchat, more cooking!" she said in her best drill sergeant tone. "I printed out a copy of my recipe for you. It's on the counter. You sure you want to do everything yourself?"

"Yup." He scanned the recipe and instructions. "So it's the four of us, right? This looks like it'll feed a small army."

"Actually, it's six. Remember the newlyweds,

Tessa and Tom Monello? We saw them making out on the path the other day. I invited them, too. They're having issues, and I kind of helped Tessa with a little advice—not that I know anything about marriage, but my advice seems to have helped. She came to tell me yesterday, and I ended up inviting them. I think Axel will feel it's less like a double date that way."

He stared at her. "Is that how you saw it? A double date?"

Well, when he put it like *that*. "Well, no, of course not. We're not dating."

"I know, but we're *something*, Daisy."

"Yes, we're something. But we're not dating. Or friends," she added with a smile.

All I know is that I love you, she thought, wishing she could scream it from the rooftops. Wishing she could know what the hell was going to happen when all was said and done.

"Speaking of dating, have you heard back from Robert Chang, by any chance?" She really should let the chef get busy, but she was dying to know.

He shook his head. "I'm figuring he'll call back tomorrow when he's had a chance to settle back in and digest the news that Lolly's nephew wants to talk to him. I really hope that doesn't blow up in my face."

She nodded. "I feel that way about tonight."

"Well, I can promise you I'll follow your recipe to the T, so at least your famed stir-fry and special recipe rice should still manage to wow the crowd."

"I wouldn't go that far," she quipped as he started pulling out pots and bowls and utensils. He went to the fridge and got out all the vegetables for the stir-fry and eyed the knives in the block on the counter.

"Second one down is great for fine chopping," she said.

"Oh wait, I should probably get the rice going first, right?"

She nodded, mesmerized by the sight of him in her apron, zooming about her kitchen. She wished she could take a photo. Oh hell, why not. Her cell phone was right in her pocket. "I'll get a photo of you hard at work on the recipe, your ingredients all around you," she said super casually, as if she just didn't want a photo to remember him by before things went really south. And they would, she knew. There was no other way for the situation to go.

He turned, holding the big glass jar of rice that she kept on the counter, surrounded by broccoli and snap peas and mushrooms and carrots. "Cheese," he said, and she laughed and snapped the photo. She'd ogle it later.

Once the rice was going, he started chopping

away, maybe chopping the broccoli a little too much, concentrating so hard on what he was doing that she stayed quiet and just watched him. He did great with the mushrooms.

"I'll make the sauce," she said, getting up and realizing she did so without reaching for her lower back. "Hey, the twinge is gone. I think whatever knot that was worked itself out. Last night's hot bath and spending most of today lying on the sofa with Tony must have helped."

"Glad to hear it. But I still want to cook. One wrong reach and you could reinjure whatever you pulled. I'll collect what you need for sauce, though, and you can make it from the table."

My hero, she thought. She watched him read over the ingredients, then get out the garlic and ginger and sesame oil and everything else. He brought it all to the table, leaning over so close that she could reach up and kiss his cheek, which she wanted to do. He brought over the knife block, a chopping board and one of the dish towels, and she was so overwhelmed by his nearness and his thoughtfulness and his sexiness that she stood up and took his face and kissed him. Really kissed him—on the lips.

He kissed her right back. She leaned him against the counter, vaguely aware that she was glad she hadn't yet touched the garlic, because her hands were all over the part of his shirt not covered by the apron. Then in his hair. He held her so close, and she felt the most wonderful sensation of desire and safety and pure happiness.

She barely heard the front door opening and closing. Work boots being kicked off in the foyer.

"Daize?" Axel's voice rang out. "Need help with dinner?"

Double drat. She pulled away. Harrison stepped back just as Axel came into the kitchen.

"Oh," Axel said, giving Harrison the usual stare of death. "Guess you have help."

"You're a guest tonight," she told Axel, "so go relax. Come down at seven. I invited Hailey Appleton, by the way. And the newlywed guests—the Monellos. Know them?"

"Why'd you invite Hailey?" Axel asked, narrowing his gaze at her.

"I realized I hadn't gotten a chance to talk to her in a while even though she's often right here on the ranch, so I figured I'd just ask her to dinner. Lucky Hailey was free since I asked her so last minute." Not a word of that was a lie. And it seemed to soothe Axel away from thinking she was trying to fix him up with Hailey.

"If you need any help, let me know," Axel said, eyeing Harrison before leaving the kitchen.

Harrison glanced at her, then turned back to the recipe. "I feel lucky I'm still alive."

She smiled. "Well, the situation is what it is, as they say. Axel and Noah are very, very wary of you. They don't love what I've been trying to do—trying to get you to like us so much that you'll just disappear."

He turned and looked at her. "Is that what you want, Daisy? For me to disappear?"

"What I want is for you to rip up the napkin," she said, wondering if she should be really honest and say the rest of the sentence out loud. She hesitated, then added, "And then *not* disappear."

"So I rip up the napkin or it's see ya." He stood stock-still, and she really hoped he didn't walk out.

Tears pricked her eyes out of nowhere. "This is really hard, Harrison. What do you expect me to do or say? The ranch is everything to me and my family."

He turned back to the counter, where vegetables were awaiting the pan. "Let's get back to cooking. Your guests are coming in forty minutes."

She nodded, relieved he was staying, but her stomach was all twisty now. He went to the fridge and got out the chicken, and for the next ten minutes, neither of them said a word.

Finally, he asked her a question about when to turn the chicken, and that kind of broke the ice since she got up to look, and then they were back to chatting away about light stuff, like the time her brother Rex accidentally fell on her with an open-faced peanut-butter sandwich that landed hard on her head. They laughed and traded funny stories, but the tension never left either of their voices, and Harrison's shoulders never quite relaxed.

And she thought the two of them would be the anchors of the dinner party? Oh boy.

"Ooh, this is delicious!" Hailey said after taking her first bite of stir-fry.

Harrison grinned. "I'm very, very relieved. I did the cooking from Daisy's recipe."

"It's not bad," Axel said with a nod.

Harrison would take that as high praise. He and Daisy sat at either end of the rectangular table in the dining room as if they were married and this were their house, the Monellos across from each other on his side, and the would-be couple on Daisy's end. The flowers he'd brought were in the center, along with the bread, which he'd sliced. The stir-fry and rice were on a big platter, and he was glad to see that everyone was eating heartily. He hadn't burned any part of dinner, and Daisy, who still seemed a bit strained, had told him everything was perfect. Food-wise, she'd added.

As Axel took a slice of the bread, Harrison noticed Hailey looking at him—with interest. Harrison couldn't get a read on Axel at all. He'd been polite since he came down, offering to set the table, but Harrison had already taken care of that. Axel had offered him one of his favorite craft beers, which Harrison had accepted, but there was no clinking of bottles. Harrison had never seen Axel out of his ranch duds, but now he was in dark gray pants with a pale gray collared shirt. Hailey wore a sundress, her red hair long and loose. Daisy looked stunning in her own sundress, hers white with tiny straps and embroidered with little flowers along the hem and neckline. The Monellos were decked out for a nightclub.

"So, Hailey," Daisy said, pushing stir-fry around her plate. "Noah mentioned you're taking all the guests out on a wilderness tour tomorrow up into Clover Mountain. That's great that all the cabins signed up—even the youngest kids are going."

"I was so happy to see the sign-up sheet," Hailey said, her brown eyes glowing. "Many times the guests really just want to relax or take a quick hike up the creek."

"You'll have a partner, right?" Axel asked, his gaze on Hailey.

Hailey took a sip of her wine. "Yup. Dylan, the ranch hand, will be assisting."

Axel nodded. "Good. Better to have two skilled

trail leaders with a group that size, particularly with kids."

"Oh I know," Hailey said. "My toddler can dash away so fast, and he's only eighteen months! One second he's there, the next I find him playing hide-and-seek in the coat closet, scaring me to death."

Daisy hadn't mentioned that Hailey had a child. Harrison glanced at her, and she looked surprised. He then eyed Axel, who was sitting as ramrod straight as Harrison had been earlier when all that tension had flared up between himself and Daisy in the kitchen. Interesting.

"See!" Tom Monello said to his wife, his hazel eyes triumphant. He then looked at Hailey. "You're what, twenty-five? And already have a toddler. You and your husband are probably already planning the next baby when the little one turns two, am I right?"

Hailey lifted her chin. "Actually, I'm not married. So it's just me and Jonathan."

"Oh," Tom said.

"That was a lot to assume," Tessa said to her husband through gritted teeth. She shoved her long dark wavy hair behind her shoulders, her eyes flashing.

Tom shrugged. "But she started young. Now she has time to find a new husband and have another kid."

"Um, Tom, seriously!" Tessa snapped. "I'm so sorry—uh, what was your name again? Bailey?"

Hailey turned bright red. "It's Hailey."

Daisy looked mortified and like she was clamping down on saying what was bursting inside her. "More stir-fry, anyone?"

No one seemed to hear her. Axel was staring at his plate and pushing rice around. Hailey had that deer-in-headlights look. Tessa seemed about to stab her husband with her fork. And Tom was busily eating.

Tom finally put down his fork, then sipped his beer. "I'm just saying, Tessa. If we start having kids now, we can have three by the time we're thirty. That's ideal."

"According to whom?" Daisy asked.

"His mother," Tessa said.

Daisy's expression said she was sorry she'd asked. "So, Axel," she said brightly, turning her attention to her brother. "Back to the wilderness tour Hailey's leading tomorrow. Are you free to join them?" she asked. Very casually.

Despite the bickering going on at Harrison's end of the table, you could hear a pin drop at Daisy's side. Axel and Hailey were both dead silent.

Daisy seemed to be holding her breath.

Axel glanced at Hailey, then at Daisy, then sort of at the two of them. "I'll have to check my calendar. I'm going to an auction with Noah tomorrow, but I'm not sure of the time."

"I'd love for you to join us," Hailey said, but her voice was a little unsteady. "I've been leading tours a long time, but a search-and-rescue specialist could give a great talk at our rest stops about hazards. Plus, we really could use the extra set of eagle eyes."

Axel nodded. "I'll let you know in the morning. I'll get your number from Daisy."

Hailey seemed to perk up a bit at that. But if someone took a photo of the dinner party guests right now, there wouldn't be a smile on any face.

Harrison glanced at Daisy. She did seem about half-pleased. Half that there was a potential get-together on the table. Half that Axel had seemed so…lackluster about it. Of course, that could just be his way.

Tessa stood. "Daisy, thank you so much for inviting us. Everything was delicious. But we actually have to get going."

Tom grudgingly stood, then took one more bite of stir-fry. And then finished his piece of bread. "You said we should say what we feel, what we want," he complained. "That's what I'm doing. Suddenly I'm the bad guy?"

"But what you want is not what I want!" Tessa said, tears glistening.

This wasn't going well.

"Well, what you want isn't what I want," Tom said, crossing his arms over his chest.

"Guys, look," Daisy said, standing up. "You two love each other. You do know that, right? You love each other. If you each want something different, you're going to have to learn to compromise."

Tessa glared at her. "Um, Daisy, no offense, but this is kind of personal, so…"

Harrison could see Daisy was fighting not to roll her eyes. Hard. "But Daisy is right. You're either at a stalemate and it tears you apart. Or you compromise and it brings you together because you had to work together to get there."

"I guess," Tom said—grudgingly.

"Let's go," Tessa said. "None of these people are even *married*," he heard Tessa mutter under her breath to her husband, who scowled at Daisy and Harrison before putting his arm around his wife's shoulder.

"We'll walk you out," Harrison said, getting up, too.

He and Daisy led the way to the front door, and then finally the Monellos were headed up the trail toward their cabin.

Daisy let out a long breath. As guest relations manager, maternity leave or not, she'd have to smooth things out with them in the morning, and

she would. For the sake of the ranch and their online reviews.

"Think they'll make it to Christmas?" Harrison asked.

"Yes, actually," Daisy said. "They're immature
and young, but they do love each other. I honestly
think they'll bicker their way to their sixtieth wedding anniversary."

"A romantic like me," Hailey called out. "And I
agree. Tom and Tessa were in my tour group a couple days ago, and they had three arguments within
a half hour. The way back—they never stopped
kissing. How they didn't trip was beyond me."

Axel laughed. "I actually did see them trip yesterday—well, more like walk right into a half stone
wall. They were lip-locked and *bam*—suddenly
both rubbing their knees."

"I'm sure they kissed each other's boo-boos,"
Hailey said on a chuckle, but then her eyes widened and two splotches of pink appeared on her
cheeks.

"No doubt," Axel said, lifting his beer to Hailey.
She lifted hers back with a happy smile.

And just like that, this dinner party was back
in business. Daisy brought out three desserts—
starting with the coffee cake the Monellos had
brought. His aunt had always loved that brand of
coffee cake, and Harrison had had many a slice in

his lifetime. He would definitely partake tonight. Hailey had brought a homemade peach pie, one of Harrison's favorite kinds. And Daisy had baked chocolate chip cookies. Harrison got up to make a pot of coffee as if this was his house—a thought that only occurred to him after Axel glared at him.

This *would* be his house. Now that was a thought that sobered him up real fast. He stood in the kitchen, staring at the coffee dripping into the decanter, his collar tightening on him. He was going to take Daisy's house? Tony's house?

Daisy came into the kitchen, and he tried to shake off how unsettled he felt. "I'll get the cream and sugar. Leaving Axel and Hailey alone for a bit seems a great idea about now," she whispered with a smile.

"You might have had to suffer through the Monellos," he said, "but this dinner party seems to have served its purpose."

"I hope so. I have a good feeling."

A few minutes later, they brought in the coffee, and they all dug into dessert, swapping stories. Hailey had everyone in stitches about the antics of her little dog, a beagle mix whom her toddler adored. Then Axel told the tale of trying to hide a huge stray dog on the ranch for a week when he was a little kid. His grandparents wouldn't allow dogs and arranged for their closest neighbors to adopt the giant stray, and they'd hired Axel to be their daily dog walker and afternoon feeder, so it had all worked out. Hailey was beaming. Axel seemed relaxed and happy. Daisy was thrilled.

On cue, as if he knew they were talking dogs, Dude came over to the table and put his chin right on Harrison's lap.

"Aww," Hailey said. "Dude sure does like you, Harrison."

Axel scowled, staring at his yellow Lab, then at Harrison. "Yeah, a little too much for comfort."

Daisy bit her lip.

"Am I missing something?" Hailey asked, looking between Axel and Harrison.

All eyes swung to Axel. Harrison looked down at sweet Dude with a sigh.

"Yes," Axel said, "but be glad you are, because it's ugly. Really ugly."

Hailey looked confused. Daisy looked nervous. Axel looked ready to punch the wall.

And Harrison figured he'd better leave, give Daisy a chance to calm things down, save the night for her brother and Hailey.

Axel glared at Harrison. "How the hell can you sit there and eat our food, laugh at our stories, and do what you're planning to do? How the hell can you? I think you should leave."

"I think so, too," Harrison said, standing up. "This was a nice night. I don't want to ruin it."

"Harrison," Daisy said. "Wait—"

"Yes, wait," Axel said suddenly. "I have an idea."

He stared at Daisy's brother. It clearly wasn't an idea that made the guy any less angry.

Axel rounded the table and stood inches from Harrison. "Hit me. Punch me square in the face like your father was supposed to do to my father. Then we'll be even. That was the original payment, right? A knockout. The bet came later when Bo Dawson was drunk off his keister. It's why he lost the poker game, by the way. So hardly fair. Hit me and rip up the napkin."

Harrison looked at Daisy, who bolted up and rushed over.

"No one is punching anyone!" she shouted.

"Um, I think I'd better get going," Hailey said and practically ran out the door.

Daisy threw up her hands. "Great. Now the fix up is ruined! Great going, guys!"

"Wait—you were fixing me up with Hailey?" Axel asked.

"Duh!" Daisy said. "Now she thinks we're people who go around screaming and yelling and fist-fighting and sending newlyweds running for the hills."

"I'm sorry this didn't go the way you'd hoped, Daisy," Harrison said, so heavyhearted he was surprised he didn't crash through the floor. He turned to Axel. "I understand why you're so angry, Axel. I do. I wish things were different, but they're not."

Daisy's eyes glistened as she stared at Harrison. "*What?* Are you telling me you're actually *really* still planning to take the ranch from us? Try to, I should say. Because you won't! No court will agree with you!"

That heavy heart of his split in two. He turned and walked to the front door. With his hand on the doorknob, he turned to look at Daisy, to implore her to understand—as if she could. But she was sobbing against her brother, who was hugging her protectively and telling her they'd fight Harrison—in court—with everything they had. And they had a lot.

They did. The six Dawsons had one another.

Chapter Thirteen

Daisy hadn't slept much last night, but she was out cold when Tony's cries from the nursery made their way into her brain from the baby monitor on her bedside table. She eyed the clock—6:14 a.m. She'd been up with Tony just after three and had finally fallen asleep at right before four. No wonder she was bleary-eyed.

Oh, and the crying she'd done.

She shoved off the quilt and went into the nursery, the sight of her baby boy making her so happy she forgot how exhausted she was and cuddled him against her. "How about a change and then some breakfast, my sweet?"

Once he was changed and dressed in a cute blue-and-green onesie with stretchy shorts, she headed downstairs for the coffeepot. Why she thought two or three mugs of decaf would wake her up was beyond her, but drinking hot coffee always faked her brain.

With Tony in his bassinet, she made the coffee and toasted a sesame seed bagel, getting out the cream cheese, which of course reminded her of Harrison.

He'd been all over this fridge last night. So helpful. So wonderful.

And then blammo. The whole thing had come crashing down on her head, which it could have done at any moment. Last night had just been pushed along by Axel—something that needed to happen so she'd wake up and actually smell the coffee. Which she literally and figuratively did right now.

The plan to make Harrison like them had worked. He liked them. No one doubted that.

The plan itself? Did not work. Had no effect on the outcome. He was still going to try to take the ranch from them. She should have seen that coming, but she'd been too blinded by a pair of intense green eyes and the tousled, sexy blond hair and the great jawline. And the great body. And the great kissing.

She grabbed a mug from the cabinet and poured her coffee, adding cream and sugar, and then took a satisfying few sips. The heat helped clear her mind even if the lack of caffeine meant no boost.

She sat down with her bagel and coffee, watching Tony stare at his gently spinning pastel mobile with the little farm animals. At least she was all cried out. Axel had let her sob all over his shirt last night after Harrison had left. Dude had felt so bad for her he'd lain at her feet, his chin on her foot.

Well, Daisy had to admit that Harrison McCord's presence on the ranch—and in her life—had actually managed to bring her and Axel closer, so that was a major positive. When she'd finally stopped crying, she and Axel had gone onto the back deck with Dude and they'd talked for a long time. Daisy had told him everything. How the plan had never gone off track, exactly, but that she'd actually managed to fall madly in love with the guy.

Because he was her brother and he loved her, Axel had said that if Harrison McCord weren't trying to ruin their lives, he'd be a great guy. Axel had even admitted to finding himself forgetting who Harrison actually was during dinner and enjoying the conversation—when it hadn't gone off the rails in some way or another.

She and Axel had been up past midnight talking about the ranch. Axel had told her that, like their brothers, who'd been talking about the "McCord Problem," as they called it, the threat of losing the ranch had made them realize that they actually cared much more about the place than they'd understood. They'd thought it was about their grandparents, their hard work, their family legacy. But it was much more. It was about *now*. It was about all six Dawsons rallying and investing in rebuilding the ranch. About Noah coming into his own while renovating. About Daisy finding a safe place to land when she was pregnant and felt so alone. About the future they'd created and were creating for the next generation.

"I won't start building that fancy log cabin until a judge orders McCord to rip up that napkin," Axel had said. "But I'm not going anywhere."

Her heart had soared at that. One mission accomplished. They weren't going to lose the ranch because they were Dawsons, dammit, and she wasn't going to lose Axel. He was staying. He'd even promised to apologize to Hailey when he texted her about whether or not he could go on the wilderness tour with her.

She had lost Harrison, though. Whatever they'd had—and they did have something truly special—was over. If he could actually try to steal the ranch out from under them, he wasn't the man she thought he was. His father's last request or not. It wasn't a fair request.

"I don't know if that's fair of *me*," she said to Tony. "But it's how I feel."

Daisy looked at the baby boy in the bassinet, his gaze moving to hers. She had her precious son. She had her family. She had this ranch. That would get her through, heart imploding and exploding all over the place.

Harrison was holed up in the cabin, trying to figure out what the hell to do. Last night, since he'd spent hours tossing and turning and not getting any sleep, he'd vowed to stay at the ranch instead of hightailing it back to Prairie City before five Dawson brothers came after him. He had today and tomorrow left on his stay at the ranch. On the deal, too. He wasn't leaving. Not when everything was so awful between him and Daisy.

He needed to go see Lolly. If she was sleeping, he'd gently wake her and ask her what she thought he should do about the ranch. He wouldn't tell her about falling for Daisy. He'd just ask her what she wanted. If the ranch belonged to anyone right now, in his eyes, it was Lolly. It hadn't passed from his father to him—it went to his aunt, then to him. That was how Harrison viewed it. He'd get his cues from Lolly. Then go from there.

His phone rang, and he lunged for it, hoping it was Daisy. But it was an unfamiliar number.

Then he realized it was *Robert Chang's* number.

"Thanks for calling back," Harrison said, feeling as though a lifeline was on the other end. "Your message said you were on vacation."

"I needed to get away, someplace where I could completely forget my troubles at home. But I guess you know all about that."

I do? "What do you mean?" Harrison asked.

There was hesitation, and then Robert said, "I just meant I assume you know about the end of my relationship with your aunt, since you called. Is something wrong? Is she okay?" Harrison heard warmth in the man's voice but also wariness.

It struck then that Harrison wouldn't have known about Robert at all had the dog-walking neighbor not been visiting Lolly when he happened to stop by. Lolly never would have brought up Robert's name. This entire conversation wouldn't be happening.

It was because someone had cared about Lolly and had come to see her. The neighbor with the dog Lolly liked. That meant something, something important in a philosophical sense, but right now Harrison had to focus on the phone call.

"Actually, no," Harrison said. "I'm very sorry to let you know that she's in hospice—at Gentle

Winds here in Prairie City. She was diagnosed with stage-four ovarian cancer about six weeks ago, and it was too late for treatment. Her brother, my father, passed away very recently, and Lolly took a turn for the worse. She's been at Gentle Winds for almost two weeks."

"Oh no," Robert said, his voice unsteady. "I had no idea."

"What happened between you two?" he asked. "I actually don't know. She didn't tell me anything."

"Lolly told me it wasn't working between us after all, and she was sorry but she didn't want to continue seeing me. I was blindsided. She refused to discuss it and wouldn't return my calls or answer the door."

So Harrison was right—Lolly had kept her illness a secret. "When was that—that she ended the relationship?"

"Almost two weeks ago. Must have been the day before she moved to Gentle Winds. Why didn't she tell me? We were getting so close. I thought we were serious."

"I think she didn't want to cause you pain," Harrison said, his chest tightening.

"But she did. I was so broken up I took two weeks' vacation and went to Machu Picchu to immerse myself in another world."

Harrison got it. He'd wanted to do something like that when he'd discovered his ex-girlfriend had been using him. "So things were good between you two until she suddenly ended the relationship?" Harrison asked. That was key.

"Yes. Things were great. I was even thinking of proposing, even though we'd only known each other a few months. Life is short. Unfortunately."

Robert had been thinking of proposing.

Oh, Lolly.

And yes, life was short. Too short. And unfair.

"Robert, I'm going over to see Lolly today. I'll call you back within the hour. I just need to see her first and let her know I've been in touch with you."

"I understand," he said. "I hope you decide to let me see her. I truly love her, Harrison."

His aunt was loved. She hadn't been alone while at Gentle Winds. From a great distance, Robert had loved her, even if Harrison hadn't known it. Somehow, it comforted him.

Harrison pocketed his phone and raced out the door. He couldn't get to Gentle Winds fast enough. But first, he had to text Daisy. He knew she'd want to know what Robert had to say.

He sat in his SUV and sent the text, all but holding his breath while waiting for her to text back. Would she? Maybe she was done with him completely.

He wouldn't blame her.

His phone pinged.

Invite him to visit her!

He wrote back, I'm going to see Lolly now. I'll tell her I think she should let him visit. I just need to see her first.

Sounds good.

He sucked in a breath. She was distancing herself. Of course she was.

I'm sorry for everything, he texted. Not everything. Not all the good stuff.

You can stuff your sorries in a sack, mister, was her reply.

He hung his head, missing her so much his chest ached.

She thought she'd be saving him from a world of hurt, and he was so hurt he had to go on a spiritual quest in Peru! Her plan backfired just like mine did.

Take knife, insert into his chest.

There was so much he wanted to say, to write, but his thumbs were too big to type well on his phone, and nothing he could say—other than the obvious—would get Daisy back in his life.

He knew exactly what she wanted to hear him say: *I would never, could never take the ranch away from you or your family. I thought I could, but I love you and I can't. Even if I didn't love you or respect your siblings, I still couldn't do such a bastardy thing. It's not in me.*

She'd never said that outright, of course, but he knew that was what she wanted. Word for word, really.

If he made things right with Daisy, he'd know deep in his heart for the rest of his life that he'd let down his father. And Lolly.

He leaned his head back against his car's seat rest.

His phone pinged. I have to go—Tony's getting fussy in the bassinet. Good luck.

And that was that.

Harrison gave a gentle knock on Lolly's door at Gentle Winds, but there was no answer, which meant she was napping. He stepped inside, closing the door behind him, then brought the chair he always sat in very close to her bed. He sank down on it.

He looked at her lovely face, her curly blond hair in its little ponytail. Lolly had always looked younger than she was, and the unfairness of it all gripped him hard now. She was only sixty-five. She was too young.

"Aunt Lolly," he said, his voice unsteady. She didn't wake up. He gently shook her shoulder. "Aunt Lolly, it's Harry."

Her eyes fluttered open, and for a moment she looked straight ahead as if she didn't even realize he was there, but then she slightly turned her head, and she strained to smile. "My sweet nephew," she said. She slowly moved her hand to touch his, and he wrapped his around hers. She kept her gaze on him, her eyes so much like his and his dad's.

"Aunt Lolly, remember when your neighbor came to see you? After you fell asleep, she told me you had a boyfriend."

Lolly's face crumpled, and his heart ripped into shreds.

Oh no. No. What had he done? Why had he brought this up? He was the worst. Daisy thought he was the worst? She was right.

"Robert," Lolly whispered. "I hurt him terribly. I told him we were through."

Tears misted her eyes, and she shook her head. *Don't jump in yet*, he told himself. *Let her talk when she's ready.*

"I didn't tell him I was sick," she continued. "Oh, how I miss him, Harry. But it's for the best. He needs to move on."

He almost gasped. It wasn't for the best! Not by a long shot. "Lolly. I took a chance, and I called him. He wants to see you right away."

Her eyes lit up, but she started to cry. "I miss him so much." She wiped at her eyes and then closed them and turned away.

"I'll be right back, Aunt Lolly," he said, not sure if she was even listening.

He went into the hallway. He texted Robert and asked him if he could come to Gentle Winds right now. Robert responded immediately that he would. Harrison was so relieved that he actually felt his shoulder muscles loosen from their knots. He quickly called the reception desk to put Robert Chang on Lolly's visitors' list, then stepped back inside and sat down at Lolly's bedside.

"He's coming, Lolly. Robert is coming to see you."

Her eyes fluttered open again, and she sat up slightly, tilting her head. "He's really coming? Do I look all right?"

He smiled. "You look beautiful. As always."

He could ask about the bet and Bo Dawson, but this wasn't the time. Lolly was emotional and spent enough. He'd wait. Right now, this moment was about the reunion with Robert. Not the past.

He had his fingers crossed that this reunion with

Robert would boost her spirits to the point that Harrison would have more time with her.

Five minutes later, there was a knock on the door. Harrison looked at Lolly, and she nodded, her eyes misty again.

Harrison went to the door and opened it. Robert Chang looked to be around Lolly's age, maybe a bit older. He had thick salt-and-pepper hair and dark eyes and wore round silver eyeglasses. He held a bouquet of red roses. "I'm Harrison McCord. It's very nice to meet you."

Robert extended his hand. "Robert Chang. I can't thank you enough for getting in touch with me." He rushed over to the bed and sat down in the chair Harrison had been sitting in, his gaze misty on Lolly. "I know how you love red roses, Lolly."

"Robert," she whispered, holding out her hand.

He took it in both of his and kissed the back. "I didn't know you were sick. I wish I had. I would have been with you every step of the way. I would have never left your bedside. I love you, Lolly."

"I love you, too, Robert. Too much to burden you with so much sickness and watching me get weaker and weaker. I couldn't do that to you."

Harrison, who'd moved into the bathroom, ostensibly to fill the vase with water for the flowers, but really to give them some privacy, almost broke down.

"But I was wrong, wasn't I?" Lolly said. "I got so used to being alone that I forgot how good it felt to love and be loved, to need and be needed. I thought I could go back to how things were before I met you, but it was terrible. No one should live in the past."

"I'm so grateful your nephew called me." Robert stood up as Harrison came back into the room with the vase of water. He put the flowers in and set them on Lolly's table. "Thank you, again, Harrison."

"Call him Harry," Lolly said with a smile.

Harrison smiled. "Call me Harry," he confirmed to Robert. Then he turned to his aunt. "Love you, Lolly. I'll see you tomorrow morning."

She smiled back, then gave her attention to her beloved.

He left Gentle Winds, everything inside him churning. He'd done right by Lolly. That he knew. He needed to drive with the windows open, feel the wind rushing around him, but he couldn't go back to the ranch right now. He drove aimlessly down Main Street, passing right by Franny's Fish and Chips.

Suddenly he knew where he wanted to be.

He drove to his father's condo. He hadn't sold the apartment yet. Or even emptied it out. Harrison hadn't been able to. He used his key and went inside, taking in the big living room with its sliding glass doors to the back patio, the living room with the black leather couch and his dad's favorite chair, the big black leather electric recliner with its heated seat and massage options. He'd bought the chair for his dad for his birthday four years ago. His father had told him that he often slept in it because it was so great.

He sat down on the recliner and pressed some buttons until the neck and back massage made him say *ahhh*. He reclined back a bit. The chair smelled like his dad, like his aftershave that he always wore. He'd donate a lot of his father's things, but he'd keep this chair and a few other items that represented his dad to him. The navy blue sweater Eric McCord's grandmother had knitted him one Christmas. A painting he fell in love with when they'd been on vacation together in New Orleans. Some family photo albums, though Lolly was the keeper of the ones going back generations.

"Lolly has a boyfriend, Dad," he said into the stillness of the room. "A nice guy named Robert. Came bearing red roses. You would like him." He stared out the window at the big oak. "She wasn't alone, after all. She took a chance on love. And even if it can't be for all that long, she's happy again, Dad."

And Harrison was anything but.

What the hell am I supposed to do? You asked me to get the ranch for you. Your last request. Among your final words, Dad. How do I let that go? How can I? What do I do?

He tried to imagine himself sitting at Franny's Fish and Chips with his father. Telling him this whole story. About Daisy. Her brothers. How Bo Dawson had stayed by eight-year-old Axel's side on a mountain ledge into the wee hours because of a goat. How he'd bequeathed Sara Dawson's mother's garden bed behind the foreman's cabin to her. How he'd never sold Daisy and Noah's mother's wedding rings. Ever. And left them to Daisy in his will, knowing how much they meant to her. He wouldn't leave out the bad parts, either. Selling all their fishing rods, likely for drinking or gambling money. Drunkenly crashing into outbuildings. Loving and leaving women. He'd say it all. The good and the bad.

What would his father say to all that? he wondered. He stared around the room, at the painting from New Orleans. At the big-screen TV where his dad had watched every episode of every iteration of *Law & Order* there was.

He pictured his father sitting across from him, taking a bite of his fried haddock with lettuce and tartar sauce, his side of fries with the spicy mayo. *What would you say, Dad?*

And then it hit him.

He knew exactly what his father would say.

It was like a bolt of lightning struck him.

His father would say, *The ranch belongs to us fair and square. So take ownership—and then sell it back to the Dawsons for a dollar that same day.*

He turned the idea around in his mind. Yes—it would let him honor his father's last wishes *and* let him walk away from the ranch, leaving it with the Dawson family. It was a good compromise. And one he believed his father would approve of.

But taking ownership at all would mean losing Daisy. For her, insisting on taking the ranch would be a betrayal. It was the principle of the thing, and she'd be furious and hurt.

He would lose the love of his life. And he didn't know how he'd ever recover.

Chapter Fourteen

Daisy walked along the creek, Tony in the baby carrier on her chest. It was a gorgeous afternoon, sunny and warm but not humid, the canopy of trees providing lots of shade for her and the baby. She wasn't going to lie—she'd been walking around, particularly in this area of the ranch, because of its proximity to the guest cabins, and because she knew Harrison loved the creek. She'd kept hoping she'd run into him today so that they'd be forced to deal with each other. But she wanted to leave it to chance, because she had no idea what she'd say to him.

She'd been too glad to hear from Sara that he

hadn't checked out today. He'd promised he'd stay through the end of his booking, and he was likely making good on that, even if she'd ordered him out of her house last night. Twice in just a few days, actually.

"What would you do in his place?" Sara had asked earlier. "If Bo had been the best dad in the world and asked you, on his deathbed, to do something for him, something that had always bothered him that he'd left unsettled."

Daisy's mouth had dropped open. "You can't be serious! You think Harrison is right?"

Sara had shaken her head. "No, of course not. But what would you do, Daisy?"

"If everything else was the same? If I'd gotten romantically involved?"

"Yup," Sara had said.

Daisy chewed her lower lip.

"Who would you choose?" Sara pushed. "The man you love or fulfilling your father's last wish?"

"Sara!" Daisy had snapped, more than royally pissed off. But she did stop to think about it. How *could* she choose?

"Sorry, babe, but this is what best friends are for—pointing stuff out even when it's not fun to hear. I'm not trying to play devil's advocate, and

I'm not saying he's right. But neither are you. Just think about it."

She was. And what she was thinking was that Harrison McCord had chosen. And he wasn't choosing her. He wasn't choosing *them*. He knew they had something very special, and he was ready to walk away.

Humph! "So I shouldn't be furious? I shouldn't be scared to death? I shouldn't be brokenhearted or wish I could hate him?"

"Daisy, I'm just asking you to look at it from his perspective. None of us, the Dawson brother I'm married to included, has done that."

Forget her almost relationship with Harrison. Take that out of the equation altogether. Just strictly on the stupid napkin and the *old* condition of the ranch, which was what the napkin had been referring to—the ranch on that date ten years ago—Harrison McCord was dead wrong.

"Because we shouldn't have to!" Daisy protested. "A drunken bet about something that didn't even exist anymore shouldn't be our fault once we rebuilt the ranch. This ranch is not the same one his father won in a bet." The more she thought about that, the more she realized it was true. She'd been truly worried about how any lawyer they'd hire would defend them in court, if need be, and she was pretty sure she'd lit upon it.

The ranch wasn't the same ranch. They weren't the same people. They'd all changed.

Including Bo Dawson. The man who'd left them each personalized letters, bequeathing them something special to them, was not the same man who'd driven them all away, one by one.

"Just putting it out there," Sara had said, squeezing her hand. "Don't be mad at me."

Daisy had hugged her sister-in-law. "I know. And I'm glad you did. Because my mind just went in some new directions."

She'd thought of little else all day. Looking at things through other lenses. Even Harrison's.

Now, Daisy stopped in her tracks along the creek, thunderstruck by something. Somewhere in these days, she'd gone from thinking he couldn't take the ranch from them because it was wrong to thinking he couldn't because it would mean he didn't love her.

Like she loved him.

Harrison McCord wasn't in love with her. He'd lived up to his end of the deal they'd made by sticking around, and she'd "won" because he most certainly did like her and the ranch and the Dawsons that were here. But that was as far as it went for him. He didn't love her.

She closed her eyes and took in a deep breath, dropping her chin down to the top of Tony's head and wishing it reached, because she desperately needed even a chin-to-baby-head hug right now. She turned and headed in the opposite direction, back toward her house. She just wanted to fling herself on her bed and pull the covers over her head for a half hour.

"I'm sorry I've been such a brat," she heard a girl say, and Daisy peered down past the curve on the path, where she could see the mother and teen daughter duo, Christy and Macy Parnell, walking just ahead of her. Sixteen-year-old Macy had blond hair dyed purple on the ends, which looked fabulous. Daisy stopped behind a tree, wanting to give the family privacy and not interrupt them or do anything that would come between their moment. Daisy had caught them bickering several times over the past few days, Macy stomping off in her black Doc Martens. And now here was Macy apologizing for her behavior.

"I'm sorry I haven't been listening, *really* listening," Christy said. "But I really heard you this morning. And I understand how you feel."

Macy hugged her mom. "I'm so glad you talked

me into coming here." Christy put her arm around her daughter, and the two kept walking.

Daisy smiled. At least two people on the ranch were communicating and coming together. She even hoped Tessa and Tom Monello, obnoxious newlyweds, were making compromises they both could smile about.

When Daisy came through the clearing in the trees to turn on the path toward her house, she gasped—because she'd run smack into Harrison McCord. They were so close they'd almost smashed into each other. For once, he was actually dressed for the ranch, in faded jeans, cowboy boots and a navy blue Henley. Maybe that was a bad sign. She hadn't even known he owned cowboy boots. Now he looked like he belonged here. Because he believed the ranch was his?

"I was hoping to run into you," he said. "Not literally. You okay? I didn't bump Tony, did I?"

She shook her head, barely able to form words. Despite being hurt and angry, she still managed to notice how the sunlight glinted in his thick blond hair and on his forearms. How remorseful he looked, the sincere apology in his gorgeous green eyes. How would she ever get over this man?

"The reunion between Lolly and Robert was everything, Daisy. They were both so happy and emotional and just glad to be together again. It's going to change Lolly's last days."

Daisy smiled. "I'm really glad to hear that. A second chance for them both."

"I've come to a decision about the ranch," he said. "One that makes sense to me."

She held her breath and stared at him. "Okay," she said, waiting.

"I'm going to fulfill my father's last request to do right by him and my aunt—then sell the ranch back to you and your brothers for a dollar."

Relief hit her so hard that her knees almost buckled. They wouldn't lose the ranch. Well, they would for a few hours. But they were getting it right back. Unmarred, unchanged.

But then she realized she hadn't been wrong about how Harrison felt—or didn't. He didn't love her. Because if he did, he'd never be able to take ownership—not for a dollar, not for a second. Was she being stubborn? She didn't think so. Sara might. But with everything they'd shared—from Harrison helping to deliver her baby to her helping him find Lolly's mystery boyfriend to those kisses that had made her toes curl—he shouldn't be able to take the ranch, even on paper, even for a few hours. It would always be between them, and she'd always doubt him.

So no, she wasn't being stubborn. She was being realistic.

But they wouldn't lose the ranch.

She cleared her throat. "It's a good compromise." Which it was, really. "I think my brothers will be very relieved. I assume our friendship had something to do with the dollar idea, so thank you for that."

Then, her heart bursting, she walked around him and hurried as fast as she could with a baby strapped to her chest up the path and away from him.

You don't love me.

She had to accept it, and she had no idea how to do that.

Or maybe she did. A new idea started forming. One she wasn't sure about at all. One she wasn't sure that Harrison would agree to. But if she was going to put this all behind her—put Harrison behind her, which she couldn't even imagine—there was only one way she could think of to start.

When Harrison's phone rang ten minutes later, he expected it to be anyone but Daisy. But it was her. He was sitting in the overstuffed chair by the window, staring out at nothing in particular, because all he could see was the look on Daisy's face when she'd barreled past him a little while ago.

She'd still seemed so upset, and he couldn't figure out why. She wasn't getting exactly what she wanted, which would be for him to just tear up that napkin into tiny pieces, but the Dawsons were keeping their ranch. He'd found a way to satisfy both their needs, hadn't he?

"I'd like to visit your aunt," she said. "I want to introduce myself and apologize for my father's behavior."

He stood up, clutching his phone a little too tightly. "I don't know, Daisy. Now Lolly is reunited with Robert. I'm not sure I should even bring up bad old memories. I'm comfortable with how I'll proceed with the napkin and the ranch. I don't think I need to even mention it to Lolly. It has no bearing, no place in her life right now."

But he realized with absolute clarity that he *did* want to introduce Daisy to Lolly. His aunt was his last surviving relative, and Daisy meant so much to him. He wanted them to know each other, however briefly. However briefly he had Daisy in his life, too.

"Oh," she said. "Okay." She sounded so disappointed.

"Actually, I would love for you to meet her.

But as someone close to me. Not as Bo Dawson's daughter. I mean, I know that's who you are. And I'm sure your name will register with Lolly. But, Daisy, you're also—"

"Also what?"

The woman who means so much to me that I can't think straight. "Forget what I just said. You're everything you are, including Bo's daughter and all that that means. Are you free to go see Lolly now?" he asked, hoping she wouldn't press him on the *also.*

She hesitated, and because he did know her so well, he was one hundred percent sure that she was deciding whether or not to demand he finish what he'd been about to say.

"I'm free now. Axel can watch Tony. He actually just asked a few minutes ago if he could take Tony on a walk, and I know he has a few free hours. I think he's hoping to run into Hailey when she returns from leading the wilderness tour. To apologize in person."

He recalled the way Hailey practically flew out the door last night when things got really out of hand. "So Axel didn't go with the group? I guess with the way things went last night, it probably wouldn't happen."

"Hailey told Axel that our ranch hand Dylan

had already asked another hand to join and that they were all set for an extra expert," Daisy explained. "I think Hailey is probably going to cross Axel off her crush list. At least for right now. And I think I'll hang up my matchmaking hat."

"Sorry," he said. "I know you were hoping a romance would give him a reason to stay in town." Besides, Axel didn't strike Harrison as all that interested in a relationship anyway. He knew another lone wolf when he saw one, and Axel Dawson was very much on his own right now—and wanted to be.

"Here we are," she said, "chatting away like everything's just peachy between us. How does that keep happening?"

"Because at the core, we're true friends, Daisy. And no matter what else, there is something very special between us."

"Fat lot of good that's gonna do us," she said.

She had a point, but he didn't want to think about that or talk about it. "I'll pick you up in fifteen minutes."

"See you then."

When she ended the call, he kept the phone in his hand for a moment to keep even a semblance of connection to her.

He really hoped introducing her to his aunt

wouldn't go terribly wrong. That Lolly wouldn't hear the name Dawson, recall the name Daisy as one of her ex-boyfriend's kids and become agitated.

For a man who'd always been sure of himself, he was doing an awful lot of questioning and second-guessing.

As Daisy walked beside Harrison into the Gentle Winds hospice, she realized her hands were shaking. What if Lolly didn't accept her apology? What if she told Daisy to get out?

"Harrison, maybe this isn't a good idea. If I upset Lolly, I'll never be able to forgive myself."

"Emotionally, she's in a good place. I think this might even give her a sense of closure. Not just about her past, but because of how my father held on to it—the bitterness, all of it. It'll allow her to put that part of her life away for good, you know?"

"That makes sense," she said. "Thanks." She looked down at her hands, which were a lot less trembly. Phew.

From the moment he'd picked her up at the house until now, there hadn't been any time or space to focus on them, which was a good thing.

They stopped at the elevator. "Robert is visiting Lolly right now. I texted him, and he'll step out when we get there. He added that he hates leaving her side for a minute."

"That's some love story," Daisy said. "I'm so glad that worked out the way it did."

If only ours could.

They arrived at Lolly's room, and Harrison gave a soft knock. Robert came out and shook Harrison's hand. After introductions, Robert said he'd go to the cafeteria for a while and for Harrison to let him know when they were heading out. Robert struck Daisy as kind, polite and warm, and meeting him helped buoy her right now.

When Harrison pushed open the door, Daisy's heart started hammering. *Please let this go well*, she thought.

Lolly was sitting up, lots of pillows behind her, and there was a bouquet of red roses on the table. Daisy definitely saw the family resemblance in the two McCords—particularly the gorgeous green eyes. Lolly's hair was ash blond and just past her chin.

"Aunt Lolly, I'd like to introduce you to someone special. This is Daisy Dawson. Daisy, my aunt Lolly."

Lolly peered at Daisy, then at Harrison. "Special?" she asked with a sly smile.

"Yes, special," Harrison said. "We'll leave it at that."

Lolly raised an eyebrow, a gleam in her eyes. "I know how that goes." She smiled and then held out her hand toward Daisy.

A whoosh of relief flooded through Daisy. Lolly was funny and kind. Maybe the woman hadn't heard her last name clearly or connected it to the man who'd broken her heart ten years ago, but for now, Daisy felt a lot more comfortable. She took Lolly's hand, and Lolly gave it a light squeeze.

"Come sit," Lolly said.

Daisy sat down beside the bed. Harrison was standing behind her, and she could feel his hands on the back of her chair. Bracing himself, she knew.

"Dawson, huh?" Lolly said. "Any relation to Bo Dawson of Bear Ridge?"

Daisy bit her lip and sucked in a breath. "My father."

"Really?" Lolly exclaimed, looking from Daisy to Harrison. "Did you know I used to date your dad? About ten years ago."

Oh boy, did she know. "Yes. Harrison told me."

"Is he still as good-looking as ever?" Lolly asked. "Don't tell Robert I said that." She winked at Daisy.

Daisy almost gasped. *She's not upset. She's not demanding I leave at once.*

"Well, he actually passed away back in December," Daisy said.

Lolly patted Daisy's hand. "I'm sorry to hear that. The two of us didn't have a happy ending, but that's how things go. Sometimes they work, sometimes they don't. Took me a long time to let go of him, but that's also how things go."

"I'm sorry he hurt you so badly," Daisy said, hoping she wasn't overstepping by saying so.

"Well, in the end, the very end, I learned what was important and nonnegotiable to me in a relationship. Someone I could count on. Trust. Took me a while to trust myself, but when I finally let go of the past, I found everything I wanted in Robert. I almost lost him because I was so stubborn, but Harry here saved the day. Sometimes you have to know better than the people who *think* they know better. Right, Harry?"

Harrison moved beside Daisy and bent down to give his aunt a kiss. "You're absolutely right."

Daisy wondered if Lolly knew about the bet. In fact, she just realized that Harrison's aunt might not know anything about it. Her protective brother might have tried to avenge his sister's broken heart, the strain on her bank account and the loss of her friendship with the woman Bo had been three-timing with, on the down low.

"Ah, there I go getting all tired again," Lolly said. "I keep falling asleep on poor Robert as he talks or reads to me, but does that man have a melodic voice or what?" She smiled, her green eyes that reminded Daisy so much of Harrison's twinkling.

"We'll let you rest," Harrison said.

Daisy stood. She gently squeezed Lolly's hand. "I'm so glad I met you."

"Me, too," Lolly said. "And I'm very happy that Harry has someone so special in his life."

Daisy felt tears sting her eyes. She managed something of a smile, and then Harrison was ushering her out.

In the hallway the dam burst, and tears streamed down her face, and Harrison held her. She swiped at her eyes and got herself together. "I'm okay. Text Robert to come back. I don't want them to miss too much time together."

Harrison smiled and nodded. He texted Robert, and then they headed out.

The sunshine and fresh air felt good on her face. "I can't believe I just cried like that. I guess I'm crying over a lot of different things for a lot of different reasons."

"You can always be yourself with me, Daisy," he said as they walked to his SUV. "Happy, sad— the gamut. Angry, too. And I know I've made you angry."

"I don't want to talk about that anymore. It's settled, right? We keep the ranch, so all's good with that."

They both got inside and buckled up. "And what about us? I know we're not friends," he said with a smile. "But we're something, right?"

He was doing what he felt was right. For his family and for himself. He'd take the ranch, then sell it right back to them. But she couldn't live with that. The man who loved her would rip up the napkin. Call her stubborn. She'd been about to settle for a life with a husband who didn't love her so that Tony would grow up with his father. She wasn't about to settle again.

She didn't respond and he didn't press her, just drove out of the Gentle Winds parking lot. She figured he was digesting all that Lolly had said. His aunt had said quite a lot.

And Daisy was trying not to think about the moment Harrison would check out of Cabin No. 1 and she'd never see him again.

Chapter Fifteen

As Harrison pulled up to Daisy's house, Axel came out with Tony in his arms. The little guy was wearing a blue-and-white onesie, a tiny straw cowboy hat on his head. Man, that was cute.

"He's officially a cowboy now," Axel said as Daisy stepped out of the car.

Harrison wondered if he should just drive off or get out and talk to Axel. The last time hadn't gone well. But things were at least settled now as far as the ranch was concerned. Axel wouldn't be asking Harrison to punch him in the face.

He got out of the car and came around. "Hey, Tony. I like your hat."

Axel gave Harrison something of a smile, which was a big improvement over the usual scowl and death stare. "It's lined in very soft cotton to keep his little head safe."

"I love it," Daisy said. "Thanks, Uncle Axel. And thanks for watching him."

Axel nodded at his sister, then turned to Harrison. "So I hear you're going to sell us back the ranch for a dollar thirty seconds after you take ownership." He extended his hand, and Harrison shook it. "It's a good compromise, and on behalf of my brothers, we appreciate it. You certainly didn't have to do that. But we're damned glad you are."

"It's the right thing to do. I'm satisfied, and I think my father would be, too."

Axel handed over Tony to Daisy. "I'm headed out with Noah to look at a new hay baler. See you later, little nephew." He nodded at Daisy and Harrison and got in his truck.

"Your brothers believe it's a good compromise, Daisy. I wish you could see it that way. It's the best thing I can do in the situation."

Her eyes flashed. "You've made your decision. We're through talking about the ranch, then. You're checking out today, right?"

"Right," he said, his heart shredding as he stood there.

"Then I guess this is goodbye. Wave goodbye to Harrison, Tony," she said to the baby.

Okay, now his heart just completely tore into pieces.

She turned and walked up the porch steps, Tony's little cowboy hat bopping a bit.

He wanted to follow her inside and talk, but what was there to say? He got back in the SUV and drove down to the cabin. He didn't want to leave this place. This ranch. He didn't want to say goodbye to Daisy or Tony.

He stood in the main room of his cabin, taking in the walls, the furnishings, the care that had gone into building this cabin—rebuilding it. He thought about the main house and the barns and the animals. He could barely believe he'd shown up here planning to wrest the ranch away from the Dawsons—and not sell it back—but he himself had been a different person then. A person holding on to bitterness—from his breakup with the woman who'd used him to his grief over losing his dad and then being faced with losing his aunt.

Now he was losing Daisy. And nothing about that was right. He felt like Lolly must have ten years ago, giving up on love and romance because she'd been so hurt and betrayed. Then giving up on love a second time, breaking her own heart because she didn't want the man she loved to have to deal with all the pain, angst and suffering.

Sometimes you have to know better than the people who think *they know better. Right, Harry?*

That applied to a few different scenarios, he thought, his head about to explode.

It's wrong to take the ranch at all, Dad, he realized with such force of clarity that he had to sit down as the truth sank in. *It's wrong to take the ranch because it's not ours—never was. For a lot of reasons.*

But one of the biggest reasons was that the Dawsons had invested in rebuilding and had made it happen—the ranch wasn't the same one Bo had bet and lost. That ranch was gone. And all those old, bad memories weren't used in the renovations.

Harrison knew better now, and that was all that mattered. That had nothing to do with honoring or dishonoring his father; it had to do with what was truly right. Whether Lolly had been speaking of the bet and the ranch when she'd said that people had to know better than the people who thought they knew better, he had no idea. He wasn't sure if she even knew about the bet. He didn't think so, but she did seem to be trying to tell him something important.

Another reason, perhaps the one that mattered

most: he'd fallen in love with Daisy Dawson and couldn't touch her family's history and legacy and present and future. The ranch belonged to the Dawsons—fair and square.

He was pretty sure he'd already lost her, for not having understood this before now, when it was likely too late. But he couldn't wait to tell her.

That was some cruddy goodbye, Daisy thought as she helped herself to one of Cowboy Joe's chocolate-chunk scones. Heartbreak eating, for sure. At this rate, she'd never lose the baby weight, but she'd rather have the scone than fit into her old jeans right now.

Harrison's handsome face, and tousled blond hair and warm green eyes flashed in her mind, and she took a big bite of the scone. Could she really let that awful goodbye be it? The last time she'd see him? Talk to him? *We did have something, something very special, and I may be upset, but that was goodbye. We went through too much together for that.*

They did. Oh foo, she was going after him. At least to say a kinder goodbye, one that she could feel good about when she thought about Harrison in the days and weeks and months to come. Oh God, maybe years.

She sipped her water. "Looks like we're going for a walk down to Harrison's cabin," she said to Tony, who was being adorable by just existing in his bassinet.

She strapped the Snugli on to her chest and then scooped up her boy and put him inside.

She wanted to put on the precious and tiny cowboy hat Axel had bought his nephew, but the brim was a touch too wide to fit while he was in the carrier, so she put a floppy white sun hat on Tony's head. "Let's go see Harrison and say a goodbye we both deserve. That man helped bring you into the world. He made my stir-fry and secret recipe rice when my lower back was aching. He made me believe I could love again—he *made* me love again. And like his wise aunt Lolly said, sometimes it doesn't work out."

She walked down the path, holding back tears, hoping he hadn't already packed and left. She needed one last Harrison McCord hug. A real goodbye. And then she'd focus on Tony and her family and the ranch and maybe ease back into her duties as guest relations manager early so that Sara could take on the job as forewoman sooner than she'd expected. Her sister-in-law was so excited about the promotion. Between the great sitter they all used and one another, there'd be solid childcare for Tony and his little cousins.

"Daisy!"

She turned around and saw the newlyweds, Tessa and Tom Monello, waving and hurrying over to her. They were in their city clothes, sharp and monochromatic, Tessa's heels at least three inches. How she didn't sink into the grass was beyond Daisy.

"We're checking out today," Tessa said, "but we both wanted to thank you for that dinner party from hell, which actually ended up saving our marriage! We talked for hours that night. And we're going to see a marriage counselor at home and make sure we work through our differences. You were right when you said that what mattered was our love for each other, and we've got that by the truckload."

"I'm really happy to hear that," Daisy said. Dinner party from hell? Yeah, she'd agree with that.

"Tessa, I still can't believe you could have one of these adorable tykes and you want to wait," Tom said to his wife as he made peekaboo faces at Tony. "But I'm willing to wait until you're ready. As long as it's not *that* long."

Tessa bopped him on the arm, slipping her hand in his. "Thanks, Daisy. We had a great time here. The ranch is really beautiful and restful."

She watched the Monellos kiss their way up the path toward their cabin, so wistful she just stood there staring long after they disappeared down the slope.

"It's amazing they didn't trip," said a familiar male voice.

Harrison! "I was just coming to see you. To say a proper goodbye. Yes, I'm mad at you, but whatever."

"I was just coming to see you."

"For the same reason?" she asked. At least he wasn't going to just leave with things so awful between them. Yeah, they weren't friends—although, dammit, they were—but they needed to smooth things over for peace of mind. For both of them.

"Actually," he said, "I'm hoping you won't say goodbye, Daisy. Because the thought of losing you—for real and for good—made me realize I can't. I can't lose you."

Her heart pinged with hope. This was a very good start.

"I love my dad, but I love you, too," he continued. "And I love that little boy right here. I can't bear the thought of taking the ranch, even on paper for an hour. I respect you and your brothers too much for that. Like you said, the ranch isn't the one your father bet. And none of us is the same person." He stepped closer and took both of her hands in his. He kissed each one. "I love you, Daisy Dawson. So, so much. And I love Tony Lincoln Dawson. With all my heart."

Daisy gasped. "Did you hear that, Tony? He loves us!"

Harrison reached into his jacket pocket and pulled out the napkin. Her father's handwriting made her smile instead of want to cry. Then he ripped the napkin into pieces and shoved the mess into his pants pocket. "I wanted to throw up the pieces like confetti but then realized one of the employees would have to clean it up. I also thought about just giving you the napkin as some kind of weird keepsake, but this is part of a bitter past, and I think it's better just gone."

Someone pinch me. Can this really be happening? "I agree, Harrison." She put her arms around him, the baby between them. "I love you so much."

He tilted his head down and kissed her, then looked into her eyes, and she saw so much in his— love, desire, happiness, relief, warmth…her future. "My dad would be standing up on his recliner chair and cheering me right now. I know it's true. Why didn't I realize that before? I have no doubt Lolly would be, too."

Daisy reached up on her tiptoes and kissed him.

"I'm doing that now, too—in my head. So is Tony. And my brothers. And Sara. I'll bet even Cowboy Joe is cheering you."

He laughed. "I want us to be a family. You, me and Tony—oh and your five brothers and their wives, when they get them. I never want to leave this ranch, because I love it. Not because it was ever mine or my family's. I love the Dawson Family Guest Ranch, and I love you."

"Let's go home, then," Daisy said and they turned toward the farmhouse, hand in hand.

* * * * *

COMING SOON!

We really hope you enjoyed reading this book. If you're looking for more romance, be sure to head to the shops when new books are available on

Thursday 16th April

To see which titles are coming soon, please visit
millsandboon.co.uk/nextmonth

MILLS & BOON

Coming next month

BABY ON THE TYCOON'S DOORSTEP
Nina Milne

Isobel headed to the kitchenette, scooped powder into another bottle and handed it to Jake, waited whilst he poured the water in from the kettle.

Took it from him and stepped closer to demonstrate. Too close—she was way too close.

Focus. But not on his body, the sculpted forearms, the swell of his upper arms, the strong thighs. Not on his smell, not on the way his hair spiked up— This was a bad idea but for the life of her she couldn't figure a way out of it.

'Put your thumb over the top of the teat, so you're blocking the hole. Then you shake' Like this.' Her voice emerged squeaky…breathless…*ridiculous*.

He'd moved even closer to her now and his eyes held a wicked glint that ripped the breath from her lungs.

'So it's all in the wrist action,' he said dead pan and her gaze flew to meet his, in shock at the double entendre.

'I—'

Then he grinned and wiggled his eyebrows. 'Sorry I couldn't resist. Puerile but—'

'Yes,' she said, trying to keep a straight face. 'Definitely puerile.' But be that is it may she succumbed to a giggle, which morphed into a full-blown laugh. And in seconds he had joined in.

Now their gazes locked and she could feel the shift in the atmosphere, the swirl of desire, the fugue of need. They were even closer now. His scent tantalised; the warm smell of baby milk mixed with a hint of citrus clean sharp shower gel and a whiff of bergamot. Her head whirled and there was an utter inevitability about what happened next. She wasn't sure afterwards who initiated it, who made the fatal decision or whether it was a completely synchronised movement.

But one step took them closer and then she was in his arms and her lips met his and oh god it felt so good. His lips so familiar and yet so new, and her lips tingled as tremors of raw desire shuddered her body. Gentle, hesitant at first as if they both feared rejection and then the kiss deepened, intensified, sent a sear through her veins. His fingers tangled in her hair, she pressed her body against his wanting more, her pulse rate accelerated at his taste, his scent, the way his kiss could drive her to the edge of desperate need for more. Her body alight and craving more of him—of Jake—she wanted his touch, wanted the satisfaction her body knew and remembered.

Continue reading
BABY ON THE TYCOON'S DOORSTEP
Nina Milne

Available next month
www.millsandboon.co.uk

LET'S TALK

Romance

For exclusive extracts, competitions
and special offers, find us online:

f facebook.com/millsandboon

🐦 @MillsandBoon

📷 @MillsandBoonUK

Get in touch on 01413 063232

MILLS & BOON

THE HEART OF ROMANCE

A ROMANCE FOR EVERY KIND OF READER

MODERN

Prepare to be swept off your feet by sophisticated, sexy and seductive heroes, in some of the world's most glamourous and romantic locations, where power and passion collide.
8 stories per month.

HISTORICAL

Escape with historical heroes from time gone by. Whether your passion is for wicked Regency Rakes, muscled Vikings or rugged Highlanders, awaken the romance of the past.
6 stories per month.

MEDICAL

Set your pulse racing with dedicated, delectable doctors in the high-pressure world of medicine, where emotions run high and passion, comfort and love are the best medicine.
6 stories per month.

True Love

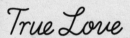

Celebrate true love with tender stories of heartfelt romance, from the rush of falling in love to the joy a new baby can bring, and a focus on the emotional heart of a relationship.
8 stories per month.

Desire

Indulge in secrets and scandal, intense drama and plenty of sizzling hot action with powerful and passionate heroes who have it all: wealth, status, good looks…everything but the right woman.
6 stories per month.

HEROES

Experience all the excitement of a gripping thriller, with an intense romance at its heart. Resourceful, true-to-life women and strong, fearless men face danger and desire - a killer combination!
8 stories per month.

DARE

Sensual love stories featuring smart, sassy heroines you'd want as a best friend, and compelling intense heroes who are worthy of them.
4 stories per month.

To see which titles are coming soon, please visit

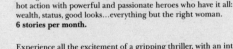

millsandboon.co.uk/nextmonth

JOIN US ON SOCIAL MEDIA!

Stay up to date with our latest releases, author
news and gossip, special offers and discounts, and
all the behind-the-scenes action
from Mills & Boon...

 millsandboon

 millsandboonuk

 millsandboon

It might just be true love...